Heaven
Forbid

D0557150

Also by Lutishia Lovely

Sex in the Sanctuary
Love Like Hallelujah
A Preacher's Passion
Heaven Right Here
Reverend Feelgood

Heaven Forbid

LUTISHIA LOVELY

KENSINGTON PUBLISHING CORP.
www.kensingtonbooks.com

This book is a work of fiction. Names, characters, places, and incidents either are products of the author's imagination or are used fictitiously. Any resemblance to actual persons, living or dead, events, or locales is entirely coincidental.

DAFINA BOOKS are published by

Kensington Publishing Corp.
119 West 40th Street
New York, NY 10018

Copyright © 2010 by Lutishia Lovely

All rights reserved. No part of this book may be reproduced in any form or by any means without the prior written consent of the Publisher, excepting brief quotes used in reviews.

All Kensington titles, imprints, and distributed lines are available at special quantity discounts for bulk purchases for sales promotion, premiums, fundraising, educational, or institutional use.

Special book excerpts or customized printings can also be created to fit specific needs. For details, write or phone the office of the Kensington Special Sales Manager: Kensington Publishing Corp., 119 West 40th Street, New York, NY 10018. Attn. Special Sales Department. Phone: 1-800-221-2647.

Kensington and the K logo Reg. U.S. Pat. & TM Off.

ISBN-13: 978-0-7582-3867-2
ISBN-10: 0-7582-3867-3

First Kensington Trade Paperback Printing: August 2010
10 9 8 7 6 5 4 3

Printed in the United States of America

For my mother, Flora Louise,
whose common sense, "mother wit" wisdom,
and ongoing support is the wind beneath my wings . . .

ACKNOWLEDGMENTS

It's hard to believe that I've reached book number six in this series. Wow! There's no doubt that without the love, support, and encouragement of so many people, this would not have been possible. I don't have enough time or space to thank everybody whose name deserves to be listed, so along with the "A" Team (including Selena and Natasha), let me just send a HUGE blanket thank-you to my family and friends, my Facebook family (for supporting me as I launched the TishTVNetwork, available on youtube.com, and for participating in the "Talk About It Tuesdays" discussions that transform the storylines from the Hallelujah Love Series to real-life issues), and all of the other Internet sites, such as Twitter, MySpace, and BlogTalkRadio, that help us authors promote our work. And what would these thank-yous be without a book club roll call? Here's my standing "o" to just a few of these fabulous organizations who support this series: Reading Is What We Do, F.A.M.E. Book Circle, Women of Faith Turning Pages, W.E.B.B. Book Club, Black Women Who Read, Urban Divas Book Club, Urban Fire Books, Da Story Book Club, Women Enlightened by Books, S.I.S.T.E.R.S. Book Club, Urban Soul, Urban Street Lit Book Readerz . . . I love you. It's that simple. Six books into this series, here's another reason why I'm thankful. I am seeing huge increases in the crossover success that I always envisioned for this work—that it not only be read by people who are religious and/or go to church, but by everyone who likes a good story filled with drama, humor, excitement, edutainment, and inspiration. As the number of fans for this series grows, you give me strength to do the same—to grow, evolve, stretch myself, push the limits, speak the truth, and be the voice of love on this planet. And speaking of love . . . Spirit . . . you are my boo . . .

1

If God Can't Fix It . . .

Anyone watching the two men conversing quietly in the corner booth of the dimly lit restaurant would have thought their discussion serious. They would have been right. The seasoned seventy-something, gray-haired minister, looking important and dignified in his black, double-breasted suit, listened intently as the younger man, displaying a rugged handsomeness in his navy blue, tailored Kenneth Cole design, used his manicured fingers to underscore a point.

"Number one," Stan Lee said, his finger in midair, "*all* sexual misconduct is sin, whether or not your members want to hear it. Before you came and laid down the law, the Gospel Truth congregation was way out of hand, from the pulpit to the vestibule. You know I'm right about it. Number two, it takes a tight rein to straighten out this kind of mess. And number three, Reverend Doctor O, I think you are the only preacher alive who can hold the rein tight enough to pull this backslidden church back in line with the Word." Secretly, Stan wished the doctor could put somebody else in line—his wife. But that was another story.

Obadiah, officially known as the Reverend Doctor Pastor Bishop Overseer Mister Stanley Obadiah Meshach Brook, Jr., and affectionately called "Reverend Doctor O," nodded in understanding. He liked this young man's fervor when it came to strong morals, and he couldn't help but agree with him. Doctor Stanley Morris Lee, the forty-eight-year-old pastor of Los Angeles's Logos Word Church, was a prolific preacher in his own right. Obadiah affectionately called Stan his namesake, even though he'd gone by his second name, Obadiah, since childhood. He respected the Logos Word ministry and viewed Stan as a spiritual son.

Obadiah knew that Stan spoke truth: Gospel Truth Church was in a gospel mess following the nationally televised scandal of its former pastor, Nate Thicke, and it took a preacher well worth his salt to pick up the shattered pulpit pieces. Something of this magnitude was the only thing that could have pulled him out of retirement, though truth be told, he'd missed the pulpit and was glad to be back.

Obadiah ran a hand over his weary eyes as he remembered the fiasco. How one of Nate Thicke's many women had managed to secretly videotape them during a sexual tryst, and how a portion of said tape was spliced into a holiday cruise promotion that was then shown during a national church convention. For about five seconds, Nate's glistening, bare backside had been seen by many of the twenty thousand attendees before a quick-thinking technical director stopped the tape. It didn't matter; the damage had been done. Nate was forced to resign, and his mother, Nettie Thicke Johnson, had immediately placed a call to her good friend Maxine, Obadiah's wife. Nettie, like Stanley, had been convinced that someone of Obadiah's stature, experience, and wisdom was the only one who could lead the congregation back down the straight and narrow. Goodness knew that during Nate Thicke's pastoral reign, the members—and the minister—had gone buck wild.

Obadiah cleared his throat and leaned toward Stanley, his powerful orator's voice near a whisper. "I know in my heart that every rule I've put in place and every change I've implemented at that there church is absolutely necessary. Narrow is the road that leads to salvation," Obadiah continued, his voice rising slightly as he quoted scripture. He looked around the sparsely populated dining room, took in the rich chestnut walls accented with deep red–covered chairs and tablecloths and sipped his coffee. "But as right as I am, the church is failing. The Sunday offering is shrinking faster than a jackrabbit's peter. And I'm losing the regular parishioners, especially the young folk. That's why I brought you here, to lead a revival and staunch the flow of fleeing fornicators. If they end up over at that funeral home Jenkins is masquerading as a house of God, Thomas will turn over in his grave."

Stanley's chuckle was low and deep. "Aw, c'mon now, Reverend Doctor O. Why are you so hard on Reverend Jenkins? He's doing the best he can. Besides, he's older than you are, and most of his members have probably been with him the entire forty years he's pastored that church."

Obadiah let out an uncharacteristic snort but otherwise remained silent. He didn't care to share the beef he had with Reginald Jenkins, a beef that went back those forty years of which Stanley spoke, a situation where Reginald took something that at the time Obadiah thought belonged to him.

"Young women don't listen to old men like me," Obadiah said after a pause. "Especially since I'm telling them to close their legs and take the 'for sale' and 'for rent' signs off their hot-to-trots and whatnot. This medicine will go down better coming from a young, handsome man such as yourself." He looked over at Stanley, took in the sleek bald head, the smooth, honey-brown face, the square-jawed strength settled under dark brown eyes, and nodded his approval. "Yes, they'll listen to you."

Both men paused while the waiter came and took away their dinner dishes. They declined dessert but said yes to more coffee.

Stanley looked down at the outline Obadiah had brought him: a recap of the rules outlined in the newly developed Gospel Truth Member Manual. Among the dozens of the now forbidden activities for church members was wearing makeup or outlandish jewelry; getting tattoos; watching television (except for a list of family programs sanctioned by the committee); and touching, besides handshakes, any member of the opposite sex who was not their spouse.

"I'm going to come with the unadulterated word of God," Stanley said. He leaned back casually in his seat while his countenance remained serious. "I'm not going to leave them with any questions in their mind. When I get done this week, they'll understand that being saved and sanctified means no fornication, no adultery, no pornography, and definitely no masturbation." His lips curled into a snarl as he all but spat out the last word, several unfortunate memories rising up unbidden in his mind. "If these women *and men* want to call themselves children of God, then they've got to live holy!"

The wives of Stanley Morris Lee and Stanley Obadiah Meshach Brook were visiting in the Brook home and having their own conversation on sexual matters . . . from quite a different point of view.

"He hates it!" Passion said passionately. "How can a grown man with three kids and oversized, working plumbing, if you know what I mean, abhor the natural act of sex so much? I just don't get it, Mama Max." Passion had been sitting on the plush, cream-colored chenille sofa, but now she paced back and forth across the carpet in Maxine Brook's living room.

"Humph, that would be a blessing for some women. There's plenty more that could go wrong in a marriage, child." Mama Max tamped down the thought that had been nagging her since moving to Texas, about what could go wrong, and refocused her attention on Passion. "Now lookie here, is the man hitting you, abusing you?"

Passion stopped in her tracks. "No. Whatever would make you ask that question?"

"Because I want to know, that's why."

The truth was, she and Stan had begun to argue more, and once, just once, he had advanced toward her as if to strike. But he hadn't. "No, Mama Max. Stan isn't abusive."

"Is he a responsible man, keeping food on the table and money in the bank?"

"Yes, ma'am, but—"

"But nothing. Is he a good father to his children?"

"The ministry keeps him busy, but, yes, when he's around them, he's a good dad."

"Then count your blessings and get you a good book to read at night. Drink some of that camouflage tea so you can sleep easy."

Passion didn't try to hide her smile. "You mean chamomile, Mama Max?"

"Yeah, that too. Drink it and cool your frisky behind down!"

Passion returned to the sofa and sat close to Mama Max. "Mama, I'm only thirty-four years old. I want to share physical intimacy with my husband, not continue with this forced celibacy that Stanley has mandated. I was celibate for five years before I got married. I don't intend to be horny and wanting with two hundred pounds of prime beef lying next to me! I'm sorry to be so blatant, Mama Max, but I haven't been able to talk about this with anyone."

"No apology needed, Passion. You can speak your mind in my house. Now, I can tell you're frustrated, and I wish there was something I could say to make you feel better. I haven't felt the flame of desire for nigh unto twenty years, and was never too crazy about the act of procreation when Reverend and I were busy creating King, Queen, Daniel, and Esther. *Maybe I should have been.* But as a wife, you do have certain rights. Have you tried talking to Stan about it?"

"Until I'm blue in the face," Passion said, standing to pace again. "But he won't even have the discussion anymore—says that as a first lady, I shouldn't have such animalistic desires.

"It's not like Stan can't perform. Our sex life was fairly good right after we got married. Nothing too risqué, you understand, and only once, maybe twice a week. But we did it."

"And then what happened?"

Passion hesitated. She respected Mama Max and her counsel, but could she share everything with her? Like what she'd discovered in Stan's luggage after he'd returned from a minister's conference three months ago? And how, upon further investigation, she'd found similar items hidden in a rarely used gym bag on a top shelf in their garage? And how any doubt as to the use of these items was cleared up when Passion came home one day, early and unexpected, and was shocked senseless by what she saw? Passion decided she wasn't ready to tell anybody what she'd learned about Stanley Morris Lee. . . . She was barely able to admit this truth to herself.

"Passion, baby . . . you all right? I asked you a question, about what happened to change how you and your husband . . . know each other."

Passion shared what she could. "Stan has been traveling a lot, so I didn't really notice it at first. When I finally asked him about it, he made excuses. Then, about three months ago, he started spouting Bible verses and using Scripture and religion as the foundation for denying me what is rightfully mine. He hasn't touched me since and has made me feel guilty for wanting something perfectly normal!

"Things can't go on this way," Passion said, almost to herself, as she looked out Mama Max's large picture window and beheld a beautiful, Texas fall afternoon. But the burst of color from the autumn purple ash tree in the Brooks' front yard, the profusion of purple, red, yellow, and orange, was lost on Passion. Her eyes weren't looking at the scenery out front, but rather at a scene from her past, the pictures she'd taken with her cell phone camera that had changed so many lives. She felt a strange camaraderie with Stan's ex-wife, Carla Lee, now Carla Chapman, along with the guilt that never totally went away, guilt from what she felt was her part in Stan and Carla's divorce.

"Passion, you need to take this burden to the Lord and leave it there," Mama Max said into a room that had suddenly become overwhelmingly quiet. "God can fix whatever is broken."

When Passion turned to face Mama Max, there were tears in her eyes. "I sure hope so, Mama," she said in a whisper. "Because if God can't fix it, a divorce court can."

Shortly after divulging her dilemma to Mama Max, Passion asked to be driven to the guest pastor condo. Her marital admissions had made her tired, and she wanted to spend some quiet time alone with her thoughts before Stan arrived. Once inside the comfortably decorated abode, Passion undressed quickly and took a shower. She had no reason to believe that tonight would be any different from all the others, but she wanted to be clean . . . just in case.

As Passion walked into the closet to don a nightgown, Stan's unlocked luggage caught her eye. Without pausing to think, she stepped over to it and lifted the lid. Inside, everything was compartmentalized and organized, much like Stan's life. His underwear, including briefs, were neatly folded, his socks paired and lined against the side. Not wanting Stan to know that she'd snooped in his belongings, Passion gingerly lifted the undershirts, T-shirts, and casual polos. She ran a hand inside the zippered compartment and came up against belts, handkerchiefs, and ties. She was just about to pull out her hand when her fingers felt something else.

Passion closed her eyes and took a breath. She slowly pulled out what her hands clutched. Swallowing, she opened her eyes and sighed. The pink silky fabric was trimmed in frilly black lace. Passion didn't have to hold them up to know, but she did anyway. It was just as she'd expected. The panties were extra large . . . just Stan's size.

2

Looks Can Be Deceiving

Stan eased up the privacy partition in the limo that had picked him up. The meeting he'd just had with Obadiah was at once invigorating and exhaustive. He loved spending time with this elder in the faith, loved sharing the Word with and learning from someone of Doctor Obadiah Brook's caliber. Often, Stan didn't feel on the same page with men his age, like KCCC's pastor, Derrick Montgomery, or Mount Zion's King Brook. True, they all preached from the same Bible and basically shared the same religious tenets, but whenever the talk turned personal, especially regarding the opposite sex, Stan shut down. How could these two virile men, who made love to their wives on the regular, understand what he was going through?

Stan smiled, remembering Obadiah's comment about the only other Black Baptist minister in Palestine, Pastor Reginald Jenkins. The man was eighty if he was a day, which would have made him about forty when he took over First Baptist. *That would have made Doctor O around thirty during that time.* Stan remembered the snort and the frown that had flitted across Obadiah's face before he covered it with his usually stern countenance. At one time, Obadiah had been a young man. It was the first time Stanley had given this fact any consideration. Maybe King Brook was more like his father than Stan realized.

Why am I thinking about that man's past? Whatever happened forty years ago with him and Old Man Jenkins is none of my business. Maybe not, but what happened to Stan almost forty years ago was haunting him more and more these days. He'd successfully shut out what started on that rainy day in April, and the chain of events that followed, for a very long time, decades, in fact. *Why are these memories coming back now?* But Stan knew why—it was because he'd come face-to-face with his past three months ago, when souls weren't all that had gotten revived in Detroit.

Luke Wilkes, the pastor of Spread the Word Cathedral, Detroit's newest megachurch referred to simply as the Cathedral, could barely contain his excitement. He'd been trying for months to get one of the city's most prominent and richest politicians, Bryce Covington, to join the church's board. And now it looked like that just might happen. During a casual conversation a month before, Luke had mentioned Stan Lee and the upcoming revival. Turns out Bryce Covington had heard of Stan Lee, was impressed with his ministry, and wanted to meet him. Luke was also talking to Stan about being a board member at-large. It would be wonderful to have either of these men's counsel, particularly regarding the business and outreach aspects of the ministry, but if he could get both, Luke knew it would be quite the Cathedral coup. He was hoping this meeting would solidify these desires.

Luke's assistant tapped him on the shoulder. "Excuse me, Pastor? Mr. Covington is on the line for you." Luke excused himself from the elite gathering of people in his office to take the call confirming the city councilman's attendance at the luncheon.

"Bryce, it's Luke. Hope this call doesn't mean you're not coming."

"To the contrary, Luke, I'm on my way. I just called to see if Stan had made it there yet. I'll have only about ninety minutes before having to leave to catch a plane to D.C. Wanted to make sure my timing was right."

"Your timing is perfect. Wish you could stay for the service."

"I'll be back to praise the Lord. In the meantime, make sure my office gets DVDs of these services."

"Will do, brothah."

"Appreciate that."

"No problem, just come on through. We're waiting."

Twenty minutes later is when the world that Stan had carefully constructed over the past twenty-five years came crashing down on him. As soon as he saw Bryce's face. As soon as he saw the man with whom he'd had his one and only homosexual encounter, the one and only time he'd truly been sexually satisfied.

"This is the surprise I told you about," Luke had announced during introductions, proud that he could have a part in bringing together two such important men. "Stan, Bryce is a staunch supporter of the Cathedral and what we're trying to do in the community. Bryce, Stan is one of the finest men of God—or of men period for that matter—that I know."

After the luncheon, and the formal announcement that both Stan Lee and Bryce Covington would be joining the Cathedral's overseer board, the two men found a moment to speak privately.

"Did you know I was coming?" was the first thing Stan said to this former friend and college roommate from two decades ago. Not "Hi," "How are you doing?" "Kiss my ass" or "Hey, what's up?" He wanted to know if he was the reason Bryce had shown up at church.

"It's the only reason I'm here." Bryce's dark brown, almost black, pupils bore into Stan's equally chocolate ones. Stan fought hard to maintain his composure as he stared at the man nicknamed PB—Pretty Boy—by those in the close-knit circle to which these men once belonged. Bryce had only gotten better-looking with age. His curly black hair was shorn almost to his head, but his eyelashes were just as long and thick as ever. A thin mustache framed his succulent lips, the bottom one larger than the top, just as Stan remembered. The faintest crow's feet appeared around Bryce's eyes, and the slightest wisps of gray brushed his temples. Stan's heart skipped a beat, in spite of itself.

Stan turned away from the love he saw in Bryce's eyes and found his voice. "I'm a long way from whatever you're thinking," he said, looking past Bryce to the group of men laughing on the other side of the large conference room. "What happened back then was a mistake, one I've not repeated. I'm married—"

"For the second time," Bryce interrupted. "To Passion Lee, who used to be Passion Perkins. Before that, you were married to the talk show host Carla Chapman. You had two children with her and adopted her oldest child, a daughter."

Stan's eyes widened. "How in the world—"

"Don't panic, Stanley. It's not too hard these days. Besides, I've never forgotten you, have followed you off and on for years. Remember Eddie?"

"Eddie West?" *Of course,* Stan thought belatedly. Eddie, a successful attorney in Washington, D.C., and head deacon at a megachurch there, was the only man from those days with whom Stan had kept contact. He'd had no idea that Eddie and Bryce were also in touch. Stan never brought him up, and Eddie had never mentioned him either. So he had no way of knowing. Until now. "What do you want, Bryce?"

"You," was Bryce's immediate response. "I've never stopped loving you all these years. Never stopped hoping—"

"I'm a happily married man," Stan said, even as Passion's frowning face swam into his consciousness. He lowered his voice to a whisper. "A happily married, *heterosexual* man." Stan threw a head nod at one of the preachers across the room who'd waved his good-bye. Determined to regain his composure, Stan forced himself to look Bryce dead in the eye. "Believe it or not, it's good to see you, Bryce. I hope we can work together to benefit the kingdom and the citizens of this city. But that's all we'll do together, understand? If you exhibit one hint of impropriety with me, or ever bring up our past again, I'll resign the seat I just accepted."

"Damn," Bryce whispered, his voice like silk, his demeanor unruffled. "Your forcefulness, that brute strength, is what always turned me on so much. You haven't changed a bit." He laughed loudly and held out his hand. Stan had no choice but to shake it because others had turned to see what was funny, as Bryce had intended. Stan pasted a smile on his face, even as he felt the jolt of electricity when the two touched palms. This long-ago lover then walked away, and after shaking a few more hands and thanking the host, Bryce left the room.

He left the room, but not Stan's thoughts. Seeing Bryce again opened a door Stan had thought locked and bolted, with the key thrown away—a door that was created forty years ago, when Stan was eight years old. Since this surprise meeting with Bryce, Stan had begun doing things he hadn't done since college, and he hadn't been able to make love to Passion since he'd shaken Bryce's hand. He thought he'd been delivered from this desire. Now Stan knew he had only been fooling himself. . . .

"Doctor Lee? Doctor Lee?" The limo driver tapped on the partition, and after not getting a response had lowered the glass just enough to speak to his client. "We're here at the condo, sir. Unless there's somewhere else you'd like me to take you."

Stan looked up at the well-lit complex with its stone architecture and neatly trimmed bushes. He'd been totally unaware of the passing scenery during the twenty minutes it had taken to get from the restaurant where he'd met Obadiah to the condominium that housed guest pastors. He nodded at the driver, and once the door opened, stepped out and took a deep breath of the cool evening air. Stan thought of his wife waiting inside the apartment and shook his head, as if doing so would rid him of the memory of Bryce and their shared history. If only it were that easy.

3

Preach, Preacher

Nettie and Mama Max beamed from the back of the church. If this first night of revival was any indication, the month-long promotional campaign announcing this impromptu round of meetings was a success.

"The church hasn't been this full since Nate left," Nettie gushed.

"Those flyers the girls passed out did the trick," Mama Max said, her thoughts slightly distracted as she eyed every person who walked through the door. "I knew putting Stanley's face on the paper would draw these women to the pews like bees to honey."

"Now you just go on, Mama Max. I'm sure these women have gathered to hear a good sermon and praise the Lord. No doubt it's remembering his preaching skills from Nate's anniversary celebration that has them flocking like flies to poop."

"Uh-huh, and if you believe that, I've got some oceanfront land in Mississippi to sell you." Nettie joined Mama Max in laughter. "That's a handsome man if there ever was one," Mama Max continued. "It's such a shame that . . ."

Nettie quickly looked over at Mama Max. "Shame that what?"

"Nothing." Mama Max shared almost everything with

Nettie, but she would never dream of breaking a confidence. What Passion Lee had told her would go no further than the distance the words had traveled from Passion's lips to Maxine's ears.

Conversation dwindled as the two women watched the mostly female audience vie for the few remaining seats in the eight-hundred-seat sanctuary. In addition to the flyers, the Gospel Truth Church had bought air time on a couple of AM radio stations and cable channels in Dallas and had posted the news about Stan Lee's guest minister appearance in the surrounding area's local papers. Stan's office had sent out an e-mail to all of their ministry partners in Texas, Louisiana, Oklahoma, Arkansas, and Mississippi. Everyone intimately involved in the Gospel Truth ministry knew the importance of a full sanctuary every night of this five-night revival. Tithes and offerings had fled along with the saints running from Obadiah's fire-and-brimstone teaching. Attendance had dropped almost fifty percent in three short months. A successful revival would ensure that the Gospel Truth bank account was saved right along with the saints' souls. Failure was not an option, because not only was the mortgage late, but the insurance, utilities, and employee paychecks were also past due.

Thirty minutes later, a poised and confident Stan Lee took the pulpit, along with Obadiah and several associate and visiting members. Stan sat in the large middle chair. Its high back of intricately carved oak and its plush, deep blue velvet cushion held to the wood with solid-gold fasteners was a throne fit for the main speaker of God's Word. He perused the crowd briefly before closing his eyes and resting his chin against strong, steepled fingers. As the choir neared the end of their song, Stan rose slowly from his seat, crossed the podium, and took the microphone, joining in effortlessly with his melodious baritone and singing the words to the song he requested, a song he hoped would prepare the palates of those attending the night's service. "Lord, I want to be a Christian," he sang, "in my heart."

Passion Lee sat in the front row, between Nettie Thicke
Johnson and Mama Max. She watched her husband as he or-
chestrated the setting, looking fine, fit, and fabulous in a tailored chocolate-brown suit that accentuated both his shoulders
and his honeyed skin color. His face was clean-shaven, save for
a neatly trimmed goatee that he'd grown at Passion's suggestion. Six feet of manly muscle, his look was the epitome of a
lover who could more than please, a man who could take you
in his arms, place you up against the wall, and . . . Passion
shook her head to rid herself of such thoughts. Stan hadn't
placed anything anywhere in way too long. Here she sat looking the part of happy first lady in her matching Lane Bryant
chocolate-brown suit, wearing the diamond earrings and
necklace Stan had given her for Christmas, wishing for a present that cost nothing—physical love from her man.

"First giving honor to God, who is the head of my life,"
Stan began as the choir sat, "and to the esteemed man of God
who leads this flock, the Reverend Doctor Obadiah Brook."
Doctor O nodded somberly. Stan continued in his acknowl-
edgments of the ministers on the roster before turning his gaze
toward Passion. His face lit up with a smile, and his eyes took
on a bedroom quality. "Lastly, I'd like to acknowledge my wife,
Passion Lee. Stand up, beloved."

*Beloved? Please. Bewildered maybe. Befuddled, yeah that'll work.
I wonder what these women looking at you with lust in their eyes
would think if they knew you hadn't screwed me in months. And you
have the nerve to call me beloved? Like you mean it? I don't think so.*
No one looking would have guessed that these were the
thoughts flitting through Passion's mind as she dutifully stood,
turned with a smile, and acknowledged the crowd before
blowing a kiss at her husband. *Liar! Hypocrite!* She could barely
keep the smile pasted on her face as Stan delved into the meat
of his sermon: How To Be A Real Christian? Just Do It.

How about being a husband and just doing "it" to me? Passion
had a hard time not squirming through the sermon, as Stan ad-

monished both single and married alike to take their minds off self and focus on God. She all but rolled her eyes when he suggested that married couples take a break from "physical pleasures" and seek God's face. She thought she'd lose her dinner when he suggested that for the next thirty days, members of Gospel Truth focus on purifying their minds, hearts, and bodies. He promised those listening that if they were obedient to the words of God being delivered through His servant, then those willing to sacrifice could have a more abundant life.

"The wages of sin is death," Stan admonished before softening his rebukes with a killer smile, "but the gift of God is eternal life. Sin is separation from God. When the devil gets in between you and what you know is right to do. But you are to put on your whole armor," he espoused, prowling the pulpit like a panther searching for food, "so that you can withstand the evils of this day." Passion watched as Stan left the pulpit, entered the aisles of the sanctuary, and began directly asking the congregants if they were willing to be true Christians.

"Yes," one woman whispered, her eyes fixed on Stan's luscious lips. "I will, I mean, I am."

"What about you, sistah?" he asked another. "Are you ready to let your light shine for Jesus, to say no to the flesh and yes to God?"

The woman swallowed visibly before responding. "I'll try," she said in a soft voice.

"Woman of God, you've got to do more than try. You must have a made-up mind to live for God." Stan knelt down until he was eye level with the woman, whose eyes were tearing up. "Will you do that? Will you do it for God, and for me?" His voice was barely above a whisper, but he made sure the sincerity of his plea was captured in the microphone. "Because God has been too good to you, my beloved. He's been too kind. He deserves the best that you can offer. Am I right?"

The woman nodded.

"Then . . . will you give it to Him?"

"Yes," she said, whispering back, and then again with firm resolve. "Yes! Thank you, Jesus! Yes!" The woman continued to boohoo so loudly, she was finally escorted from the main sanctuary.

Stan continued in this way for more than ninety minutes, mixing stern mandates with humor and hiding criticism behind witticism. He interchanged twenty-dollar words with ones costing fifty cents, catering to both the learned and unlearned. When he'd worked up a sweat, he paused and dramatically took off his suit jacket, showing off a body that didn't miss a meal or a workout. His sermon was punctuated by encouraging comments from the ministers in the pulpit, most on their feet as Stan built toward his finale.

"Teach the Word!" one exclaimed.

"Preach, Preacher!" Obadiah intoned, taking a couple steps toward Stan and swiping at him with a large, white handkerchief.

When Stan suggested women stop lying on their backs and start fighting on the Lord's battlefield, two of the younger associate pastors jumped up and high-fived. The pianist and organist added their musical punctuations as Stan whipped the congregation into a spiritual frenzy. When he concluded his sermon, Stan received a word from the Lord to take up a special, purifying offering. He admonished listeners to not "tip" God, to leave their ones in their wallets and pull out Jackson, Grant, or Benjamin Franklin. The aisles clogged with guilt-ridden givers. Doctor O watched carefully as the baskets overflowed with green. There was no doubt he'd enjoyed Stan's sermon, but he was enjoying this impromptu giving frenzy even more. Doctor O smiled, his heart happy for two reasons—the size of tonight's offering, and the unexpected sighting of the person who was even now smiling back at him from the back row.

4

In the Biblical Sense

They'd been riding in the rental car for ten minutes, but Passion remained silent. Stan, who'd showered and changed from the suit he preached in, now wore a cashmere sweater, jeans, and Nikes. He looked good. He smelled good. His prolific preaching had gotten Passion all riled up, as it often did. She'd been wondering since the church said "amen" if there was any way she could have her man tonight . . . and if he was wearing the pink underwear that were no longer in his suitcase.

Finally, Stan cleared his throat and spoke. "You're awfully quiet."

"A lot on my mind."

"Feel like sharing?" If what was on her mind was what Stan thought was on it, sharing with him was the last thing he wanted. But he felt it a proper question to ask, even if he didn't want to hear the answer.

"Not really." Passion squelched the urge to sigh and instead turned and looked out the window. The night was dark and cloudless, the air warm.

"The doc is happy. Tonight's special offering was well over ten thousand dollars. The church was hanging on by a wing and a prayer, everything past due, folks not paid. If this keeps up all week, Gospel Truth will be back in the black. God is good."

This time Passion couldn't stifle her annoyance, which came out as a snort.

"Look, what is it? Just spit it out, okay? As if I don't already know."

"My beloved," Passion said, mimicking the seductive whisper Stan had used on her and other females in the audience. She knew how well those tactics worked. She was once the female in his congregation, hanging on to Stan's every word, ready to do all that he had asked. In fact, she'd done what he'd asked, and what his interpretation of the Bible had demanded, for five, long years. Passion had done the work. Now she wanted the reward.

"Can you live right for God, for me?" Passion shifted in her seat to look directly at Stan as she threw his words back in his face. "What about you, Stan? Can you live right by God? Can you honor your wife, our vows, and our marriage bed? Because your old-time religion preaching has got me as horny as hell and—"

"Watch your language, woman of God."

"Horny as *hell*," Passion repeated for emphasis. "I want you in my bed tonight, Stan. And I want us to make mad, passionate love to each other the way God intended, the way marriage ought to be."

"There's more to marriage than screwing."

"That may be true, but those other things aren't on my mind right now." *Sex is . . . and pink panties.* She knew the underwear conversation would have its day, but Passion wanted to handle one problem at a time and right now—her wet panties were the priority.

Stan muttered under his breath.

"Excuse me? What did you just say?"

"I said you're just like her."

"Oh, no, he didn't," Passion whispered to the trees

whizzing by as they sped down the highway. "I am not just like Carla," she continued, knowing Stan was referring to his ex-wife. "If I were, I'd be in another man's bed right now, instead of here supporting your monkish ass!"

"I said watch your language! No wife of mine is going to talk like that!"

"I'll talk however I want, Stan. I've already got a daddy and you ain't him!"

"Not in my car you won't!"

"Kiss my ass!"

"What?" Stan turned widened eyes on his wife.

"Now that I think about it, will you *please* kiss my ass, as well as the surrounding area!" Passion began to laugh hysterically at the irony of the statement. "Please, pretty please with a cherry on top," she eked out between gales of laughter. "Kiss my ass and my assets, *Doctor* Stan Lee!"

Between the pressure from Passion and the phone call from his church secretary he'd received earlier, it was too much. Stan quickly decelerated, changed lanes, and with his foot steadily on the brake, eased onto the highway's shoulder.

"Stan, what are you doing?" Passion asked, wiping laughter-induced tears from her eyes.

"I'm putting you out."

"Whew, you're about to crack me up again. Don't be ridiculous."

The car came to a stop. Dust from the gravel billowed around them. Stan kept his hands on the wheel and stared straight ahead as he spoke. "I've asked you to stop cursing, and you insist on being disrespectful and disobedient. Now get out."

Passion crossed her arms and shook her head, convinced that her husband had now lost his mind along with his libido.

Stan sat for a second longer before snapping off his seat belt, opening his car door, and marching over to Passion's side of the car. "Get out."

"What are you going to do, Stan, leave me here on the side of the highway?"

"That's where most trash ends up, isn't it?" Stan reached into the car, undid Passion's belt, and grabbed her arm.

"Let go of me, fool!"

"Get out of the car!"

Passion grabbed a hold of the steering wheel, leaning her body away from the door. She was determined to stay in the car.

Stan was just as determined to get her out of it. He grabbed her leg and pulled. Passion started kicking. "Let go of my leg!" Her skirt rode up to around her waist as she continued kicking and screaming. One kick landed on Stan's thigh, another one precariously close to his manhood. Stan grabbed Passion's ankles with one hand and with the other, reached under his wife's buttocks and pulled her out of the car. Passion managed to stay on her feet and immediately tried to get back in the car. Stan grabbed her around the waist, swung them both around, and pushed Passion several feet away from him.

Heaving for breath, Stan turned and walked toward the driver's side of the car. But he didn't get far. Two hundred pounds of pissed-off female jumped on his back, and arms became death grips as Passion held on for dear life.

"You're not going anywhere without me," she panted. "Understand that, nucka. *Nowhere!*"

Stan tried to turn and loosen Passion off his back at the same time. Had there not been a rut hidden in the grass, he might have been successful. But his foot hit the crease in the earth, and both he and Passion fell to the ground. The only thing missing from the picture was a voice crying "timber!" They landed with a thud and began wrestling and rolling in the grass. Passion pummeled Stan with her fists while he hid his face and deflected her blows. Using his foot as leverage, he once again grabbed her arms and rolled them over until he was on top. "No wife of mine will talk like a trollop," he huffed, using the word his grandmother flung regularly at the girls in the neighborhood where he grew up. He felt a strange sense of empowerment—and arousal—as memories of wrestling with someone else came into his mind.

Passion's head hit a rock. "Ow!" Her scream brought Stan back from the crazy place his mind had gone. He suddenly became aware of his surroundings and realized with horror that not only was he, a prominent man of God who'd just preached the Word to hundreds, wrestling with his wife on the side of the Interstate, but also that in a hideously sadistic way, he was enjoying it. *I'm losing it. I've got to get a grip!*

Stan became very aware of Passion's presence underneath him. "Passion, sweetheart, I'm so sorry. I don't know what got into me. Are you all right?" His deep chocolate eyes bore into Passion's lighter ones, darkening even more as his body responded of its own volition to Passion's softness and heavy breathing from the wild-world-of-wrestling episode they'd both just re-created.

"Shh, Passion, don't cry. I didn't mean this. I didn't mean any of this." Stanley kissed Passion's eyes, where tears pooled at the corners before sliding into her ears. "I'm sorry, darling." He kissed her nose and mouth.

Suddenly, Passion didn't feel the pebbles or grass beneath her. She only felt Stan's hard body on top of hers and knew this may not be where she wanted it, but this was what she wanted. Her premenopausal hormones were like those of a raging teenager, and at the moment she didn't care that her behavior matched them. She shamelessly opened her mouth, sucking Stan's tongue in, grinding into his manhood, pressing his head more firmly down on hers. Stan gave as good as he got, both of them now totally oblivious to everything but each other. Neither of them heard the car that drove up and parked just behind their rented Cadillac. It was the red lights, however, that got their attention. Both of their eyes flew open as they sensed flashing lights and heard hard-soled shoes stepping onto the gravel. Stan rolled over and Passion scooted to her knees, rearranging her skirt and trying desperately to rise quickly in her three-inch heel. The other shoe rested on its side near the pavement.

Stan and Passion looked up sheepishly at the cop, a hysterical laugh lodged in their throats.

"What in the Sam tarnation is going on here?" the senior officer asked in a Texan twang as he approached, keeping a hand on the butt of his gun. His partner stood next to the patrol car talking into the car radio.

Stan and Passion could only imagine how ridiculous they looked, and the officer's question made it clear that they had some explaining to do. As Stan whipped up a creative explanation to appease the cop, something about going through with a bet and a dare, Passion's mind whirled with what had just happened. She'd witnessed something from her husband that she hadn't seen much of outside the pulpit—passion. Passionate anger to be sure, but it was passion nonetheless. Considering the circumstances, she should have been angry, but instead Passion was hopeful. Maybe tonight would be different than the others. She ignored the warning bells going off in her head and held on to the desire pulsating throughout her body. Perhaps tonight, she thought, she'd know her husband—in the biblical sense of the word!

5

A Stranger's Confession

"He did what?" Mama Max paced her living room floor much as Passion had the day before.

"I know it sounds bad, Mama Max, but I started it." Remembering how the night ended, Passion almost laughed. It wasn't the best sex she'd ever had, but Passion knew that if she could ever teach Stan to properly use what God had given him, she'd be in seventh heaven.

"Ain't no such thing as a woman starting nothing that ends with a hand upside your head."

"Wait a minute, now. He didn't hit me, Mama Max."

"Hit, pushed, shoved—he put his hands on you, didn't he?"

Among other things. Belatedly, Passion remembered she was talking to a revered mother of the church and forced her thoughts away from last night's bedroom antics, the first such experience in a little more than three months.

"You're right, Stan should not have threatened to kick me out of the car, and he most definitely shouldn't have made good on his threat and landed us both on our hind ends. But everything worked out all right."

"How you figure?"

"Because Stan and I were intimate last night, Mama Max. For the first time in a very long time."

"Humph, you young women amaze me."

Passion knew that there was no changing Mama Max's mind, so she didn't try. "I just called to thank you, Mama Max. God must have heard you. I also called to see if you wanted to share a light dinner before church tonight. Since Stan is with your husband—"

"Who told you Stan was with Obadiah?"

"You mean he isn't? Stan left here over an hour ago, said he had a meeting. I just assumed it was with Reverend Doctor O."

"No, child, Reverend Doctor was in his study most of the night and is there right now. He's been bombarding the throne of grace on behalf of these backslidin' saints here in Palestine. If Stan shows up here, I'll have him call you."

"That's okay. I'll try his cell phone. And on second thought, I need to watch my waistline. I'll just have some of the salad Miss Nettie had delivered last night."

"All right, baby."

Passion pressed the END button and immediately called Stan. When the call went to voice mail, she didn't leave a message.

"Forgive me, Father, for I have sinned." Stan squirmed uncomfortably in the tight quarters.

"How long has it been since your last confession?"

"I'm not Catholic. I just want to confess my sins before you and the Lord. I saw this church and stopped."

"Very well. What is the grievance against God that you've committed?"

"I pushed my wife."

"You pushed your wife?"

"Yes, I was trying to get her out of the car."

"How badly was she hurt?"

"I didn't hurt her—I mean, not physically. But I've never

laid a hand on a woman in my life. She just kept pushing my buttons, has been pushing them for months. And that's not all, Father."

"Go on."

"I had sex."

"I see. With whom, son?"

"My wife!"

There was a long pause before the priest continued. "Your wife."

Stan nodded, unable to answer for fear of breaking down and crying "like a bitch," as he'd heard a teenager at church say while among his schoolmates, a phrase he himself would never voice because he didn't allow profane words to come out his mouth. He also knew that if he opened his mouth, he might confess his other sins, the ones that had haunted him for more than forty years.

"And having sex with your wife is a sin because . . . ," the priest prompted.

"Because I'm supposed to live holy! How am I going to lead a backslidden congregation back to Christ if I'm sweating between my wife's legs? Father God, forgive me! And give me strength to withstand the wiles of the devil!"

Father Flannigan took off his glasses and wiped his eyes with a handkerchief. The Catholic population was quite small in Palestine, most confessions boringly routine. Kelly Munson confessed weekly to gambling on the boats in Louisiana. Her son, Patrick, owned up to cheating on his school exams and having lustful thoughts about his school's head cheerleader, and Jim O'Reilly admitted giving in to the pleasures of alcohol, often making this confession while reeking of liquor. Admitting affairs was fairly common, as was guilt for lying, cheating, and stealing. For the most part, these admissions were perfunctory, confessed again and again. But this man, this stranger's confession, was different. Father Flannigan perceived a deep hurt in this man's heart and pain from his past, pain so severe it clouded his judgment to the point that he felt it was wrong to make love to his wife.

"As a man of the cloth, you know the word of God," Father Flannigan said. When the stranger on the other side of the partition remained silent, he continued. "And you probably also know that the marriage bed is undefiled, that sex was given to married couples as a way to show their love for each other. It is a totally blessed act in the eyes of God."

"It is a necessity to be used for procreation only," Stan countered. "This was a mistake. I've got to get out of here." Stan ran away from the priest and from the power of that which he hadn't confessed.

"Wait, son!"

Father Flannigan heard the outer door slam. He crossed himself and prayed for the tortured soul of the man who'd entered his chamber.

6

A Secret Place

Mama Max hummed a lively tune of "Old Time Religion" as she prepared another loaf of banana nut bread. The revival had ended, and to everyone's profound relief, it had been a huge financial success, partly due to an anonymous donation of twenty thousand dollars that Nettie had confided to Mama came from her son, Gospel Truth's former pastor, Nate Thicke. Nobody could question that the revival was timely and had led to financial prosperity, as least for the time being. Mama Max knew that only time would tell whether it would lead to spiritual prosperity for the Gospel Truth members and whether such growth was temporary or permanent.

"Give me that old time religion," she sang as she squished the last of the bananas and began folding them into the batter. "Old time religion like it used to be. Yes, Lord." Mama Max felt good this morning. This feeling was much different than it had been just a month ago, when collectors threatened to turn off the church's electricity, or a week ago, when she fretted over who might or might not come to the revival, and definitely different than the sinking feeling she'd had after the Reverend Doctor preached his first sermon as pastor of Gospel Truth.

★ ★ ★

Mama Max had had gas all morning on that particular Sunday, a sure sign of trouble if there ever was one. Nevertheless, she'd dressed up in her Sunday best, a spiffy long dress bursting with flowers in primary colors, and a red straw hat boasting flowers as well. She was greeted warmly, probably reminding more than a few attendees of their grandmothers. The church was almost full, she remembered, and the choir had "sang their way on up to heaven" as Mama Max's father used to quip. But shortly after the side door opened and her husband entered the sanctuary, the atmosphere changed. Mama Max had immediately gotten the sinking feeling that things weren't going to go over very well. That her husband walked into the church carrying an oversized broom was her first clue. The title of his sermon, "Sweeping Satan out the Church," was her second.

Nobody would argue the point that the reverend doctor being back in the pulpit agreed with his health. Until he was called out of retirement, Reverend Doctor O seemed to have one ailment after another: high blood pressure, heart palpitations, arthritis, back pain. But from the time Nettie Johnson called with the request that Mama Max's husband come out of retirement to save a church, Obadiah had been the picture of health.

That first Sunday Obadiah preached was no exception. He brought forth the word of God with fervor, shaking the rafters with his booming voice. Looking back, Mama Max thought he would have hailed down fire and brimstone for real if he'd been able to. As it was, his sermon sufficed, as he admonished the people to "get right with God or get left behind." But when he brought out the new Gospel Truth Member Manual, the massive document that even she hadn't known about, well, that's when Mama Max's gas started acting up for real!

"Whew, it's long," Nettie had leaned over and whispered as she began thumbing through the pages. When asked by the reverend, she'd offered her advice on what she felt were the "dos and don'ts" of godly living. She knew others had been questioned and had contributed their two cents as well. Nettie had no idea, however, that their suggestions were going to become a behavioral bible of sorts, a rules-and-regulations manual to be followed without question. But Reverend Doctor O was making this fact plain, bellowing the threat that members were to adhere to the Word, or else. Nettie swallowed hard as she read some of the page headlines, knowing even as strict as it appeared, the handbook was probably for the best.

"Lord have mercy," Mama Max said softly as she read the table of contents. "Even Jesus better stay up in heaven. 'Cause if he comes down here to Gospel Truth Church, the Reverend Doctor might not think him holy enough to get back in!"

It wasn't the "known sins" Mama Max read that she had a problem with. Nobody wanted to go against the Ten Commandments, and everybody knew that fornicating and masturbating and most other kinds of "atings" were abominations before God. Nobody had to think twice about homosexuality and pornography. Anybody with an ounce of home training didn't have to be schooled about these.

But some of the other ones on the list were bound to cause problems, items added to the list—according to the reverend—to "help with housecleaning." Mama Max enjoyed an occasional splash of Baileys Irish Cream in her coffee, but the rules outlawed any and all forms of alcohol, including beer, wine, even NyQuil. Smoking anything except some meat on a grill was forbidden, as was cursing (*I'm sure as hell going to have problems with that one,* Mama Max thought with a giggle), gambling (including the lottery, bingo, and card playing . . . and Mama sure liked a scratch-off now and then), wearing makeup, and watching television(except a list of shows sanctioned by the Gospel Truth Moral Board). For women, dresses had to be worn loose and hang below the knee, and arms were to be covered to the elbow, even in summer. For men, ties were required at all times, except when involved in physical labor, such as repairing or cleaning the house of God, and jewelry was limited to watches, cuff links, and sensible chains. Earrings on men—forbidden. Hair for both sexes was to be neat and trim, and tattoos, especially new ones done after hearing the word of God as delivered by Obadiah Brook, were expressly forbidden. Hugging between male and female church members who were not married to each other was no longer allowed, and when conversing, a distance of two feet must be maintained at all times. The new Gospel Truth Member Manual, passed out to members at the end of Reverend Doctor O's first sermon, was fifty pages long. Many of the members who read it—the table of contents, much less the whole book—hadn't bothered to attend the following week, and ever since, attendance had continued to dwindle.

Mama Max set the last loaf of banana bread into the oven, took out the two that had been baking, wiped her hands on an apron, and looked at the clock. "Reverend!" Mama Max went into the hallway and called again. "Obadiah!" A slight frown creased Mama Max's forehead as she walked toward the study. *That man has been closeted away in there for hours.* She stopped in front of her husband's home study. Just as she raised her hand to knock, she heard a low moan.

"Reverend, you all right in there?" Mama Max tried to open the door but it was locked. "Obadiah!"

"Oh, God," she heard her husband whisper.

Mama Max pressed her ear against the door. "Got some warm banana bread out here whenever you're ready."

Mama Max listened for another moment but hearing nothing more, shook her head and walked back to the kitchen. Obadiah had always had a strong relationship with God. For years, his study had been his sanctuary, and for the most part, Maxine left him alone when he was preparing to deliver the word of God. But it seemed like ever since they moved to Texas, Obadiah had been spending more and more time cloistered behind those doors. Mama Max wasn't one to get in the way of the Lord's work, but she worried about how hard her husband was toiling to save, she sometimes felt, ungrateful saints.

She worried about other things, too, but most of the time was able to chase away the devil's thoughts. "That rascal's even been plaguing my dreams," she'd recently confided to Nettie. And while Mama Max tried to do her part in aiding the ministry, and was delighted to be living close to her good friend Nettie, she still had to admit one thing—she was lonely. Back in Kansas, she had any number of church members she could call and gossip with or invite over for coffee. Once or twice a week, sometimes more, she'd gone to the gym or out to the movies with her daughter-in-law, Tai, and her grandkids were always stopping over. She hadn't thought she'd miss them so much. But she did.

"Now, you just shape up, Maxine Fredonia Brook. God has been too good to you to even think about sulking." Maxine began bustling around the kitchen, cleaning up and thinking about Passion and the marital problems she was having. For the most part, Maxine was satisfied. She decided to be thankful that things were as well as they were, and after finishing up the dishes, picked up the phone.

"Nettie, this here's Maxine."

"Hey, Mama Max!"

"Girl, I got a loaf of banana nut bread over here that will make you slap your mama and some ice-cold milk to go along with it."

"What kind of nuts did you put in it?"

"Black walnut, child. Ain't no other kind of nut for banana nut bread. Should I cut you a slice?"

"I'm on my way."

Obadiah leaned his head back, thankful for the cool leather of the navy blue sofa in the library portion of his study. This small room was his sanctuary, filled with books, about a dozen different Bibles, study guides, concordances, tapes, and DVDs—everything a man might need to prepare to preach. But this room also contained other things, things that had nothing to do with Obadiah's fiery sermons, things that nobody, not even Mama Max, knew anything about.

Obadiah reached up and wiped the sweat from his face, closed his eyes as his breathing returned to normal. Once his heartbeat slowed and the shaking stopped, Obadiah got up, put everything back in its secret place, scanned the room to make sure all was in order, and went to break bread, banana bread to be exact, with his wife.

1

God's Princess

Princess Brook stared long and hard at her grandmother's number. "Grandmama Max will understand," she whispered, trying yet again to convince herself to make the call. She picked up the receiver and had punched in nine of the ten numbers needed to complete the call before she hung up the phone and placed her head in her hands. "Father, Mother, God," she prayed, "please give me the strength to do Your will."

God's will. This was whose will she'd been trying to live by for the past two and a half years, ever since she'd closed the door on her own desires and declared herself to be "God's Princess." Ever since leaving college in shame and after a summer surrounded by her father's sermons and her mother's love, returning in victory. Princess walked to the minifridge in her cluttered UCLA dorm room, grabbed a soda, popped the top, and remembered.

The future had looked bright that sunny day in August three and a half years ago, when her mother and father had driven her to Kansas City's international airport for her LA-bound flight. She was leaving home for the first time, shaking with excitement at the prospects of her first year as a freshman at UCLA and at the blank canvas called "adult life" that stretched before her. Those first days of college had been all that she'd dreamed and more. And once she hooked up with basketball star, campus heartthrob, and almost-a-cousin-but-not-quite Kelvin Petersen, Princess's life had never been the same.

The ringing phone jolted Princess out of her reverie. She looked at the caller ID and smiled. "No, I haven't called," she answered.

"I knew it!" Joni screamed. Joni was Princess's best friend, former roommate, and former favorite party partner. When Princess decided to turn her life around and live a Christ-like lifestyle, she figured her days with "ole Joni girl" were num-bered. But Joni had surprised her. Joni had not given Princess a hard time for "finding Jesus," and after seeing the change in her former roommate, Joni had allowed Princess to lead her to Christ some months later. The shocks continued when, during their junior year, Joni confided that she had led someone else to salvation, her former weed-smoking, pill-popping boyfriend, Brandon. Joni and Brandon were now married, with plans to start a family after Joni graduated college. Brandon, who came from old money and had bypassed higher education, was al-ready making a name for himself in the world of finance.

"I'm going to call her," Princess whined. "I just know that once I tell her—"

"Yeah, yeah, the entire world will know. Or, more specifi-cally, Tai and King Brook will find out that at one time you were a very, very bad girl!"

"Quit playing," Princess admonished, but the reprimand was halfhearted. At one time, she *had* been a bad girl. And out-side of Kelvin; Brandon; Joni; Kelvin's mother, Tootie; and a few people in Germany, nobody knew just how bad Princess had been.

"Look, you're always telling the girls that who the Lord sets free is free indeed. Am I right? Well, you're not going to be totally free of your past until you are ready to not only face your history but also *embrace* it. You know that there are other girls out there just like you, suffering from the guilt and shame of their secrets. These are the same women who look up to you, because in their eyes you've got it so together. Just think of how much more they will respect you once they find out how far you've come. They'll figure that if you did it, turned your life around, then they can do it too."

"I agree with everything you're saying. It just seems so hard to put everything out there. Grandmama Max will be so disappointed. And I don't even want to think about Mama, or Tee . . ."

"That's exactly who you should be thinking of. The best way for your baby sister not to follow in your footsteps is for her to know about the path that she shouldn't go down." Joni softened her voice. "Princess, you can do this. You've got to do it. Because only then can you follow the voice of the Spirit . . . and write that book."

After a few more minutes, Princess disconnected from Joni and dialed her grandmother. She paced the floor, waiting for the phone to be picked up on the other end. After five rings, she was about to give up. What she had to say could not be left on voice mail.

"Hello?" Mama Max sounded out of breath as she answered her phone.

"Hey, Grandmama."

"Princess! Child, as I live and breathe, I just asked Tai about you this morning. Whew, let me catch my breath. I was just coming in from the store." Mama Max was quiet for a moment, taking off her shoes and fanning herself with a hastily grabbed newspaper. She plopped down on the sofa and took a long swallow from the ever-present glass of water on the coffee table. "Now, that's better. Okay, baby. You've been coming to me in my dreams. I was wondering when you were going to call and tell me what's what."

Princess smiled in spite of her nervousness. "Well, since you knew I'd call, do you know what I'm calling about?"

Mama Max's pause was short. "My guess is that it involves God, men, and probably some stuff you either should or shouldn't have been doing with one or the other. How right am I?"

Too right. "I'll have to talk to God about His sharing my business with you. But since you've pretty much sketched out the general picture, you might want to sit down, Grandmama Max. Because I'm getting ready to color it in for you."

8

His Baby's Mama

Kelvin Petersen leaned his lanky, six-foot-five frame against the shower tiles. He closed his eyes as the water pulsated over his body, and then turned so that his knee would feel the liquid massage. He'd just finished another round of physical therapy with the team doctor and wasn't too happy with what he'd heard: It would be another month before his knee was a hundred percent. The doctor was recommending that Kelvin's modified practice schedule continue and wouldn't confirm that he'd be ready to start at the beginning of the NBA season.

Kelvin turned so that the hot, pulsating water worked the muscles in his back, much as his masseuse would do in another hour. He didn't want to think about what the therapist had said, because that would mean thinking about Guy Harris, the man who dared threaten him for the position that last year was his alone—right point guard. Nobody questioned that Kelvin started in this position, every game. Not only did he dominate it on the team, but he was a dominating force in the league as well—that is, until the benefit game played a month ago, when the Denver Nuggets' lumbering center had become a tree, one that had sent Kelvin's attempted layup into the stands while the center became entangled in Kelvin's feet. All three hundred twenty-five pounds of this former Nebraskan came crashing down hard on Kelvin's right knee. Word had it that Guy was on the phone to their coach the very next day. And as of right now, Kelvin's nemesis was also in the starting lineup. Kelvin abruptly turned off the water, toweled off, and moments later was dressed and heading out of the training facility.

"KP! What up, dog?" It was Kelvin's friend and fellow baller, Jakeim.

"Nothin' to it, son," Kelvin said, reaching out for a brother's handshake.

"There's something to it, to hear your boy Guy talkin'."

"Aw, I ain't worried about that fool. He'll get put back in his place as soon as my knee's straight." Kelvin stepped back and feigned a fade away jumper. He tried not to wince as an ache sliced through the lower portion of his leg.

"Take it easy," Jakeim cautioned. "We got a long season ahead of us, and I'd definitely prefer to have you healthy for the homestretch."

"Don't worry, Keim. I'm going to be back on the court, full press, in three weeks. And I'm planning to work my way back into that starting position before the first game."

"Just know a brothah has your back," Jakeim said. He cocked a knowing smile at one of the secretaries who worked in the building and was looking at him the way a thirsty man would water. "Lookie here, dog, let me get with this feline and hollah back atcha."

"Aw-ight, Keim. Later." Kelvin deactivated the alarm on his cherry-red custom Ferrari Fiorano Coupe, opened the door, and slid inside. Something about sitting down in this creamy, off-white leather always made him feel good. But once his iPhone vibrated and he looked at the caller ID, his feel-good didn't feel so good anymore.

"What." Kelvin voiced the word like a statement, instead of a question. A man heading to the electric chair would have sounded happier.

"Is that any way to greet the mother of your child?"

The woman's silky voice grated like steel wool on soft skin. "I ain't up for no yakkity yak, Fawn. What do you want?"

"What I want," Fawn spat, all pretense of friendliness gone, "is some time and attention for me and my child. Little Kelvin hasn't seen you in a month! He misses his daddy!"

"That boy barely knows me."

"Yeah, and whose fault is that?"

"Look, I'm not in the mood for this bullshit, Fawn. I'm not the one who spent the end of last year in Miami, chasing another jock, courtesy of my child support. You weren't worried about me seeing my son then, now, were you? But now that he got cut and I'm healing, your ass is back on my side of the world talking about your son miss his daddy. You think I'm 'bout to bite down on that bullshit, you out your muthafuckin' mind."

"You know why I went to Miami, Kel." Fawn turned her voice silky again, almost childlike. "I was trying to get back at you for fuckin' my best friend."

"If she'd been your best friend, then she wouldn't have been in my bed, now, would she?"

"Any woman who gets the chance will climb into your bed, Kel. You know you've got it like that. Now, baby, can we come over? Please! Your son misses you; he really does. Here, baby, talk to your daddy."

Kelvin rolled his eyes. *Aw, here we go. This son-as-a-pawn bullshit all over again.* He tried to steel himself against the range of emotions he knew would accompany hearing his son's voice.

"Hi, Daddy!"

Kelvin's heart melted. "Hey, Little Man. What you doing?"

"Nothin'."

"You been a good boy?"

"Uh-huh." Kelvin heard Fawn's voice mutter something in the background before his son continued. "We comin' over, Daddy?"

I can't stand that bitch. "Put your mama on the phone."

After agreeing on a time and giving Fawn his new gate code, Kelvin ended the call. He reached into the console and pulled out a blunt, breathed in the smell of pungent weed mixed with vanilla-flavored tobacco and lit up. He loved the smell of vanilla. It had been one of his ex-girl's favorite scents. His ex-girl Princess. Kelvin allowed his mind to roll back as he took a long drag off the cigar-wrapped weed, punched in his iPod, and cruised through Phoenix's light afternoon traffic. At one time, he'd had Princess Brook wrapped around his finger. When he told her to jump, she'd simply ask "how high?" At one time, that girl would have done anything for him—and had. But that was almost three years ago, before Fawn got pregnant, and before Princess turned into a Holy Roller. That's what he'd heard, that Princess was like a campus preacher, trying to convert the campus crowd to Christ. Kelvin took another long hit off the blunt before rolling down the window and flicking the small remainder out the window. He turned up Lil Wayne and bobbed his head to "Lollipop," remembering when Princess had treated his body like one. But that seemed as if it had happened a whole other lifetime ago. Because in their last conversation, Princess had made it clear, in no uncertain terms, that what they'd had was over. . . .

"What do you mean, you're not coming down here? After I had to call all over LA to track you down? Why aren't you and Joni in the condo? And why aren't you using the cell phone I sent you? Look, never mind that. I just set up a round-trip, first-class ticket for you, woman. You better get your ass on that plane."

In the beginning, during those first few weeks back at UCLA following their breakup, Princess had considered Kelvin's offers. But she'd known those gifts came with strings attached. It had taken all of the previous summer to get him out of her system, and truth be told, he still wasn't completely gone. All the more reason for her to do what she knew she had to do—stay strong. "Things are different, Kelvin. I'm living for God now."

"Living for God?"

"I'm not the same girl who left college in May. For instance, I won't continue this conversation if you insist on using foul language. I'm God's Princess now."

"Oh, so I'm supposed to believe you all, what, celibate and shit? That you're not getting your smoke on, your drink on, or fuckin'? Oh, my bad, *making love?*" Kelvin looked in the mirror at his rock-hard abs as he paced the floor of his home gym. "This is Kelvin Petersen you're talking to, baby. I know I turned that shit out right there. You gotta come, because the 'KP' is callin'."

Silence had filled the air then, and Kelvin remembered how strong Princess's voice had sounded when she finally responded. "This conversation is over, Kelvin. Have a nice life."

"Have a nice . . . What the hell is that supposed to mean?"

"I can show you better than I can tell you, Kelvin, and I want you to listen up: Jesus is my boo." The click in his ear signaled her good-bye.

That was the last time he'd spoken to Princess, almost two years ago. He'd called again, but the number had been disconnected. Later, he found out she'd moved back on campus. According to Brandon, who kept him informed on all things Princess, she'd moved back so she could better minister to her fellow students. Fawn thought she knew everything, but she didn't know this: while almost any woman who had the chance would climb into his bed, Kelvin's mind was on the only woman who had climbed out of it . . . and stayed out.

9

Just the Two of Us

Carla Chapman turned on her side and raised her thick leg high in the air. Some people might have been surprised at how limber this size 18 body was, but her insatiable husband was more than enough reason for this cushioned sister to keep her body pliable. She moaned with pleasure as Lavon parted her flesh, sank in to the hilt, pulled out, and sank in again.

"Is this what you've been waiting for?" he whispered, his breath hot and wet against her ear hole.

"All d-day," she stuttered as Lavon shifted strategically to hit her sensitive spot.

"Uh-huh, well I'm going to give you as much as you can stand." Lavon lifted Carla's leg higher, settling into a smooth lovemaking rhythm. He reached up and tweaked one of Carla's luscious, forty-four double d's before running his hand over the chocolate belly he loved to jiggle and down to the folds of her feminine paradise, where he heightened her pleasure with a finger working a rhythm all its own.

"Oh, baby . . ." Carla could barely get out the words, so expertly was Lavon playing all her keys. Her moans continued as he found another sensitive spot and massaged it the same way his penis massaged her insides. Lavon pulled out suddenly and handled her body as if she were a size 6. He turned her on her side, directed her to her knees, grabbed a hold of her shoulder-length weave, and entered her from behind. Soon, almost four hundred combined pounds of sexual healing and body slapping had the springs creaking, the windows shaking, and the four-poster bedposts hitting the walls. It was a good thing these adults had the house to themselves, because based on the sounds emitting from the home's master suite, one of Carla's kids may have dialed 911. Fortunately, Brianna, Shay, and Winston were spending the week with their other family: Stan; Passion; and Passion's daughter, Onyx. Carla could only imagine their Huxtable-like activities. Hers and Lavon's alone time, however, resembled *Sex and the sho'nuff City!*

"Oh, baby, that was so good." Carla cuddled her gleaming body into Lavon's equally perspiring one and gave him a sloppy wet kiss. "I don't know how you keep getting better, but you do."

"This inspires me," Lavon said, playfully pinching Carla's ample butt cheek. "And this," he said, patting her furry mound. "And this," he whispered, licking her neck.

"Stop, that tickles."

"Oh, you want me to stop now?" Lavon playfully pushed Carla away from him.

"Don't even think of getting out of this bed." Carla rolled over and threw her leg over Lavon's as she faced him. She took in the ordinary-looking, extra-dark face that turned her on more than Denzel Washington—either the actor or her so-named former rubber friend—ever could: the bushy eyebrows, beady eyes, thick nose and lips. Lavon wasn't your typically handsome man, but he could give any pretty boy a run for his money below the waist. She reached up and wiped away beads of sweat, smiling at the man who'd replaced her prudish, frigid ex-husband and finally allowed her to throw her dildo away. *The real thing is definitely better than the imitation, and close to the nine inches the manufacturer made.* "I love you so much, Lavon Chapman. I didn't know a woman could feel this much love for a man."

"So, was I worth it?" Lavon's tone was playful but his eyes were searching.

Carla knew what Lavon was thinking about—the very public scandal, church ouster, and subsequent divorce she'd endured over three years ago. Lavon, on the other hand, had come through the ordeal fairly unscathed. Except for the hurt he felt for what she went through, hurt that he obviously still felt. Carla caressed his cheek tenderly before kissing his juicy lips. "I'd go through everything again to end up right here, right now, with you."

"What did I do to deserve you?" Lavon kissed Carla's nose and enveloped her in his strong, meaty arms. "I love you, woman."

The two satisfied adults lay in each other's arms, catching their breath and thanking God that they'd found each other. For each, it had been quite the journey, one that both thought might be the end of Carla Danielle Ellison Lee Chapman. Neither was proud of the fact that their love affair had begun when Carla was married to Doctor Stan Lee and was copastor of Logos Word Interdenominational Church. Lavon had gone to the church to produce a series of inspirational DVDs for the ministry, but he ended up with the minister instead. It hadn't been pretty, and both were sorry that the affair had happened, but neither was sorry for the outcome. They'd asked forgiveness for their former transgression—from God, from Carla's former husband, and from her children—and then they'd moved on to embrace the love that God had given.

That they were soul mates was not even a question. Carla and Lavon fit together like white on rice, eggs and bacon, chicken and waffles, sausage and grits. That their professional lives melded together as easily as their private ones was further proof that theirs was a love meant to be. Lavon was the executive producer of Carla's nationally syndicated talk show, *Conversations with Carla,* a show that had flourished under his hands-on guidance. Carla knew many of her Christian friends would disagree with her, but she believed it was God who had sent Lavon to their church to film the Logos Word ministry. And as hard as the subsequent disgrace had been to endure, Carla felt God had a hand in that too. For the prize she now held, and who held her in his arms, she'd again endure the cross of persecution. *Must Jesus bear the cross alone, and all this world go free. . . .*

"A penny for your thoughts, Puddin'."

"Is that all they're worth?" Carla reached over for a sheet to cover them. "I was just thinking about a message left earlier, on my private line at the studio."

"Who was it?"

"Believe it or not, it was Maxine Brook, Tai's mother."

"Girl, I know who Mama Max is. I once belonged to King and Tai's church, remember?"

"Oh, yeah, I forgot that you're a church ho, changing your membership like women change shoes." Carla laughed when Lavon pinched her tittie.

"Your fine butt is what pulled me away from Mount Zion, believe that. What'd Mama Max want?"

"Wants me to call her. Says she just heard a story that needs to be told, and she thinks my show is the place to tell it."

"Oh, Lord. With Mama Max, that tale could be just about anything, especially if it has anything to do with her sleep-around son."

"King? Not anymore. He's being faithful to Tai, at least he'd better be." Carla was silent for a moment as she thought of Tai Brook, her sister in the Lord, who'd endured her own share of pulpit pain down through the years. "No, I don't think it's about Tai and King. But whoever or whatever it's about, Mama Max will have my ear. But not until Monday because," Carla purred, kissing Lavon's chest, "this weekend"—she kissed his neck—"is all about . . . just the two of us." Carla kissed Lavon's lips and continued singing the Grover Washington classic as she eased off the bed. She turned, jutted out her sizeable assets, and put her hand on her hip. The stance was saucy and seductive. "I'm going to take a shower. Care to join me?"

Anyone watching would have been surprised to see a big man move so fast. "Baby, this sounds like round two." Lavon sidled up behind Carla and rocked her in his arms. "Just the two of us . . ." The lovers hummed and two-stepped their way into the shower.

10

A Different Kind of Meal

Passion pushed away from the computer. She was trying to come up with a Thanksgiving menu, but her heart wasn't in it. Stan had asked her to fix an intimate, preholiday dinner for the associate ministers and their wives, to be served the Saturday before Thanksgiving. It wasn't that Passion had a problem cooking. She was a Georgia peach who felt she could throw down with the best of them. No, the turkey in the pan wasn't the problem, but the turkey sleeping in her bed was. Stan wanted her to keep on the happy-first-lady face, let the world believe that theirs was a happy marriage. But Stan was finding more reasons to stay at his church office, while she'd found more unmentionables in his office at home. The truth of the matter was that Passion was becoming unhappier with each passing day. And she didn't know what to do about it.

Unbidden, a picture of the man who got away came into her mind, the man whose photo she'd recently seen in *LA Gospel,* escorting his wife to the NAACP Image Awards. *Don't, Passion, don't even go there.* Even as her head said no, her heart said yes. She closed her eyes and remembered Lavon Chapman's deep kisses and probing tongue—remembered the night they both lost control and almost had sex. Unlike Stan, Passion had no doubts Lavon knew how to use the massive gift

God had blessed him with. And now someone else was getting all that good loving, and she was left with that woman's languid leftover.

"Mommy! Mommy, it's me. I'm home!"

Thank God for diversions. That line of thought will lead to nothing but trouble. Passion smiled as her pride and joy bounded into the den. At eight years old, Onyx was a braided bundle of energy: smart, inquisitive, and, if Passion didn't rein her in, as rambunctious as all get-out. Onyx had adjusted well to having a father figure in the home, and Stan seemed to shower the same love upon her that he did his own kids. *I have to give him that—he's a great father.* She only wished he was a great husband as well.

"Hey, sweetie pie, how was your day?"

"Not too good, Mommy."

Passion watched with humor as Onyx pasted an exaggerated frown on her face. "It's Charlie McPherson. He keeps pulling my braids at recess, and I don't like it. I know you told me that fighting isn't ladylike, but if he does it again, I'm gonna knock him on his behind!"

Passion stifled a smile. "Now, Onyx, you know you can't do that. What about Mrs. Abrams? Did you tell your teacher about what little Charlie is doing?"

"Only a hundred times," Onyx said, rolling her eyes and crossing her tiny arms for good measure. "But all she does is stomp her foot and say, 'Charlie, stop it right this minute. Be a good boy.'"

Onyx's mimicking Mrs. Abrams was spot-on, and Passion didn't try and contain her laughter. "Well, I tell you what. The next time Charlie pulls your braid, just tell him he's doing that because he likes you and thinks you're the prettiest little girl at Rolling Hills Elementary. I bet that will put a stop to his bothering you."

"Yuck! I don't like Charlie. His hair is red, and he has

freckles and wears braces! But he better stop messing with me, Mommy. Or I'm gonna knock him out!"

"All right, Michelle Tyson. What do you say about a little snack to tide you over until dinner? Would you like a couple chicken fingers with some chips?"

"Can I have them with barbeque sauce, my favorite?"

"Yes, honey."

While getting the frozen fingers from the freezer, Passion's eyes fell on the twenty-pound turkey Stan had bought for the dinner he wanted. The holiday dinner that was supposed to be filled with joy and cheer. Passion's smile became sinister as a plan unfolded in her head. If Stan wanted his little we're-one-big-happy-family dinner, then there was something he'd have to give Passion in return. Sure, it ached her heart a little to have to bribe her husband into having sex with her, but the dildo she'd purchased mere months into her marriage wasn't working out. She didn't like masturbating, couldn't help but feel it was wrong, even though she was married. And the further truth was, she loved her husband and she loved making love to him. Stan had the equipment. If he really wanted to, Passion felt he could be an excellent lover . . . like that last time after the fight in Texas. He'd actually hit her G-spot for the very first time. But after returning to Los Angeles, Stan had reverted back to his old self, not wanting to have sex and not wanting to talk about their Texas rendezvous. That was already more than a month ago. In Passion's mind, it was way past time for the two to become one again, and as she sat Onyx's plate on the dining room table and walked back into the den, she had two things in mind: the pre–Thanksgiving Day menu saved on the computer and a different kind of meal that she'd be requesting just as soon as Stan got home.

11

Lightning Done Struck

Nettie Thicke Johnson took a long swig of sweet tea and leaned back against the fluffy floral sofa her son Nate had gifted her two Christmases ago. She'd been on the phone for the past two hours, calling members, especially those she hadn't seen in the past three months, and encouraging them to come out for the early morning Thanksgiving Day service. "Break bread with Christ before you break bread with your family," she'd gently admonished, referring to the special Lord's supper that would be offered Thanksgiving morning. Most people had made a halfhearted promise to be there. Others told her they'd moved their membership, either to Reverend Jenkins's church, the Methodist church, or a church out of town. Nettie gazed into the distance, remembering how just two short years ago, there would have been standing room only at any service her son conducted. Nate Thicke had been the drawing power, no doubt about that. Things had not been the same at Gospel Truth since he and his family had left Palestine and moved to Turks and Caicos.

Nettie picked up the phone to dial again, but it rang before she got the chance. "Hello?"

"Miss Nettie? This is Anne Black, returning your call."

"Hey, Sistah Black, how you doin'?"

"Doing fine, Miss Nettie, miss seeing you, though."

"Well, child, that's just why I'm calling. To find out why we haven't seen you at church lately and to invite you to early morning service Thanksgiving Day."

"Miss Nettie, no disrespect, but I'm not too keen on the new pastor."

"Now, baby, Revered Doctor O—"

"You mean Reverend Doctor Oh *No?* Because that's his favorite word. You can't even breathe and be a Christian according to the way he preaches."

"The good reverend doctor," Nettie continued without acknowledging Anne's dig, "is preaching the unadulterated word of God. It might not taste good going down, but this religious medicine is good all the same."

"All he does is tell us what we can't do. Why can't I buy a lotto ticket? You can't win if you don't play!"

"He's preaching Bible."

"Where in the Bible does it say I can't watch *Grey's Anatomy?* What's wrong with enjoying *The Price Is Right?* And who's this 'Moral Board' that decided what is and isn't sinful on TV? It doesn't matter, Miss Nettie," Anne continued, her voice softer. "The TV shows weren't even the last straw."

"Well, what was, baby?"

"It was when Sistah Jones escorted me back to the choir room so I could cover my arms. Miss Nettie, it was ninety-five degrees that day!"

"But the book plainly says 'no elbows can show.' "

"Doctor Oh *No's* book, not the Good Book. I'm sorry, Miss Nettie. I'm going home for Thanksgiving. But even if I was going to be here, I wouldn't be attending Gospel Truth on Thanksgiving, or any other day. Again, I don't mean no disrespect to you. I've always admired your faith. Even after Reverend Thicke resigned, you know I was still in that choir stand every time the church doors opened. But I have to tell you something. When it comes to Doctor Obadiah's heaven, I don't think anybody in Palestine, save for you and Mama Max, can make it in."

Nettie's heart was heavy as she hung up the phone. She understood Anne's frustration; the new Gospel Truth rules were stricter than normal. But desperate times had called for desperate measures. Reverend Doctor O had done what he felt necessary to to bring order back into the house of God. "Humph. Those folks better off keeping their money in their pockets rather than wasting it in slot machines and bingo halls," Nettie muttered to herself as she walked to the bathroom. "And who cares about an anatomy—gray or any other color?"

The tires on Mama Max's jet-black Thunderbird had barely stopped rolling before she opened the car door and hurried to Nettie's front door. She didn't notice that her usually perfectly coiffed hair was coming down in the back or that she wore one black sock and one navy blue one underneath her charcoal-gray warm-ups. She huffed up the steps, crossed the porch, and punched the doorbell three times in a row.

"Hold your horses!" Nettie shouted, drying her hands and walking quickly to the door at the same time. She never stopped talking as she opened the door. "Where on earth is the fire? I tell you the tru—Mama Max? Is that you running up those steps as if lightning is about to strike?"

"Lighting done struck, child, and Satan's on the loose. Open up this here door 'cause you ain't gonna believe what I just heard."

Nettie quickly opened the door. The hug she meant for Mama Max's shoulder barely touched her back as Mama Max hurried past Nettie into the living room. "Lawd, I know you ain't got no Baileys Irish Cream but I sure could use some in my coffee right now!"

"Come on back to the kitchen while I put on a pot, Mama. And tell me what on earth has you in such a state!"

Mama Max followed Nettie to the kitchen. "We're the only ones here, right?"

"Uh-huh. Some of the churchwomen are coming over in an hour or so, but it's just you and me until then."

"It's them Noble bitches, stirring up my blood again!" Mama Max's face contorted as she fairly hissed out this news. The Nobles were a family of beautiful, cultured, and some would say conniving women who'd lived in Palestine off and on for decades.

"Katherine?" Nettie hadn't seen Katherine for over a year, since the former church member had relocated to New Orleans to live near her daughter.

"Worse, her sister, Dorothea."

"Dorothea Bates? What on earth about Dorothea has your blood riled?"

"She's here in Palestine, that's what!"

"Are you sure? Dorothea's shadow hasn't darkened these parts in ten, twenty years. Besides, if she were here in town, I'm pretty sure I'd know about it. Her grandniece is my daughter-in-law, after all."

"Well, she's here. Heard it with my own ears."

"From who?" Nettie handed Mama Max a steaming cup of coffee, then reached into the refrigerator for flavored creamer. "This Irish Crème creamer is as close to your Baileys as I can do."

Mama Max was too wrapped up in her thoughts to hear her. "Now, you know I'm not one to be nosy. . . ."

Nettie hid a smile.

"But I passed by the bedroom and heard the reverend doctor talking all lowlike. So I tiptoed into the guest room and picked up the receiver. Now, you know I'm not one to be nosy, but when the Spirit nudges me to do a thing, I try and be obedient. So I picked up that phone, yes, I did. And I heard her."

"She was on the phone with your husband?"

Mama Max nodded. "And that ain't all. The phone hadn't rung, which means she wasn't the one who'd done the calling. I just can't believe this!" Mama Max set down her mug so hard that coffee sloshed over the sides. "How long has he been consorting behind my back?"

Nettie frowned. "You mean . . . cavorting?"

"That too. How long has he been in touch with Dorothea?"

"Now, Mama. It's obvious you have some kind of history with this woman but—"

"Forty years! That's how long it's been since I laid eyes on her. Ever since I caught my husband in her room all those years ago. He promised me that he'd never see her again, and I believed him!"

Nettie was shocked but not surprised at Mama Max's revelation. Unfortunately, she was all too familiar with how men of God sometimes strayed. It had happened with her own preacher husband, who'd carried on a lengthy affair with Dorothea's sister, Katherine Noble. The two saw each other until his untimely death from a car accident. "Maybe he's told the truth," she finally offered. "Maybe he hasn't seen Dorothea in all these years."

"Then how'd he get her number? How does he know anything about that . . . Lord, it ain't worth losing my religion to call her what she is, God forgive me for the truthful name I used earlier. But I'm telling you, this has got me powerful upset! Reverend ain't said a word, ain't mouthed a peep about who's in town for Thanksgiving."

"Well, now, you just pray on it, Mama Max. Then maybe she'll be long gone by Christmas time."

12

Still My Princess

Today, I'm proud to call myself God's Princess. I've always been a princess—that's what my parents named me—but I didn't always belong to God. I thought I did. I got baptized, went to church, sang in the choir, and attended revivals. I had the Lord in my head, but not in my heart. I found this out the hard way, during my first year at college, my first time away from home and away from the watchful eye of my parents. What happened during this year is what I'm about to share with you. I'm not going to lie, sharing my shortcomings is not an easy thing to do. But living with the guilt of being disobedient would be harder. And I believe God wants me to share my testimony to maybe help someone else. To maybe help you. He wants you to know the backstory so you'll understand the love story . . . so that you'll know why, in no uncertain terms, that Jesus Is My Boo.

Princess sat back against the wall in her old bedroom and read what she'd written, the prologue to her self-help memoir. She felt safe here, surrounded by childhood memories and familiar sights and sounds. Her parents hadn't done much to her room since she'd left that first time three years ago, nor had they changed the family routine. Her mother was downstairs cooking up a Thanksgiving storm. Her brother, Michael, was in his room, the pounding bass of whatever he was listening to vibrating through the walls. And the twins, Timothy and Tabitha, or Tee as Princess and her friends called her, three years her junior, were deep into a Wii tennis match. No, things hadn't changed much, and this was just the way Princess liked it. That's why she'd waited until the Thanksgiving holiday to begin to write. She wanted to begin working on her book in the same way her journey into womanhood had begun—at home. And she'd wanted to begin it now for another reason— so she could share the first chapter with her mom, after she'd shared the secrets she'd told Mama Max. *I'll do that later . . . maybe tonight.*

Princess looked at her table of contents. The first chapter was titled "The Journey Begins." In her outline, Princess had decided to write about the excitement of the months leading up to her leaving home, beginning with the day she'd learned her application to UCLA had been accepted. Smiling, she began typing on her laptop, recording her memories from that happy time.

"Yo, Princess!" Michael opened her door without knocking, something else that was just like old times.

"How many times do I have to tell you to knock, fool?"

"At least one more time, evidently. If you don't want to be bothered, then lock your door."

"What do you want?"

"The telephone. It's for you." Michael threw the cordless on the bed and walked out of the room.

Princess hesitated on taking the call. More than likely it was Rafael, the boy she'd dated in high school and who was still a good friend. They'd reconnected after her breakup with Kelvin and had agreed to get together while both were home for the holidays.

I'll make it quick. "Hello?"

A voice as smooth as liquid poured into her ear. "Hey, baby. How's my princess?"

Kelvin! As if on cue, her heart began pounding in her chest. She'd forgotten that he had her parents' number. Had she remembered, she would have made it clear to all concerned that for anybody answering to the name Kelvin Petersen, she was not available. It had been two years since she'd talked to him, and now she remembered the reason. Because no matter how much her mind said she was over him, her body always betrayed her. She thought seriously about hanging up the phone.

"Princess? You still there? Don't hang up, baby."

"What do you want?" Princess asked, gripping the phone as if it were a lifeline.

"Just wanted to talk to you, baby, to hear your voice."

"Don't 'baby' me, Kelvin. We've been over for a while now."

"Don't matter. You'll always be my princess."

"I'm going to hang up now, Kelvin. Please don't call my parents' house again."

"No, wait!"

Against her better judgment, Princess remained on the line. "What?" She didn't mean for her voice to get whispery; it did so of its own accord.

"I've been thinking about you, Princess. I just wanted to find out how you've been, what you're up to. Just because we're not dating anymore doesn't mean we can't be friends."

Princess closed her eyes against her feelings and the memories his voice evoked. She searched for a memory that would be useful in this moment. And then one came to her—Fawn. "No, Kelvin, we cannot be friends. I'm living a different lifestyle now, a Christian lifestyle, and my friendships reflect my values."

"I'm a Christian. Remember the rev baptized me after I moved into his house, during my junior year of high school."

Princess remembered. Her play-uncle, Derrick Montgomery, had baptized Kelvin shortly after moving him into the Montgomery household, which was shortly after finding out he was Kelvin's father, the product of a casual relationship before he'd married and took a church. She could have looked no further than her uncle to see the grown-folks pain that came with grown-folks pleasure. But she'd been eighteen with a bullet the summer she moved to Los Angeles. Nobody could have told her a thing.

"Being a Christian and being Christ-like are not always the same thing. Are you still getting high, Kelvin? Drinking, fornicating . . ."

"Forna-who?"

"Having sex outside of marriage. The people I hang around now don't do any of those things. And neither do I. So I really don't see what we have in common to constitute a friendship."

"We loved each other once." Kelvin's voice dropped and stroked Princess's ear. "I still love you."

Jesus is my boo. Jesus is my boo! "Somebody else has all my love right now, Kelvin."

For the first time since they started talking, Kelvin's voice became stern. "Who is he? Is it that dude you used to date back in high school, the one at KU? I bet he's home for the holidays, talking a good game and whatnot. Baby, come spend Thanksgiving with me. I can give you the world, Princess, treat you better than any other man can even think about treating you. I'll buy you whatever you want: cars, furs, diamonds, trips, you name it, baby, and it's yours."

"See, this is the difference I'm talking about, the one you can't understand. I'd rather have Jesus, Kelvin, than silver and gold."

Damn, her voice sounds good. "Baby, why can't you have them both—"

"Kelvin, where are you?!" In the background, Fawn's voice could clearly be heard. "What are you doing sitting in the dark? Who's the bitch on the phone now?" Her high-pitched voice rose even higher as she yelled louder. "Whoever you are, he's mine, bitch. I ain't going nowhere so you might as well back your shit—"

That was the last word Princess heard. She did what she should have done moments earlier—ended the call. But she'd heard enough to know that Kelvin was still Kelvin, the big baller with all the chicks, all the weed, all the money, and all the baby mama drama.

Thank you, Jesus. Thank you for reminding me what I left, and why I left it. Princess lay down the phone, picked up her laptop, and looked at the title of Chapter Two: "My First Love Wasn't Jesus, but It Should Have Been."

He'd been raised to be a gentleman and would never consider bodily force when dealing with females. But in this moment, Kelvin swore he understood how a man could hit a woman. He was so mad at Fawn he couldn't see straight.

"What did I tell you about that, huh?" Kelvin shouted. When Fawn didn't answer, Kelvin walked over to the couch and stood over her. "What did I tell you about doing that shit when I'm on the phone?"

"You just mad because I interrupted whatever rendezvous you were planning with some ho. Ain't no bitch out there as bad as me, who'll put up with your bullshit and still give you the best pussy you ever had. You remember that."

"Oh, so that's it. You think your shit's golden, huh?"

"You must think so, since I'm still here."

Kelvin picked up a glass and threw it across the room. It hit the wall and shattered into dozens of pieces. Fawn hardly flinched.

"I must have been outta my muthafuckin' mind to let you move in here. And your lyin' ass saying Little Kelvin was sick."

"He was, he—"

"Stop lying, Fawn! I know you haven't been to the doctor's. I talked to Brandy."

On hearing that name, Fawn rolled her eyes. Brandy was a twin who joined them regularly for a ménage à trios—one of the many women he'd slept with during his college days, and now. "You gonna listen to that ho over me?"

"No, I didn't listen to her. I listened to the doctor's office after talking to her."

Fawn looked up quickly.

"Yeah, that's right. Did a little detective work. I've been thinking y'all was at the hospital, and instead your ass was at the mall."

"Look, Kelvin, Little Man was sick."

"So was I. I was sick as hell to let your ass move in here. But I tell you what. I'm better now. And just as fast as your ass moved in here, you're moving right back out. You said you needed a place to stay until our son got better? Well, he's better now. So you need to get your shit and get out."

"If you want to keep seeing your son, I don't need to do a damn thing."

"Oh, I'll keep seeing him, believe that. But it won't be because you're in my house. It will be because you want to keep getting a check every month, the one that is going to cease until I get visitation, in writing, and until you get the fuck out!"

"I ain't going nowhere."

Kelvin stared at Fawn a long moment. She was fine, he'd grant her that, but other than looks, he didn't know what he'd ever seen in her. And all he wanted now was a life without her in it. "Fine! Then I'll leave."

Kelvin walked out of the den and into his bedroom. He

called his uncle Geoff, the one who was always just a phone call away when he needed to be bailed out of trouble.

His uncle picked up the cell on the second ring. "Happy holidays, Kelvin! You coming this way for Thanksgiving?"

"As a matter of fact, I am, Uncle. And by the time I get back to Phoenix, I need you to have found me a new house."

B

Written All Over His Face

Obadiah's movements were slow as he made his way to the hall and down the steps. He could hear his wife humming from the kitchen, even as the smell of collard greens and candied yams wafted up to greet him. *She's gonna be mad as all get-out. But I've got to tell her.* "Probably knows already," he mumbled as he reached the bottom stair.

Mama Max looked up briefly before placing the pan of freshly made biscuits into the oven. Just because service started at 8 a.m. was no reason for her not to make breakfast as she had almost every morning for the last fifty years. As she turned to flip the sausage, her mouth fixed into a frown from what she'd seen when she glimpsed the reverend: a fine man looking as spiffy as ever. Mama Max wouldn't even try and lie to herself by saying the doctor wasn't a handsome man of seventy-two. For one, he looked ten years younger, especially dressed up as he was now in his Sunday go-to-meeting clothes. Two, unlike other men his age, Stanley Obadiah still stood an unbent six feet tall. All of that preaching had kept his paunch to a minimum, although he put on some pounds with his sicknesses a while back. But he still had a head full of gorgeous gray hair, eyes that twinkled, and except for a crown and bridge on the back right side, all of his own teeth. Yes, her husband still cut quite a swath. Unfortunately, she knew she wasn't the only one who thought so.

"Coffee's on," Mama Max said over her shoulder while reaching up in the cabinet for the sorghum molasses.

"Um."

So you ain't gonna tell me, huh? Mama Max began to hum as she set a bowl of sugar and a carton of half-and-half on the table. *Jesus keep me near the cross. There's a precious fountain . . .*

"Somebody might be at church this morning," Obadiah began in his deep, raspy voice. "You ain't gonna like it if she shows, but I want you to know she might be there."

"Who is it?" *The wicked witch of the south?* "I know you're not going to say Dorothea Bates. Ain't no husband of mine would have the nerve to come in here and tell me that."

Obadiah sighed heavily before taking a drink of coffee. Mama Max pulled the biscuits from the oven and slammed the tin down on the stove. Obadiah jumped.

"Now, Maxine, I'm telling you so you don't go off. She wants to come praise the Lord, thank him for bringing her through some things. How could I deny her the right to come to God's house?"

"Why can't she praise Him somewhere else? What's she doing here, Obadiah?"

"She's here to see Jenkins—the two of them have been . . . courting."

This news stunned Mama Max into silence for a moment, and she decided she'd have to digest what she'd heard before talking about it. "Then why ain't she heading to his church this morning?"

"First Baptist don't have early morning service, and Jenkins has been a little under the weather, or so I hear."

Mama leaned back against the counter, crossed her arms, and glared at her husband. "You heard it from Dorothea, no doubt. How long have y'all been communicating, Obadiah? And why did she feel the need to tell you her business?" In her anger, Mama Max began wiping off an already clean counter. "She's got nerve, coming in my face."

"Maxine, what happened between y'all was a long time ago. Let it rest."

Mama Max brought over a homemade sausage biscuit, piping hot, and set it in front of Obadiah. "I'll let it rest, Stanley Obadiah. Question is, will you?"

An hour later, Mama Max sat next to Nettie on the front pew. She swore to herself that she wouldn't turn around, but rather, she'd watch her husband. If Dorothea Noble Bates showed up at church this morning, the news would be written all over Obadiah's face.

The headline came across his forehead about thirty minutes later. Any other time, Mama Max would have thought it funny how Obadiah tried to keep his face neutral. But she saw it: how his eyes narrowed, just the littlest bit, and how his lips went into a hard line. There weren't that many people at early morning service; she guessed around a hundred. So it wouldn't be hard to see Dorothea when the chance to turn around came. Not that it would have mattered, Mama Max thought wryly. *Could have been a thousand people in this here building and Satan would still stick out like a sore thumb.*

The choir stood as the offering was lifted. Nettie resisted the urge to cringe. She knew that the Lord could use anybody, but the truth of the matter was, most of the good voices had been swept out of the church with Obadiah's broom. Those in the stand now were the ones who wouldn't have had a shot when Nate was around. "It's all right anyhow," she said with fervor, as the off-key soprano soloist began a Baptist classic:

> There is a Name I love to hear,
> I love to sing its worth;
> It sounds like music in my ear,
> The sweetest Name on earth.

People began fanning even though it was forty degrees outside and no elbows showed. A few children giggled and were quickly shushed by stern looks and a couple open palms meeting chubby cheeks. The choir, such as it was, joined in with the chorus:

Oh, how I love Jesus,
Oh how I love Jesus
Oh, how I love Jesus,
Because He first loved me.

Mama Max almost smiled when she saw her husband rise from his chair and gesture for the microphone. *I knew he wasn't going to let them butcher one of his favorite songs.* Then she remembered who was in the audience . . . watching. *Humph. Sucka probably just showing off.*

It tells me of a Savior's love,
Who died to set me free;
It tells me of His precious blood,
The sinner's perfect plea.

There was no denying Obadiah's powerful voice. A few parishioners stood and raised their arms toward heaven. Nettie joined in with her vibrant alto, and soon Mama Max was swaying and singing along with the rest of the crowd. They'd almost gotten through all of the verses, when a strong, pulsating soprano rose above the rest of the voices:

It bids my trembling heart rejoice,
It dries each rising tear,
It tells me, in a still small voice, to trust and never fear.

Mama Max gritted her teeth, resentment and jealousy jumping into her heart before she could stop it. She remembered the woman who'd chased her man in Dallas: tall, buxom, with long, thick black hair, plush red lips, and velvety light skin. And that voice. It was as strong and melodious as it had sounded forty years ago, as if an angel had come down from heaven to serenade. Mama Max could feel the presence of the Spirit, even through her annoyance. *Bless your enemies. Do good to them that persecute you.* Mama Max gave her head a little shake, trying to tune out the voice of God. *She needs your forgiveness. Give it to her.*

As Dorothea continued to sing, Mama Max slowly turned her head toward the sound, along with the others. Her eyes widened briefly before she forced a neutral expression on her face. There, standing in the last row of the church, was Dorothea Noble Bates, a shadow of her former, beautiful self. The thick, shiny black hair that was once the envy of females was now white and thinning, pulled back in a sharp bun. Her face was sallow, with wrinkles and bags that hinted to a story of a difficult life. Dorothea had always been slender, but now she looked almost anorexic, her collarbone protruding from the neck of her dress in a grotesque fashion. But her voice was clear, pitch-perfect. And as she sang the last verse, she opened her eyes, looked directly at Mama Max, and then moved forward to the front of the church. Dorothea looked at Obadiah, whose voice matched hers perfectly, and at that moment, it was as if the two sang only to each other.

> *And there with all the blood-bought throng, from sin and sorrow free,*
> *I'll sing the new eternal song of Jesus's love for me.*
> *Oh how I love Jesus, oh how I love Jesus, oh how I love Jesus*
> *Because he first loved me.*

Mama Max lowered her head, as if to hide behind the wide-brimmed, bright orange felt hat she wore. But there was not enough lace in Palestine, let alone on the front of this headpiece, to shield her from what was in her own heart. The temporary pity she'd felt for Dorothea Bates had been replaced with intense anger, and she envisioned a scene that included her giving this nervy songbird a good thrashing. *How dare that hussy come to this church and take over the service like I'm not here!* Dorothea sang her heart out, and tears rolled down her eyes as she stood in front of the church. Obadiah remained in the pulpit and finally tore his eyes away from Dorothea to aim them toward heaven. Mama Max would never have admitted it, but the duet was beautiful, and many in the congregation were heartily enjoying Obadiah and Dorothea's blatant worship of God, and subtle worship of each other.

The last note hung in the air, joined by choruses of "Amen" and "Thank you, Jesus." A few of the older women got happy, and two nurses hurried over with Kleenex and fans. Nettie, one of only a handful of people who knew the Dorothea/Maxine history, wiped her eyes, even as she could almost feel Maxine's anger burning the arm that touched her sleeve. Still, she felt the spirit of God even more and waved a hand in the air. "Hallelujah!" she said once, and then again. But those who hadn't felt the Spirit, or weren't caught up in their own personal praise, looked with curious eyes between Dorothea and Gospel Truth's first lady.

Obadiah clearing his throat caused Mama Max to open her eyes and look up. The way he looked at her was hard to discern, and that made Mama Max, who always felt she could read her husband like a book, uncomfortable. She broke the stare with Obadiah and watched as Dorothea began walking to her seat.

"Praise the Lord!" Obadiah said in a booming voice. Various responses were shouted from a majority of the early morning worshippers. "Praise Him again, I say!" A louder chorus of "Amen" and other terms of agreement ensued. "I want to take this time to thank an old Gospel Truth member—well, when the church was Palestine Baptist—for letting God use her and the voice He gave her. Mrs. Bates, would you stand again?"

Dorothea had just sat down, having received a variety of handshakes and arm pats on the way back to her seat. She slowly and somewhat shyly stood up, acknowledging the claps and grins directed at her. She also made very sure not to look anywhere near the direction of Maxine Brook.

"I hope I'm not out of order in announcing this news," Obadiah continued. "But Sistah Bates is back in Palestine for a happy occasion." He looked questioningly at Dorothea and when she nodded slightly, continued. "Most of you are too young to have known Sistah Bate's late husband, but he was a fine, God-fearing man."

He couldn't have feared God too much if he married that husband-chasin' heifah. Mama Max reached into her purse for a peppermint, hoping that sucking on it would prevent her from cursing this woman out in the sanctuary. She kept a slight, appreciative smile on her face, but Nettie could almost feel the anger pulsating from her friend. She reached over and gave Mama Max's arm a little squeeze. Mama Max kept sucking and picked up a fan, trying to cool herself down.

"Well, God has once again blessed Sister Bates with a godly man, Reverend Reginald Jenkins." At this news, a small murmur began, especially among the older members. "As y'all know, Reverend Jenkins has been widowed for some years now. So let's praise the Lord for his faithfulness, that he can bring love into your life no matter your age. Reverend Jenkins would have worshipped with us this morning but is under the weather. Please keep him in your prayers."

After nodding politely, Dorothea sat down. So far, the service had gone as she and Obadiah planned. She'd wanted her impending marriage to Reginald announced publicly, and she'd especially wanted Maxine Brook to be there. Dorothea didn't want there to be any suspicions that the flame between her and

Obadiah burned brighter and hotter than ever. Dorothea would have done anything to be near Obadiah, including marrying his one-time rival. Hopefully today's announcement would put to rest any doubts of why she'd returned to Palestine.

Mama Max listened to Obadiah's sermon on being thankful and nodded in all of the appropriate places. Anyone observing her would have a seen a dutiful, if not doting, wife. But looks can be deceiving, because underneath the façade whirred thoughts that were more determined than doting. The news of Dorothea's impending marriage to a man who was closer to dying than living did nothing to lessen Mama Max's distrust. Like Obadiah, Reginald Jenkins had long carried a torch for his now fiancée, forty-plus years that she knew of. Dorothea had chosen a married Obadiah over a single Jenkins then. Mama Max was determined to make sure history didn't repeat itself.

14

Most Precious Love

"How about you come over for brunch tomorrow?" Princess said, reaching for her laptop. "You know Mama's famous breakfast casserole is going to be front and center. And the fried turkey turned out delicious!"

"I'm only about ten minutes from your house," Rafael countered. "I could swing through, grab a fried turkey sandwich now, and we could go hang out. C'mon, Princess, I've only seen you once since we've been home. And I'm leaving on Saturday to spend a few days in Saint Louis before going back to school."

"Uh-oh. Are you getting ready to meet the folks? You and Lauren must be getting serious." Lauren is the woman Rafael told Princess he'd been dating the past year. From what she'd heard, their both being from the Midwest and attending KU was about all Princess thought they had in common.

"No, nothing like that. She just couldn't believe I've never hung out in Saint Louis. She wants to show me the sights, take me up in the arch and whatnot. Besides, I've already met her parents."

"How do they feel about their daughter dating a brothah?"

"C'mon now, what's not to like? I'm handsome, articulate—"

"Conceited . . ."

"With a bright future in politics ahead of me. Any mother would consider it a blessing that I grace their daughter with my presence. Just ask Tai."

"Whatever, okay?" Her voice held agitation but Princess smiled because Rafael was telling the truth. Her parents had both given their seal of approval when she and Rafael started dating her junior year in high school. His parents were long-time members of Mount Zion. King had baptized Rafael and occasionally golfed with Rafael's father. Tai and Rafael's mother worked together on Sanctity of Sisterhood regional conferences. The families had been friends for years and had been pleased when Rafael asked Princess to the prom. Both sets of parents hoped it was the beginning of something long-term.

And while Princess liked Rafael's sense of humor and thought he was cute, she always looked at him more like a brother than a boyfriend. Yes, they'd grown closer after attending the dance together, but aside from tongue dueling and a little touchy-feely, their relationship had not been physical, not that Rafael hadn't wanted it to be. Princess still felt a little guilty about how she'd used Rafael as a smoke-screen when she started dating Kelvin during her freshman year at UCLA. Her parents had thought the two were carrying on a long-distance relationship, but Princess had been carrying on with Kelvin instead. *If I'd known then what I know now . . .*

"So, what's up? Am I coming through or what? I'm only five minutes away now."

"I have to write this chapter, tonight, while things are fresh. We'll hang out all day tomorrow if you want, promise."

They hung up a moment later, and Princess slid off the bed and walked over to the desk she'd had since turning thirteen. She plugged in her computer, sat back, and took a deep breath. The glare of the numbers on the digital clock suggested it might be too late to begin writing, but at nine-thirty, Princess was too jazzed to be tired. She and Tai had talked tonight, after King had left to golf off the massive Thanksgiving meal, Michael and Timothy had hooked up with their respective friends, and Tabitha had gone to a movie/sleepover with a group of hers. Princess had been helping Tai put away food and tidy up. Her heart had beat rapidly in her chest as she gathered the nerve to have "the conversation." But Mama Max's words had given her strength: *She's your mother, baby. Ain't nothing that a mother's ear can't hear, and a mother's love won't cover.*

"Mama, I need to talk to you."

"What about, baby?"

"About the book I'm writing."

Tai remained silent having already been told by Mama Max that Princess would be sharing something with her soon. Mama Max had gone quiet, however, when Tai had asked for details.

"Would you like to take a break?" Tai asked Princess. "I can put on water for tea, and we can finish cleaning the kitchen afterward."

A few minutes later, mother and daughter settled into the well-worn Brook den. Many a movie had been watched while nestled into the soft tan leather of the large sectional couch. Princess pulled on the comfort of those memories as she sipped her orange spice blend.

"The book is an autobiography," Princess began softly.

"Right, you told me that," Tai replied in an equally subdued tone. She took a sip of her mint medley and waited.

"It's mostly about what happened to me during my first year of college . . . things I'm not too proud of."

"Most kids who are away from home for the first time do things that they later regret."

"Remember what you whispered in my ear that day you and Daddy came to the condo and met Kelvin? You said that since I was experiencing grown-folks pleasure, you hoped that I was ready for grown-folks pain. Remember?"

Tai nodded slowly.

"Well . . . this book talks about the grown-folks pain you warned me about."

The memories of that tense afternoon flooded Tai's mind. The day she and King had flown to Los Angeles unannounced and found out their daughter had lied about living with a female friend and was instead living with the son of a woman Tai had despised for years. The day this son, Kelvin, had brought eighteen years of swagger into the room, defiantly pledging his love for Princess. The day King learned that his "little princess" had become a woman, and he'd come precariously close to a beat-down of the man who'd help take her girlhood away.

"You're no different in that regard, Princess, from a majority of kids. We often listen to life instead of our parents. That's a part of spreading your wings and coming into adulthood."

This subtle empathy and encouragement opened the conversational floodgates, and for the next half hour, Princess gave Tai a glimpse into her life as the partying, drinking, weed-smoking girlfriend of the big man on campus, Kelvin Petersen. Princess shared her hesitancy at becoming sexually active, and how she'd thought this gift to him would solidify her place in his life.

"I thought he'd be my one and only, Mama," Princess said. "Like Daddy was for you."

Yeah, but I most definitely wasn't your daddy's one and only . . . is what Tai thought. "Yes, your father is the only man I've ever known," is what she said.

Princess continued, telling Tai about the scores of women who'd constantly thrown themselves at Kelvin, often right in front of her face, and how Princess had been determined to keep her man. Tai had almost cringed then, because some of her daughter's words could have been her own. She told her mother about the night she'd discovered Kelvin and Fawn screwing in the laundry room while Princess had been partying just feet away. Finally, Princess told her mother the secret she'd not even shared with Mama Max. And then she waited for the rebuke. It never came.

"I'm so sorry," Tai said, pulling Princess to her chest and rocking her softly. "I wish that you would have told me then and that I could have been there for you."

"I couldn't," Princess whispered, silent tears streaming down her face and soaking Tai's blouse. "I was so ashamed. . . ."

"We've all done things we're ashamed of, honey," Tai said, stroking her daughter's hair and back. "That's when we have to remember it's not how often we fall down, but how many times we get back up again."

The two women enjoyed a silent embrace for several moments. Their tea grew cold. Neither noticed.

"The thought of what happened crossed my mind," Tai said finally, as both women wiped away tears and Princess sat back against the sofa. "When you went to Germany and didn't tell anybody, and then came home from college and were so emotionally distant. Remember me asking you about it?"

Princess nodded.

"I knew that you'd gone through something and that it had been deep. I'm sorry that it happened, but I'm glad you told me about it. I want you to know I'm always here for you, Princess, your daddy too. It doesn't matter how old you get. You'll always be our little girl."

Taking a deep breath, Princess placed her hands on the keyboard. Even with her mother's knowledge about what happened and her approval that Princess share with others the trial that became her testimony, Princess was hesitant about how to begin. The other chapters had flowed easily, how she fell in love with Kelvin, believed his lies, dabbled in drugs, and lied to her parents—in short, how she'd thrown away all her home training for a walk on the wild side. After each incident, however, she'd written about what happened on the other side, the lessons she'd learned and the Scriptures God had used to bring her out of her darkness into His light. Again, Mama Max's voice came into her consciousness. *Just tell it,* she'd said to Princess, after suggesting the young woman's journey be shared on the popular TV show *Conversations with Carla.*

"That's what I'll do," Princess said out loud. She took a long swallow of soda, said a brief, silent prayer, and began to type:

> *I had an abortion. Until now, this has been my secret shame, the burden that I bore alone. Nobody in my family knew about it; in fact, I just told my mother tonight, before sitting down to write this chapter. It's a hard one for me, y'all. Not because of the debate on whether abortion is right or wrong, but how the procedure affected me. See, I didn't really want to do it. I'd hoped that my boyfriend at the time, the father of the child, would declare his undying love for me and encourage us to get married and continue this family that had already begun growing in my belly. But he didn't. He told me that it wasn't a good time, that along with school and sports, a baby was too much to deal with. I convinced myself that he was right and that I wanted what he wanted. But you know what? I think about my baby almost every day, and definitely when I see a little chocolate boy running around. I got rid of the baby before its sex could be determined, but my heart says it was a boy. I even went ahead and named him after his father and mine. No one knew that, either, until now. But you see, losing my child is what led to me turning my life around and developing*

the relationship I now have with Jesus Christ. I learned a valuable lesson while dealing with this horrible drama, while paying this high price to try and secure the love of a man. I learned that God's love is the greatest, most precious love of all, and it's free. . . .

15

Every Now and Then

Kelvin looked every bit the king of the castle as he lounged by his uncle Geoff's swimming pool. A large, black-and-white-striped umbrella covered most of his lanky frame, and a large pair of Spy sunglasses shielded his eyes from the glare of the bright sun. The only thing missing from this kingly picture was a bowl of grapes and servants to fan him.

"All right, kids, calm down now. Don't make me have to come out there." He laughed as Brandon and Joni sprayed each other with large, powerful water guns. They got closer and closer to each other in the pool, ending up in a tousling match, turned kissing match near the shallow end. The two, though opposite in looks, complemented each other perfectly. Joni's petite frame, dark hair, and dark skin, evidence of her Latina heritage, somehow balanced blond-haired, blue-eyed Brandon, who stood six foot one.

"Come join us, buddy," Brandon called out, his arms still around the wife he adored. "That chocolate won't melt. Get in here."

Instead of answering, Kelvin repositioned the pillow behind him, tilted his head back, and closed his eyes. In the two days since arriving in Los Angeles, he'd been with four differ-

ent women, including the well-known-around-campus sex-
crazed twins, Sandy and Brandy. And while no one could miss
the love felt when Brandon and Joni looked at each other, the
only thing Kelvin felt was tired.

Brandon put a finger to his lips as he eased his lithe frame
out of the water. His blue eyes sparkled as he loaded up his
water gun. Joni stifled a giggle as she, too, gathered ammuni-
tion, while the handful of other adults, teens, and children
continued to talk and play normally, thereby assisting with the
ambush.

"Ow! Damn it!" Kelvin cried as two powerful streams of
water blasted him from head to toe. He jumped up out of the
lounge chair so quickly that it toppled over. Ignoring it, he
gave chase to the culprits, Brandon and Joni, who wisely ran in
opposite directions. "That's your ass," Kelvin shouted, jumping
into the water behind Brandon. The two men stroked the
length of the pool, with Kelvin getting a hand on Brandon's
foot, just as Brandon sought to make his getaway out the other
end of the pool.

"It was Joni's idea, man!" Brandon was laughing so hard he
could barely defend himself against the wave of water Kelvin
pushed in his direction. Joni, wrapped in a towel now, laughed
uncontrollably from her relatively safe poolside perch. Geoff,
his wife, and all other onlookers shared in the glee.

After feeling he'd properly avenged himself for having
been thoroughly soaked, Kelvin pulled himself from the pool
and bowed to the still-laughing audience. "That's all, folks," he
said, languidly walking in Joni's direction. Joni's eyes widened,
and she sought shelter behind Kelvin's aunt. "Oh, I'ma get
you. But not now. When you least expect it, girl, I'ma get you."

Kelvin smiled as he walked by family and friends, rustling
hair here, giving a hand pound there. It was good that he could
now handle laughter at his expense. Growing up as one of only
a handful of Blacks in Germany, this had not always been the
case. Especially when he was younger, he got teased and beat

up on the regular. Many a day he'd come home crying or cursing, depending on the circumstances. But his mother had encouraged him to be strong and stand up for himself. His stepfather had assured him that one day things would change. He'd been right. Everything changed when, for his tenth birthday, Kelvin's uncle Geoff sent him a basketball, signed by none other than Shaquille O'Neal and Kobe Bryant, who at that time were the Lakers' golden boys. From that moment, Kelvin vowed to follow in Shaquille's footsteps and go pro. And he decided to follow in Kobe Bryant's footsteps and excel at point guard.

When Kelvin turned thirteen, it was like a magic wand was waved across his body. He grew three inches in one summer and two more the summer after that. Almost overnight, he went from being teased to treasured, as his voice deepened and his body filled out. At fifteen, a cute German girl helped him lose his virginity and in the process, develop the male swagger that continued to this day. He became the most popular kid in the private, international prep school he attended and was the star of the basketball team. That same year, as his uncle Geoff watched his nephew's skills progress, he offered to take care of him so that Kelvin could attend school in Los Angeles and improve his chances of getting seen by scouts. The year after that, he met his biological father, Derrick Montgomery, and six months later, he met Princess. The year after that, he accepted an offer to play point guard for the UCLA Bruins.

"Baby, do you want a beer with your sandwich?" Joni had taken full advantage of Geoff's suggestion that she make herself at home. She'd pulled a container of turkey salad from the refrigerator, found a bag of chips in the pantry, and was placing a large dill pickle slice on each plate.

Kelvin stopped swigging his own Corona. "Uh-huh! I knew the truth would come out!"

"What are you talking about?" Brandon nodded at Joni and looked questioningly at Kelvin.

"I knew that whole 'I'm a Christian now' nonsense you and Joni been spouting was just an act!"

Joni brought a plate of turkey sandwiches over to the table. "How do you figure that?"

"Yeah, how do you figure that?" Brandon echoed as he reached for the chips.

" 'Cause, you're sitting up here about to get your drink on, that's how! Ha! I knew y'all hadn't changed all that much."

"You don't think so?" Brandon had the urge to argue with Kelvin, defend himself, but decided to handle the conversation a different way. "You think that Joni and I are the same as when we all lived together at college?"

"Well, you don't get high anymore, and you're married now, so I guess the fuc—" Kelvin looked around sheepishly, hoping none of the other adults had followed them inside. "I mean, the screwing is legal. But look at y'all. You're still drinking. I thought drinking was a sin."

"If that were the case, Jesus wouldn't have performed his first miracle," Joni stated calmly as she poured herself a chardonnay. "The sin isn't in drinking—it's in getting drunk and letting the liquor control you, or change who you are."

Brandon chimed in. "Now, don't get me wrong, if it makes you uncomfortable, or hurts our testimony in any way, we'll put the drinks down right now. Joni and I know who we are in Christ, but you don't. So if it makes us less Christian in your eyes . . ." Brandon stood, preparing to replace his and Joni's alcoholic beverages with soda.

"Aw, sit your ass down, junior. Ain't nobody sending you to hell for having a drink. But to hear your girl Princess tell it, she's as pure as the driven snow."

"Princess doesn't drink," Joni acknowledged. "But that is her choice and the decision she made based on her relationship with God. But that's just it—all decisions regarding one's relationship with God are personal. Nobody can tell you how to live your life for Him. I mean, they can direct and instruct but in the end, nobody knows enough to know the mind of God. If they tell you they do, they're lying. As much as I respect your father, Kelvin, and as much as we enjoy being members of Kingdom Citizens, I don't even think *he* knows everything that God is thinking."

"Joni and I are the same fools you clowned with at school," Brandon said after taking a long swig of beer. "Crazy is how God made us. We still love a good time, love to laugh . . . and to love. We've just toned it down, that's all. She might drink a glass of wine or have a margarita if she's chillin' with her family. I'll have a brewsky if I'm hanging out with friends. It doesn't change the fact that I'm saved. Nor does it make Princess wrong for choosing not to drink. She has her reasons for how she's living for God. Like Joni said, it's personal."

"Yeah, I can see y'all a little on the subdued side, damn near boring, matter of fact." Brandon delivered a playful punch to Kelvin's arm. "I don't think I've heard you curse once, Joni," Kelvin continued. "And I still can't believe this fool turned down my weed. So, I guess I'm seeing a little sumpin, sumpin . . ."

Joni smiled and changed the subject. "You talked to Princess, didn't you?"

Kelvin looked quickly over at Joni. "She talk to you?"

"I called her on Thanksgiving. She told me you'd called."

"Well, did she also tell you that I called back and got blocked like a bill collector? First her brother told me she wasn't there, and then her mother told me straight up to stop call-ing!"

Joni shrugged. "I guess she doesn't want to talk to you, Kelvin. She's moved on."

"If that's the case, then why can't she even speak to me? We got history. Just because we broke up doesn't mean we can't be friends."

The three munched on their sandwiches in silence. Kelvin got up for another beer. "You want one?" he asked Brandon.

Brandon motioned to the half still left in his bottle. "No, dog, I'm good."

"You ask me, I think she's seeing that fool back in Kansas, the chump I took out of the lineup as soon as Princess got to LA."

"Rafael?"

"Uh-huh. I'm right, huh?"

"I don't know," Joni said, wisely choosing a neutral answer. "She's so busy these days, with her campus outreach program and the book she's writing—"

"She's writing a book?"

Oh, shoot. "Yeah."

"What kind of book?"

"An inspirational book, like a self-help book, a guide for young women to live godly lives."

Kelvin snorted. "Ha! I bet I'm all up in that shit, as the example of who not to date! She bet not call me out, though. I'll sue her fine ass."

"Kelvin! Would you really sue Princess if she talked about the two of you dating?"

"Hell, no. But I'd let her think I was going to, just so I could get back in those panties."

Joni laughed and shook her head. "I think that would take more than a lawsuit, homey." She gathered their empty plates, listening to Kelvin wax poetic about getting Princess back.

"All that money and fame and your butt is still ignorant." She bent down and gave Kelvin a hug. "Thank goodness that in that respect, you haven't changed a bit."

Kelvin turned down Brandon and Joni's movie invite and spent the evening relaxing with his relatives. He'd planned to fly home the next day, Saturday, but after talking with his father and ignoring Fawn's incessant calls, he ended up spending the day with Derrick, his little brother, D2, and the rest of the Montgomery clan. That he was still at their home on Sunday was even more surprising. But the fact that he'd joined the

Montgomerys and attended Kingdom Citizens Christian Center's Sunday morning worship services—and found himself enjoying it—was the biggest shock of all. *I can go to church when I get back with Princess,* he thought. *Every now and then.* When Kelvin finally boarded a Phoenix-bound plane late Sunday night, he was more determined than ever to get back the love he'd lost.

16

A Strong Deliverer

Stan was nervous. He paced the plush, carpeted floor of his Detroit hotel suite, wondering for the umpteenth time if he'd done the right thing by agreeing to meet with Bryce. But the truth was, for the past five months, his curiosity about the last twenty-five years of Bryce's life had gotten the better of him. Plus, he'd calmed down from their initial meeting the previous July. He'd not seen him since that meeting, and while they'd participated in teleconferences concerning the Cathedral ministry, Bryce had kept his distance, only calling Stan's church office one time, and even that call stayed mainly business, with only perfunctory pleasantries spoken at the beginning and ending of it. But then, last week, a holiday card had arrived in the mail. It was elegant yet simple, wishing Stan and his family a merry Christmas and happy new year. Stan had immediately recognized Bryce's fluid, calligraphy-like handwriting and had felt the same, uncomfortable fluttering that had happened when he first saw Bryce after so many years. When asked, he'd truthfully told Passion that Bryce was a former college roommate with whom he'd reconnected during a business trip to Detroit. She'd commented on how nice the card was and had praised Bryce's handwriting. Stan had thought ironically, *If she only knew . . .*

The next day, Stan had called Bryce's office to thank him for the card. He was put through immediately, and after a moment of small talk, Bryce took control of the conversation.

"I want to see you," he'd said simply. "It's fine if you just want to talk, Stan, but I need to see you. So much between us remains unsaid, at least for me. Like I told you before, I've never forgotten about you, but only recently felt I was in a place to try and reenter your life. I want to hear about what life's been like for you, learn about your family, tell you about mine. I want to see if we can reestablish the friendship we once shared, in whatever way you'd feel comfortable. Just tell me the time and the place, and I'm there."

Life had played its part after that when two days later, Luke Wilkes called and requested Stan's presence at an emergency board meeting. There'd been a problem with a certain report that threatened about a million dollars of the Cathedral's outreach budget. Luke needed the wisdom of his counsel and called the meeting, even though Christmas was just days away.

The meeting would happen tomorrow. Stan had purposely flown in the day before, after agreeing to meet with Bryce. Now he wondered if his actions were wise.

"Maybe I should call and cancel," he whispered aloud. He walked over to his briefcase, pulled out his cell phone, and began looking for Bryce's number. At about this same time, Bryce was entering the elevator on the way to Stan's room. A moment later, there was a knock on the door.

"Hello," Stan said simply. He stepped away from the door, allowing Bryce to enter. He scanned the empty hallway quickly before shutting the door.

Bryce stared out the window a moment before turning around. "It's good to see you, friend."

Stan walked over to the minibar to hide his nervousness. "Can I get you something? A soda? Water?"

"I'll take a shot of brandy, neat, if you have it."

Stan smiled. This was Bryce's drink of choice in college.

"Some things never change," he said while fixing the drink. After pouring himself a ginger ale, he brought both glasses over to the small dining table in the corner of the room. Handing one to Bryce, he said simply, "Cheers."

Bryce looked at Stan a long moment, his drink untouched. "To renewed friendships," he said finally, and took a sip of the strong drink.

Stan sat down at the table. Bryce quickly joined him. "You look good, Stan," he said. Both men took another drink.

"How long has it been, twenty-five, thirty years?"

Bryce set his glass down, leaned back in the chair, and linked his hands behind his head. "Before this past July, it had been twenty-three years since I saw you. In person, that is. Like I said before, I've followed your career, seen you several times on the religious networks. You can't imagine how many times I looked you up, almost called you. When I heard about your divorce from Carla, I actually flew to LA. I even attended a service at Logos Word."

"You were at my church?" Stan was incredulous, as much by the fact that Bryce had been in LA as by the fact that Stan had been totally oblivious to the danger that had sat unnoticed in his pews.

Bryce nodded. "Came there with the intention of making you feel better after the breakup. I'd divorced recently myself, and while leaving Sheila is what I wanted, it was still a painful time."

"Why didn't you approach me, after coming to Logos Word?"

Bryce shrugged and took a sip of his drink. "Figured that wasn't the best way to reconnect—in public, at your church, and by surprise. Was I right?"

"Probably." The two men eyed each other knowingly before Stan looked away, changing the subject as he did so. "Any kids?"

"A daughter, Jasmine. She's in college now, at Howard. Once we got her up and out of the house, I knew I had to take my life back, stop living a lie."

Stan nodded, looked at the ice cubes melting in his ginger ale, and wished he were a drinking man.

"What about you?" Bryce asked.

"What do you mean, what about me?"

"This marriage, to Passion. Are you happy?"

Stan fought the urge to squirm, but instead, he finished off his ginger ale and rose to pour another. "More?" he motioned to Bryce's glass.

"I'm fine for now."

"Passion is a good woman," Stan said after returning to the table. "She's good with her daughter and with my children when they're with us. She's a godly woman, *for the most part,* and loves working in the ministry. And she's from the south, so you know she can cook!"

"I see." Bryce slowly sipped his drink, his eyes boring into Stan. "She sounds like the perfect minister's wife. But . . . are you happy?"

Stan nodded but didn't trust himself to speak. The problems between him and Passion were escalating, and after a comment she'd made recently, he suspected her of knowing about his fetish.

"You've never had another relationship . . . like ours?" Bryce asked softly. "Not in all these years?"

"Haven't had one, and haven't wanted to have one," was Stan's quick reply. "What happened between us was a mistake on my part, the simple act of satisfying a young man's curiosity."

Bryce's laugh was immediate and genuine. "Man, I think you actually believe what you just said. But I was there, remember? And while our time together was definitely satisfying, there was nothing about you and me that was simple."

"I asked God's forgiveness for my actions back then," Stan

continued, without acknowledging what Bryce had said. "I asked to be delivered from any desires that were . . . sinful. And God answered my prayers."

"So, you've never once, in all these years, thought about what we shared together or desired to be with me again."

"No." It seemed as if time stood still while Stan's one-word answer—which both knew was untrue—permeated the room.

"I see." Bryce rose from the table, leisurely took off his sports jacket, grabbed his glass, and walked over to the bar.

Stan tried not to watch as Bryce sauntered to the counter. His friend had stayed in good shape over the years, his body lean and compact. Bryce wore jeans that complemented legs that seemed long for someone under six feet. The black polo shirt he wore was tight, emphasizing the muscles in his back and shoulders. Bryce had let his hair grow out since Stan had seen him at the Cathedral. His curly black locks tickled the shirt's neckline. Bryce had gone from a pretty boy to a gorgeous man.

Bryce turned unexpectedly and caught Stan staring at him. His smile was slight, yet knowing. "Refresh your drink?"

Stan shook his head and got up to look out the window.

"I was so hurt when you left me," Bryce said, joining Stan at the window. "I went through a slew of unfulfilling male relationships, looking for what we had. After grad school, I spent a year in London and another in Africa, working for conglomerates. That's where I met Sheila. Her father was a big shot at one of the companies. He barely approved of our union, didn't think I had enough money to take care of his daughter in the style to which she was accustomed. But that didn't matter." Bryce chuckled softly. "I could take care of her in other ways.

"We dated for years, but Sheila finally issued an ultimatum. She was nearing thirty and heard the proverbial biological clock ticking in her head. It wasn't like I didn't love the woman, and to this day I respect her. But I'd experienced a deeper level of love, and that's what I was holding out for. Anyway, I finally ran out of reasons to say no. And her father offered me a ridiculous salary to become president of one of his companies. So I did it. We were married for twenty-one years."

"And then what happened?"

"I turned fifty." When Stan turned to Bryce with a questioning look, he continued. "I don't know, man, but something happened. I went away, by myself, shortly after that birthday. Went to Mexico for a week, just me and my thoughts. I looked at my life, what worked and what didn't. And I thought about you . . . a lot. By the time I came back home, I'd decided to take down the façade I'd created and live life on my terms, the way I want it"—Bryce looked at Stan—"the way I know it can be. I filed for divorce and resigned my position the same week. On the one hand, it was one of the most painful times in my life, but now I'm truly happy. And as soon as I get the love I want, my life will be complete." Bryce stepped toward Stan. Stan took a step back.

"Will you hug me?"

"That's not me anymore, Bryce. I've already told you that—"

"Just a hug, nothing more. I've missed your arms around me."

Stan's mind said no, but his arms said yes. They seemed to open of their own volition, and Bryce immediately stepped inside his embrace.

Bryce's scent was intoxicating, his touch electric, and after a long moment, Stan stepped away from him. He walked to a chair in the living room and sat down, physically signaling that the moment was over. Bryce said nothing, but rather followed him to the sitting area and sat down on the love seat opposite the chairs. They discussed many things: Stan's marriage to Carla and the subsequent, very public divorce; Stan's rise in the ministry; Bryce's rise in politics; mutual friends; former teachers and their passion; the New York Knicks. As the hours went by, the two men conversed like the old friends they were, comfortable and easy, often finishing each other's sentences as each man knew the other's story.

After laughing at memories of the down-the-back Jheri curl and Shaft-style leather coat that Bryce used to wear, Bryce asked Stan a question. "What about you? Do you still wear the panties? Remember how I used to rub them when you put them on?"

Stan sobered for a minute.

"Aw, c'mon, now. You can't be embarrassed about that. There was something ultrasexy about a strong man like you wrapped in silk. That used to turn me on like nobody's business!" Sensing Stan's discomfort, Bryce stopped. "I'm sorry, Stan. I didn't mean to make you uncomfortable. Really, man, sorry about that."

Stan rubbed his thin mustache a moment, before a smile scampered across his face. "Funny that you should mention those," he said finally. "After I saw you in July, I went and bought some, started to wear them. I'd only done that occasionally over the years, and hadn't at all since being married to Passion. But, yeah, after I saw you . . ."

"You're fighting it, aren't you? What you're feeling, between you and me?"

Stan swallowed, hard. "There is no feeling between you and me, Bryce. Other than brotherly friendship and Christian love."

"Okay, man, if you say so. But for the record, I'm here, ready and waiting for you. If you ever decide differently, I think you and I could have something very, very special. We did once."

"That was a long time ago, during a time of experimenta- tion—"

"That lasted off and on for five years! It only ended be- cause that's what you wanted. You might call that an experi- ment, but I call it something else."

"I call it over," Stan said finally. "I've changed. I am a hetero- sexual, period, with no desire to be with a man. And I am a husband who has always been faithful to his wife and who will continue to cleave only unto her.

"You'd like Passion," Stan continued. "The next time you're in LA, please let me know. I'd love to invite you to the church and then over to our house for dinner. And in case you decide to marry again, a woman, there are several upstanding women at Logos Word who would make fine wives. God can change you, Bryce," Stan finished. "The same way he changed me. If you let him."

"That's just it," Bryce countered quickly. "You felt that our love was something that needed to be changed, that it was wrong. I know differently. I know the truth. Our love was pure and magical. And it is the memories of that love that has given me the courage to make huge changes. Only my change wasn't to run away from who I am, but rather to embrace it."

Conversation became sporadic after that, and before long, Bryce left the room. The next day, when they saw each other at Spread the Word Cathedral, the men were cordial and professional. Stan's handshake was genuine as he bid Bryce good-bye and once again invited him to LA and Logos Word. "He's a strong deliverer," he whispered in Bryce's ear as they shared a brief, brotherly embrace.

"Good," Bryce whispered back. "Then I'll ask God to deliver you . . . into my arms."

Stan thought about Bryce all the way back to Los Angeles. He'd forgotten how much fun Bryce could be and admitted he'd missed their intelligent, spirited conversations. Even so, Stan knew that without a doubt, all future interactions with Bryce would be limited to the boardroom or a dining room boasting a meal that Passion either prepared or attended. Stan wanted to believe what he'd so confidently told Bryce, that he was a different man now, with no desire for what had once been between them. But had he really, truly changed? Stan didn't want to put himself in the position, no pun intended, to be tested.

17

Some Explaining to Do

Passion smiled as she watched Onyx cut out paper snowflakes. She'd learned how during a classroom project, and ever since, Onyx had been transfixed with the art. Half the kitchen and most of the downstairs great room were covered with her handiwork.

"Do you like this one, Mama?" Onyx held up another of her masterpieces, this one looking more like a badly mangled scrap of paper than a flake.

"It's beautiful, darling," Passion said. "I think that's your best one yet!"

An hour later, Passion had packed her daughter's overnight bag and dropped her off for a sleepover. A Logos Word church member who worked in the office had a daughter Onyx's age, and after a church trip to Disneyland, the two became best friends. One was at the other's house at least twice a month. Stan had encouraged Passion to befriend the mother, a single woman who was roughly Passion's age. But old habits died hard, and Passion had never been one for too many women friends.

Passion returned home and began to clean up the mess her daughter had left behind. They had a cleaning woman, but Passion picked up out of boredom more than anything else.

Things slowed down at Logos Word around the holidays, and no meetings were planned for the weekend. There would be a slew of rehearsals in preparation for the Christmas program, but Passion didn't attend any of those.

After tidying up the dining room, Passion went into the kitchen. It was Friday night, a noncooking day for Mrs. Lee. Passion, Stan, and Onyx usually went out to eat on Friday nights, along with Stan's children if they were visiting. Other times it would just be her and Onyx, or like tonight, just her and Stan. Passion wasn't particularly looking forward to dinner tonight, because after coming clean with what she knew, neither she nor her husband would have much of an appetite.

Stan came home from the church office and, after a quick shower, donned a pair of dark gray slacks, an icy-gray shirt, and a black sports coat. Passion was dressed casually as well in a pair of black slacks with a multicolored sweater sporting a Christmas theme. Ever mindful of her status as prominent first lady, however, she'd carefully applied her makeup and had swept up her freshly permed hair into a simple yet stylish ponytail that she thought made her face appear slimmer. She'd gained fifteen pounds during this latest round of marital problems, specifically since about six months ago, when Stan had deemed sex "unclean."

These were Passion's thoughts as Stan navigated the heavy Friday-night traffic, making his way to Beverly Hills and one of their favorite seafood restaurants. After their tussle in Texas and subsequent night of lovemaking, Passion had backed off with her demands, hoping that her husband would take the lead. But they'd only made love once since then, Thanksgiving night, again at Passion's pleading.

Since then, Passion had focused on church matters, Onyx, and preparing the house for a slew of visitors during the holiday season. All year, but especially now, Stan would often invite visiting ministers, special guests, or loyal church members over for coffee and conversation. Next week was her "sistah soiree," when she invited the pastors and deacons wives over for a formal tea. She'd often been too busy to remember that she was not happy.

"I think the Christmas program is going to be great this year," Stan said.

"Just like all the others," Passion responded. "They're always beautiful."

"The choir is working on a classical medley. I heard part of it and couldn't believe those were singers I knew. Sounded like something you'd hear at Carnegie Hall or Lincoln Center in New York. But right after that, they're singing some contemporary originals that the kids will like—R & B, hip-hop-sounding songs. I'm really impressed with our new minister of music. She's a godsend."

"She's very talented," Passion agreed.

They continued sharing small talk until they arrived at Crustaceans. After a generous tip to the mâitre d', Stan and Passion were seated quickly, at an intimate booth near the back of the room, where they could see and be seen, yet still enjoy a private conversation. The next few minutes were consumed looking over the menus, and after ordering appetizers, Passion decided to take the conversation to a more personal level.

"I've been thinking."

"Oh, Lord . . ."

Passion laughed. "I've been thinking about the holidays. Our three-year anniversary is coming up, and I thought about us taking a little getaway. Nothing too far away, but somewhere we can unwind when the holiday programs are over. What do you think about that: a weekend getaway, something romantic, just the two of us?"

Stan took a sip of lemon water. "Something to think about," was his noncommittal answer. "But I've got to coordinate it with Carla and the church. You know I work weekends, and that's also when I have the kids."

After terse negotiations, Stan had finally conceded that

Carla had as much right to their children as he did. The first year following their divorce, the kids had stayed with him and Passion, spending weekends with their mother. The following year, it had been about fifty-fifty, the children spending three days a week with Carla and four days with him. This year, with their heavier school loads, it had been decided that they would spend weekdays with Carla and weekends with the Lees. The arrangement had worked out, for the most part.

Passion resisted the urge for a sarcastic comeback. She knew more than anybody how committed Stan was to his "weekend work," and since she cooked and cared for the kids when they came over, she was more than a little aware of their schedule too.

"I thought about that," she replied instead. "And thought that maybe a middle-of-the-week getaway would be easier, someplace really nice and reasonably close, like Vancouver or Mexico."

"I don't know, Passion. I'm pretty busy right now. Maybe we can take a trip in the summer, include the family."

Passion was grateful that the waiter came just then, delivering their appetizers and taking their dinner orders. Passion enjoyed some of her perfectly cooked baguette and crusty shrimp. "How are the satays?" she asked.

"Delicious," Stan replied, taking a hearty bite of the grilled beef that had been marinated in lemongrass and Asian herbs.

After enjoying a bit more of the appetizer, Passion wiped her mouth with a napkin. "You know, Stan," she said softly, "I think it would be good for us to spend some time together, alone. Your schedule has been so busy all year, and mine, too, between the church and the kids. I think there are some things we need to talk about, and it would be good to get away and have some meaningful conversation."

Stan wiped his mouth and tossed down his napkin. He spoke low but clearly. "You know what? I knew this reprieve was too good to be true, that it would only be a matter of time before you started hounding me again about taking care of your needs. We just did it, woman! But there's never enough for you, is it? You are never satisfied."

"Don't make me laugh," Passion growled, her voice barely above a whisper. "What, are you a holiday husband, giving up the nooky the way the government gives days off to celebrate? Am I to expect us to make love on Christmas and New Years, and then have to wait until Valentine's Day? Humph. If that's the case, I need to get me another calendar. One that records *all* the holidays, those in our country and all of the other countries as well."

Stan took a deep breath. "Let's not do this, Passion. Let's not fight. I don't think now is a good time for a vacation. And I don't think it's a good time for deep conversation either; there's too much on both our plates."

"Well, let me put something else on your plate," Passion said pleasantly. She reached into her purse and pulled out a pair of silky white thong panties, extra-extra-large. "These aren't mine," she hissed as she discretely tossed them to Stan.

Stan caught the incriminating garment, quickly pocketed the panties, and looked around the room. It seemed that no one else had noticed; each table seemed focused on its own party. "Woman, have you lost your mind?"

"I haven't lost my mind, but you've obviously lost your drawers. Oh, wait, rather hid them. I found your little treasure chest, the duffel bag on the top shelf of the garage. Now, you may not want to talk about anything deep, but Stanley Morris Lee, I think you've got some explaining to do."

18

Just Dropped By

"Page five, paragraph two!" the woman shouted as a young woman walked into Gospel Truth wearing makeup. She was referring to the Gospel Truth Member Manual that she'd pored over since receiving it four days before.

"Twenty-five and three," her cohort echoed, tsking a man who entered with an earring in his ear. The contents of this manual had occupied the conversation for most of their visit to Palestine. They'd not only discussed it, but obviously memorized much of it as well.

"Oh, no, you don't, sistah," the first woman admonished, stepping in front of the couple about to enter the sanctuary. "Your elbows and knees must be covered, and, sir, if you two aren't married, you need to take your arm out from around her waist!"

Oh, Lawd, Mama Max thought as she hurried from her car to the sidewalk leading up to the church. *I should have known that inviting these two biddies down here was a bad idea!*

It hadn't seemed so at the time. After a lengthy conversation with these good friends who were members of her church back in Kansas—Mount Zion—Mama Max had thought it would be a treat to have Elsie Wanthers and Margie Stokes (or Sistah Alrighty and Sistah Almighty respectively, as a former church member had aptly named them) join her and the reverend for the holidays. Both women were elderly with not much extended family. The previous year, they'd joined the Brooks for Thanksgiving and had spent Christmas with another Mount Zion family. This year, they'd had no plans. So Mama Max, in a moment of spontaneity, invited them to bring in the New Year in Texas.

"Now look, sistahs," she said, grabbing both ladies' arms and pulling them to the side. "Not everyone coming in here has read the Gospel Truth handbook. These are the holidays, after all. Some of them are here visiting, just like you. Others are members who haven't been here in a while."

"Don't make no never mind," the shorter, stout woman countered. She'd been so busy checking out the other women that she'd failed to notice that her white stockings had a run that snaked up her leg or that her salt-and-pepper afro wig was askew. "The good reverend doctor has written a manual for these here Christians to follow. It's the truth I tell ya, every blessed word. This manual should be adopted across the nation."

"I've already put a call in to Queen Bee," the taller, rail-thin woman added, referring to Mount Zion's first lady, Tai Brook. "I told her that her father-in-law has written a book that needs to be adopted by our church *immediately*. I even offered to FedEx her a copy, but she assured me she could wait until I got back."

Mama Max stifled a laugh even as she recalled the humorous conversation she and Tai had shared shortly after she'd heard the manual suggestion. Tai knew hell would freeze over before King adopted any such manual for his church, but she had humored the old women by omitting this fact during their conversation.

"The good Lord appreciates your dedication, surely he does," Mama Max assured them. "And I'll be sure and tell Reverend how you're soldiers on the battlefield, fighting for the Lord. But let's go inside now. The services are about to begin. We have a place of honor for you two ladies, right down front."

This praise seemed to pacify the women, for the moment. Elsie "Sistah Alrighty" Wanthers straightened her wig, and Margie "Sistah Almighty" Stokes readjusted her scarf and hat. They followed Mama Max down the sidewalk.

"Page sixteen, paragraph one," Sistah Almighty whispered loudly as a young man sporting a cross tattoo held open the door for them.

"Page eleven, verse one and nine," Sistah Alrighty said, forgetting what she'd read was a book, not a Bible. "She probably don't even realize she's on her way to hell," she continued too loudly as they were ushered down to the front row. "But I know a lotto ticket when I see one, and the place holder in her Bible definitely looks likes a Powerball!"

Later, after services, the two sistahs from Kansas joined the Brooks and the Johnsons—Nettie and her husband, Gordon— for dinner at Nettie's house. Nettie's massive Christmas tree was still up and lit, its blinking lights creating a festive atmosphere in the dining room scented with pine boughs.

"Lord, this smothered chicken looks delicious," Sistah Almighty said as she placed a generous portion on a bed of rice. "The Lord bless you, child, for feeding us old folks."

"Well, I'm no spring chicken," Nettie countered. "In two more years, I'll be threescore."

"Baby, I'm fourscore," Sistah Alrighty responded with a wink. "You just a babe." She clucked her dentures as she placed a spoonful of steaming candied yams next to a serving of greens.

"Ooh, I can't decide between the rolls or the corn bread," Sistah Almighty exclaimed, looking from one to the other.

"Might as well have one of each," Mama Max hinted, hiding a smile.

"Wouldn't want to be impolite and not take your suggestion," Sistah Almighty readily agreed. She hurriedly scooped up two of the freshly baked rolls and a big slug of corn bread. She dipped a roll in the gravy and placed almost half in her mouth. "Lord, this is the day the Lord has made," she professed around the mouthful. "And I'm rejoicing!"

"Sistah, we haven't yet blessed the food," Obadiah admonished.

"God forgive me." Sistah Almighty bowed her head, but not before she'd placed the other half of the gravy-soaked roll into her mouth.

Everyone continued small talk until all were served. After a quick blessing of the food, conversation resumed. As was often the case, Obadiah was front and center in the conversation, telling one of his lame jokes and acting as if he'd been born a comedian.

"It was during Sunday school," Obadiah began after a drink of sweet tea. "And they were teaching about how God created everything, including human beings. Little Johnny seemed especially intent when they told him how Eve was created out of one of Adam's ribs. So, later in the week, his mother went to look for him and found him lying down in bed. His face was all scrunched up like he was in pain. His mother sat on the side of the bed and asked him, 'Johnny, what's the matter?' He rolled over and told her, 'I have a pain in my side. I think I'm going to have a wife.'"

Those around the table laughed at the enjoyment Obadiah got from telling the joke as much as from the joke itself. The table was so noisy that they didn't hear the doorbell the first time it rang.

"Hmm, wonder who that is?" Nettie said as she rose from the table. But unexpected company wasn't unusual. People in this small town often just dropped by, especially church members needing counsel or a friend looking for a casual chat. She knew it could be almost anybody. But she wasn't prepared for the faces that greeted her on the other side of the door.

"Reverend Jenkins, Dorothea, uh, y'all come on in."

19

God Don't Like Ugly

"I told Reginald we should call first," Dorothea said, still standing on the other side of the doorjamb. "But I made these fresh, this morning before service." Dorothea held out a foil-covered tin. "A small thank-you for the kindness you and Gordon showed while my husband was in the hospital."

Nettie smoothly recovered from seeing Dorothea on her doorstep. She found first her tongue and then her manners. "Oh, you shouldn't have," she said, taking the pan from Dorothea and motioning with her arm for the couple to enter. "But we sure appreciate it."

"Well, I'm nowhere near the cook that you are, but this praline recipe has been in the family for years. I'd like to think I've gotten pretty good at making them."

Jenkins stepped around his wife and whispered loudly in Nettie's ear, "Don't let her modesty fool you—those things will make you hurt yourself. And speaking of, something sure smells good in here!"

Even as Nettie prayed they'd decline, she felt she had to do the Christian thing and invite them to dinner. "Oh, just some chicken and rice. Y'all welcome to join us. We haven't been long sat down."

"Oh, we couldn't," Dorothea said.

Please don't. Nettie didn't have anything against Dorothea, but she knew the atmosphere would change as soon as Mama Max learned the identity of these visitors.

"Well, now, it sure smells good," Jenkins said, already making a move toward the dining room. "If you're sure it won't be an imposition . . ."

Nettie said a quick prayer as she led Jenkins and Dorothea back to the dining room, asking God to help everybody hold their tongue and their tempers.

Mama Max sensed something before she knew why. She put down her fork and stared at the entrance to the dining room. No one else noticed the change, but Mama Max's stomach flip-flopped. Obadiah and Gordon were in a deep conversation about fishing, and the two church mothers were recapping their favorite rules from the Gospel Truth manual. Mama Max reached for her purse to take an antacid, forgetting that she'd left it in the living room. She took a swallow of sweet tea instead and was thankful that she didn't drop the glass when Dorothea rounded the corner.

Dorothea Noble Bates Jenkins's look had totally changed. Gone was the gaunt, mousy-looking woman who'd sung at Gospel Truth on Thanksgiving. Dorothea wasn't the raving beauty she once was, but it was obvious she'd taken pains with her appearance and the work had paid off. The thinning white hair had been colored and cut: a short, almost pixie look that enhanced her high Creole cheekbones and hollow cheeks. Her brows had been arched, and it looked as though she may have gained a pound or two. The makeup she wore had been expertly applied, accenting the good, camouflaging the bad. She was dressed simply yet elegantly in a peach-colored Chanel suit, with low-heeled ivory shoes and accessories, the biggest one being the huge diamond sparkling from the third finger of her left hand. And while anyone looking would have labeled her an elegant older woman, there was something else about her, as there was with all the Noble women, something mildly intoxicating, alluring, mysterious, especially to men. As if her thoughts brought on the action, Mama Max's perusal was interrupted by both Obadiah and Gordon jumping to their feet.

"Hello, Dorothea," Obadiah said, reaching for her hand and gawking like a teenager. "You're looking well." Mama Max cleared her throat, breaking his trance. "Uh, Reverend," he said, releasing Dorothea's hand and shaking Jenkins's.

"How y'all doing?" Gordon piped up immediately, barely giving Obadiah's last syllable the chance to clear his mouth. Though the greeting was inclusive of both newcomers, Gordon's eyes were solely on Reverend Jenkins's wife.

"Y'all, have a seat," Nettie interrupted, working to find the temperance she'd prayed for. She'd never seen Gordon make a fool of himself over no woman, and she most definitely didn't intend for the foolishness to start today. "Let me refresh this platter of chicken."

"I'll grab the rice," Mama Max added quickly, almost knocking her chair over from getting up so quickly.

"Please, let me help—"

"No, never mind, Dorothea," Mama Max interrupted. "Help yourself to the tea there while we heat up the food."

"Father, Jesus, Mary, and angels, I need all of y'all to help me!" Mama Max was whispering, and pacing the floor, leaving Nettie to do all the actual work. "Of all the people to stop by your house today, why does it have to be her? And why in the hello saints should I care? That ring Jenkins gave her is almost weighing down her left side.

"I'll tell you why," Mama Max continued, not letting Nettie get a word in edgewise. "It's because Obadiah's nose flew open as soon as she turned the corner. I swear I don't know who I want to slap harder, her or him!"

"Now, Mama Max, don't get your pressure up," Nettie cautioned. "Like you said, it's a small town and Jenkins is the only other Baptist pastor here. It stands to reason that we'd fellowship together from time to time."

"Oh, really? So this is normal? Jenkins stops by your house all the time?"

"Not exactly." In fact, she couldn't recall the last time Jenkins had been to her house, but if memory served, she still had had kids at home. So that had to have been ten, fifteen years ago at least. Nettie kept her mouth shut about this little tidbit, surmising that some things were better left unsaid. "Me and Gordon visited him in the hospital several times. I prayed with him and some of the sistahs from his church, and Gordon helped some of the men from the congregation tidy up the churchyard. I think this is just gratitude showing, Mama Max. Let's not make a mountain out of a molehill."

"Lord, how long must I endure this woman?" Mama Max strung out the word *long* for so long, Nettie stopped to stare at her. "I just don't like her," Mama Max concluded. "God forgive me, but I can't stand her thievin' behind."

For all the drama happening in the kitchen, another episode brewed in the dining room.

"You say your name's Dorothea?" Sistah Alrighty asked yet again.

"Yes, ma'am." Even though at sixty-six she was a senior citizen herself, she deferred proper respect to the woman who was fourteen years her senior, even if she'd have rather ignored her completely. This senile-acting woman made her skin crawl.

"Dorothea, that name sure sounds familiar. You ever been to Dallas?"

Dorothea glanced over at Obadiah.

"Now, sistah," Obadiah interrupted, placing one of his large hands on top of the church mother's bony one. "You've met so many people over your lifetime, you're probably thinking about another Dorothea."

"Humph, could be . . . could be not. You grow up in the church?"

Dorothea squirmed slightly, not sure why she was so uncomfortable with an old biddy she didn't know. "Yes, I've attended church all my life." *Not that it's any of your business.*

Sistah Alrighty reached into her purse and pulled out a pair of very thick glasses. She put them on and stared openly at Dorothea. "I know you," she finally concluded, pointing a bony, accusatory finger at the woman sitting across from her. "Sure as I live and breathe, I know you. And the Lord is going to help it come to me just where I know you from."

The investigation was interrupted as fresh, piping-hot platters were set on the table. Sistah Alrighty's attention was temporarily diverted. "More?" she asked simply, before piling second helpings on her plate. Conversation was forced but pleasant enough. Jenkins proudly recounted his and Dorothea's Christmas Day wedding. He assured everyone at the table, even those who could not have cared less, that a honeymoon was imminent just as soon as the doctor gave him a clean bill of health. Obadiah changed the subject, asking Jenkins about a pastor who'd recently died. Nettie and Mama Max listened as Sistah Almighty recounted her favorite passages from the Gospel Truth Manual while Sistah Alrighty ate . . . and thought.

"The devil is a lie!" Everyone jumped at the unexpected outburst and stared at Sistah Alrighty as her fork clattered to her plate. "I remember! I said the Lord would help me recollect and I remember!" She pulled off her glasses and squinted her eyes. "You've got a lot of nerve, woman, coming in here."

Sistah Alrighty had reached back forty years for the incident that forever etched a woman named Dorothea in her mind. It was in the early sixties, back in Dallas, Texas. She'd been young then, and anybody who knew Elsie Wanthers knew that she was on fire for God. Every year, she took her vacation during the National Baptist Convention, and this particular year had been no different. She'd signed up to volunteer, as always, and had been assigned to work as a hostess in the pastor's lounge. That's when she'd first seen her, acting what was in her opinion a little too friendly with Reverend Obadiah Brook. Elsie knew Reverend Brook in particular, because the year before, she'd met his wife, Maxine, and their two eldest children when she'd volunteered and been placed in the nursery and day care.

She'd asked another woman about the beauty sidling up to Sistah Brook's husband and was told that Dorothea had known Obadiah a while. It seemed that many of the workers knew about this inappropriate friendship. But one woman didn't know, and Elsie thought she should

Later that evening, Elsie and another woman from the convention sipped colas in the hotel lobby. She'd been just about ready to go to her room when Obadiah and Dorothea walked into the lobby. Her mouth almost flew open: They were laughing and cuddling, not even trying to be discreet! Before she could think about the consequences, Elsie walked to a hotel phone and asked for Maxine Brook. As soon as she answered, Elsie whispered, "I don't mean to be nosy or rude, but I just saw your husband come into the lobby, and I don't think he's headed to your room."

"Who is *this?*" a sleepy Maxine had asked.

"You can just say . . . I'm my sister's keeper."

Elsie heard about the fallout the next day. Dorothea disappeared, but not before Elsie had a chance to track down the hotel she was in and share a piece of her mind. It was the last church convention Dorothea attended, at least that Elsie knew of.

Elsie had no intention of telling Mama Max of her role in Mama Max finding out the truth, but the last day of the conference, Mama Max had joined her husband in the pastor's lounge.

"I heard about what happened, and I'm sorry," Elsie whispered into Mama Max's ear.

Mama Max's eyes widened, and she quickly pulled Elsie to the side. "It was you, wasn't it?"

"Ma'am? I don't know what you're—"

"I recognize your whisper. It was you who called. And I want to thank you."

Mama Max and Elsie Wanthers never had another conversation about what happened that night in Texas, even when Elsie married, moved to Kansas, and joined Mount Zion, which was pastored by Obadiah Brook at the time. But she'd had Mama Max's back since 1963. And she had it now.

Obadiah tried to defuse the situation. "Mother, here, let me take you out on the porch to get some fresh air. I think your medication is acting up."

"Ain't nothing wrong with my medication or my mind!" Sistah Alrighty insisted, shooting daggers at Dorothea. "God don't like ugly, and ain't enough makeup in the world—"

"Mother, it's getting late. We're going to head back to the house," Mama Max interjected. She became more concerned for this elderly woman's health than her own demons. She helped Sistah Alrighty to her feet. "Let's go."

Nettie rushed around in the kitchen, placing a sizeable amount of peach cobbler into a Styrofoam box. By the time she finished, Mama Max had maneuvered a mumbling Sistah Alrighty out to the porch, joined by Sistah Almighty and Gordon. Obadiah lingered behind in the dining room with Jenkins and Dorothea. He wished for a moment to talk to her alone, but he had no way of knowing when that would happen, especially now.

He put his hand on her shoulder. "I'm sorry," he said simply.

When his hand lingered a bit too long for Jenkins's taste, he removed it. "Apology accepted," was his terse reply.

Outwardly, Dorothea was a study in calmness, but inside, her peace was shattered. Because during all the commotion involved in escorting the old woman outside, the puzzle pieces had come together. She'd mentioned Dallas, Texas, and for Dorothea, there was only one unfortunate memory, besides Kennedy's assassination, that was linked to that place. Dorothea knew she'd just come face-to-face with that memory.

20

Get Me Some Peace

You could cut the tension with a knife. Obadiah drove with both hands on the wheel, staring straight ahead. For the first time since they'd arrived a week ago, the two church mothers were as quiet as church mice. Mama Max looked out the window at the bare tree limbs. Fall had turned to winter, and other than the holidays, Mama Max had barely noticed. She still didn't. She looked at the scenery, but instead of seeing brown bark, green grass, and blue skies, she saw peach, ivory, and big diamonds. Even more, she saw what Elsie "Sistah Alrighty" Wanthers had seen, that which had sent her into a tizzy. She saw memories.

What could have passed for a funeral procession continued once Obadiah pulled into the Brook driveway and parked the car. Mama Max helped Sistah Alrighty while Obadiah escorted Sistah Almighty. Once they got inside the house, Obadiah walked directly to his study and closed the door. Mama Max asked the church mothers if they cared for dessert. Both declined, saying they were tired and wanted to nap. Mama Max felt they wanted to gossip, but she had other matters to be concerned about.

She settled the ladies into the guest bedroom, took a deep

breath, and walked straight to the study door. "Obadiah," she said, knocking. "We need to talk."

"I'm with the Lord," Obadiah replied after a moment.

"Not in the way you're going to be if you don't open this door!"

It seemed as if forever passed, but actually a minute later, Obadiah opened the door. He'd taken off his suit coat and tie, and undone the first few buttons on his shirt.

"Don't come in here yapping at me, woman. I'm not in the mood."

"Why? What's got you in such a bad mood, Obadiah?" *As if I don't know.*

"Those nosy church mothers, that's what. It was uncalled for how they embarrassed Dorothea. I'm putting them on a plane first thing in the morning."

"Any embarrassment that happened don't have a thing to do with no old ladies. I think it has to do with an old man— who did what *you* always wanted to do, to marry her."

"She's married, Maxine. Why can't you just let it rest?"

"Because you can't! You've been acting strange since before she arrived in Texas, all holed up in this here study for hours at a time. Coming to bed all late and leaving the house before your breakfast has digested good. I've called the church during those times, so don't tell me that's where you were."

"I ain't been with Dorothea. That should satisfy you."

"Humph. It sure don't satisfy you. I can see that."

"But what you can't see is how you're getting on my nerves right now. You wonder why men flock to women like Dorothea? This here is why." Obadiah tapped his four fingers against his thumb, simulating a mouth talking. "You don't know when to shut up, Maxine, or when to back off. I'm telling you—now is the time!" Obadiah put a hand to his chest then and closed his eyes in pain.

Mama Max's chagrin quickly turned to concern. "Are you

all right, Obadiah? Want me to get you some water or some-thing?"

Obadiah walked over to the large black recliner behind the equally massive oak desk. He sat there a moment, breathing evenly, in and out. "I want you to get me some peace," he said finally. "Please lock the door on your way out."

21

What's Going On?

Things hadn't been the same since Stan caught the panties Passion had thrown at Crustaceans. The holidays had ended, the kids had gone back to school, almost a month had passed, and the silence continued. When he wasn't out of town, which was often, he was in his church office or down in the den, watching television. Aside from dinner with the family when his children were over, he rarely interacted with anyone at all. He'd taken to sleeping in a guest bedroom mostly, and any questioning by Passion only served to increase the emotional distance between them. Passion was losing patience. She had wanted their marriage to change, but this wasn't the change she'd had in mind. Things had gotten worse, not better, and she didn't know what to do about it.

Compounding matters was the isolation that Passion increasingly felt. She didn't have anyone to talk to about what was going on, at least not in her mind. Sure, some first ladies, including Vivian Montgomery of Kingdom Citizens Christian Center and Mount Zion's Tai Brook, had reached out to her following her marriage to Stan. But she hadn't felt those overtures sincere. After all, Passion knew for a fact that Vivian and Carla were very good friends and that Carla and Tai had gotten closer while working together on an SOS conference. She felt dubious about speaking to any of the associate ministers' wives about it. The last thing she wanted was others in the church knowing the true state of her marriage. She'd found out Mama Max was too old to understand her urges, and the one woman who would totally understand her situation was the woman she dared not call. Passion would love to talk to Carla, but she knew that that was not an option.

Passion walked up the stairs and crossed into the kitchen. She was looking in the refrigerator, deciding what to fix for dinner, when Stan came through the front door.

"Passion, where are you?"

Passion looked up from the steak she was holding. *Is that my husband actually calling out to me?* She was so shocked, she almost forgot to answer. "I'm here, Stan. In the kitchen."

Stan stepped just inside the kitchen door. "Are you cooking dinner tonight? I'd like to invite a guest over."

Oh, so that's what this is about, fronting for the masses. "Don't I always cook dinner, Stan? Except on Fridays?"

"I'm just asking as a courtesy. If this is going to cause an argument, I can switch these plans to a restaurant. Matter of fact . . ."

"Wait a minute, Stan. I don't have a problem adding a plate at dinner. Onyx won't be here. Their class took a field trip, and they're stopping for pizza afterward."

Stan stepped farther into the kitchen and leaned against the counter. "Okay. What are you fixing?"

"I was thinking about fried steak. . . ."

"Do we have any lobsters left in the freezer? Or what about those thick cuts of salmon—have we eaten all of them?"

Passion immediately wondered who Stan was trying to impress. Most of the time, he was more than happy with whatever she prepared, especially if it was a Southern dish. But this was more conversation that didn't involve children than they'd had in two weeks. She decided to keep her curiosity to herself. "I'm pretty sure there's some salmon left. I could marinate and bake them, fix a light pasta to complement it, and add salad and French toast. How does that sound?"

"Good. What about dessert?"

"I'll come up with something. Who's coming over?"

"An old friend of mine from D.C. We're both working on that Cathedral project, in Detroit. He's in town on business and I . . . want him to meet you."

Passion couldn't help but raise her brows at this statement. Hell, Stan barely saw her, and now he wanted to introduce her to an old friend? "Will his wife be joining us?" she asked.

"No, Bryce is divorced. It will be just the three of us. Does seven sound good?"

"Sure. But I'd better get started."

A little over two hours later, a freshened-up Passion smiled as Bryce Covington entered the Lees' living room. She was immediately taken with the debonair man who gently kissed her hand upon introduction. She'd never really been into pretty boys, but there was something about this one that made her tingle just a little bit. Of course, as the guests were seated in the dining room and Passion went to the kitchen for salad and bread, she reasoned that her flutters could have simply been because after kissing her hand, the person who'd come with Bryce had hugged her. It was the most contact she'd had with an adult male in two months.

"Stan tells me the two of you have known each other a long time," Passion said, once she'd poured lemonade for everyone and sat down.

"Yes, we were roommates in college." Bryce speared a broccoli flower onto his fork and ate it. "This dressing is delicious. A vinaigrette, correct?"

"Uh-huh." was all Passion said as she ate her own bite of salad.

"Where'd you buy it? I'd like to take some back to D.C. with me."

If she could have, Passion would have blushed. She took a moment to wipe her mouth with a napkin. "I made it."

"You're kidding me. It's divine." Bryce took another bite and savored it fully. "Man, looks like you found a keeper here. You might want to hold on to her."

Right now, Stan was simply trying to hold on to his composure. He'd been totally unprepared for the surprise guest Bryce had chosen to bring along to dinner. Evidently he'd called the house while Stan was in the shower and asked Passion if another guest could be seated. Passion had forgotten to pass this bit of news on to him, though, granted, he'd been in his office until just before Bryce arrived.

While Passion and Bryce chatted, Stan took the opportunity to check out Bryce's "business associate." He was a handsome, dark-skinned brother with perfect white teeth and manicured hands. Stan guessed him to be an inch or so taller than himself, six-one or two. If he didn't work out, he'd been born with a perfect metabolism. Stan couldn't detect an ounce of fat anywhere. On top of that, from an earlier conversation he knew that Ryan had graduated from Stanford with a degree in international business. He had a home in Los Angeles and a condo in London. He'd never been married and had no kids. Stan could not find one thing that was wrong with the brother, and it drove him crazy. That and the fact that he and Bryce made a perfect couple, and Stan would bet his ministry that that's what these two were. He'd caught the subtle look that had passed between them when they moved from the living room to the dining room, the subtle touch when Ryan had let Bryce walk ahead of him into the room. And why did Bryce have to look so devastatingly handsome tonight, in his black Armani suit, stark-white shirt, and silver cross necklace, a gift that Stanley had given him almost twenty-five years ago?

Later, if tested, Stan would not have been able to recall a major part of the dinner conversation. He'd never felt so conflicted and battled so many emotions: anger, jealousy, fear, guilt.

He breathed a sigh of relief as it neared an end. The dinner had not been at all what he intended, a chance to show Bryce what a happily married man he was.

"The dinner was lovely, Mrs. Lee," Ryan said as he cupped her hand.

"Please, call me Passion." She eased her hand out of his, less she embarrass herself. Ryan was handsome but rugged, more her type. And she'd noticed something when he sat down in the den. The brothah was packing a weapon for which a license was not needed.

"Passion, the pleasure was mine," Bryce said, forgoing her hand to hug her instead. His scent was woodsy with a hint of something else. Passion wanted to bury her head in his neck, while he buried something elsewhere. Passion kept trying to rein in her sexual thoughts. She didn't know why, but the last two months without intercourse had bothered her more than the five years she had been celibate before marrying Stan.

After a few more pleasantries, the men departed. Stan's mood seemed to change instantly, and after thanking her for the dinner, he said he was tired and went to bed.

Passion's mind whirled as she put away food and placed dishes in the washer. *What on earth is going on?* It was obvious something was troubling Stan, but she couldn't for the life of her imagine what it was. She went back over the evening in her mind. It had been engaging and entertaining; she'd thoroughly enjoyed both Bryce and Ryan's company. These were smart, successful men, like her husband. She and Stan had interacted easily throughout the dinner, and once he'd even placed his hand on top of hers as he made a comment. Passion was so caught up in enjoying the evening that only now was she questioning the sincerity of his actions. It was obvious that he'd set out to impress his guests, and by their accolades at the end of the night, that mission had been accomplished. *But look how different he became the moment they left the house. Something is going on.*

Before she could ponder the mystery further, Onyx burst through the door. The rest of the evening was filled with baths and bedtime stories. But as Passion lay down, alone, in the master suite, she continued thinking. Maybe Stan was working on a business deal, and these men were investors. Bryce was a politician; maybe Stan was thinking of running for office and gathering information. But in all the years she'd known Stan, both as a member of Logos Word and then as his wife, she'd never seen this old friend from college before. Bryce Covington was the type of man people remembered. If he'd been at the church before, his was a face she wouldn't forget. As she drifted to sleep, a question swirled in her head: *Who is Bryce Covington, and how does he fit into Stan's ministry?* Only time would tell how she'd act when she found out.

22

When I Would Do Good

Stan paced the floor of his church office. He'd told his secretary that under no conditions was he to be disturbed. "What if Sistah Lee calls?" his assistant had questioned.

"No one!" had been his bellowed reply. He'd apologized, blamed it on pressure regarding the upcoming church anniversary, and closed his door. That was an hour ago, and he was no less wound up now than he was then.

It had been two days since Bryce had swept into LA like a whirlwind, bringing all kinds of emotional, physical, and spiritual debris with him. After Bryce and Ryan had left the house that night after dinner, Stan had gone to his home office and after a few minutes, called Bryce's cell. Bryce didn't answer— not that time or the five or six subsequent times Stan called, late into the night and the next day. Stan never left a message, and after trying one last time in the early afternoon, he had given up.

He'd basically closeted himself away since then, trying to sort out the mess himself, yet desperately longing to talk to somebody. But he couldn't talk to anybody about a problem that he wouldn't even acknowledge to himself.

Seconds later, Stan was sprawled out on his carpeted office floor, prostrate before God. *When I would do good, evil is always present.* "Help me!" he whispered fervently. "Help me withstand the wiles of the devil! I am here to do Your will, Lord. Only Your will." Stan talked and prayed in the holy language for fifteen minutes, and while this act brought him comfort, it did not bring him peace.

Stan decided to go home. He'd just walked over to get his suit jacket when his assistant's voice came over the intercom.

"Bryce Covington for you, sir," she said tentatively. "I told him that you were not taking calls and to leave a message. But he insisted on being put through."

"I'll take it."

"Stan, I'm so sorry. Ryan and I left Los Angeles and flew directly to Mexico. I didn't pick up my cell phone for two whole days. Talk to me, friend. What is going on with you?"

For the first time in six months, Stan's strong façade broke. "That's what I'm hoping you'll help me find out."

Bryce left the bedroom where Ryan lay sleeping and walked into his gourmet kitchen for a glass of freshly squeezed juice. "I'm here for you, Stan. You know this."

"I can't be with you!" The statement came out of its own accord, but Stan was grateful for its truthfulness. "It's against everything I stand for, everything I've been taught."

"That's why I moved on," Bryce replied after a long hesitation. "I realized that you would never acknowledge what we both know—that you're in love with me and have been for the past twenty-five years."

"No, Bryce—"

"Don't try to deny it, because I know it's true. I could feel it when I showed up to your house with Ryan, my new man. I sensed the tension between you and Passion. I know how you look when you're in love, and that is not the expression I saw on your face when we dined at your home in Los Angeles."

"This phone call was a bad idea," Stan admitted after a lengthy pause in which he heard their favorite jazz artist, Earl Klugh, playing in the background.

"For who?" Bryce responded. "Ryan is quite the catch, Stan. I'll admit it. But he pales in comparison to you. Just say the word, and he's gone. I only have one request, one mandate: that you be here to take his place."

Stan squeezed his eyes tight, looking for Jesus. He allowed the censoring voice of his grandmother, and the voices of fire-and-brimstone preachers who'd mentored him, ring in his ear. *The wages of sin is death, but the gift of God is eternal life. That which is not of God is sin! Don't give in to the pleasures of the flesh! Be dead to sin, but alive in Christ!* Stan wiped his eyes as his resolve strengthened. "Have a good time with Ryan," Stan said with a courage he did not feel. "And please make sure that any and all calls in the future pertain to Cathedral business."

Stan sat motionless after ending the call, his fingers steepled, his brow knit in fervent thought. *This is a test. This is a temptation of the devil no less than what Adam experienced in the garden of Eden.* After several long moments, Stan rose from his chair and paced the room. He thought of all he'd been through in the past twenty-five years: the ministry reaching its fifteen-year milestone, his marriage and divorce from Carla, the promising educational path of his children and the fact that a godly woman, a patient woman, waited for him at home. Stan's grandmother's voice rang again into his consciousness. *Anything that is not of God is sin.* This thought gave Stan the courage to go home with the determination to love his wife, no matter how much he actually abhorred the act. His grandmother's memory gave him another thought: Where was she when he was being raped . . . in her house?

23

Will You Pray?

Princess stood up from her desk and stretched. The stretch turned into a praise, as she extended her hands toward heaven. *Thank you, Jesus.* She'd done it. She'd just e-mailed the manuscript of her book, tentatively titled *Jesus Is My Boo,* to the editors at Praise Publishing. Her part was over. Now all she had to do was sit back and wait to see what the company thought of her work.

Well, not exactly. Princess's brow furrowed as she thought of everything that had transpired over the past few days and how quickly she had learned that writing a book was only half the job. She'd gotten two unexpected phone calls in as many days, regarding marketing and publicity for the book's upcoming release: one from her aunt Vivian, who had a publicist she wanted Princess to talk to, and the second one a total shock . . . from Carla Chapman.

Princess plopped down on her single bed and grabbed one of the throw pillows. She almost wanted to be pinched to confirm she wasn't dreaming. *Carla Chapman wants to talk to me about being on her show?* Like many college students, and most adults between the ages of twenty-five and seventy, *Conversations with Carla* was must-watch TV. And after being nominated twice in a row, *Conversations with Carla* had won its first Emmy last year. Princess knew that getting this kind of national exposure could make her book a bestseller and hers a household name. But everyone would know her secrets as well. "Be careful what you ask for," had been Mama Max's response when Princess told her she wanted to be on Carla's show, during the same conversation she'd confessed almost all. She'd repeated the desire to her mother when she was home for the holidays. Princess had met Carla a couple of times while with her mother and knew that Tai and Carla talked fairly often. "Finish the book first," had been Tai's advice. "Then we'll see."

Princess mindlessly played a computer game as she pondered her grandmother's words. Was she really ready to share her story, the good, the bad and the ugly, with the rest of the world? "Only one way to find out," Princess said aloud as she reached for her cell phone. She tapped a mindless rhythm on her leg while waiting for the call to be answered. After announcing her name, several minutes passed. Finally, she was transferred to Carla's private voice mail:

"Hi, uh, Mrs. Chapman? This is Princess Brook. Thanks so much for calling me! I'd love to be on your show, I think. People will be all up in my business, but maybe my story can help someone. I look forward to talking to you and can be reached at . . ."

Princess finished the call. She knew she should be studying for a test in advanced marketing research, but she decided to check her e-mails instead. She clicked Yahoo! on her tool bar and waited for the page to open. Staring at her from the top of the page was the last face she needed to see: Kelvin Petersen. She meant to click on the mail icon, but almost of its own volition, her hand moved the mouse to the story's caption: KP IS BACK! She clicked on the link and read about how after being sidelined for almost three months with a knee injury, Kelvin would see limited play action in the Suns' upcoming game against the Los Angeles Lakers. "I'm glad to be back," Kelvin was quoted as saying. When asked how the injury would affect his ball playing, Kelvin quipped, "I'm coming back better than I was before I left." The article quoted his doctor and coaches, before going on with more general information about team standings and the rest of the basketball season.

Princess closed the article and once again looked at the photo of a smiling, confident young man. At one time, Kelvin had been her world. The sun had risen and set on him, and when they broke up, it left a huge void in her life. Kelvin was energetic and charismatic, there was always something going on when he was around. And for all his promiscuity and self-centered ways, there was also a generous, compassionate side. Kelvin made Princess feel special when she was around him—his presence was addictive. When he wrapped her in his strong, long arms, or used his tongue on either set of lips, it was as if nothing else in the world mattered, for either of them. There was no denying how thoroughly he could love her. Princess knew that in all of her partying, drinking, getting-high days, Kelvin Petersen's skilled dick had been the most dangerous drug she'd taken.

"Satan, get behind me," Princess whispered, closing out the page and trying hard to ignore the tingling between her legs the forbidden memories had caused. This was one of the reasons she stayed so busy, and why, if not studying or proselytizing, she surrounded herself with like-minded friends. Besides Joni, there was one other girl on campus with whom she'd grown close, Sarah Kirtz. Like Princess, Sarah was a preacher's kid. Her father, Jack Kirtz, had a ministry in San Diego and had even worked with her play uncle, Derrick Montgomery. Sarah was two years younger than Princess, but she had an intensity about God that belied her age. Sarah had worn a commitment ring since she was fifteen, and aside from a quick peck, had never kissed a man. She was determined to remain a virgin until she got married. Princess believed that she would, and she believed something else—that she needed someone with that kind of unbendable will to help her through this moment of weakness. Once again, she reached for her cell phone.

"Hello there, God's princess!" Sarah fairly sang the greeting. Her smile was evident though the phone.

"Hey, Sarah." Princess felt better already.

"Are you looking for someone to minister with you today? I'm almost done with this research paper but can meet you in the courtyard in about an hour."

"Actually, I'm calling about something else. The devil is busy and I'm battling temptation. Will you pray with me?"

24

Here Comes Trouble

Kelvin sipped his drink and surveyed the scene in Myst night-club's VIP room. There was the usual bevy of beauties that always surrounded pro players, and there were various levels of decadence that routinely took place in rooms that were off-limits to ordinary folk. He watched a hip-hop star light up a blunt as he swigged Cristal from a bottle, a popular young businessman snorted cocaine from a stainless-steel vial, and a buxom redhead with a four-leaf-clover tattoo on her cheek was giving serious head to one of his teammates.

Jakeim burst out laughing. "That shit is scandalous," he said, motioning to the athlete whose head was thrown back in pleasure. "Boy out here acting like pussy ain't free."

"He needs to check himself for real," Kelvin replied. "That shit end up on the Internet, it'll reflect on the whole team."

"Then again, it might be good for your boy to end up on YouTube. He'd get more face time there than he's getting on the team right now." The two men laughed and pounded fists.

Kelvin looked at his watch and contemplated leaving. The whole VIP club scene had gotten old. It wasn't like the first year he was drafted, when he partied until the break of dawn and was the life of the party in city after city and state after state. Three years in, and the thrill had gone. What other youngbloods now found exciting almost bored him to tears.

"Aw, shit," Jakeim drawled before finishing off his bottle of beer. "Here comes trouble."

Kelvin didn't even have to turn his head to know who Jakeim was talking about—his baby mama. It didn't surprise him to run into Fawn; she was never far from where money was being flung around. Things had quieted down between them since the holidays. After he'd returned to Phoenix from LA, his attorney had arranged to meet with Fawn. They'd drafted up an agreement whereby she would remain in the home that Kelvin had recently vacated and would receive a generous monthly allowance to take care of their son. In exchange, she was to have no contact with Kelvin Petersen, other than that which involved Kelvin Petersen, Jr. These exchanges were to take place in her home. She would have absolutely no access to Kelvin's new residence. She'd pouted for about two weeks, until she got the first check. Since then, things had been civil. Kelvin had hired a nanny for when Little Kelvin stayed with him, and a maid service, a chef, and a personal assistant to run the household otherwise. But as Fawn headed his way, Kelvin could tell by the look in her eyes that she wasn't over him. Obviously she was trying a new strategy to get the ring and become wifey—the only thing in life she wanted—or so she'd said at one time. Kelvin finished his drink and reached for the car keys lying on the table. If he'd thought it was time to leave earlier, he was sure of it now.

"Hey, Jakeim, what's up?" Fawn and one of her ballplayer-chasing sidekicks stood next to the table.

"Hey, Fawn."

"Kelvin."

"Fawn." Kelvin looked up and took in Fawn's appearance. As usual, she was dressed to impress and provoke. She'd cut out her weave, and the new short haircut framed her face nicely, emphasizing her perfect bone structure and well-defined lips. Her bronze skin looked silky smooth and was amply displayed in a short, tight, white minidress. The strappy, jeweled four-inch sandals she wore were outshone only by the two-carat, teardrop-diamond necklace she wore. Fawn looked good, Kelvin admitted to himself. So did her friend. But for him, their looks just proved how money-hungry, drama-starting bitches often came wrapped in pretty packages.

When no further conversation ensued, Fawn's friend piped in. "I was at the game the other night, Jakeim. You were amazing!"

Jakeim nodded. "I try."

"She's right, Jakeim," Fawn added. "You were the best thing on the floor that night."

"Glad to see you back, Kelvin," Fawn's sidekick said coyly. "You looked good—"

"Well, I'd love to stay and chat," Fawn said, obviously not wanting to hear any accolades her friend had for Kelvin. "But I'm meeting someone." Without waiting for a response, she turned and walked away, swaying her ample behind seductively. Kelvin watched impassively before a waitress came over to their table, blocking his view.

"The lady over there wants to buy you a drink," she said, looking at Kelvin.

Kelvin looked in the direction the waitress pointed. His eyes landed on a beautiful brunette, with dark, tanned skin and luscious black hair. He couldn't tell whether she was Latina, Greek, or Middle Eastern, but he liked what he saw. He nodded to the woman and placed his order. She simply nodded back in return.

"Ha! I know Fawn will fuck any nucka now," he said once the waitress had moved away from the table.

"What?" Jakeim asked as he looked around. "Aw, that shit's messed up right there." Fawn was sitting on a teammate's lap, outlining his ear with her tongue.

Kelvin shrugged. "It's a free country."

"Yeah, but Guy Harris? His wife just had a baby, what, last week? That shit's foul, man, I'm telling you."

"Whatever, dog, I'm gone." Kelvin placed a fifty-dollar bill on the table. The waitress came up with his drink. He took it, walked toward the exit, and nodded subtly at the woman who'd purchased it to follow. She slid off the stool and followed him out.

An hour later, he was eight inches deep into the woman whose name he'd already forgotten. But there was another woman he couldn't forget, who'd been on his mind constantly since the holidays. And as he found his release, Princess was who he was thinking about.

25

Healthy Appetites

Obadiah leaned back against the black leather chair and closed his eyes. The Lord had given him a powerful scripture to preach from on Sunday, and he'd been working on his text for the past hour. As he gently rocked the chair beneath him, he meditated once again on the passage, Romans, chapter six, verses six through twenty-three:

> *Likewise reckon ye also yourselves to be dead indeed*
> *unto sin, but alive unto God through Jesus Christ our*
> *Lord. Let not sin therefore reign in your mortal body,*
> *that ye should obey it in the lusts thereof. Neither yield*
> *ye your members as instruments of unrighteousness*
> *unto sin: but yield yourselves unto God . . . for the*
> *wages of sin is death; but the gift of God is eternal life*
> *through Jesus Christ our Lord.*

Obadiah rocked forward and picked up his pen. *The wages of sin is death.* He put down the pen and rubbed his eyes, knowing that one living in a glass house should not throw stones.

It had been a month since Jenkins and Dorothea had shown up unannounced at Nettie's house, but Dorothea had called regularly since then, with a singular focus: She wanted to be intimate. So far, Obadiah had kept her at arm's length. After all, he was the senior pastor of a local church. He had his reputation to consider. Not to mention the fact that he was a married pastor. When Dorothea had countered that that hadn't mattered before, Obadiah had replied, "It matters now. All those other times, I was out of town. Maxine's here, Dee. And she's mighty suspicious already. You know that."

"I need you," Dorothea had responded, acting as if she hadn't heard what Obadiah said. "Jenkins is as limp as cooked spaghetti. And I know Maxine ain't working that weapon you got. Let me do it, Obadiah. You know I can make you feel good, Daddy. I can make it feel real good."

Obadiah had hardened in spite of himself. Unlike some of his peers, his healthy sexual appetite had not diminished with age, a fact that made Maxine's stance on lovemaking—or rather lack thereof—that much more difficult. He knew several men his age who still liked to dip the pole in the hole, and he couldn't understand why the thought of old people having sex seemed so astonishing. Given the gist of his sermons, Obadiah could understand why people might raise a few eyebrows at his having sex, but like he'd told a preacher friend just the other day, his motto was "use it or lose it."

It was time to take control of his lust; Obadiah knew that. He'd managed to be with Dorothea only once every two to three years or so, getting his pleasure elsewhere the rest of the time. But things couldn't go on this way. He knew as well as anyone that where there was smoke, there was fire. And he had no doubt that Dorothea's poontang was piping hot!

Obadiah rose from his chair and walked to the corner of his office. He poured himself a glass of water and drank it slowly, trying to get his mind off having sex and back on fighting sin. He went back to his desk with resolve and had written another quarter of his sermon when his cell phone rang.

"Doctor Brook," he said in his staid, preacher voice, even though he knew who was calling.

"Oh, really," Dorothea purred. "Well, Doctor, I've got a prescription that needs filling. Can I come by your office?"

"You know you can't come by here, woman. Why do you keep trying to tempt me?"

Dorothea's laugh was throaty, sultry. "You know why!"

Obadiah smiled in spite of himself. He'd had a thing for Dorothea for more than forty years, but before, it had always been manageable. In all these years, they'd never lived in the same town, and with the exception of an occasional phone call between the two, it was out of sight, out of mind. Now, even though he'd forbade her from ever coming to the church without his knowledge or purposely showing up anywhere he was, she was still pulling his strings. He knew he shouldn't, but he looked forward to her phone calls, talking sexy, and sometimes dirty, in his ear. He wanted her as much as she wanted him, and in rare moments, he admitted the truth to himself: it was only a matter of time.

Two hours later, having warned Dorothea yet again not to come by the church, Obadiah left the church office and made the drive to the Brook residence, less than ten minutes away. When the ministry had offered the parsonage to house them, both he and Maxine had decided against staying next door to the church. They'd learned from experience that it was good to have a little distance between the parishioners and their personal lives.

He'd put Dorothea out of his mind to finish the sermon, but now that he was finished and heading home, she crowded Obadiah's thoughts again. As soon as he'd started the car, he turned on a CD to tamp down the thoughts. Within seconds, the voice of his favorite singer, James Cleveland, poured from the speaker. "Master, the tempest is raging, the billows are tossing high," Obadiah sang along with the CD, his voice clear and melodious. He sang "Peace Be Still," but even as he pulled into the driveway, his mind was in torment and he was more than a little relieved that he didn't see Maxine's car. *Probably over at Nettie's.* Again, Dorothea's flirtatious laughter drifted into his ear.

Once inside the house, Obadiah walked straight to the kitchen. As usual, Mama Max had cooked and left the food on the stove. He washed his hands and made himself a plate of fried pork chops, green beans with new potatoes, macaroni and cheese, and topped the menu off with large, juicy slices of marinated tomatoes. Fifteen minutes later, he wrestled the last piece of meat off the pork chop bone, finished his glass of cola, and let out a satisfied belch.

After placing his plate in the sink, Obadiah poured himself another glass of soda and headed to his office. Considering the topics that had occupied his thoughts all afternoon, he felt more than a little discomfort for what he was about to do. But as sure as he knew his name, he knew that what he was about to do had to happen. He'd taken care of one type of appetite; now it was time to take care of another one.

26

The Devil Is a Lie

Mama Max hummed a tune as she turned into the driveway. Visiting with Nettie always did a world of good for her spirits. She'd especially liked Nettie's suggestion that Mama Max take over teaching the adult Sunday school class. She shook her head at seeing Obadiah's car parked in the drive, instead of in the garage like most proper folk. She punched the button and waited for the door to open, looking around and continuing to hum as the creaking, wooden garage door slowly lifted from the ground. She noticed that one of the porch lights was out and made a mental note to tell Obadiah so the deacon who handled house repairs could replace it. She was just about to pull her car into its space when she noticed something else, and frowned. *Why is he keeping that study window open?*

There were two sets of windows in Obadiah's study that faced the street. The open window was in the library section of the large L-shaped room. Mama Max had first noticed it open last week, when she walked over to chat with the neighbor. The fact that it was open stuck out, because Texas had experienced an unusually cold February. She'd meant to mention it to the reverend but had forgotten. *And it's open again?*

A thought occurred to Mama Max that almost made her hit the gas pedal and crash through the slow, still-opening garage door. "The devil is a lie!" she said, pulling into the garage and screeching to a stop just shy of the back wall. She entered the kitchen from the garage and walked straight to the study, not even stopping to take off her coat or set down her purse. She turned the knob and wasn't surprised to find the door locked. "Reverend?" She tried the knob again. "Obadiah!" she shouted, pounding on the door at the same time. "You better open up this door and I mean right now. And if there's anybody in there with you, they'd better give their soul to God 'cause their butt is mine!"

Mama Max waited, hands on hips, shoulders heaving, foot tapping. "Stanley Obadiah Meshach Brook! You'd better open this here door. What's going on in there?" Her imagination ran wild with images of Dorothea sprawled across the couch in Obadiah's study with the hem of her skirt somewhere around her waist, and Obadiah grunting like a pig in mud. Mama Max pounded on the door again. When a few more seconds went by with no response, she stormed through the living room and out the door. She didn't even notice the bushes snagging her pants or the cold wind that whipped around her calves and ankles. Her focus was singular: to get inside Obadiah's study and to do it right now!

By the time she arrived at the window, it had been closed. *Uh-huh, you're up to something, and I bet it's with that hussy!* Mama Max was fit to be tied. She was more determined than ever to get into that study, and for the first time in her life pondered the thought of breaking and entering. The owner of the home had installed new storm windows just prior to renting it to the Brooks, and they were designed to not only keep the elements out, but intruders as well. The screen was a mesh of strong wire, the frame made of steel. The frame could be raised, but only from the inside. *I can't raise this here window, but I can sure raise holy hell!* Mama Max took a deep breath and bellowed, "Obadiah! You better come to this window and I mean now!"

A couple lights went on, one next door and the other across the street. Mama Max looked in time to see the same neighbor she'd discussed rosebushes with last week sheepishly peek out the window and wave.

Mama Max ignored her. "Obadiah!" A strong hand on her shoulder caused her to almost jump out of her skin.

"Woman, what in the hell is wrong with you?"

"Where is she?" Mama Max panted, breathing heavy from her screaming exercise.

"Get a hold of yourself, Maxine," Obadiah cautioned. "Don't go making a fool of yourself out here."

"Humph, like you're making a fool of yourself in there?" Mama Max's eyes narrowed as she looked from Obadiah to the window and back. Suddenly her eyes widened, and she raced toward the door, entered the house, and raced toward the back door. "What's this back door doing open?"

Obadiah ignored her, instead walking up the stairs toward their bedroom. "You need to find a hobby, woman, or get some business to tend to. Because you'll drive yourself crazy trying to tend to mine!"

By the time Mama Max had calmed down and gone up to bed, Obadiah was already snoring. He left around five-thirty the next morning, before Mama Max had put coffee on. She sat at the table alone, sipping and thinking. Life had basically been good with Obadiah. They'd had their ups and downs, and a large part of their marriage had been spent with him on the road. But she'd enjoyed her role in raising the children, ministering to the women in their various congregations, and taking care of her husband the best she could. Except for Dorothea, Mama Max had never suspected Obadiah of being with another woman. Which is why she was determined to get to the bottom of how Dorothea had gotten into his study and, more importantly, how she'd escaped.

Once Mama Max had finished her breakfast and washed the dishes, she headed to Obadiah's study. She knew the door was probably locked and was fully prepared to call a locksmith if she had to in order to get in. If Dorothea had indeed been there, as Mama Max suspected, she believed there would be some kind of evidence to prove it. Mama Max had already decided that if she found the proof she was looking for, the Brooks wouldn't see their fifty-third anniversary.

She turned the knob on the study, and to her surprise, the door opened. Mama Max took a deep breath and stepped inside. The office smelled like Obadiah: a blend of Listerine mouthwash and Old Spice cologne. She looked around slowly. The space seemed in order, the way Obadiah preferred things. Yesterday's newspaper lay folded in the center of an otherwise bare desk, save for a pen-and-pencil set, a praying-hands paperweight, and three manila folders on the desk's right side. Mama Max walked the length of the room, looking in every nook and cranny for she didn't know what. But she didn't see or sense the presence of a woman anywhere.

The office was L-shaped, the smaller portion being a second room that served as the library for Obadiah's extensive collection of texts and study guides. Mama Max eyed the well-worn leather couch that took up one side, with shelves of books on the back wall. She walked over to the couch. Nothing looked out of order. She bent down, smelled the leather. No scent of perfume clung to either the seats, the throw she'd knitted and given to Obadiah, or the pillows that decorated the otherwise staid room.

Once Mama Max had gone over the entire study with a fine-tooth comb, a wave of guilt settled over her. Dorothea hadn't been in this room. If she had, Obadiah had eliminated all evidence, and when could he have done that? She'd gotten up when he did this morning, and he beat her to bed last night. *Could I have been paranoid, making up an affair in my head?* "Oh, Father, forgive me," she said aloud. "And I need to ask Obadiah's forgiveness when he gets home."

Mama Max looked at the filled shelves around the room.

"He's right. I need to tend to my business," she said, walking over and fingering the hundreds of books. "And I'm going to start right now." She decided to get a jump on teaching Sunday school by studying one of her favorite Bible passages—Proverbs 31. After finding pen and paper to write an outline, she began pulling out various concordances, textbooks, Bible versions, and other study aids. She walked over to the shorter wall and began looking at those books. One in particular jumped out at her. It was on one of the higher shelves, but Mama Max felt if she reached on her tiptoes, she could get it. She gripped the side of the shelf and reached up, leaning into the shelf itself for support.

That's when it happened. The entire bookcase moved, almost causing Mama Max to tumble over. "The blood of Jesus!" she cried, even as the case continued to swing open. Mama Max went stumbling into this secret chamber, almost falling down. Fortunately—or unfortunately—her fall was somewhat stayed and totally cushioned by the competition she'd feared—but not who she'd imagined. Her fall was stayed by a blue-eyed, life-size rubber sex doll.

Mama Max pulled her face from between the enormous, jiggling globes, and within seconds, her mouth soon resembled the doll's open O-shaped lips. She screamed and jumped up at the same time, her mind barely able to register what her hands were feeling and her eyes were beholding. Mama Max eyed the five-foot, six-inch creation, from the long black human hair on its head to its red-painted toes. Her lips formed a straight line as she took in the realistic-looking, pink vagina. This wasn't some cheap blow-up doll. It was a new-and-improved, twenty-first-century version, so lifelike it was scary. Mama Max's hand went to her chest as comprehension dawned and the lights came on in this seventy-year-old mind. She slowly backed away from the "companion" that had been keeping Obadiah company in the late-night and early-morning hours when he'd been locked away in his study. *A doll?*

Obadiah has been cheating on me with . . . some rubber? For a moment, Mama Max thought she'd be ill and wanted to run away, but as she looked around, the other items in this small room kept her glued to the spot. A look of horror replaced that of shock and awe as her eyes took in row after row of pornographic books, DVDs, and sex toys. On the other wall was a flat-screen television, within perfect viewing sight of a large recliner Mama Max had never seen before. *When did he have time to purchase that chair, let alone bring it in here?* Then she remembered the outing several months back: when she and Nettie had done an overnight trip to Dallas, a girls' day out. *Well, obviously there had been a boy's night out too. . . .*

"Jesus, have mercy, Jesus," Mama Max whispered as she slowly put one foot in front of the other. As she got closer to the magazines, she was appalled by what she saw. Breasts, vaginas, and rear ends were splashed across the covers in various poses. Mama Max closed her eyes and pulled one of the DVDs out. The title, *Tits and Tushes,* was juxtaposed over a pair of enormous breasts. That cover was the tamest of the three or four she pulled out. By the time she eyed the last one, where several couples were splashed across the cover in the very act of fornication, she'd seen enough. She turned to leave, but on her way out, a small leather toiletry bag caught her eye. With fear and trepidation, Mama Max picked it up and unzipped it. "Viagra!" she shrieked, when among the contents of latex condoms, disposable gloves, mouthwash, and deodorant, she'd pulled out a large bottle of small blue pills. Mama Max's eyes grew wide as she threw down the pills, stumbled over the hastily tossed DVDs, and ran from the room as if the devil himself were chasing her.

27

Sordid Revelations

"Ain't no fool like an old fool," Mama Max said, her voice sad and weary. She sat at the table in her dining room, still wearing the house dress she'd donned just before coming downstairs more than four hours ago. The coffee Nettie had poured for her remained untouched, as did the slice of fresh strawberry-rhubarb pie she'd brought to try and cheer Mama Max up. She'd been so distraught when she'd phoned Nettie that Nettie offered to come to the Brook residence as opposed to Mama Max coming to her. Nettie wasn't sure her dear friend would be safe behind the wheel of a two-ton vehicle.

Nettie remained quiet, not knowing what to say. Her mind was still reeling from what she'd seen with her own eyes, the secret room in her pastor's study, the man of God who'd been brought to Gospel Truth to preach the unadulterated Word, the man who brought a broom into the pulpit to sweep Satan out of the church. Obviously the pastor had failed to heed the old saying "sweep around your own front porch before you try and sweep around mine."

"I never thought I'd divorce him, not after all these years," Mama Max continued in the same dry, lifeless tone. "Next year we'll have been married fifty-three years. And for what? For me to find out I don't even know the man I've called my husband?" The first show of emotion came to her face then, a single tear that ran down, hovered on her chin, and then dropped on her dress. "It's a shame before the living God. I will not live a lie." Mama Max brought her fist down on the table for emphasis. "Trying to teach others to live holy. I will not live a lie," she repeated in a whisper.

Nettie took a deep breath and chose her words carefully. After all, this sordid revelation of Obadiah's activities affected not only his marriage, but his ministry as well. If this got out to Gospel Truth, let alone the nation, her son's past sin might pale in comparison. "I can't imagine the hurt you feel," she began, her voice soft, soothing. "You have every right to be upset."

"Upset? You think I'm just upset? I've a mind to go to that church right now and beat that man like he stole from me. Because he did—he stole the trust I had in him right out my heart. I'm beyond upset, Nettie Jean. I'm madder than a bunch of red hornets right now."

"I know you are," Nettie said quickly. "That's the natural reaction of any wife who'd find this type of, uh, stuff in her house."

Mama Max snorted. "Here I am worried about Dorothea's shriveled behind and all along my competition has been a plastic pussy. Have you ever heard of such? It would be funny if it wasn't so sad and disgusting. I oughta grab that thing and take it right on up there to the church. Tell Obadiah if he wants to keep her, that's the office she'll have to stay in because she's getting the hell out of my house!" Mama Max pushed back abruptly from the table and started toward the hall.

"This will bring an awful hurt to the ministry if folk find out," Nettie said as she hurried to catch up to Mama Max.

Mama Max whipped around. "The ministry? What about my marriage? Do you think I give a damn about the church right now, when my whole life lies in shambles? To pull the

covers off this hypocritical SOB will be just what he deserves."
Mama Max hesitated before entering the study, but then lifted
her chin and marched forth with resolve.

"Now, Mama, just think on it a minute. It will affect everything y'all do in the future."

"Y'all? Or Reverend? Because I have nothing to be
ashamed of, unless you think being ignorant a shameful thing.
Now that the eyes of my understanding have been enlightened, I'm going to brighten a few others too." Mama Max
pulled on a pair of the disposable gloves she'd seen earlier in
Obadiah's toiletry bag. After putting them on, she grabbed the
naked doll by the hair and began dragging it through the
house.

Nettie prayed feverishly under her breath. She was thinking about the future of Gospel Truth, as well as how a scandal
like this would affect Mama Max, her children, and her grand-
children. "Wait, Mama, hold on a minute."

Mama Max walked through the kitchen, grabbed her car
keys off the table, and opened the door to the garage. The
silicone-filled breasts of the doll continued jiggling when
Mama Max stopped to speak. "Wait for what? I'm getting this
slimy piece of sin out of my house and taking it to its owner,
where it belongs." She opened the back door of her Cadillac
to push the doll inside, but just before she did, Nettie grabbed
the doll's foot.

"Let go!" Mama Max tried to jerk the doll out of Nettie's
grasp.

"I think you need to think on this, Mama!" Nettie huffed,
tightening her hold on the thick rubber.

"I don't need to think on anything!"

"Well, pray, then!"

The two women wrestled with the life-size doll, both trying to take it from the other. The doll twisted and turned with
the motion of the women, its O-shaped mouth an appropriate
expression to being pulled in opposite directions.

Mama Max soon tired from trying to hold the doll. "Fine," she said, and let it go so abruptly that Nettie stumbled back, tripping over a box and almost falling into a basket of clothes for charity. She half sat, half stood, trying to steady her breathing. Mama Max fell back against the car, her always perfectly coiffed hair coming out of its chignon and her dress askew. The doll leaned facedown against the door, momentarily forgotten. If one were looking in on this scene, it would have been hard to tell who won the battle: Mama Max, Nettie, or the doll.

After a moment, Mama Max stood. "This is my house and my business. Don't try and stop me, Nettie." She pushed the doll into the backseat and slammed the door shut.

Nettie watched helplessly as Mama Max slid into the driver's seat, hit the switch to open the garage door and turned the keys. "Are you sure?" she yelled through the glass.

Mama Max looked at Nettie a long moment, and then rolled down the passenger side window. "What am I supposed to do? Just let that man treat me any kind of way?"

"Most certainly not! This matter must be dealt with, Mama Max—"

"Datgum right—"

"But I just think you might want to handle it in private before you take it public. Think of that grandbaby who you said might be on TV." Nettie was talking fast, afraid Mama Max would put the car into gear any moment.

Mama Max reached for the keys and turned off the engine. "You're right," she said with a sigh. "Thank you, Nettie. I appreciate you saving me from embarrassing myself and my family. You go on home now. I'll be all right."

The calm with which Mama Max spoke frightened Nettie more than her earlier screaming had. "Are you sure?"

"I'm sure." Mama Max opened her car door and got out. "You go on home now," she repeated.

"Promise me you'll call me back over if you need me, and

take time to pray. The devil's got your husband trippin', Mama. Don't let him get you too."

Several hours later, Obadiah entered the front door. His face formed an immediate scowl for two reasons: one, the house was dark even though Maxine's car was parked in the driveway, and it was only six-thirty; two, the smell of dinner that usually greeted him was noticeably absent.

"Maxine?" he called out tentatively, sensing something wrong. Aside from when Mama Max was sick or out of town, Obadiah never walked into a house devoid of the smell of his dinner cooking. He turned on the hall light. "Maxine?" he called again.

When Obadiah turned the corner into the living room, he gasped. There, sprawled spread-eagle on the floor, was the doll he used almost nightly to relieve the sexual tension that plagued him. Scattered around his fake friend were DVDs, magazines, and videos, and sprinkled throughout were his little blue pills.

Obadiah tentatively stepped into the darkened room. He was so focused on the pile of porn that he didn't see Mama Max sitting at the corner telephone table until she spoke.

"We need to talk, Reverend Doctor," she said in a voice that was deadly calm.

"Maxine, I can explain," he began, his hands put up in a sign of surrender.

"Ain't no explaining to do on this one, Obadiah. I've got my mind made up. It's either me or that disgusting plastic pussy and repugnant porn. This house ain't big enough for me and . . . all that."

28

A Funky Valentine

Passion read the hastily scrawled note for the umpteenth time and wiped away tears. If only she could wake up and find that the past twenty-four hours were just a dream. But that was the problem—she was awake. And the craziness of her life was all too real. She forced herself from the bed she'd crawled back into as soon as she'd gotten Onyx off to school and canceled all of her ministry-related engagements. It was the fourteenth of February, and while she'd always enjoyed listening to Ella Fitzgerald's rendition of "My Funny Valentine," Passion found herself getting ready to experience a very funky Valentine's Day instead.

The drama started yesterday morning with what she thought an innocent question regarding an early morning call on Stan's cell phone.

"Who was that?" she'd asked in a sleepy voice, about the caller who'd awakened them at six-thirty in the morning.

"Bryce," Stan said curtly, not unlike many of his answers in the months since the panty toss. They'd silently declared a truce but obviously hadn't cleared the air.

"Kind of early for business calls, don't you think?"

"What's it to you?" Stan threw back the covers and

bounded out of bed. "Back in here for two nights and you're already nagging."

Passion sat up. "What's with the attitude? I just asked a question. How would you react if one of my friends called at this hour?"

"I don't know, Passion," Stan sneered. "Do you even have friends?"

Where did that come from? Passion took a deep breath. Tomorrow was Valentine's Day. She'd planned an intimate dinner, for just the two of them, at a Malibu hideaway. On a recent *Conversations with Carla*, a guest had talked about being responsible for one's own actions and how the only person one could change was oneself. Passion had taken those comments to heart, decided to put her ego aside, and do whatever it took to get her marriage back on track. She'd planned to take the blame for why the marriage wasn't working, apologize for the panty throw, agree to counseling to deal with her sexual appetite, and maybe later, if she could arrange it secretly, ask one of Stan's peers to talk with him about his . . . issues.

She followed him into the bathroom. "I'm sorry, Stan—"

"I'm getting ready to take a shower. Do you mind?"

Passion took a step toward him and forced a smile. "No, in fact, I'll join you if you'd like."

Stan simply stared, waiting for his wife to leave the room so that he could take off the T-shirt and large boxer shorts that served as pajamas. Instead, Passion threw off her cotton nightgown and leaned into her husband. "Just a shower," she whispered. "Nothing more. Let me take care of you, honey. The coffee timer's set, and there's a freshly made coffee cake to go along with it."

Stan grabbed Passion's arms and pushed her away with such force that she stumbled into the clothes hamper. "Stan! What is wrong with you?"

Stan appeared stunned that he'd pushed her, but his resolve

did not waiver. "I have a lot on my mind, Passion. Please, just get out."

Stan had left the house shortly after that, barely after seven a.m. and without stopping for his usual cup of joe. Passion had arrived at the church about an hour later and had been in either meetings or counseling sessions the whole day. When she arrived back home in time to greet Onyx, around three o'clock, she found the note on the kitchen's gray-and-black-streaked granite island:

Passion: Emergency meeting out of town. Will be back on Friday. Can be reached by cell. Stan. PS: Sorry for earlier.

"Sorry for earlier . . . That's it?" Passion asked the empty room. "And is this earlier for just today or for the last six months?" Passion reached for the note and tore it into shreds, while calling Stan every name but a child of God. After she'd shredded the note, she picked up the pile and threw it like confetti all over the room. Before she knew what was happening, she was throwing anything that wasn't tied down or too heavy—dish towels, pot holders, a roll of paper towels. She picked up a glass and was about to hurl it toward the cabinet when she caught a glimpse of her reflection in the mirror that hung above the sink. Passion's arm stopped in midair as she took in the vision staring back at her: the wide red eyes, wild hair, and wrinkled gown. She took a closer look and determined that the twenty pounds she'd put back on since remarrying did not become her. She stepped up to the mirror. *Where is Passion? Where is the bold, confident, in-control woman who came into this marriage?*

Passion frowned, determined to find out. "I can't keep doing this. I've got to do something about it." Passion left the room and headed downstairs to retrieve the information she needed.

29

Who I Am?

"Thanks for coming," Bryce said as soon as Stan had walked through the doorway. "Don't I get a hug?" he continued once Stan was inside.

"I don't feel right being here."

Bryce came to stand directly in front of Stan and fixed him with a compassionate stare. "But you came anyway. I'm glad to see you." Bryce stepped closer, his stare penetrating and unblinking into his friend's eyes.

Finally, Stan could resist it no longer. He fell into the arms he'd dreamed about since January. They hugged a long moment, and then Stan, feeling something growing that shouldn't, abruptly broke away. "I can't do that. You know that I *cannot* do that." He walked to the other end of the room, putting space between them. While regaining his composure, he took a look around. "Nice place. Good taste. But, then, that was always you."

"It took me a while to get used to the smaller space, but it's growing on me."

Stan laughed. The smaller space Bryce referred to was almost three thousand square feet.

"Hey, c'mon! The home I left was twice this size. The girls still live there."

"Your wife and—"

"*Ex*-wife. And my heart, Jasmine. Thank God we're still close. I'd heard horror stories about what divorce could do to a child. It's one of the reasons I waited until my daughter was grown before leaving. But then again, you know a little something about it." Bryce turned toward the kitchen. "Drink?"

"Water's fine." Stanley walked over to the fireplace, which covered almost the entire back wall. The ledge was filled with photographs, mostly of a beautiful young woman he correctly assumed was Jasmine. "She's beautiful, your daughter. Looks like you."

"Thanks. She's definitely Daddy's little girl. Has her mother's temperament, though—focused, determined." Bryce returned to the room with a glass of lemon water for Stan and a tumbler of brandy for himself. "To life," he said somberly. The two men eyed each other a long moment, clinked glasses, and drank.

Bryce sat on a long, tailored sofa while Stan chose one of two gray-upholstered wingback chairs. "How is he?" Stan asked into the silence.

"He's hanging in there, waiting for you if you want to know the truth. Otherwise, I think he's ready to go, man, ready to check out."

Stan put down his drink and rose. He looked out over the well-tended, landscaped backyard. He imagined flowers in spring, the water gurgling from the lion head over the stone pool. But now things were barren, the way Stan felt, paying homage to the season of winter. "I can't believe that Eddie has AIDS. He was married, with a lovely wife and those four beautiful children. . . ."

"We were all married, Stanley. Doesn't stop the truth."

"Speak for yourself . . ."

"Eddie was on the down low for the entirety of his marriage, ironically with a man he met at his and Donna's wedding reception. He's told me time and again that if he'd met Phil before marrying Donna, that marriage never would have happened. The thought made him sad, but then he'd think of his children and remember why everything had been worth it."

"Donna never suspected?"

"Did you?"

"Eddie 'Hound Dog' West?" Stan responded, referring to Eddie's college nickname. "Not even once."

"Neither did Donna, at least not that Eddie knew of. Donna always had her own life, raising the kids and then striving for her PhD. She's a force to be reckoned with in her own right, lecturing and teaching in underdeveloped nations all over the world. She spends considerable time in Africa and also the Caribbean. But aside from the physical aspect, she and Eddie have always been good friends. That's one reason he never thought about divorcing her. He loves Donna. But then last year, when he got diagnosed with full-blown AIDS . . ."

"I didn't think that happened anymore. People get tested, and when HIV is discovered, there are procedures, medicine. People live full, long lives now. Look at Magic Johnson."

Bryce snorted. "Magic Johnson . . . Everybody throws him up as the poster boy for AIDS. Man, everybody's story isn't like Magic Johnson's. Everybody doesn't have millions of dollars for the best treatment, doctors, physical and emotional therapy, diet. I'm not hatin' on the brother, but I'm just saying, all people living with HIV aren't living a stress-free, worry-free life. People with HIV get sicker, suffer horribly, react negatively to medications and treatment, go through hell. And then the disease advances to full-blown AIDS. Like Eddie. Because of how fast the disease has progressed, the doctors believe he was infected for years and just didn't know."

"I don't get it. How . . ."

"Phil cheated."

"Lord have mercy."

"With a young, strapping twentysomething he met at a conference. According to Phil, they only met a few times. But as we hear over and over, one time is enough."

Stan resisted the urge to ask Bryce about the strapping thirtysomething who'd joined them for dinner when Bryce was in LA. Instead, he stayed focused on the conversation about their mutual friend. "I can't believe Eddie wasn't protecting himself."

"Me neither. But he and Phil have been together for almost twenty-five years. Eddie was committed and thought Phil was too."

"Donna must be devastated. And she's negative, correct?"

"So far, but it hasn't been quite a year. I think she will get tested for a while, until she's convinced that the disease didn't spread to her."

Stan plopped back down in the chair. He hadn't seen Donna in years but had been there when she and Eddie got married. In fact, he'd been one of the groomsmen. That was also the last time he'd seen Bryce, until last year. He stared out the window and remembered. Stan, Bryce, and Eddie had been like the three musketeers, not only hanging out and partying together but also sharing hopes and dreams. Stan knew that Eddie always suspected something between Stan and Bryce, but Stan never confirmed it. By the time of Eddie's wedding a few years after college, Stan had left the lifestyle behind, had embraced God and ministry, and was on his way to being one of the country's preeminent preachers.

"I wonder why Eddie didn't call me?" Stan asked, almost to himself.

Bryce reared back on the couch and fixed Stan with another penetrating stare. "You know why. He's a practicing Christian, just like you. He's heard the fire-and-brimstone sermons on homosexuality and other acts you deem immoral."

"Not me, Bryce, God."

"Oh, really? Whose God? Because I love God, too, man, and He loves me back. He hasn't once told me to stop being what I am. In fact, He is the one who gave me courage to stop insulting His creation by lying about who I am!"

Stan got up from his chair. "Look, Bryce, I'm not going to argue with you about this. The Bible—"

"Oh, would that be the King James Bible? You do know the good old king was a faggot, don't you? The man who commissioned the very book that you and others so self-righteously use to denounce people like him was gay, homosexual, a lover of other men, just like you and me."

"I am not a homosexual! You know why I was that way in college, because I was raped!"

"Oh, so that's it. Everybody who's gay has been molested. That's bullshit and you know it."

"Not for all of us, Bryce. My story is a lot like Donnie Mc-Clurkin's. You know about him, right, the singer?"

"I've heard his story, but I'm not sure I buy it. Wait." Bryce held up his hands when Stan tried to interrupt. "I'm not saying he wasn't molested, and feels that turned him gay. But every man who's raped by another man doesn't fall into a homosexual lifestyle, and everyone who is gay has not been molested. Besides," Bryce continued, in a soft voice, "we're not talking about Donnie. We're talking about you. I was born to love you, Stanley."

The air fairly crackled as the two men eyed each other. Once again, Stan broke the stare. "I was delivered from that lifestyle many years ago," he answered. "Since then, I've loved only women."

Bryce clapped twice, smiled, and clapped twice more. "Very good, Stan, convincingly delivered. But you and I know that there is only one person who you will ever truly love, with your heart, soul, mind—and that's me."

Bryce's words hit a nerve, but Stan was determined to make Bryce understand that he was not the same man he was twenty-five years ago. "Bryce, you were the only man I was ever with . . . in that way. It was a long time ago, and I've been changed."

Bryce looked into Stan's eyes, saw a gaze that begged his

understanding. He didn't believe Stan for one minute, wasn't sure Stan believed it either. Bryce knew he would never give up on him and Stan being together. But he'd pushed enough . . . for now. "Well, I guess Eddie has changed, too, because there was once a time that brothah would have crossed the street to avoid a preacher. And now he's called for you."

Stan took a deep breath, glad the subject had changed. "I hate that it took this illness, but I'm glad that Eddie has seen the light and wants to get right with God, confess his sins, before it's too late, before he takes the final journey into eternity and meets Jesus."

"I hope that one day we all see the light and embrace our truth. And I also hope that when you get to the hospital, you'll bring prayer and compassion and leave that judgmental, sancti-monious bullshit you're spouting right here."

30

Somebody Else

Passion looked at her watch. Was the second hand moving at all? It seemed like forever, but only five minutes had passed from the last time she'd looked at it. She hated that she'd been in the shower when Stan had called, but he said he'd call back in half an hour. That was almost twenty minutes ago.

Passion thought about Stan's message and smiled. "Just wanted you to know that I got your message from yesterday. I owe you an apology too. Might be able to get a flight out early, so we can go to a belated Valentine's dinner. Will call back in thirty . . ."

Thank you, God. Thank you, thank you, thank you . . . Passion almost shuddered when she thought how close she'd come to making a very big mistake. She'd been just about to dial Stan's ex-wife, Carla Chapman, when she'd received a call from out of the blue: her assistant with a very distraught church member on the phone. Passion knew the call was important; her assistant would never have bothered her otherwise. It was indeed. On Valentine's Day of all days, the woman had just lost her mother to cancer and was furious with God. The woman's husband had just left her last year, and she'd suffered a miscarriage the year before that. She was understandably at the end of her rope. Her mother had been this sister's rock. Passion had ministered over the phone for thirty minutes before deciding that this was a job that needed personal attention. Helping this grieving Logos Word member took Passion's mind off of her own troubles and caused her to rethink things once she got home. Here she was, upset about a man-made holiday that was probably overrated, when she had her health, strength, and a mother who lived. She'd prayed, asked God's forgiveness for focusing on what she didn't have instead of being grateful about what she had, and left a long message on Stan's cell phone that ended with sincere Valentine's Day wishes. And now he'd called her back. She shook her head again, thinking how close she'd come to ruining it all. Stan would have been furious if Passion had involved his ex-wife in their private affairs. True, he and Carla were amicable for the children's sake, but Passion knew Carla's past behavior and subsequent success still rankled Stan. And he couldn't stand Carla's husband, Lavon. As far as Passion could tell from the few times the four had been in the same room, those feelings were mutual.

The telephone had barely stopped ringing when Passion picked it up. "Hey, Stan!"

"Hello, Passion," was Stan's weary answer.

Concern replaced excitement. "What's wrong?"

"I'm in Chicago, where I've been ministering to an old friend who was on his deathbed. He died a few minutes ago."

"Oh, no!" Passion thought of the Logos Word member's mother passing yesterday and about the saying of how death comes in threes. She relayed the news about the member, even as she offered condolences for Stan's friend. "Did your friend have cancer too?"

"No, he had . . . another terminal illness."

Passion's brow furrowed. Something about the way Stan answered the question set her wheels to turning, and she couldn't figure out why. But she was always pressuring him to talk to her, be with her, let her in. She didn't want to do that now. She wanted to show him the supportive, understanding wife who would be waiting with open arms when he got home. "I know the family needs you, Stan. Just know my prayers are joined with yours—for their strength and your safe return." Passion slowly placed the phone on the receiver and looked out the window on a clear, starless night. *Thank you, God, for my mother . . . and my husband. Keep me focused on what's truly important, Lord. Amen.*

Stan got off the phone, rubbed weary eyes, and walked back into Eddie's private room. They'd removed the body, but the room was still buzzing with the friends and family who'd gathered to be with him in the end, people who loved him in spite of how he died.

He walked over to Donna. "I just let my wife know that I'd be staying the night. Would you like me to come over to the house and pray with you?"

"Thanks, Stan, but no. I don't think I'm much up for prayer tonight. We've been praying so hard this whole time, and Eddie is still gone. Don't get me wrong. I'm not blaming the Lord. It's just that I'm tired and there is so much to do. Relatives are coming in, and logistics need to be worked out. But it would be a blessing if you could stay until Saturday and perform the service."

"What about his pastor?"

"Eddie wanted you. He didn't tell you?"

Stan shook his head. "I'll stop by tomorrow. We can discuss it then." In all honesty, Stan didn't know if he could preach his old friend's funeral. He didn't think some of those attending would want to hear about the wages of sin being death, when death was lying in a coffin. And he surely didn't think he could dilute the word of God. But right now his friends needed him. And he'd be there for them, in whatever ways he could.

Bryce walked up and put a hand on Stan's shoulder. "You all right?"

"No," Stan honestly responded.

"Please stay with me tonight," Bryce whispered. When

Stan started to protest, Bryce held up his hand and leaned in closer. "Not like that. I have two guest rooms. I just don't want to be alone tonight. Plus, Donna has asked me to help her plan the service. I could use your help in that regard."

Stan gave a slight nod, and then continued to offer support and prayer to those in the room who'd receive it. Finally, he made eye contact with a tall, attractive woman who'd been eyeing him all night, and walked over to her.

"I'm Stan Lee," he began, with hand outstretched.

"So I gather," the woman answered, her countenance guarded. Still, she reached out and shook his hand. "Sheila Covington."

Bryce's ex-wife. "You were good friends with Eddie?"

"More so with his wife, Donna. What about you? How did you two . . . know each other."

Stan's eyes narrowed. Then he dismissed her statement and blamed his reaction on paranoia. "Bryce didn't share this with you?"

"Besides a daughter, Bryce and I don't share much."

"We went to school together," Stan continued casually. "Many years ago."

"You don't say."

A little of Sheila Covington and her haughty attitude went a long way with Stan, and for the first time since learning of her, he not only empathized with Bryce, but also understood why it hadn't been hard to leave her. He looked at his watch and after a few parting pleasantries, bid her adieu. He walked over and hugged Donna, shook the hands of a few of the relatives gathered around her, and, after looking around the room again, walked out the door. Bryce had purposely left shortly after their whispered conversation. He'd meet him at the hotel, and then ride with him over to Bryce's house, where he would spend the night. He refused to vent the myriad of thoughts running around in his head and kept focused on one and one alone: *He who the son sets free, is free indeed.* Stan had been delivered from the wiles of Satan, and with God's help, he would withstand any snare the devil tried to set.

Sheila watched as Stan said his good-byes and then left. She'd noted that Bryce had left earlier, after the two had a whispered conversation in the corner. When it came to Bryce, even as an ex-husband, Sheila didn't miss much. She'd always been curious about Stan Lee, the ex-roommate turned mega-minister who Bryce spoke of so highly. What Bryce didn't know was that one day, when cleaning out some papers in a spare bedroom, she'd run across an old, yellowing letter that Bryce had written but never mailed. It was to Stan Lee and professed a little more love from one man to another than Sheila thought it should. Another time, in the heat of an argument, Bryce admitted to her that there was no way she or anybody else would ever have his heart, that somebody else already had it. Sheila believed she'd just shaken hands with that "somebody else" and wondered if Stan's wife knew that as much as Stan had her heart, he had somebody else's as well.

31

A Special Someone

Princess rushed into her dorm room, reaching into her back-pack as she did so. She'd been expecting to hear from Carla Chapman and hoped this was the call. They'd played telephone tag for a month now, but Carla had spoken to Tai, and through her, Princess knew that Carla had plans for her book beyond just being a guest on her show. Her mother had said Carla didn't go into details but did convey how much she'd enjoyed the manuscript Praise Publishing had sent to her.

"Hello!" Princess plopped down on the bed, not even bothering to check caller ID.

"Princess Brook, are you sitting down?"

"Adele?"

Adele Simms was the head publicist for Praise Publishing. Princess had only talked to her once but had heard great things about how hard she worked to get publicity for her authors. Besides, she had this deep, raspy voice that was easy to recognize.

"The one and only. I know that Serena will be contacting you shortly, but I wanted to call right away. Do you have an agent?"

"Uh-uh."

"Well, you're going to need to get one. Earlier today, I spoke with Lavon Chapman, executive producer for Carla's show."

"She's been trying to get a hold of me! The producers left three messages!"

"I didn't know you knew her. Girl, you can't be holding out with this type of valuable information. Do you know how many books you'll sell by being on her show?"

"Hopefully I'm getting ready to find out."

"I just hope you know how lucky you are, how most authors would kill to get the kind of publicity you're about to receive for your debut. Princess, what's getting ready to happen can set you up in the literary world for years to come. That's why you need an agent. Because if you work this right, it can turn into a variety of different opportunities: speaking engagements, guest appearances, maybe even your own talk show!"

Princess's head was spinning. She really hadn't thought much beyond writing the book and sharing her testimony. As for speaking engagements, she'd been ministering on and off campus for two years. That would be easy. But television? Her own show? Princess felt a combination of excitement and fear.

For the next twenty minutes, Princess sat stunned as Adele shared the plans that the producers of Carla's show had for her. The more Adele talked, the more Princess's exhilaration and trepidation grew. Shortly after ending the call with Adele, Princess got another call. It was her editor, the woman who'd held her hand and walked her through the writing process, step by painful step.

"Serena! I just got off the phone with Adele. I can't believe this!"

"Well, you'd better start believing it," Serena said in her soft, calm voice.

Princess smiled as she calmed down. She'd often joked that Serena had definitely been named correctly. The sky could be falling, and Serena's demeanor would remain serene, telling everyone as she so often did, "No matter how it looks or feels, God is in control."

"We've just finished a meeting to discuss these new developments concerning your book."

"New developments? Like what?"

"Like moving the pub date up from September to June. Put your roller skates on, young lady, because you're getting ready to have a very busy summer."

As soon as Princess hung up with Serena, she dialed her mother. "Mama, thank you!"

"Thank me for what?"

"For whatever you said to Miss Carla. Mama, I'm not only going to be a guest on her show, but they also want to try me out as a recurring cohost!"

"What?" *My daughter, on television?* Tai had talked to Carla but had simply said that she knew about the book and about her daughter's testimony, and that she was very supportive. After that, the topic had changed to their husbands, and plans to try and get the Brooks to join the Chapmans in Turks and Caicos the following Thanksgiving.

"You know how Doctor Phil and those other people used to be on *Oprah,* as a cohost? Well, Carla wants to have one day a week focused solely on young-adult issues, and for that show, they're wanting a cohost in that age range. And they're thinking about me!"

As Tai's surprise and delight wound down, motherhood kicked in. "What does this mean for your schooling, Princess? You still have a few months left, and this is your hardest year. Are you going to be able to handle school and this book stuff too?"

"Believe me, Mama. I'm not trying to come back here after this semester. I fully intend to graduate in June."

"Don't get me wrong. I think your working with Carla will be wonderful. I just want you to keep your eye on the prize."

"I will, Mama. Most of this stuff will be happening in the summer, after graduation."

Tai hesitated before changing the subject. She was very aware of how much Princess had matured in the years she'd been away at school. She also knew how close her daughter was to her grandmother.

"Mama, you still there?"

"Yes, honey. But I'll let you go, okay?" Tai hung up the phone without sharing the burden that was on her heart: Mama Max had moved back to Kansas and was filing for divorce.

Princess hung up the phone. She called Joni and got her voice mail, and she knew that Sarah was studying with Joel, who was part of the male ministry team. Princess thought about calling Rafael, but his girlfriend was giving him grief about his women friends. Princess knew what it was like to have your man receiving female callers, so even though theirs was a strictly platonic relationship, she'd decided to let Rafael call her if he wanted to talk. She scrolled through her phone book, checked her e-mails, and still was restless. She could always go out and witness; there was always a student or two who would help her do that. Fact of the matter was, however, Princess didn't feel like doing any of those things. She felt like celebrating, sharing her joy with somebody special, somebody in person. Most of the time, Princess could keep her focus on either study or God. But in this moment, although Jesus was her boo, Princess was desirous of a special someone in her life.

Princess lay back on the bed, closed her eyes, and whispered softly, "If it is Your will, God, please let me meet someone, a friend, a man who loves You as much as I do. Amen." A face flitted into Princess's consciousness as she lay there, meditating on God. But she quickly shook away the image. It didn't matter how much she had once loved Kelvin; he was the last man she needed to be with—now or ever.

32

Just Live Your Life

Life was good for Kelvin Petersen. He'd met a luscious Caribbean sistah at the mall the previous weekend. She was still at his house. Pursuing married Guy Harris had not only left Fawn little time to bother him but had also given him quality time alone with his son. But his real reason for celebration had to do with the phone call he'd just received. It was time to celebrate! Nothing major—there was a full day of practice tomorrow—but a little something to mark the occasion. He got into his car, plugged in his phone, and hit speed dial.

"My man," he said as soon as Jakeim answered.

"Playa, playa. How you livin'?"

"You ain't heard? I'm back in the starting lineup, dog!"

"Word?"

"Guy Harris is getting ready to warm the bench, son."

"Congratulations, bro."

"I'm heading to the club for a little low-key celebration. You down?"

"I'm there, dog. Hold my spot."

Kelvin smiled as he disconnected the call. Finally, all the pieces of life's puzzle were coming together for him, especially in the female department. He felt he deserved it, after what

went down with Princess and the drama he'd endured with
Fawn for the past three years. Stephanie was the type of sistah
he thought he could hang with for a minute. She was smart,
beautiful, confident, and had her own life and her own money.
Her father was a diplomat with the Bahamian government, and
her mother was a doctor. Baby girl had been raised in the lap of
luxury, so she wasn't chasing the dollar signs. For the first time
since dating Princess, he felt he was with a woman who was
about the love, not his paycheck. Life couldn't get much better.

Kelvin reached into his console and then, on second
thought, nixed the idea of lighting a blunt. He was content
jamming with the sounds of T.I. and Rhianna and was content
with how he planned to live his life from now on—drama free.
He joined in, singing at the top of his lungs, banging out the
beat on the steering wheel of his cherry-red Ferrari, smoothly
swerving in out of traffic on the I-10, cutting through Phoenix
on the way to the suburbs and the Myst club, less than fifteen
minutes from his house. Kelvin cranked up the music even
more and settled into the vibe of his good mood. He was less
than five minutes from the club, and when he saw the green
light at the intersection, he changed into the straight-ahead
lane and increased his speed. Out of the corner of his eye, he
saw something coming at him and only had time to utter one
word before the crash: "God!"

The car came out of nowhere, doing sixty in a forty-five-
mile-per-hour zone. The young driver of the other car had been
texting on his cell phone and hadn't seen the red light until it
was too late. He tried to swerve but still broadsided Kelvin on
the driver's side. Another car was clipped, spun around, and hit
Kelvin from behind, pushing his car another twenty feet. T.I.'s
and Rhianna's voices continued in the otherwise deadly silence,
encouraging all who listened to live their lives. The music played
on, but Kelvin could no longer hear it. . . .

33

We Need to Pray

Joni's hands were shaking so much she could barely dial Princess's number. Had she not been so frantic, she would have remembered that Princess was number three on her speed dial. But the news she'd heard had nearly rid her of the ability to think.

Princess had barely answered before Joni began talking. "Princess, have you heard what happened? Kelvin's been in a bad car wreck. It doesn't look good, Princess. We need to pray."

Princess grabbed her throat, trying to dislodge her heart from there. Instant panic set in at Joni's words. She jumped off the bed, where she'd been studying, and began to pace the floor. When she could finally breathe again and found her voice, Princess's question was simple: "What happened?"

Joni filled her in with what she'd heard on the news: After the accident, Kelvin had been airlifted to Maryvale Hospital and was in a coma. "Brandon's flying out tonight," Joni finished. "And I'm going to fly down tomorrow. I know there's been a lot of bad blood between you and Kel, but at one time we were all best buds, and he's still one of my husband's best friends. I know it's a lot to ask, Princess, but—"

"Book me on the same flight you're taking," Princess interrupted. "I'll call my prayer circle and—wait, Mama's on the other line. Let me call you back." Princess clicked her call-waiting button. "Mama, I just heard . . ."

"Oh, Lord, I was hoping to reach you before you heard it on television."

"I just got off the phone with Joni. That's how I found out. How's Uncle Derrick doing?"

Tai paused as she thought about the conversation she'd just had with her best friend, Vivian Montgomery. Vivian was concerned about her husband, Kelvin's biological father. Even though Kelvin was sixteen when Derrick found out he existed, they'd created a strong father/son bond since then. He'd taken the news hard and had canceled a trip to South Africa to fly to his son's side. Tai relayed this information to Princess and could hear her daughter sniffling in the background. "What about you, baby? I know you still have feelings for Kelvin. One always does, for their first love."

"I'm flying to Phoenix tomorrow, Mama. Me and Joni."

"Are you sure that's wise, Princess? We're all concerned for Kelvin's well-being. In fact, your father and I will be there in a few days to pray for Kelvin and to be there for Viv and Derrick. Maybe you should wait until then to come visit." Tai didn't know what would be worse for Princess—if Kelvin lived and they rekindled their tragic romance, or if he died, leaving Princess with a lifetime of what-ifs.

"I already told Joni to book my ticket. I know Brandon needs her and she needs me. I'm going to be there for her . . . and for Kelvin."

Tai couldn't argue with her daughter. That rationale was exactly why she was dropping everything to be by her best friend's side. "Well, keep me posted, baby. I'll also e-mail you our travel plans as soon as they're confirmed."

They talked a little bit more, and then Princess's phone started blowing up with one call after another—all fellow students or friends who knew of her and Kelvin's shared past. She talked to a couple and then put her phone on vibrate so she could process the roiling emotions that were running through her. A part of her despised Kelvin and the things that had happened while being with him. But her mother was right: Another part of her still loved him. She was about to get on her knees to pray in earnest when her phone vibrated. It was Rafael.

"Yeah, I know about it," Princess sighed into the phone. The tears that had threatened to erupt since Joni's call now ran down her face. The familiarity and comfort she found in hearing from this old friend finally gave her the space to cry out loud. "I'm scared, Rafael."

"Don't cry, baby girl. It's gonna be all right. It's messed up, though. I can't lie about that. I don't know why these fools keep trying to text and drive at the same time. If they're making it a law not to *talk* on your phone while driving, how does one then think they can *type* while behind the wheel?"

"I don't know," Princess whispered.

"Princess, do I need to worry about you? Now, don't get me wrong—I feel bad for dude and all—but it took you a long time to get over what happened between y'all. I don't want to see you get hurt again."

"Kelvin's in a coma, Rafael," Princess said harshly. "I don't think he's in a position to hurt anybody."

"I know what I'm saying might sound cold, but you're my best friend. So I have to be one hundred with you and say what's on my mind. Don't let your sympathy turn into something else. That's all I'm saying."

"I'm doing my duty as a child of God," Princess countered. "This isn't about any personal feelings I have for Kelvin. It's about being there for my friends and praying for someone in need."

"Okay, you remember that," Rafael replied, not backing down one bit from his position. "And remember, too, that I'm the brother whose shoulder you cried on when that fool pushed you to the curb for baby mama. Be careful, Princess."

"Look, Rafael, I gotta go." Princess hung up the phone, cried, prayed, and remembered the good times—when Kelvin was her prince.

"I'm worried about Princess," Tai said, having called Mama Max as soon as she'd hung up with her daughter.

"I thought something about that youngster was familiar," Mama Max replied. "It stopped me in my tracks, hearing his name on the news. I was making dinner, and it stopped me right where I was. I'll sure pray for that young man, sure will."

"Pray for Princess too," Tai said. "We all need to be strong during this very difficult time." Tai felt her words ironic, considering the hard time her mother-in-law was facing. "What about you, Mama Max? How are you doing?"

"As well as can be expected," Mama Max said conversationally, as if she were discussing the weather. "For a woman whose husband is a plastic-pussy-poking preacher."

34

His Eye Is on the Sparrow

Tai paced her floor again, much like she had when talking to Princess. "Mama, I'm really concerned about you. You didn't come to church last Sunday, and you haven't been to work out with me all week. You might as well admit it—you miss the reverend. It isn't a sin to miss the man, you know," she continued quietly. "Y'all have been together for more than fifty years."

"Don't matter, we ain't together now. And it looks like things might stay this way. I need to think about putting this house up for sale, think about getting something smaller, a condo perhaps."

"He hasn't called at all?"

"He's called a few times, but I've ignored them."

"Why?"

"Because he still hasn't gotten rid of that disgusting doll. Talking 'bout he can't find a way to get rid of it. I told him to take it out of the house the same way he brought it in there. Besides, according to him, it ain't sinning since she ain't real. I told him, 'Trust me, if you have to hide it behind a fake wall, you can pretty much bet it's sin.' The nasty scoundrel. Look, child, I need to check on my rump roast. Let me call you back."

Mama Max's face was fixed into a frown as she basted the

rump roast with the succulent juice at the bottom of the pan. Eight hundred miles away and almost three weeks later, and she was still very angry at Obadiah Brook. It had taken her exactly forty-eight hours to pack up some clothes and her favorite cooking utensils and fly back to Kansas, forty-eight hours after finding the doll, confronting Obadiah, and demanding that he get that filth out of her house immediately.

Mama Max didn't have to put him out of the bedroom that night. They'd been sleeping in separate rooms for almost fifteen years. It started when they moved into their latest, three-bedroom home. Mama Max had set up a "sanctuary," a place where she could do her crocheting, knitting, and sewing. But very quickly, the bed she'd bought for guests became the one she slept in each night. After falling asleep there after a late-night prayer session, she realized she appreciated a sound sleep uninterrupted by Obadiah's loud farts and even louder snores. She didn't have to worry about him pawing on her or waking up to find something hard and long poking her in the back.

The decision to stop having sex was never discussed. Obadiah kept asking, and Mama Max simply kept having a headache, or a backache, or a don't-feel-like-it ache. Once he stopped asking, Mama Max was so thankful for the silence that she never questioned why. The thought of him cheating came up from time to time, but as they both grew older, and with no evidence to suggest the validity of such a thought, those worries faded. Mama Max thought Obadiah had finally reached the place she'd been for years, done with intimate encounters. Their lives had settled into a peaceful pattern. During the day, Obadiah spent a considerable amount of time in his study, while a majority of her time was spent in either the den watching television or the kitchen. Several times a week, Obadiah met with a group of seniors who played golf at a nearby course, and occasionally he'd grab a fishing pole and go in search of catfish, black bass, bluegill, or perch. They'd eat most of their meals together: breakfast between five-thirty and six-thirty, lunch around noon, and dinner at seven. Afterward, they'd usually watch a television show together, normally one from the sixties or seventies on TV Land or a religious channel, and they'd discuss various goings-on of the day and within the family. After that, Obadiah would retire to his study or bedroom, and Mama Max would fall asleep watching television, before finally going to bed around nine-thirty. She'd thought theirs was a simple life, but a good life. Now she didn't know what to think.

Mama Max had just put on a pot of coffee when the phone rang. Without even realizing it, she wished it was Obadiah telling her that he'd thrown the trash out and purchased her a ticket back to Texas. She was half right: the caller was in Texas.

"Hey, Nettie."

"Mama Max, how you doing?"

"Tolerable, can't complain."

Nettie had been worried about Mama Max since before she'd left Texas, and while Mama Max tried to keep up a strong front, Nettie heard the strain in her voice. And she'd dreamed about her too. "I saw Reverend Doctor last week. Took a casserole over to your house, a pan of corn bread and an apple cobbler. He seemed real appreciative, Mama Max. He's lost without you around."

"Might be lost, but he ain't lonely. Was the girl still there?"

"Even if she was, I don't think he'd have her in either the living room or the kitchen, and that's as far as I made it into the house. But I can tell he misses you, Mama Max. It seemed like he wanted to talk, but he just wouldn't open up, beyond church matters."

"Who wants to open up about the type of stuff he's doing?"

Nettie paused, looked out her window, and watched two sparrows fly in and out of the two large oak trees that framed her window. The birds chattered as they danced along the leaf-less branches, seemingly content to simply enjoy the beauty of the day. If only man could be more like the animals in God's creation: taking no thought for the morrow, knowing that each day was sufficient unto itself. Mama Max was already making plans for something that hadn't happened—a divorce.

"His eye is on the sparrow," Nettie found herself saying out loud. "And I know God is watching over you and this situation, Mama Max. I don't need to tell you that tongues are wagging. People are naturally wondering where you are, especially since you've been at the church practically every time the door opened since y'all got here. The reverend doctor hasn't said anything from the pulpit, and I don't think it's my place to say anything either. But people know we're friends . . . and they're asking."

"Lord have mercy." Mama Max sighed. "This whole thing is a hot mess. But I'm not ready to come back, not until the reverend changes his ways."

"There's one more thing you should know," Nettie continued after a slight hesitation. "Dorothea has been over to your house—at least twice."

35

It's Her Fault

Obadiah looked at the frozen dinner in disgust. He'd never eaten such a meal in his life, but even at the age of seventy-two, he was discovering that there was a first time for everything. It wasn't like he couldn't have eaten a home-cooked meal. Nettie had called earlier and asked if he needed anything, and one of the church mothers had invited him over for dinner. But he didn't feel like talking to anybody who knew Maxine, didn't feel like fielding questions or coming up with explanations regarding her abrupt departure and continued absence from Gospel Truth. He'd passed several fast-food places on the way to the store, but for Reverend Doctor Pastor Bishop Mister Obadiah Meshach Brook, Jr., such an establishment was out of the question. He could count the times on both hands that a Big Mac, a Jack or anybody else in a box, or a slice of pizza from a hut had passed his lips. He'd always felt sorry for folks who thought that such fare was good eating. The only reason they did, he knew, was because they'd never had Maxine fix them a burger. He thought that the colonel did all right with a piece of chicken, but even that bird, made with "twelve secret ingredients," was only good in case of emergency. So for the first time in five years at least, the reverend doctor had gone into a store and walked up and down its aisles in search of food. The experience had promptly given him a headache, which is why he'd gone to the frozen-food section, picked up a "gourmet" meal of Salisbury steak, gravy, mashed potatoes, and green beans, and was now standing in a kitchen he also rarely visited, using a stove he'd rarely used, to cook his dinner.

"Let me see," he said, putting on his glasses to read the box. "Preheat the oven to three hundred fifty degrees." Obadiah peered down at the knob in the center of their industry-sized steel range. "I guess this is it." He bent down farther so he could better see the numbers. "Yes! This is it. Here's three fifty, right here!" Obadiah smiled as if he'd discovered a cure to cancer. He turned the knob until the desired number was lined up exactly with the line on the stove.

After reading the rest of the instructions and having frowned severely at the suggestion that he could microwave the meal, Obadiah pulled the platter out of the box. He pulled back the plastic covering the food and frowned again. "This looks just about good enough to feed a dog," Obadiah mumbled to himself. " 'Course, Maxine would probably think that just about appropriate." He shook his head and looked at his watch to see if the required ten minutes were up, the time the box suggested the oven heat before placing the food contents into it. He had another five minutes to wait and decided to check the refrigerator for the umpteenth time to see if he could find a Maxine-cooked-it leftover. There were none, so instead he settled for a handful of cookies and a glass of milk. It seemed that since Maxine had been gone, he was hungrier than he'd ever been. And it wasn't just Maxine Brook's cooking he missed. He missed Maxine.

A few minutes later, Obadiah placed the tray in the heated oven. He sat down at the kitchen table to wait for his dinner, rubbed a weary hand over his equally tired eyes, and tried to figure out how he'd gotten to this place. He recalled the evening two weeks ago, when he'd come home to find his companion sprawled on the living room floor, surrounded by his porn collection. He'd been taken aback, to say the least, and more than a bit embarrassed. Yes, he'd acted indignant, accused Maxine of wrongdoing for going into his private domain, but Obadiah couldn't blame his wife for how she'd reacted. Discovering a dildo in Maxine's underwear drawer would probably elicit an equally appalled response.

But what does she think I'm supposed to do, shrivel up and die just because she don't want loving anymore? Obadiah munched down hard on the chocolate-chip cookie, anger quickly replacing guilt. *I'm her husband, and she ain't been with me in almost twenty years! I'm the fool here, because I should have been demanding my rights this entire time! Reducing me to using a doll—this is all her fault!* "This is your fault, Maxine! At least it was a doll and not another woman!" Obadiah's voice boomed off the soft yellow-colored kitchen walls. "All the women throwing themselves at me and I've remained faithful! *Except for Dorothea.* Having that thing there was the only way I could."

The one-sided conversation sounded good to Obadiah, so much so that he decided to try Maxine's number again. Here she was acting all sanctimonious, all high and mighty, and she had a hand to play in what had gone on in their house as well. She had abandoned her wifely duties, been disobedient to her husband; in short, she'd abdicated her wedding vows. Obadiah felt a new resolve to get in touch with his wife, to fly to Kansas if he had to. It was time to talk some sense into that woman and bring her home!

He was just about to pick up the phone in the kitchen when two bells rang at once: the food timer that he'd set for the frozen dinner, and the doorbell. He decided to get the doorbell first.

"Dorothea, I thought I told you not to come here no more," he said, once he'd looked through the peephole and opened the door.

Dorothea was nonplussed as she ignored Obadiah's comment. "Is that any way to greet the woman who's brought you dinner?"

Obadiah hadn't even noticed the tote bag at Dorothea's side. "I'm making my own dinner," he sighed. "But come on in." Instead of waiting for her, he simply left the door open and walked back into the kitchen.

"Smells kinda good," Dorothea said, looking around. Her eyes widened as she eyed the frozen dinner box sitting on top of the trash. "Obadiah Brook! Don't tell me that's what I smell in the oven." But he didn't have to; she saw it for her own eyes as he pulled the sorry-looking contents from the oven. "Lord, have mercy," she continued, placing her tote on the table and pulling out its contents. She sat down a salad, a loaf of garlic bread, and a container of spaghetti on the table. "You know I don't cook much, but I'll place my spaghetti up against any-body's—and especially up against that pitiful-looking steak."

Obadiah retrieved a fork from the drawer and poked the meat suspiciously. He shrugged his shoulders, went back to the drawer for a steak knife, and cut a small piece from the end of the meat. His bite was tentative. "Jesus!" he exclaimed after he'd chewed and swallowed. "People actually eat this stuff?" He looked at the meal that had cost him five dollars and almost threw the entire contents away right then. But he'd come up during the Depression and always cleaned his plate. So with a sense of loathing, and in the span of about five minutes, he forced down the white paste they called potatoes and the piece of shoe leather that passed for steak. But when it came to the string beans and the lump of peaches and flour that they dared call a pie, he'd reached his limit, and for the first time in well over sixty years, threw food in the trash. "Okay, let's see what you've got here so I can get that nasty taste out my mouth!"

Dorothea, who'd heated up the spaghetti while Obadiah scarfed down his food, looked at him with a mixture of com-passion and desire. "You always had quite an appetite." She made herself at home in Maxine's kitchen, looking from cabinet to cabinet until she found the dishes. She fixed both herself and Obadiah's plates and joined him at the table.

"Where's Jenkins?"

"Home, asleep."

"It's barely seven o'clock, woman!"

Dorothea sighed. "Believe me, I'm well aware of what time it is, on many levels."

"He still ain't satisfied you, huh?"

"He can't, poor thing. A wet noodle is stiffer than his little dick. He tries to make up for it with material things, and while I'm extremely appreciative, I need more."

"You can't keep coming over here, Dorothea. I told you that the last time you showed up at my door unannounced. Neighbors around here are nosy, and somebody from the church could stop by. I don't want folks talking more than they already are."

"What's wrong with a sister-in-the-Lord bringing you by a plate of food? Didn't Jesus admonish us to feed the hungry?" Dorothea rested her hand on Obadiah's thigh. "And I *know* you're hungry."

Obadiah moved Dorothea's hand off his thigh. "Stop that now. Ain't nothing going to go on here in Maxine's house."

"Fine, I understand." Dorothea thought while she chewed a forkful of food. "I think I saw a Quality or a Hampton Inn when I went shopping the other day. I know there's a Holiday Inn not far from here, but maybe we should go for something less conspicuous, a motel on the other side of town that would have little or no chance of being frequented by anybody either of us know."

"You know how small this town is, Dorothea. Ain't no place safe here. There's liable somebody watching every move you make. Which is why . . ."

"Why, what? Why we can't be together?"

"That, too, but it's why . . ." Obadiah looked at Dorothea for a long moment, a plan forming in his head behind the thought he'd just had. "I need your help with something, Dorothea."

"Anything, just ask me."

"Let's finish eating first. Then I need to show you something."

Thirty minutes later, Dorothea followed Obadiah to his study. Short of a sermon outline, she couldn't think of anything in his office that he'd want to share with her. When he walked to what looked like a library wall, pushed against the end, and walked into a smaller, secret room, Dorothea followed. And then stopped short. Obadiah's companion stared at her with sightless eyes, its large breasts displayed prominently, like two ripe melons, the lower part of her body covered with one of Maxine's knitted throws.

Dorothea recovered quickly. "Oh, my precious Obadiah," she said, walking over and putting her arms around Obadiah, who stood rigid before her. "Your marriage has come to this? Oh, baby, we can't have you resorting to this madness. Let me help you, right now." She stepped back, put her hands behind her back, and started to undo her skirt.

"No," Obadiah said, staying her hands with one of his large, powerful ones. "That's not what I meant when I asked you for help. This"—Obadiah pointed to the rubber doll—"is the reason Maxine went back to Kansas. She won't come back until it's out of the house, but I'm scared to take it any place for fear of somebody seeing me or, worse, taking a picture of me trying to get rid of it." The scandal of Gospel Truth's last pastor was never far from Obadiah's mind, and the last thing he wanted to do was bring more shame to his church. "But people aren't watching me like they're watching you. Do you think you can help me get rid of it?"

Dorothea looked from the doll to Obadiah and back again. "I'll help you, Obadiah. But what do I get out of the deal?"

Thirty minutes later, the deed was done. Dorothea was gone, and so was the monstrosity that had sent his wife fleeing for the land of Oz. For some reason, moving the sixty-pound doll had been more taxing than usual for Obadiah, possibly because other than her arrival, shortly after arriving in Texas, he'd never moved her more than a couple feet. By the time he'd helped get the doll in Dorothea's car and his accomplice had left, a sheen of sweat covered Obadiah's face and arms. He watched until Dorothea's taillights turned the corner. Then he hit the button to lower the garage door, walked back into the house, and straight to the phone.

As had been the case the last few times he'd tried his wife's number, he got voice mail. But it didn't matter. He had news, and Obadiah was sure this news would make the difference. Slightly irritated, he hit the pound key to bypass Maxine's recorded message. As soon as he heard the beep, he spoke into the phone. "Maxine, everything is outta here, and God is not pleased with how you're acting. You need to come home. Now."

36

Sleep Don't Come Easy

Passion was tired. She'd been counseling church members all day long, and the conversations hadn't been easy ones. One member was a single mother dealing with unruly children, one of whom she suspected of being in a gang. The second counseling session had involved a woman battling guilt. She'd had to move her mother into a home last year, because of her mother's increased dementia. Now it looked as though she might have to quit a job she loved to take care of her full-time. The member was torn between wanting the best for her mother and wanting the freedom to continue living her own life. There were a few less serious but no less harrowing counseling sessions before she began the final session of the day, the member who was now in her office. This member, about the same age as Passion, was considering divorce from her husband. She believed he was a sex maniac, outside of the will of God, because he wanted to make love every night, sometimes more than once in a night. Passion only wished she had this woman's "problem." After realizing Passion wasn't going to condone the woman getting a divorce on these grounds, the woman huffed out of the office. Passion was glad to see her go.

"Lady Lee, you have a call," her assistant said over the phone, just seconds after Passion sat back down at her desk.

"Take a message."

"I tried, but the woman said it was important."

Passion hesitated, not sure if she could speak to one more woman today about her problems. "Who is it?"

"Her name is Sheila Covington."

"I don't know her. Take a message."

"Ma'am, I'll have to take a message, or I can put you through to our first lady's voice mail. She is not available."

Ten minutes later, Passion walked out of her office. "Did the woman leave a message?" she asked her assistant, who responded that she had. As soon as Passion got into her car and put on her headset, she dialed the church's voice mail system and punched in her code. There was only one new message. "My name is Sheila Covington. You don't know me, but you may know my ex-husband, Bryce Covington. He's a very close friend of your husband's, and if you want him to remain your husband, you might want to keep him away from my ex. There's no use leaving my number. If you don't understand this message, you probably won't call back, anyway, and if you do understand what I'm saying, then . . . you've been warned."

When Passion turned into her driveway, she was still trying to figure out the cryptic message that Sheila had left on her voice mail. Now she wished she'd taken the call. As the first lady of a prominent ministry, Passion often received calls from women she didn't know, as well as from various ministries, charities, and social organizations. But in the three-plus years she'd taken calls at the office, she'd never had one like this. Why had Sheila Covington, Bryce's ex-wife, called to warn her about his and Stan's friendship?

Passion's thoughts continued as she went inside her home, changed clothes, and went to the kitchen. She took chicken from the refrigerator and rice from the pantry to begin dinner. Stan had rarely mentioned Bryce, who lived thousands of miles away from them anyway. Aside from their college days, there seemed to be little in common that he and Stan shared.

Bryce hadn't mentioned being in ministry, or even attending church for that matter. And while she'd enjoyed his loquacious conversation and model good looks, Passion couldn't see Bryce fitting into the Lee lifestyle on a regular basis. His and Stan's getting together had been a meeting for old time's sake, nothing more. How could that be dangerous for her marriage? Was Bryce involved in something illegal? She knew Bryce was in politics. Was there a scandal brewing on the horizon?

Conversation was light as Stan, who'd returned from Chicago several days prior, Passion, and Onyx ate a dinner that was commandeered largely by Onyx's recap of her school day. After putting her daughter to bed, Passion tidied up the kitchen and put the leftover food in the refrigerator. It had been hours, and Sheila Covington's out-of-the-blue phone call and enigmatic message made no more sense now than when she'd received it this afternoon. She had to find out what was going on, but how? The one time Bryce Covington had come up in conversation, after he'd called the house before the sun rose, an argument had ensued. *I'll just play it by ear. And in the meantime, I'll do a search on Bryce Covington tomorrow, see what the Internet can tell me about him . . . and this Sheila chick too.*

"Dinner was good tonight, Passion." Stan had finished his ablutions in the master-suite bathroom and now sat on the silk-covered bench at the end of their sleigh bed, taking off his socks. He had on his standard sleeping fare: an extra-large white T-shirt and equally large white boxers with thin black pinstripes. "Maybe we can have the associates and their wives over soon to enjoy your good cooking."

Passion warmed at the praise as she took off her robe, draped it across the foot of the bed, and climbed up on their king-sized mattress. She knew that Stan's ex-wife, Carla, was known for her culinary skills, especially when it came to Southern cooking. Passion had eaten at Carla's table and knew the hype was true. Carla was an excellent cook. So hearing

Stan's compliment was not only music to her ears, but it also gave her a way to bring Bryce into the discussion.

"You know I love entertaining, Stan. So just tell me when and how many, and I'll try my best to whip up something tasty. Speaking of dinner guests, how is your friend Bryce doing?"

Stan was walking to the clothes hamper and stopped at Passion's question. "Bryce? Why would you ask about him?"

Passion tried to keep her face passive, her voice casual. She shrugged. "Nothing in particular. It's just that he and his friend were two of the last guests we had over who weren't church members, and I know that he also knew your friend in Chicago. Even though you haven't discussed it, I could tell your friend's death bothered you. You were quiet for a few days after returning from that trip."

Stan relaxed. It made perfect sense for Passion to ask about Bryce, precisely for the reasons she mentioned. Besides, Stan knew better than anybody what an unforgettable impression Bryce made on any and everyone with whom he came into contact. Passion was also correct about how quiet he'd been after returning from his time in Chicago with Eddie and his family before he died. The conversation regarding homosexuality that he'd had with Bryce had upset him more than he realized. He'd spoken with him only once since that trip, and that was strictly to discuss matters involving the Cathedral. Stan relayed this information to Passion.

"I've decided to resign my position on the Cathedral's board," Stan said. "I'm spreading myself too thin professionally, and it's leaving me almost no time for my family." Stan crawled under the covers, lay on his back, and pulled the cover up to his chin. "I know I've been distant," he continued, looking at the ceiling. "And I know I haven't been as . . . intimate as you'd like. I'm going to try and do better, Passion. Please know that my lack of physical interest has nothing to do with you. I came up in a family where physical affection was discouraged, on all levels. My family was not demonstrative—no hugs, no kisses, even loud laughter was rare. We were extremely conservative, and, well, that's just one of the reasons why I struggle with that part of our relationship. But I want you to know that I'm aware of the situation. And I'm going to do better."

Passion lay on her side of the bed, shocked. Stan had just opened up more in the past three minutes than he had in three years. It's all she'd ever wanted, to be able to talk to her husband about their relationship, especially about what things weren't working and why they weren't working. Stan had always squashed such discussion before it even got started. Maybe, just maybe, they were turning a corner in their relationship, and Passion could have the healthy marriage she'd always wanted.

Passion wanted to roll over and kiss her husband. She wanted to put her arms around him, snuggle her head to his chest, and fall asleep in his arms. But she knew this was a delicate moment, where one wrong move could change the mood and make Stan regret what he'd revealed. So she stayed on her side of the bed, and instead of hugging her husband, hugged her full-length body pillow, turned off the light on her nightstand, and whispered into the darkness, "Thanks for sharing with me, Stanley. I love you so much and want to be the supportive, understanding wife that you need. Knowing more about the experiences that shaped who you are helps me do that. Whenever you want to talk about . . . anything, I'm here—childhood, past hurts, rejections, whatever. I've got my share too. It will only help us get closer, Stan. Stan?"

Passion became quiet and realized from his deep, even breathing that Stan had fallen asleep. Sleep always came easy for her husband, while slumber often eluded her until dawn. Passion hoped that tonight would not be one of those nights. But as she turned on her side and snuggled under the comforter, she remembered Sheila Covington's cryptic words: *If you do understand what I'm saying, then . . . you've been warned.* This would be another night where sleep would not come easy for Passion.

37

Boyfriend and Best Friend

"Princess, it's me."

"Rafael?" Princess whispered into her cell phone even as she squinted at the clock. It was one in the morning, Pacific Standard Time, which meant that in Kansas it was three a.m. Immediately alarmed, she sat straight up in bed. "What's the matter? Why are you calling so late?"

"Me and Lauren just broke up."

"Ooh, boy, you just scared the mess out of me. I thought someone had died." Princess's heart was pounding in her chest. She placed a hand over it and tried to calm down. She'd been on edge ever since getting the phone call about Kelvin's near-death accident three weeks ago. As her heart quieted, she got out of bed and went into the bathroom so she wouldn't wake Sarah, her new dorm mate. "So what, y'all just had a big fight or something?"

"You can say that. She came over earlier, accusing me of something I didn't even do."

"What's her name?" Princess asked wearily.

"Who?"

"The woman Lauren thinks you're cheating on her with."

"How'd you know that that is what it was?"

"Because, Rafael, that's always what it is."

Rafael sighed into the phone. "Aw, this other girl don't mean nothing to me. We just get along well because we work together and both love politics. She has a boyfriend, and I told Lauren that. But she wants to play the paranoid female role, and that isn't going to work with me. She was even jealous of you, and you're almost two thousand miles away!"

Princess knew this was true. She also knew that while nothing could drive a man away faster than a jealous woman, nothing could be more reliable than a woman's intuition when it came to her man's fidelity. "Were you cheating on her, Rafael? And remember, you're not talking to Lauren—you're talking to Princess."

"I know who I'm talking to." Rafael's voice took on a sultry, flirty quality. "I'm talking to my girl, from back in the day!"

"Shut up, boy. I was never your girl."

"Oh, so junior and senior year in high school was just, what, my fantasy?"

"No, that was real." Princess became quiet. It had been a long time since she'd thought back to those fun, carefree days when she and Rafael were joined at the hip. When they'd finished with their extracurricular activities—sports and the debate team for Rafael, drill team and the school newspaper for Princess—the two would spend the rest of their free time together. Sometimes they'd drive to the Plaza or head to Gates Barbeque for short ends and chicken plates to go, and then drive to either Swope Park or Loose Park, where they'd eat and share dreams. On the weekends, friends would join them as they went roller-skating or to the movies. Sometimes Rafael and Princess would just hole up in either of their bedrooms and listen to their R&B/hip-hop favorites: Snoop Dogg, Kanye West, Destiny's Child, and Fantasia. And while Princess left the relationship the same way she came in—a virgin—she not only counted Rafael as her boyfriend, but as her best friend as well.

"I didn't cheat on Lauren," Rafael said firmly, mistaking

the reason for Princess's silence. "That's what made me so mad. She's accused me of cheating ever since we got together. And I was totally faithful to her. That kind of nagging makes a brothah want to go out and do what he's being accused of doing anyway."

"Why do you think she didn't believe you?"

"Probably because it's her butt that's foul. I heard that she was rockin' it with this dude in Kansas City. Some thug life situation. I heard that about a month ago and didn't even sweat her on it because I trusted her.

"But tonight? Me and my boys was sitting here chillin', and she comes in all gangster and stuff, demanding to know where I was earlier and going into my bedroom like she paid rent, looking for somebody who I guess she'd been told was in here. It was downright embarrassing, Princess. I'm not trying to live with the female drama situation. I've got plans and I'm going places. I need a woman who's going to be with me, not fight against me."

Again, the conversation lulled as both Princess and Rafael ruminated in their thoughts. Rafael had never stopped loving Princess and had been more crazy about her than he'd let on when they dated. Princess had always viewed Rafael more as a brother than a boyfriend, but she had always believed he was a good guy. She still did. She just didn't have the depth of feeling for him that she felt one should for their man, like the way she'd felt about Kelvin, almost from the beginning.

"So how's your boy?" Rafael asked, as if reading her mind.

"Who?"

"Please, girl, don't even try it."

"Okay, I guess. He's recuperating at his father's. They've hired a full-time nurse and a slew of specialists and therapists to try and help him, you know, get back to normal."

"I never cared much for old boy, especially after how he treated you, but it's a hard thing that happened to him."

Princess agreed. It had been a hard thing that happened to

Kelvin: in a coma for almost a week, a broken left arm, broken left leg, bruised spine, and a plethora of cuts and gashes. Princess, Joni, and Brandon had flown into Phoenix the day after his accident, but after an afternoon of prayer and one-sided conversations by his side, Princess had taken a red-eye back to Los Angeles. Aside from the fact that she felt she'd done all she could, old feelings she thought dead and buried started to resurface, and after a stunning woman with an island accent arrived on the scene, Princess knew those feelings must stay buried. So she'd fled the scene and reimmersed herself in ministry.

"Yeah, it's hard," Princess said with a yawn.

"Look, it's late. I probably should let you go."

"Yeah, I've got a class at nine."

"So, Princess, when are you coming home?"

"To Kansas?"

"Yeah."

"I don't know, sometime after graduation, I guess."

"You're moving back here?"

"I don't know, Rafael. Why?"

"Just asking."

"Well, get out my business and get some sleep."

"Princess . . ."

"What?"

"Thanks."

"You're welcome."

"Princess."

"What, boy?"

Rafael paused. "I love you."

38

What's Up?

Kelvin strained against the weight of the pulley above his bed. His therapist had told him to take it easy when it came to maintaining strength in his upper body and right side, but Kelvin's mind was focused on one thing only: next year's season with the Phoenix Suns. He did a couple more repetitions and then fell back against the bed. The weights made a loud clanging noise as they fell to the bottom of the device. Kelvin wiped sweat from his brow with a fluffy white towel. He clenched his left fist and frowned at the cast that covered almost his entire left arm. His left leg was encased from his thigh to below his knee. Kelvin "the KP" Petersen looked a far cry from the ferocious ball-stealing, play-making, point-scoring guard for which he was known. Now he looked like what he was: a beat-up, scruffy twentysomething, carrying the weight of the world.

Kelvin reached for a pair of massage balls and twirled them slowly as he contemplated his life. He couldn't believe he was where he was: flat on his back instead of practicing for the game tonight. The Nuggets were huge rivals on any given day, but with him injured, the teams were swirling like vultures, each team counting the Suns out, trying to lock up the western conference early. It rankled more than a little that his point-guard replacement, Guy Harris, was doing very well and had scored double digits in the last several games. Kelvin deduced that Fawn thought she was doing well, too—Kelvin had seen her sitting in the section reserved for girlfriends. It didn't surprise him that Fawn was dating a married man. Wherever there was bling, she'd hang around. And while he felt sorry for Guy's wife and newborn baby, he was also grateful. The nanny had dropped off Little Kelvin for his last visits, and he hadn't talked to Fawn in over a month.

Which brought his thoughts to Stephanie, the Caribbean queen who'd made him smile again. As if on cue, his phone rang. It was her on the line.

"I was just thinking about you, baby."

"You only think about me now, or you haven't stopped thinking about me?"

Kelvin laughed. "I'm always thinking about you." He loved Stephanie's sense of humor, and the sexy lilt of her voice, the way she clipped certain words and left out others altogether. He wasn't in love with her, but he was definitely "in like." And while he enjoyed staying in the lavish Montgomery abode, especially since they'd practically redecorated a wing to accommodate his hospital bed and training machines, he couldn't wait to get back to Phoenix and to Stephanie. "So, what's up? Are you coming to see me this weekend? I can put you up at the Beverly Hills Hotel. It's not far from the house. You'll get to meet the one and only reverend extraordinaire, Derrick Montgomery, and his lovely wife, Vivian. And I'm telling you now, my little brother, D2, is going to fall in love with your fine ass so—"

"Kelvin!"

"What, ma?"

Stephanie hesitated. "I'm not coming to Los Angeles."

"I understand, baby. After all, it was short notice. But no worries, the ticket is fully changeable, and we can change the dates on your room as well."

"That's not what I mean, Kelvin!" Stephanie's voice was more clipped than usual, each word enunciated fully. She paused a moment and then said the words she dreaded saying. "I'm going home."

"To the Bahamas?"

"Yes."

"Okay, baby, but chill out. How long are you going to be gone for?"

"That's just it, Kelvin." Stephanie was crying now. "I'm moving back home, to stay. It's all happened so suddenly, but there is some kind of major controversy going on in the government, a scandal that involves my father. He's totally innocent, understand, but it's putting a horrible strain on my mom and our businesses, and, well, we had a family conference call last night, and it was decided that we would . . . circle the wagons, as you Americans say. My brother is coming back from Paris, my sister from Geneva, and I'm flying home tomorrow. It's a one-way ticket, Kelvin. I'm so sorry."

Kelvin was a bundle of emotions. The one bright cloud on his horizon had been the burgeoning relationship he saw happening with this woman. Being with her was one of the things that motivated him to work so hard to return to physical perfection—his livelihood as a professional athlete notwithstanding. Kelvin was disappointed and did little to hide this fact.

"So, you're going to leave me, just like that? I thought we had something, Stephanie. I thought this was more than a way to pass the time for you."

"It was, Kelvin. I'm devastated to have to leave you. But family comes first. And I don't want you waiting around for me when it can be months, or even years, before everything gets sorted out. I also know I can't ask you to drop everything and move to the island. I mean, it is paradise, but I realize it would be a lot to ask."

"But you didn't ask, did you?"

"Should I have? Really, Kelvin, would you consider—"

"No."

"I figured as much."

"So tell me something, Stephanie. Would you have been so quick to run back to Daddy if I was healthy, if I was still the starting superstar for the Suns?"

Stephanie was taken aback by his obvious insinuation, so much so that she could think of nothing else that had to be said between them. "Good-bye, Kelvin."

She hung up on me! Kelvin held the phone in his hand for a long moment before flipping it shut. He dropped the massage balls and adjusted his bed to a semiupright position. He stared at the ceiling for answers to the myriad of questions forming in his mind. *Why did this happen to me?* He'd been totally healthy before the accident, for the first time in months. He'd been prepared to celebrate his return to the starting lineup, ready to reclaim his crown. Instead, he was lying up in the home of his father and stepmother, reconciling the fact that he'd just been abandoned by the woman he'd planned to make a more permanent fixture in his life. He'd planned to ask Stephanie to move in with him when he returned to Phoenix.

"Damn." Kelvin rang the buzzer for his nurse. Stephanie's news had aggravated his leg, or perhaps that's just how it seemed. He just knew that suddenly he'd become extremely uncomfortable. The nurse came in at once, rearranged his pillows, and left to prepare a mild sedative so that he could go to sleep. Minutes later, he was feeling more comfortable and knew that sleep wasn't far away. As he closed his heavy lids, welcoming slumber's escape, it wasn't Stephanie's face that appeared in his consciousness. It was Princess.

Lord, please heal Kelvin's body and let him know that You are in control of his life. These are the words that Princess had uttered, that had pierced his unconsciousness during her hospital visit and resonated somewhere in his heart. When he'd awakened, she was gone. But she'd been there. Princess still cared about him. But did she care enough to let him back into her life?

39

We Need to Talk

Mama Max smiled as she opened the door. "Well! To what do I owe this pleasure? My world-traveling son and his busy first lady stopping by to see me is good news indeed. Come on in, y'all!"

Tai Brook and King, her husband and Mama Max's son, entered the living room.

"Y'all hungry? I just made a batch of fresh rolls, and there's some homemade strawberry jam to go with it. Beef stew will be done in about thirty minutes. You thirsty? I've got some Kool-Aid in there, though I know y'all say you don't drink it no more, as if you didn't have it almost every day of your lives growing up. Why are y'all standing there like a couple of strangers?" For the first time since opening the door, Mama Max stopped and really looked at her son and daughter-in-law. That's when she noticed they weren't smiling. "Well, what in the world? Who died?"

King stepped forward and hugged his mother. "Mama, we need to talk."

Tai gave her a quick hug and a kiss on the cheek as well. "Why don't we go into the living room?"

Mama Max put a hand on her ample hip and stood her ground. "We don't have to go anywhere. Whatever news y'all got can be delivered right here in this foyer. Now, what's going on?"

"Calm down, Mama," King said, his tone quiet but stern. "We want to talk to you about you and Daddy and this divorce situation. Now, can we go into the living room?"

"Don't know what there is to talk about. But, yeah, y'all come on in."

King and Tai sat on the couch while Mama Max sat on the love seat opposite them. "So, out with it. What do y'all think you can tell me about my marriage that I don't already know?"

Tai looked at King, who took a deep breath and began. "I talked to Daddy this morning."

Mama Max's eyebrows rose into a look of righteous indignation. "And?"

"And he said he left a message for you last week that he'd . . . cleaned the house."

"Unh-huh."

"Mama, Daddy misses you. Now, I know you've said you don't want to talk about what happened that caused you to move back here—"

"That's right, I don't. Did your daddy tell you why I left Texas and why I filed for divorce?"

King rubbed his eyes. Unfortunately, his father had told him everything, more information than a child would ever want to know about one's parent. He'd been surprised for sure. He knew his father wasn't perfect and remembered incidents from his childhood that suggested his father wasn't always faithful. *But a sex doll?* If a million dollars were on the line, he'd never had guessed that was what plagued his parents' marriage. Having this knowledge, however, didn't deter him from the goal of today's visit: to keep his parents together. If he and Tai could withstand his multiple affairs with real women, surely his staunchly Christian parents could withstand one with a doll.

"He told me about the doll, Mama."

"He did?"

"Yes," Tai answered.

"And have you ever imagined a nastier piece of filth in all your life?"

"I admit we were shocked, Mama, but—"

"Shocked? I hope you were appalled, repulsed, and disgusted! Who knows how long your daddy cheated on me with that . . . fake floozy."

King looked at Tai as if to say, "Your turn."

Tai rose from the sofa and joined Mama Max on the couch. "Mama Max, you know I completely understand how you feel. Finding out that there's another woman doesn't feel good, even if the other woman is . . . well . . . rubber." Tai fought to maintain her composure, because suddenly the entire situation seemed extremely amusing. *Reverend Doctor O?* Tai simply couldn't imagine, nor did she want to. "But you came to me many times when I was ready to leave your son, and you gave me very sound reasons for staying in my marriage. Now, I'd like you to consider those reasons for staying in your own."

"Daddy misses you, Mama," King added, feeling that Tai had gained some leverage. After all, they were a perfect example that there could still be marital life after affairs. "You know he can't cook, and he hates fast food. I think he's losing weight, not to mention sleep."

"Oh, so he didn't tell you that he's not lonely for company?"

Tai and King looked at each other with confused expressions.

"Oh, he didn't tell you everything, I see. Well, he's not alone down there in Texas. I have it on good authority that a real-life floozy has been making herself available since I've been gone, that she's been over to my house at least twice. And I haven't heard anything about him not letting her in. So, children, your daddy might have gotten rid of the doll, but there's still trash around the house."

"You don't know that, Mama," King pressed. "It's probably just some member coming by on church business. Or maybe it's one of the mothers dropping off food."

"She's a mutha all right."

King's eyes widened. His mother had always been feisty, but he'd never seen her act quite so stubborn. He decided that he and Tai had done enough for one visit and decided to leave her with some food for thought.

"You've been married a long time," he said, rising from the couch and going to stand directly in front of his mother. "And you've weathered everything from relocations to sicknesses to drama from your children. I don't think you're the kind of woman who's going to let a little *trash* drive you from your own home. You run things, Mama, always have. And you know good and well you don't want to divorce Daddy. It's time for you to start acting like the mother who raised me, the one with some sense."

Mama Max was stunned into speechlessness. How dare her son talk to her any kind of way. But by the time she'd gotten her mouth to working again, Tai and King had given her hugs and made a quick exit. Mama Max stood with hands on hips, watching her son and daughter-in-law get into their car and drive away. Finally, as she watched the taillights turn the corner, she found her voice and asked her question to an empty room. "Just who do you think you're talking to?"

40

Love You Good

"I'm coming over there." Dorothea stood and reached for her purse.

"Now, don't come giving me no sass, woman! I said I was fine, and I mean it. Besides, I can get Nettie or one of the other church members to come over if I need anything."

"Oh, only a Gospel Truth Christian can help you now? Where was Nettie or one of your *members* when you were trying to sneak that life-sized sex doll out your house, huh? Where was one of your deacons, one of your church mothers then?"

"I can't tell you how much I appreciate your helping me with that, Dorothea."

"You can show me, Obadiah. I need you."

"You've got Jenkins," Obadiah retorted. "And I'm trying to keep my wife. Don't come over here, Dorothea."

Dorothea slammed down the phone, frustrated beyond belief at how things were progressing with her long-time lover. More accurately, she was frustrated because things were not moving forward at all. Dorothea had been beside herself when she learned that Maxine had left Texas. Obadiah had this strange notion about not fooling around in the same town that his wife stayed, and Dorothea hadn't been able to talk him out of it, hadn't been able to get him to join her at a hotel, and hadn't been able to talk him into taking a trip to Dallas, where they'd have less chance of being seen by prying eyes. She'd thought marrying Jenkins would be advantageous to her financially, and she thought it would be the perfect cover for an ongoing relationship with Obadiah, with both of them living in Palestine.

Dorothea went to check on her husband. He was sleeping, as usual, the remote dangling from his limp hand. Instead of him watching the television, the television was watching him. She walked into the den, put the remote on the table, and placed a cashmere throw over his legs. *You're a good man, Reginald Jenkins. I wish I loved you more.*

Tea always seemed to calm Dorothea's nerves, but thirty minutes later, as she sat sipping her honey-lemon concoction, she was just as wound up as when she'd finished talking with the reverend doctor. She tried to tell herself it was ridiculous, that after all these years she had no right to be besotted with a married man. But Dorothea Noble Bates Jenkins knew the truth of the matter—Obadiah Brook was the love of her life, and she'd never love another man like she did him. She sat back in her chair and remembered when it happened, the night she fell in love.

"Ruthanne, why are you rushing me so?" Dorothea asked her younger sister. "It's not like there won't be any seats left when we get there!"

"You're only saying that because you haven't seen what I've seen or know what I know!"

"And what's that?" Dorothea rushed behind her sister, who was making a beeline to her new car: a shiny, red, brand-new 1961 Corvair.

"Only the finest man in Texas," Ruthanne said, shutting her car door and turning the key at the same time. "His name is Obadiah Brook. He pastors a small church near Wichita Falls."

"Country preacher?" Dorothea was aghast. Even now she could have rivaled Jackie O for the title of style icon, her powder-blue knit suit with fabric-covered buttons fitting her slender frame like a glove. Her thick black hair was pulled back into a chignon so that her white pillbox hat could perch at a perfect angle. Dorothea had been pestering her sister and friends to move from Texas. She wanted to relocate to either Harlem, Chicago, or Los Angeles and snag her a rich, sophisticated city man.

Ruthanne cast Dorothea a sideways glance. "Let's put this conversation on hold until after church—see how you're talking about this *country preacher* then."

Ruthanne didn't see Dorothea after church that night. That's because shortly after the service, Dorothea found herself at the host pastor's home, along with several other invited guests. The Noble sisters were known for their stunning good looks, beautiful voices, and refined manners. They were often invited to social functions and provided added décor to anyone's table. That's how she'd gotten invited to the host pastor's home. The fact that she ended up sitting next to Obadiah had been strictly her doing.

"Enjoyed your sermon," she said politely as she took a dainty bite of fried chicken. She was the only person at the table cutting the meat with a knife and fork.

"Uh-huh."

Obadiah said nothing further, but his dark, almost black pupils bore into her light hazel-green ones, causing a spiral of heat that began around her neck and flowed down to her stomach and beyond. She knew she was blushing but couldn't help it. Ruthanne had been right: Obadiah was the finest Black man she'd ever seen. What was it about him that made him so desirable? Dorothea pondered this question as Obadiah held court with the other ministers and deacons at the table. His voice was like butter, smooth and silky, its bass quality like a fur wrapped around one's shoulders. His lips were heart-shaped, cushiony, framed by a tidy mustache on an otherwise smooth, dark-brown face. His brows were thick, and tightly curled lashes framed his dark bedroom eyes. His hair was conked, like Jackie Wilson's, straight and as shiny as a patent leather shoe. Obadiah wore it slicked back on the sides, higher on top. He could have easily been an R&B star or given Sidney Poitier competition on the Broadway stage.

Dorothea said little throughout the dinner. Obadiah virtually ignored her, and along with everything else she noticed about him, she also noticed the simple gold band he wore on the third finger of his left hand. Seeing Obadiah made Dorothea more determined than ever to leave the South and head to the big city. She was sure that's where she'd have to go to find somebody to even come close to what she was sitting next to.

As they gathered in the living room, Obadiah appeared at her side. "Sister Noble, correct?"

"Yes, Reverend."

"Would you be so kind as to give me a ride home?"

"Well, I would love to, Reverend, except I didn't drive tonight. I rode with Brother Smith over there. I'm sure he wouldn't mind having you ride with us."

"Uh-huh." Obadiah's eyes continued to bore into Dorothea.

"I . . . might be able to get us a taxi," Dorothea offered. Her hazel greens didn't blink as she looked at Obadiah. "Would only take five minutes for a cab to get here."

"I have a wife and three children at home," Obadiah continued, changing the subject abruptly. "I'm not looking for another wife. And I won't leave the one I have. I can love you good, but I can't love you long."

Dorothea stared at him a long moment, then spoke softly. "I'll call a cab."

They made love all night. Dorothea had never felt anything like it. Not only was his penis long and thick, but Obadiah also knew how to use it. He knew how to use his mouth as well. Dorothea almost climbed the walls with pleasure. He'd screwed her every which way but loose, and when the sun peeked over the horizon in the early morning hours, she was still longing for more.

And not just the loving. In between the lovemaking, while they rested, Obadiah shared his hopes and dreams for a large ministry, one that would clothe the naked and feed the hungry. He listened as she told of her plans to pursue a singing career in either Harlem or Chicago and offered his advice and encouragement. In the span of a few hours, Obadiah had shown more care and concern for her than other men had in a lifetime of living. In the years to come, he became her everything: her counselor, her teacher, her therapist . . . everything but her husband.

From that first meeting on, Dorothea saw Obadiah every few months, often traveling to wherever he was preaching an anniversary or conducting a revival. The loving continued to be stellar, the best she'd ever had, and aside from the fact that he was married, Obadiah was all the man she'd ever wanted. She convinced herself that the physical pleasure was enough. And for two years, it was. But then came 1963 and a convention in Dallas, Texas, where something got in the way of her good loving—something named Maxine Brook. The confrontation was ugly. Fortunately for Obadiah, the fallout was minimal, but Maxine knowing about Dorothea devastated their affair. Something else devastated their relationship that year, but Dorothea kept that truth locked away deep in her heart.

It was an entire year before she was with Obadiah again, and then the time apart lengthened to two, then three, and then five years following a cancer scare that had landed Maxine in the hospital for two weeks. During this time, Dorothea moved to Harlem and sang in nightclubs. That's where she met George Bates, a hardworking man who loved her deeply. They married, and she loved him as best she could, until he died unexpectedly from a brain aneurysm at fifty-three. She relocated back to Texas, settled in Dallas, and entered another long-term relationship. A conversation with Reginald Jenkins, who she'd reconnected with when he traveled to Dallas for a preaching engagement, was how she'd ended up back in Palestine. That and a conversation she'd had with Obadiah shortly after seeing Reginald. The conversation where she found out that he'd be moving to Palestine as well.

Dorothea rose, moved to the sink, and poured out the remainder of her now-cold tea. *I can love you good, but I can't love you long.* Dorothea was wondering if Obadiah Brook would ever "love her good" again.

41

Back to Normal

Luke Wilkes looked around the conference table at the Cathedral, one of the finest, most influential churches in Detroit. He was pleased with what he saw. He'd been able to assemble a fine group of advisors, and as a result, his ministry and outreach efforts were poised to go to a higher level in the coming years. His biggest coup had been getting prominent politician Bryce Covington to join this prestigious board. Bryce was known for being extremely intelligent, deceptively shrewd, and highly connected. Luke had wanted to work with him for a long time, and now Bryce was fully on board.

"Gentlemen, I think that concludes the order of business for this month's meeting. You're all very busy men with your own successful operations, so, as always, I want to thank you sincerely for taking time from your schedules to meet here today. If there is no further business, I believe we are ready for this meeting to be adjourned."

"Excuse me, Luke," Stan spoke into the silence. "I do have something to bring before the board."

Luke's frown showed his annoyance. He ran a very tight ship and liked to know everything that was going on before it happened so he could have as much control as possible. He and Stan had spoken briefly earlier, and Stan hadn't mentioned anything that needed discussing. "Uh, sure, Doctor Lee. The floor is yours."

Stan took a moment and gathered his thoughts. He knew Luke was angry, and Stan felt bad about having to spring this news on him in this fashion. But it was the only way. Luke could sell snow to an Eskimo, and if Stan had confided in him privately, before the meeting, Luke would have convinced him to change his mind and the announcement would never have been made. "It is with a great degree of disappointment that I must tender my resignation from this illumined board, effective immediately."

There was a soft rumble among the eleven other men sitting around the table, looking from one to the other. Luke's eyes widened. A few voiced mild objections. Bryce, however, looked as cool as a cucumber. His expression never changed.

"I've thought about it, prayed about it, and discussed it with my wife. Logos Word is undergoing a series of transformations, and aside from that, our children are growing up faster than we can blink, and they, especially my sons, need more of my direct involvement in their lives. I'll still be available by phone, Luke, if you ever need my counsel. But this is my last meeting with you gentlemen. My prayers will continue to be with this exceptional board and outstanding ministry. Luke, I am honored that you asked me to be a part of it."

Shortly after the meeting ended, Luke pulled Stan away from the group. "You could have warned me, brother," he said softly, his tone belying his agitation.

"You would have talked me out of it," Stan replied honestly. "Few people can say no to you, Luke."

"I just hope you haven't started a domino effect."

"Why would you say that?"

"Bryce Covington. One of the reasons this board position appealed to him is because he knew you were on it."

Stan was taken aback by this news. Bryce had told him as much, but Stan didn't know that Bryce had told Luke. "There are many fine gentlemen on this board, Luke, and yours is a fine ministry that benefits Bryce's constituents. I can't see any reason why my leaving would change how much you two could help each other, not to mention the city of Detroit."

Luke's expression was somber as he looked hard at Stan. Then he broke into a charismatic smile and offered Stan his hand. "I hope you're right, Doctor. I sure hope you're right."

After saying good-bye to the other members, Stan exited the church's executive offices and headed to his car. He thought he'd escaped, when a voice pierced the cool, April evening.

"Stan!"

Stan stopped but did not turn around.

Bryce quickly closed the distance between them. "What? You're going to leave the city without saying good-bye to a dear friend? I noticed you hugged and communed with everyone else except me. What's that about?"

Stan turned around. "You know very well what it's about, Bryce, just like you know what the resignation is about. I won't be returning to Detroit, for any reason. And while I will always think highly of you, I won't be seeing you again. Good-bye."

Stan turned to get into his car. Bryce put a hand on the door, preventing Stan from opening it. "No, Stan. I'm not going to let you run away from us."

"I'm not running from you, Bryce. I'm running to my wife, my children, my godly life. I'll admit it, seeing you again churned up feelings I thought long gone. But God is not the author of confusion, and I will not remain in any situation that brings disorder into my life."

"You're right, Stan. God is not the author of confusion, and once a person embraces their truth, confusion disappears. You know you love me," Bryce continued quietly. "And you know you want to be with me, in every way."

Stan made another attempt to open the door. "Don't make a scene, Bryce. I have a plane to catch."

"Prove it."

"What?"

"Prove that you are delivered, that you have no desire to be with me. Spend the night with me—in my home, in my bed. If you can deny me, while wrapped in my arms, then I'll believe."

Stan glared at Bryce, his mind in turmoil. A part of him wanted to accept Bryce's challenge. Stan was a man who rarely backed down from anything, and he would take immense pleasure in proving Bryce wrong, in proving that he was absolutely, one hundred percent heterosexual. But another part of Stan was afraid that if he went to Bryce's home, he would be the one proven wrong.

"Bryce, this is over. Let me go." Stan reached yet again for the door handle.

Bryce looked deep into Stan's eyes, moving closer to him. "Are you sure this is what you want?"

Stan thought no one had ever looked more beautiful than Bryce in this moment: his eyes, full of admiration and desire; his lips, soft and wet; his body hard, emanating a woodsy, citrusy scent. "I'm sure," he finally whispered.

Bryce looked around, and seeing no one else in the parking lot, he leaned over and placed a kiss on Stan's mouth. "Give me a hug."

Stan hesitated only briefly before wrapping his friend in a hard, warm embrace. "I'll be praying for you, Bryce," he whispered.

Bryce continued the hug for a long moment, silent, savoring the feel of the man he loved. Finally, he stepped back. His smile was bittersweet, and his words were sincere. "I'll be praying for you, too, Stan. For your family and your happiness."

Bryce walked away quickly after that, and Stan opened his car door without looking in Bryce's direction. Seconds later, he was out of the parking lot, speeding toward the airport where he was hoping he could book a red-eye flight. Originally, he'd planned to leave the next morning, but Stan knew he needed to get out of the city as quickly as possible. He'd pay first class, full price if he had to. No ticket price was too high, he figured, when it came to saving his soul.

Stan gripped the steering wheel as he entered the freeway. *Thank you, Jesus, for being my strength.* Stan had stopped an affair from happening, but he couldn't stop the tears that flowed from the time he turned out of the church parking lot until he turned into the rental car parking lot. Once there, he wiped his eyes, blew his nose, straightened his back, and walked to the van that would take him to the airport and to the plane that would take him back to normal, back to the life he'd built over the past twenty-five years.

Bryce and Stan thought they were alone in the side parking lot, where they'd both parked, totally by chance. But actually, there was a third person there. And as soon as Bryce's car followed Stan's out of the parking lot, this silent observer reached for his cell phone.

42

Bedroom Business

"Hey, hot chocolate," Lavon said as he walked into his wife's spacious executive office in the MLM Network building.

"Hey, Hershey," Carla responded, using one of the many pet names she gave her husband.

"Good show today." Lavon leaned down and planted a warm kiss on Carla's waiting lips.

"You think so? My mind was so distracted that if it hadn't been for the cue cards, I wouldn't have even known who I was interviewing."

"The cameras couldn't see that, baby doll, and that's all that matters. What was on your mind?"

"Brianna. I'm not trying to be a snoop or a spy, but I just happened to look on her computer when I was in her room the other day. . . ."

"Oh, I see. That computer jump up and trip you, did it, while you were on your way out of your daughter's room?" Lavon plopped down in the large cushiony seat in Carla's brightly decorated office. The mustard-yellow chairs complemented the other bold colors of purple, red, orange, and green. Used incorrectly, these shades would have collided, but each complemented the other. An eight-foot-long striped couch using all of the colors pulled the palette together beautifully.

"More like what I saw on her computer tripped me. You know how photos from our picture file are our screen saver?" Lavon nodded. "Well, Brianna's is that same way. There was a picture of her in a bikini, in a very suggestive pose. I guess it was taken last month when she and that group from school went whale watching, because she was on a boat."

"So, she was in a bikini. Weren't they all in bathing suits?"

"I guess so, but that's not my point. This picture was overly sexual, in my opinion. Her little butt cheeks, which aren't so little anymore, were spilling out of her bikini bottoms, and she was proudly displaying her *ass*ets." Carla emphasized the first syllable while turning back with a seductive smile. "So the next thing I knew, I was looking at her MySpace account."

"Wait a minute. How did the computer jump from the screen saver to online?"

"My hand just fell on the mouse," Carla said, laughing. "And when I looked up, there was her MySpace page."

"I don't know, Carla. What you did sounds precariously close to snooping to me."

"I don't care. I'm her mother, and I don't like what I saw on her page. All of her pictures, well most of them, anyway, look as though she's advertising. I need to have a talk with Miss Thang and remind her that she's only fourteen years old."

"Now, baby, you aren't gonna like this, but the apple don't fall far from the tree. You're the sexiest woman alive. Just stands to reason that your daughter is gonna be all kinds of sexy too."

"That's exactly what I'm afraid of. I started screwing at fifteen, and let me tell you from personal experience, that's way too young to start experimenting sexually. See, the problem is, you think you're grown at that age—you think you know everything—but, baby, you haven't even begun to live. And by the time you find that out, it's too late. A woman can never get back her innocence, and nine times out of ten, the first man who pops the cherry is the least deserving of it. Because if he was, he wouldn't be popping it, right?"

Lavon leaned forward. "Do you think Brianna is sexually active?"

"I don't know, but that's why we're getting ready to start a conversation. I can't be telling millions of people how to handle their daughter if I can't handle my own. I've got a call in to Tai, to get some hands-on advice. She and Princess went round and round for a minute, but it seems the two now have a close relationship. Her younger daughter, Tabitha, is just a year or so older than Brianna, I think. So she'll be good to talk to."

Lavon rose from the chair and walked around to Carla's side of the desk. He opened his arms. "Come here."

Carla eyed the love of her life, smiled, and gladly rose to be in his arms. Lavon gave the best bear hugs. He could make a woman who weighed three hundred pounds feel as if she were light as a feather. Carla was every bit of one eighty, yet Lavon picked her off the floor and swung her around, until she squealed like a teenager. "Put me down, man!" Yet when he did, she stayed in his embrace.

Lavon kissed Carla on the lips, once, twice, and again. He kept her hand in his as he walked over to her office door and locked it. He walked to the speaker phone and pushed a button. When a voice answered on the other end, Lavon's directive was simple: "Hold our calls. We are not to be disturbed for any reason."

Once he'd ensured their privacy, he led Carla over to the sofa. He rearranged the pillows on it, lay down, and pulled Carla on top of him. They enjoyed exploring each other's mouths with their tongues for long moments. Lavon reached down and cupped Carla's thick backside. Aside from her overflowing mounds, her luscious lips, her large shapely legs, and her beautiful face, her "baby got back" was one of the things he loved best about her. He kneaded it gently, even as Carla began to grind into his already hardening manhood.

"Um, careful, you about to start something we can't finish right now." Lavon rolled out from under Carla and positioned her on her stomach. He knelt beside the couch and began a massage from her shoulders down her legs and back.

"Ooh, Lavon, that feels so good. This is exactly what I needed." They enjoyed a companionable silence, broken only by Carla's oohs and ahs.

Lavon was almost finished, when his hands went still. "Baby . . ."

"Hum?"

"I almost forgot."

"Forgot what?"

"Forgot to tell you about a call I received, something very interesting I might add."

"What?" Carla asked drowsily. Lavon's strong hands and expert ministrations were putting her to sleep, and she couldn't think of any kind of news she wanted to hear at this moment.

"Friend of mine saw Stan kissing a dude in the Cathedral's church parking lot."

This news woke Carla right up. "What?" she asked, lifting her head from her arms.

"Well, actually, the dude kissed Stan. But that was after they had some kind of intense conversation. Stan was trying to leave and the man—"

"Whoa, whoa, whoa," Carla said, sitting up. "You're talking about Stanley Morris Lee, my ex-husband, father of my three children, pastor of Logos Word Interdenominational—"

"Yes, yes, and yes!" Lavon sat down next to Carla.

"Kissing a man you say?"

"Bryce Covington."

"The politician?"

"The one and only."

"The pretty boy?"

"Ah, I don't know about all that . . ."

"That fine, light-skinned brothah who's so pretty he looks like a cross between Rick Fox and Vivica Fox?"

"Ha! Woman, will you stop focusing on fine foxes and let me finish telling you what I heard?"

"Wait a minute. Who did you hear this from? You know I don't believe one bit of gossip I hear, especially coming from church folk. I've been the subject of that, remember?"

Lavon fixed Carla with a look. "How can I forget? Anyway, this news comes from someone reliable, a friend of mine. We used to work media together in a ministry in Minneapolis. He's now the media director at the Cathedral. He was sitting in his car in the parking lot, talking on the phone, when he saw this all go down."

"All of what go down?" Carla's mind was reeling, even as her intuition had her more believing the story than not. It would explain a lot of things about Stan Lee, particularly when it came to the demise of their marriage.

"That's all. Just this dude kissing Stan . . . on the lips. Stan was walking to his car when Bryce called out to him, and my friend said at first it looked like Stan wanted to get into his car. But Bryce kept holding him back. They talked quietly for a few minutes, and then Bryce kissed him, they hugged, and then—according to my source, who shall remain nameless—they both got in their cars and left."

"Oh, my . . . ," Carla said, her hand to her chest. "My, my, my . . ."

"So what do you think? Stan's a down-low preacher? You know that as quiet as it's kept, there are more than a few—"

"I don't know if I can believe this, Lavon. Isn't Bryce married with children?"

"Isn't Stanley?"

"Touché."

"And more than that. Bryce is no longer married. He divorced his wife last year and came out."

"Came out?"

"Admitted he was gay. He didn't do it in a grand way, with a press release and news conference, but he doesn't try and hide it either. My friend tells me he's seen around town with a young, dark, super handsome brothah—his partner, I guess.

That's why my informant was so shocked to see Bryce kiss Stan. He knew Bryce was gay but had no idea that Stan might roll that way."

The intercom interrupted their conversation. "I know you said no interruptions, Lavon, but it's Princess Brook on the line and you said—"

"And I meant it," Lavon said, a smile in his voice. "Good job, Susan, we'll take the call."

Carla shifted back into talk show host mode and spent the next half hour conversing with her good friend's daughter. She could tell she was going to love doing the show with Princess, who had the right blend of straightforwardness and personality that made one a star. They decided to air the show live, on the same day the book came out. If everything went the way Carla and Lavon planned, Princess's book would make the *New York Times* bestseller list.

Shortly after they finished the call, the Lees decided to leave the office and handle anything else that needed attention from home. Aside from work, there were several matters that demanded their attention. They both were concerned about Brianna and decided to talk to her that night. For Lavon, he also wanted to finish what he and his wife had started in her office. When it came to Carla, Lavon was insatiable. There was no place he'd rather be than on top of her.

Carla was juggling those two issues, and one more. She had to find out the truth about Stan. Was he gay? Perhaps bi? And if he wasn't down low, just how much about this other relationship did his wife, Passion, know? Some would say it wasn't her business, but Carla was making it hers. She and this man had two natural children together, and he'd adopted Brianna as well. His being gay would also totally explain his aversion to having sex with her. Yes, Carla was making Stan's bedroom business her business. And soon, she knew, it would be time to have a conversation with Passion Perkins Lee.

43

Unknown Caller

Kelvin settled back into the seat of the plane he'd chartered to return to Phoenix. A pretty nurse/assistant and a personal trainer sat in the back section; his best friend, Brandon, occupied the seat next to him. It was hard to believe that he'd spent over a month in Los Angeles, but the truth was, the stay had done him good. Ever since finding out at the age of sixteen that Derrick Montgomery was his biological father, the two had experienced a turbulent relationship. He was like his father in many ways, and being stubborn was one of Derrick's traits that Kelvin had inherited.

Kelvin had gone to live with his father shortly after receiving an athletic scholarship to UCLA. At first, things had gone smoothly. While Kelvin's uncle Geoff was wealthy and lived in a very nice home in Santa Barbara, Kelvin loved the cosmopolitan vibe of his father's Beverly Hills mansion. He loved being twenty, thirty minutes from the action: Sunset Strip, Malibu, Bel Air, Hollywood, Universal City, and places to shop on every corner. Another fifteen minutes and he was in the heart of the hood, where some serious balling went on and where he continued to get his hair cut until he moved to Phoenix. Kelvin became close to his half brother and sister, and loved the homey atmosphere his stepmother, Vivian, created.

Some say nothing good lasts forever. Six months into his stay, Kelvin and Derrick went head-to-head on a matter on which neither would budge: Derrick demanded that Kelvin attend church regularly, and Kelvin countered that he didn't need God or church. Kelvin moved out, and it was a rocky road—paved with their mutual love for basketball—that eventually brought father and son back together again. But then Kelvin got drafted by the Phoenix Suns and moved to Phoenix. He and Derrick had tried to remain close, but their busy schedules made regular conversations difficult, especially since he couldn't seem to get his dad into the texting mode. Spending this time now under the same roof had helped them bond again. Kelvin was doubly thankful: for the stepfather who loved him like a son and for the biological father who'd helped the boy become a man.

"Mr. Petersen, can we get you a drink before takeoff? A light snack, perhaps?"

"Some orange juice would be nice," Kelvin replied. "Buckle up, man," he said to Brandon, who was busy doing business on his laptop. "And put away the books . . . chillax for a minute."

Kelvin's vibrating satellite phone interrupted him. He immediately thought of Stephanie and smiled when his phone listed the caller as unknown. That sometimes happened with international calls.

"Hey, beautiful!" Kelvin said, by way of greeting.

"Wow, Kelvin, I guess absence does make the heart grow fonder."

Kelvin's smile turned upside down. "What's up, Fawn?"

"Oh, so I take it that greeting wasn't for me."

Kelvin ignored her comment. "Is Little Man all right? I was going to call you anyway. I'm headed back home, to Phoenix. I was hoping the nanny could drop him off tomorrow."

"Sounds like you've missed your son."

"Of course."

"What about his mother?"

"Fawn, must we always go through the baby-mama yip-yip? I just want to have a cordial conversation about Kelvin."

"All right."

"All right? Just like that? Maybe I do need to ask if you're okay."

Kelvin and Fawn laughed. It was a rare moment of civility, reminding them that at one time they'd actually liked each other.

"I am calling about Kelvin," Fawn continued.

Kelvin sat up straighter in his seat. "What about him?"

The flight attendant stopped in front of him. "Sorry, Mr. Petersen, but we're ready to take off. If you can end this call until after we're airborne, that would be wonderful."

Kelvin nodded at the flight attendant, and spoke into the phone. "Look, I gotta go, but will call you back in a few minutes. But just tell me, is my son okay?"

"Yes, Kelvin, he's fine. But there is something going on that I need to talk with you about."

Kelvin ended the call, his brow furrowed as he looked out the window. Fawn said nothing was wrong with Little Kelvin, but she still needed to tell him something? Kelvin couldn't wait until the plane reached cruising altitude and he could call Fawn back. His heartbeat probably wouldn't return to normal until he found out exactly what was going on.

44

Back to Texas

Tai hugged Mama Max again. "I'm glad you're going back to Texas, but I'm going to miss you!"

"That simply means you'll need to bring my grandkids down more often. They'll be out of school soon, so you won't have any excuses."

"It's a date. I'll try and coordinate with King's schedule, and maybe we can all come down: me, him, and the twins."

"That would be good, honey."

"Mama Max, I know you have reservations. I've been in your shoes. But trust me, you're doing the right thing going back to Daddy O."

"I'm going back to Texas. The jury's still out on whether or not I stay married to the reverend."

Tai knew she didn't have time for a lecture. The plane was in its last boarding call. "Being in the same house is a start, Mama. I know God will direct your path from there."

Mama Max waved one last time before pulling her carry-on down the Jetway. She quickly settled into the bulkhead aisle seat that Tai had requested on her behalf, buckled her seat belt, and pulled out a Bible from her tote bag. She didn't open it right away, just rested it on her knees as she waited for takeoff. It wasn't that she had a fear of flying, per se, but it felt good to have the Word close by nonetheless. She idly fingered the book's well-worn pages as she offered a mental prayer to God. *Lord, be with me on this here journey. Help me do what's right. Help me release anger and unforgiveness, Lord. Help me to see Obadiah as You see him, Lord. Help me love him as You love him. And me, too, Jesus. Help me to love me like You love me. Amen.*

Dorothea parked the car next to the curb of the Brook residence and waited. *Am I doing the right thing?* After much prodding, Obadiah had finally met her at a hotel in Tyler, Texas, a little over an hour from Palestine. Obadiah had loved her good, but she could tell his heart wasn't in it. Afterward, they'd talked for a long while, and for the first time, Obadiah really opened up about his marriage—how guilty he felt about betraying Maxine and about not practicing on Saturday night what he preached on Sunday morning. "This is the last time," he'd told her as they made love for the second time. "I've prayed for Maxine to come back to me, and when she does, I'm going to be faithful to her."

A light was on in the front of the house. *He's in the study.* Dorothea's fingers tapped the steering wheel as she pondered whether to go knock on the door. She'd tried to stay away, as he'd requested, but here she was, parked outside like a schoolgirl after the popular jock, trying to get up the nerve to go in.

"This is ridiculous, Dorothea. You're sixty-six years old and acting like a love-struck fool." Dorothea gave herself no more time to think. She reached for the container of pralines she'd made for Obadiah and the door handle at the same time, opened it, and walked briskly up the sidewalk to the Brooks front door.

She rang the doorbell once, no answer. Dorothea impatiently waited for a few seconds before she rang it again. *Is he really not going to open the door? I know he hears this doorbell.* After ringing the bell a third time and not getting an answer, Dorothea reached into her purse and pulled out her cell phone. She dialed Obadiah's cell phone. It went straight to voice mail. After leaving a message and waiting another minute or two with no return phone call, Dorothea upped the ante and called the home phone. Her frustration mounted when Maxine's cheerful voice spilled into her ear.

"Praise the Lord, saints. You've reached the Brook residence. . . ."

Dorothea hit the pound key, bypassing the message. "Obadiah, I know you're in there. Open the door. I've got something for you, and we need to talk. Now stop acting silly and open the door. I'm not leaving until you open it."

When another minute had passed, Dorothea stepped off the porch and into the yard. She walked along the front of the house until she came to the window of the study, the same window Maxine had banged on a few months earlier. She was tall enough to look inside, and the curtain was open just enough to give her visual access to the room. When she pressed her nose to the screen, she dropped the container of sweets.

"Obadiah!"

Dorothea ran back to the porch, where she banged on the door and rang the doorbell at the same time. She frantically reached for her cell phone again, this time dialing 911.

"Nine-one-one, what's your emergency?"

"I don't know, but we need an ambulance quick. The reverend is passed out on the floor of his house. I'm outside and I can't get in. We need to get him help—quick!"

Mama Max was anxious and more than a little peeved as she waited for her luggage to appear on the baggage carousel. After begging her to come home, Obadiah wasn't at the airport to pick her up like he said he'd be, and he wasn't answering either his cell phone or the home phone. When her own cell phone rang, she hurried to get it. *I'm going to give this man a piece of my mind!* Of course, the phone was where it always was whenever she was trying to get it—*especially* when she wanted to give someone a piece of her mind—at the bottom of her purse.

"It's about time you called me, Reverend. You've got some explaining to do!"

"Mama Max, it's Nettie."

"Oh, sorry, child, and thanks for calling me back. I still haven't heard from Obadiah and I'm mad as all get-out. Did you reach him?"

"No, ma'am, but I did find a ride for you. One of the deacon's daughters lives in Dallas. We've already called her, and she's on her way to pick you up and bring you to Palestine. Do you have your luggage, Mama? Because she'll be there in about fifteen minutes, and it might be easier for y'all to see each other if she could pick you up curbside. I can tell her what you're wearing. Her name is Maylene, and she'll be in a beige Toyota Camry."

"Lord, have mercy. The reverend's got folks scrambling around after me. I sho don't like to cause this kind of trouble." She stopped fussing long enough to tell Nettie what she was wearing.

"It's no trouble at all, Mama Max. She was coming this way anyway. Can you meet her curbside? They've got those push carts in the airport to help you with your luggage, and one of those porters can help you too. It shouldn't take her more than ten, fifteen minutes to get you and then about ninety minutes for you to get here."

"Nettie, is everything okay? Oh, wait a minute. Here comes one of my bags." Mama Max turned to a tall, lanky, blond teenager standing next to her. "Baby, can you get that bag for an old lady? Thank you kindly." She placed the phone on her other ear. "Now, what's the matter? Sounds like you're in an awful hurry for me to get back there. Did you miss me that much?"

"I missed you something fierce, Mama," Nettie replied

honestly. That statement was the truth. But Nettie was battling with another truth and whether to tell Mama Max what was going on now or wait until she got to Palestine. After a few seconds of wrangling and a quick silent prayer, Nettie decided there was nothing Mama Max could do so far away, except worry herself sick for the next two hours. When she arrived in Palestine would be soon enough to tell her about what had happened to her husband. "You going straight home when you get here? Or do you want to stop by my house first?"

That's a strange question. "I guess I should stop by my house, Nettie, unless you need to see me first. What is it that you're not telling me, girl? Because if I've got trouble sitting in my living room, I'd surely like to know about it before I get on the front porch, if you get my drift."

"Well, there is something going on that you should know about, Mama. But I'd rather tell you when you get here, when we can talk face-to-face."

"What is it, Nettie? Because I'm here at the airport, and if Reverend is still acting a fool, I can turn around and get on the first thing smokin' right back outta here!"

"Now, don't go worrying yourself about it, Mama. It ain't nothing that God can't handle."

"Does it involve the ministry? Is something going on at Gospel Truth, somebody gossiping about where I've been? Because come Sunday, I'll tell anybody who's got nerve enough to ask me to my face!" Mama Max's volume had increased with her temper, so much so that several passengers waiting around her also wanted to know the gospel truth about what was going on!

Almost three hours later, Maylene turned on to Elm Street, where the Brooks lived. Right away, Mama knew something was wrong and that the gas that had started churning as soon as they'd turned onto the highway wasn't from the hamburger and fries they'd gotten in the fast-food drive-thru. And if the gas wasn't enough to allude to something being out of order, then Nettie's black Infiniti SUV parked in the driveway drove the message home.

Maylene had barely stopped the car before Mama Max opened the door. Nettie opened her car door at the same time and hurried over to Mama Max. "So good to see you," she said, hugging her. "Thanks for bringing her home, Maylene. Here, let me give you some gas money."

Maylene waved away the suggestion and told Mama Max how good it was to have met her. After the three women retrieved the luggage from her car trunk, Maylene was gone. Maylene had barely put her car in gear and drove away when Mama Max turned to Nettie. "Okay, Nettie, you can see my face. What is going on?"

"Reverend Doctor is in the hospital. He's had a heart attack."

"Jesus!" Mama Max whispered, searching Nettie's face with her eyes. "How is he? Is he going to . . ."

"By the grace of God, he's going to be fine. I haven't gone to the hospital yet. Wanted to wait for you. But I've been on the phone several times. He's in surgery—that's all I know."

The two women placed Mama Max's luggage just inside the door and then hurried to Nettie's SUV. In a rare moment for this law-abiding citizen, Nettie ignored speed limits, and after a short, quiet ride where both ladies prayed instead of talked, she pulled into the emergency parking lot at Palestine Regional Medical Center. They hurried up the sidewalk and through the double doors, heading straight to the information desk directly in front of them.

"I'm here to see about my husband," Mama Max said, trying to regain her breath. "Obadiah Brook."

The nurse behind the counter greeted the women, then looked up information on her computer. "Yes, ma'am, he's still in surgery. But if you'll have a seat in the waiting room, I'll get a doctor to come and talk to you."

"Much obliged," Mama Max said.

She and Nettie walked into the waiting room where Mama Max stopped short. Sitting in the corner, wringing her hands and wiping her eyes, was Dorothea.

"What are you doing here?" Mama Max asked, advancing on Dorothea as if ready for battle.

"Mama Max." Nettie put a hand on Mama Max's arm, trying to stop her from moving forward.

"Let go of my arm, Nettie." Mama Max stopped directly in front of Dorothea. "I'm only going to ask you this one last time. What are you doing here? Because if Jenkins ain't had a heart attack the same time as the reverend, it's getting ready to be me and you!"

45

Try Jesus

"Mama Max," Nettie whispered, trying to keep her voice calm. "I don't think this is the place for—"

"For what? To call this floozy out before God and everybody? She got the nerve to show up here when it's *my* husband on the operating table. I got the right to do a little operating of my own." Mama Max balled her hand into a fist and looked mad enough to really punch Dorothea.

Dorothea, who'd been surprised to see Maxine come through the door, regained her composure. She tilted her chin haughtily, her voice calm. "Yes, Maxine, we all know how concerned you are about your husband. So much so, in fact, that you abandoned him when he needed you most."

"Oh. No. You. Didn't!"

"Mama Max, you've got to keep your voice down. People are looking." Nettie tried once again to move Mama Max, who at the moment resembled the tree that was planted by the waters. She would not be moved.

"You're asking Maxine to use logic instead of emotion, Nettie?" Dorothea managed a tired laugh. "That'll be the day."

"Sistah, you bettah stop talking," Mama Max hissed, lowering her voice as Nettie suggested, though the action took extreme effort on Mama Max's part. "Because I am *not* the one."

Dorothea sat up a bit straighter in the chair. "Obviously."

"Oh, my God." Mama Max turned to Nettie, a frantic look on her face. "Tell her, Nettie. You better tell her fast, 'cause it's about to get ugly. Tell her don't try me, try Jesus. 'Cause he'll help her. I'm getting ready to hurt her. As mad as I am in this here hospital, they'll need to get another room ready!"

One of the nurses from the reception desk rushed into the room. "Ladies, I'll have to ask you to keep your voices down. Everyone in here is under stress. Please, Mrs. Brook, if you'll come with me. The doctor wants to talk to you."

Mama Max cut her eyes at Dorothea one last time before following the nurse out of the waiting room. After she was sure Mama Max was out of hearing range, Nettie sat down next to Dorothea. "You have a lot of nerve, sister."

"What I have is a lot of love for Obadiah Brook, more than Maxine will ever feel. Don't even try," she continued, putting a hand up when Nettie would have interrupted her. "Things are not always as they seem, Nettie Johnson. There's more to this story than you realize, and I couldn't care less whether you understand it. But know this: If it hadn't been for the fact that I love Obadiah enough to look after him when his wife ran out and went over to check on him when I did, the reverend doctor wouldn't have made it. That's what the doctor will tell Miss High and Mighty, Miss Holy Roller, Miss *Accuser*. That five more minutes, and Obadiah would have been . . ." Dorothea didn't finish the sentence. Instead, tears welled up in her eyes, and she turned toward the wall, away from Nettie. "I got there just in time," she whispered to herself.

Nettie didn't know what to think, much less say. So without another word, she stood and went in search of Mama Max. She wanted to avoid another confrontation, and after Mama Max finished talking to the doctor, Nettie suggested they go to the cafeteria for a cup of coffee.

"He had three blocked arteries," Mama Max said as they

walked toward the cafeteria. "But the doctor said he'd make it. Obadiah's going to pull through."

"Praise the name of Jesus."

"Bless His holy name."

The two ladies were quiet until they got their cups of coffee. The room was fairly crowded for a Thursday afternoon, but they found a table near the back of the cafeteria. For a couple minutes, they sat quietly, sipping their coffee.

"Thanks for helping me back there," Mama Max said finally. "Can't help Obadiah none from a jail cell, and if I ever got to beating that woman, that's where I'd be. I owe her more than forty years' worth of ass whoppins, yes, Lord . . . would be a first-time convict at seventy."

"Anyone would be upset," Nettie offered. "But I know why she's here."

Mama Max looked up from her coffee cup.

"She went over to check on Reverend Doctor O. She said that the doctor told her five more minutes without medical attention and the reverend would have died."

"So what does she want for that information, a thank-you? Probably her and Obadiah *checking up* on each other is what brought the attack on in the first place."

Nettie didn't have an answer for that comment. The ladies sipped their coffee in silence.

"I'll tell you one thing," Mama Max said. "I'm not going to keep on playing second fiddle to that woman. I'm going to help Obadiah out of this here emergency. After all, he is my husband, for what that's worth, and I'd give this kind of help to a stranger. It's the Christian thing to do. But as God is my witness, as soon as he's back on his feet, he's going to have to decide to be anonymous to me."

Nettie frowned slightly. "You mean *monogamous,* Mama Max?"

"That too. I mean it, Nettie. If that man don't convince me that an old dog can be taught new tricks, I'm going to click my heels three times and head back to Kansas—for good."

46

The Best Defense

Carla sat quietly, enjoying a rare Saturday that was totally open to do with as she wished. There was nothing pressing regarding the job, her Sanctity of Sisterhood commitments, or her children. In fact, she had the house to herself, and that almost never happened. But Lavon felt she needed some quiet time, and after he'd begun their day with a lavish love dance involving multiple orgasms, he had offered to take the kids to the mall.

At first, Carla hadn't known what to do with herself. But shortly after her family drove off, she drew a hot bubble bath, scented the water with vanilla cinnamon bath salts, put on a compilation jazz CD, and sank into the water. She'd stayed there for almost forty-five minutes, until the water had cooled and the jets had turned off. Then she'd come downstairs and made herself a vegetable omelet. Being able to cook for one instead of five was a treat unto itself. She'd taken the meal out to a deck she hadn't enjoyed nearly enough of in the three years she and Lavon had lived in the home. It was nestled in an exclusive Woodland Hills community, and the view was beautiful. Even the weather cooperated. The valley could get extremely warm in the summertime, sometimes hitting triple digits. But this April day was perfect: gentle breeze, warm sun, and not a cloud in the sky. That's where Carla still sat, a glass of chardonnay having replaced the orange juice she'd had with brunch.

While slowly sipping and savoring the taste of this rare glass of wine, Carla thought about Stan. It had been a week since Lavon had dropped his Stan-might-be-gay bomb, and Carla was still trying to figure out what to do with the news. At her request, Lavon had phoned his friend again and gotten more information about Bryce Covington as well as his friend's promise not to spread what he'd seen. The friend assured Lavon that he was the only one who knew, and because of his respect for both Stan and Bryce, it would stay that way. He told Lavon that the man Bryce was openly squiring around town was an ex-model and businessman from LA named Ryan Westbrook. Lavon and Carla had Googled his name together, and from the looks of what was on the Internet, Ryan seemed quite successful. Carla knew one thing for sure: The brothah was fine! *But, dang. Does he look good enough to turn a straight guy gay? And if not, how long has Stan been living with this secret?* Carla concluded that she never really knew the man with whom she spent ten years. *Was our marriage a lie? Was his love for me ever real at all?*

Carla looked at her watch. *Probably another hour or so before Lavon and the kids come back.* She sat back, enjoyed the wine, and tried to let her mind go blank, to think of nothing at all except how blessed she was. Lavon was an amazing man, husband, father, and business partner. Her children were healthy, and fortunately for Brianna, she hadn't acted out too badly when Carla demanded she change her MySpace pictures. Of course, the choice was either that or lose the computer, cell phone, and her freedom, but Carla had given her a choice. The show ratings were higher than ever, and Carla looked forward to helping Princess launch her literary career. That reminded her. She hadn't talked to Tai. She walked in, retrieved her cordless phone, and walked back out on the deck.

"Girl, if this telephone tag was the real thing, I would have lost ten pounds by now. I know what busy feels like, though, hope you and your family are well. I'm pretty much doing nothing all day, so it's a perfect one for catching up on my end. If you find some time, call me back."

Carla ended the call and sat the phone on the wooden patio table. She picked it up, started to punch a set of numbers, set the phone down again. She was deep in contemplation as she finished her wine, picked up the phone, and punched in Stan's home number. *Please let Passion be home, because I don't know if I'll have the nerve to call again.*

"Hello?"

"Passion, it's Carla."

"Hi, Carla. Stan's not here. You might be able to catch him at the church, or if not, on his cell."

"Actually, Passion, I'm calling for you."

A slight hesitation. "Oh?"

"Yes."

"Do you have a change in the kids' schedule? I know with summer coming, we'll have to coordinate vacations along with everything else."

"Yes." Carla decided to ease into the reason for her call, instead of blurting what could be a revelation straight out. While the lack of love between these two women was no secret, they'd always strived for civil interactions. "How's Onyx?"

"She's doing fine, starting to get a smart mouth on her, though."

"Ooh, sistah, you'd better nip that in the bud."

"Tell me about it."

Another pause. Carla and Passion remembered at the same time that at one point, theirs had been a truly cordial relationship. When Carla was Passion's first lady, Passion used to help with the SOS conferences. Passion wasn't one for having too many female friends; in fact, she had none. But there had been a time when Carla came as close to that for Passion as any woman ever had, besides a childhood friend who'd died several years ago. *Do you even have friends?* Passion remembered Stan asking her that in a heated moment. The truth of the matter was, she didn't, and this simple, casual conversation with Carla made her realize that maybe she needed one.

"There's another reason I called," Carla spoke into the silence. "It involves a matter of a sensitive nature. I'd have suggested we meet in person, but I only have about an hour of free time before the kids come back."

Passion's curiosity was immediately piqued. "We can discuss whatever it is over the phone."

"It's about Stan."

"What about Stan?"

"Passion, this is a bit difficult for me. What I'm about to share came to me as gossip at first, but Lavon has since verified the information."

Passion's curiosity was quickly turning into something else. "What kind of information?" she demanded. "What information regarding Stan could possibly be any of Lavon's business?"

Carla understood Passion's anger, especially regarding Lavon's involvement in what she was about to say. If Passion had had her way, Lavon would have been her husband, not Carla's. So she chose to ignore Passion's question and ask one of her own. "Does the name Bryce Covington mean anything to you?"

The question caused Passion's heart to jump in her chest. She didn't know why she reacted as she did, but a second later, another voice came into her head. *If you do know what I'm talking about . . . you've been warned.* "Yes," Passion answered cautiously. "He's a politician in Michigan."

Lord, please let me be doing the right thing. "Has Stan been in Michigan recently, perhaps visiting Bryce?"

"Look, Carla, whatever you've heard, or whatever you've got to say, just spit it out. I don't have time to play twenty questions. What have you heard about my husband?"

Carla took a deep breath, remembering a different time: when Stan was her husband and Passion had shared some information with him that had effectively ended their marriage. She prayed that would not be the case this time. "Stan might be gay."

There it was, the ugly truth, pushing up against a gorgeous California afternoon. Even as Passion's heart stopped, the world around her went on. She could still hear Onyx and her friend laughing in the den, could still hear KJLH playing a Stevie Wonder song on the stereo. A car went past the window she gazed out of, a neighbor walked her dog. But for Passion, the world had stopped. "What did you just say?"

Carla relayed an abbreviated story of what Lavon's contact had shared with him. "I was as floored as you are," she finished. "Not believing it for a second . . . at first. But according to Lavon's friend in Michigan, who is the media director for the Cathedral, Bryce Covington is openly gay, so what he says he saw is not totally impossible.

"I started thinking about when Stan and I were married, Passion, about how challenging our . . . times of intimacy were. I don't want to say too much here, and I definitely don't want to get into your business, but—"

"I've experienced it too," Passion said, cutting Carla off and surprising herself by blurting out the truth. "It has been difficult for Stan and I to connect intimately. There's a wall there. . . ."

Both women became silent again. Carla, suddenly warm, wiped away sweat. Passion wiped away tears.

"Stan and I have children together," Carla continued. "For that reason alone, I'll always care about him. And whether or not you believe this, Passion, I only wish the best for your marriage. Stanley is a good man, and if he's battling something like this, he'll need a good woman to help him through it. I believe you are that woman."

Carla and Passion talked for an hour. Carla shared her experiences and what she knew of Stan, including the fact that he'd been molested as a child. She told Passion the name of the therapist who'd worked with them and suggested that perhaps continued therapy would allow Stan to admit to whatever was going on with him.

"Stan's not gay," Passion said as their conversation wound down. "I refuse to believe that."

"You're probably right," Carla readily agreed. "It could have been that Bryce was simply coming on to Stan or that he and Bryce are just close friends, and their embrace was misinterpreted. But it bothered my spirit enough to call you, Passion. Again, there are kids involved here. I just think that the best defense is a good offense."

"Thanks for calling, Carla."

"You're welcome, Passion. Let me know if I can do anything else to help. I mean that."

Passion put down the phone and continued to stare out her bedroom window. She looked over at the king-sized bed, the beautiful sleigh that took up a large portion of the room. Her eyes rested on Stan's dressing room. *Will I find any more secrets if I go in there?*

Passion sighed. As he'd promised, Stan was making more of an effort in their marriage. They'd made love last night, the second time in a month. For other couples, this would be starvation, but for Passion, it was a feast. And the biggest thing was, Stan had thrown away the panties. He'd told her that last night as well, after they'd made love and while they still held each other. He'd said he wanted to take a trip together, just the two of them, and reconnect. He was finally starting to sound like the husband she'd always wanted. It had been this way since . . . since Stan came back from Detroit, after resigning his position with the Cathedral board, a board on which Bryce Covington sat as well.

"Oh, God," Passion whispered. "Oh, Jesus, please don't let what Carla heard be true." *I just think the best defense is a good offense.* Passion knew that Carla was right. Passion would not sit idly by while her husband suffered. If there was any truth to what Carla had heard, Passion was going to find out about it, and she was going to find out today.

47

Committed

Passion flinched when she heard the front door close. *He's home.* She'd both anticipated and dreaded this moment since the conversation with Carla. Postponing her talk with Stan had also crossed her mind. But Passion felt that as uncomfortable and potentially explosive as this information was, she and Stan had to talk about it. The spread of AIDS was highest among African American women because of men on the down low. Passion wasn't trying to go out like that. She had to know the truth.

"Hey, honey." Stan greeted Passion, who was sitting in the living room. "Where are the kids?"

"They're not coming over tonight. Onyx is with her father, so we have the evening all to ourselves." Passion meant for the statement to sound casual, but it did not.

Stan was immediately suspicious of something going on. "How did that happen? Did they have something special to do with Carla? Was there an activity of theirs that we missed putting on our calendar?" Stan walked fully into the living room and stood over Passion, who was seated on a high-backed wing chair facing the large picture window. "What's going on, Passion?"

This alone time was not starting out the way Passion intended. The last thing she wanted was Stan on the defensive. She tried to defuse the situation and shift the mood. "I'm actually happy we get this unexpected quiet time." She stood, wrapped her arms around Stan, and placed her head on his shoulder. "How was your day?"

Stan did not return the hug. "It was fine until I came home ready to spend time with my children, only to find out they're not here. I need to call Carla and let her know that this is not okay." He dislodged himself from Passion's embrace and headed to the phone.

"Wait, Stan. I've already talked to Carla. In fact . . . I asked her if the children could come tomorrow instead of today. I wanted to talk with you."

Stan stared at Passion. He'd tried so hard these past few weeks to live up to her expectations, to be a more caring, loving husband. And this was the thanks he got? Passion rearranging his kids' schedule to spend more time with him alone? "This is very selfish of you, Passion. I appreciate your wanting to spend time with me, but my children are with Carla five days a week and with me for two. Two!" Stan punched two lean, strong fingers in the air for emphasis. "And then without consulting me, you call my ex-wife and ask her to keep them yet another day? Whatever it is you want to talk about could have waited until Monday." Stan cast a last, hard look at Passion before walking away.

"It's about Bryce Covington," Passion said to his retreating back.

Stan stopped in his tracks and whirled around. "What about Bryce?"

"Stan, can we sit down and talk calmly, rationally? I want to talk, not argue."

Stan walked over to the other wingback chair in the room. A round coffee table holding a crystal vase filled with colored glass balls and blown glass flowers separated them. He sat down heavily and stared straight ahead.

You could cut the tension with a knife. Passion silently prayed, desperate for a different atmosphere in which to approach what she had at first guessed and now knew would be a volatile topic. "Stan, please, let me make some tea while you change clothes, get into something more comfortable. Are you hungry? I made some chicken turnovers that turned out really good, like handheld pot pies. I'd love to heat up a couple for you."

Her voice was soft, pleading. Stan knew he was overreacting and tried to change his mood. After all, whatever Passion wanted to talk about where Bryce was concerned could be no less than speculation. Bryce was a popular public figure. Perhaps she'd heard of some scandal, or perhaps she found out that he and Ryan were more than friends. But that would have no bearing on him. He'd been very discreet in his recent dealings with Bryce. Only a handful of people knew of their intimate connection back in college, and one of them was dead. Maybe he'd be better off engaging his wife in whatever discussion she wanted to have about his old lover. Stan was fighting to hold on to the heterosexual persona he'd carefully crafted over two decades. Passion was an integral part, even a pivotal part, of his being successful.

"I'm sorry, Passion. You're right. It's been a rather stressful day, and I was looking forward to releasing some energy by taking the boys out on the court. I'm happy to talk with you, but I'll change first."

"Are you hungry?"

"A little. Heat up those turnovers as well."

"Wonderful." Passion rose from her chair to where Stan still sat. She kissed his smooth, bald head. "I love you."

"I love you too."

"Let's keep it casual. I'll meet you in the den."

Fifteen minutes later, Passion and Stan were seated on the oversized forest-green sofa in the comfortably decorated den. They ate the turnovers from a shared tray, munched potato

chips, and drank lavender-infused tea. Two glasses of lemon
water sat on one of the large square ottomans that doubled as
tables. The tension from earlier had dissipated as Stan told Passion some of what had transpired at church.

"I'm glad she's active again," Passion said, referencing the
member who was the current topic of conversation. "She was
so angry when her mother died."

"It's understandable. Many people feel God has failed them
when life doesn't turn out the way they've planned, or when
our prayers seemingly go unanswered. She hasn't totally come
to terms with her mother's death, but she knows that God isn't
through with her yet."

"Maybe I should call her this week, invite her to lunch at
the church."

Stan looked up. "That would be wonderful, Passion. I wish
you would do more of that, socializing with the women in the
church."

Passion felt this was a perfect segue into more personal
matters. She had no problem being first in discussing something in her own life she'd like to change. "You're right, Stan. I
do need to reach out more—to women in general and to certain church members in particular. I never had a lot of female
friends growing up . . . friends period, for that matter. I was always overweight, tall for my age. The other kids either teased
me or bullied me, and I built up a pretty strong wall around
me.

"I had one friend growing up. Her name was Robin
Cook." Passion smiled at the memory. "She was just like me—
fat, tall, disliked. We became inseparable and unstoppable and
caused way more trouble together than we'd ever encountered
apart."

"Oh, so are you telling me I married a bully?"

"A bully and an instigator who'd beat your butt for looking at me wrong! I was not a happy kid and didn't like seeing
others happy, especially the cute, popular girls. They were the

favorite targets of my wrath. But boys were not excluded. I was an equal-opportunity beat-down artist."

Stan laughed. "You and Robin keep in touch?"

"We lost touch when I was fifteen. My family left Atlanta and moved here. Then, interestingly enough, I ran into her a few years ago, here in LA. We tried to get that best-friend camaraderie back, but our friendship was never the same. She died a short time later."

"Sorry to hear that."

"Yes, it was a weird situation, and a sad ending to a life I feel was never fully lived."

"There are some good, Christian women in our fellowship; you know who they are. I'm not sure they'll join you in a fistfight, but they would be great company and a way to widen your circle. . . ."

"I think I'll start next week. Invite the sistah to lunch and see how it goes from there."

Stan and Passion sipped their teas a moment. "What about you, Stan? I know that Reverend Doctor O is one of your mentors and that you are good friends with Derrick and King, but do you have friends from your childhood, friends outside the ministry?"

"The ministry keeps me so busy that most friends outside of that world have dropped by the wayside. Like Bryce, for instance," Stan said, deciding to start the discussion Passion wanted to have. Perhaps not running away from it would show Passion that he had nothing to hide. "He and I knew each other in college, but after graduating, I left D.C., moved here, and dove headfirst into ministry. We'd lost contact for more than twenty years, until I saw him in Detroit, at that first board meeting."

"I bet y'all were surprised to see each other."

"He wasn't. Luke had told him of my involvement."

"But you were happy to see him?"

"Why wouldn't I be?"

Passion shrugged, wanting to keep the light atmosphere but determined to not back down. That's what had been happening for the past three years, and why the effervescent woman of three years ago now seemed a shadow of her former self. "Any number of reasons. I didn't go to college, but I can think of several high school classmates I wouldn't be happy to see if I met them now. Were you and Bryce friends in college?"

"What did you hear, Passion?"

Passion looked away, then looked at Stan and told him.

Stan's emotions fluctuated from surprise, to anger, to defensiveness, and, finally, to relief. What Passion had heard was a rumor, pure and simple. He would simply deny it. "Do you believe I'm gay? Do you believe I'd actually kiss a man, or let one kiss me?"

"I don't know, Stan. That's why I wanted us to talk."

"What is there to talk about? What would make you think this is something worthy of even one minute of conversation? I'm surprised you didn't simply laugh it off and dismiss it immediately. It's ludicrous, Passion. How could you believe this gossipmonger, over what you must know about me by now? I was your pastor, for what, five or six years before becoming your husband for the past three? You saw me with Carla; you know me with my children. Now you're my wife, and yet you give this a moment's thought?" Stan laughed. "I guess you don't know me as well as I thought you did."

"Hearing about the parking lot incident isn't the only reason I wanted to speak with you, Stan," Passion replied. "I only gave it any weight at all because of a call I received from Bryce's ex-wife . . . Sheila Covington."

This was a verbal punch Stan had not expected. His ego deflated, and not even anger could fill it with air. What he realized in this moment was that he was tired of running, hiding, trying to keep up a front twenty-four hours a day. Maybe it was time to divorce Passion and live the rest of his life as a celibate minister. More and more single ministers were successfully running churches. Perhaps his life would be made much simpler if he wasn't dealing with females at all on a personal level.

"Do you want a divorce, Passion? Is that what this is about?"

Now it was Passion who was taken aback. "No, Stan. What I want is to have a real, open, honest relationship with you. What I want is to help you, in whatever way I can. I took vows for better or worse, in sickness and health, and I meant them.

"If you tell me these rumors are false and Sheila's call was bogus, then I'll believe you. But if you tell me something else, I'll stand by your side. I love you, Stanley Morris Lee. And if you'll be honest and let me in, I'm committed to being with you all the way . . . no matter what."

48

Let the Past Stay in the Past

A week later, Stan and Passion sat in the office of a leading relationship therapist who was especially popular in religious circles because in addition to being a psychologist, Dr. Ike Banner was a seminary graduate. He'd thought that traditional ministry would be his path in life, but God had other plans. Shortly after he obtained a doctorate degree, a fledging practice, owned by one of his father's dear friends, practically landed in his lap. He'd honed his skills in the quiet town of Bend, Oregon, for twenty years before relocating to Rancho Palos Verdes ten years ago.

If there was any doubt that his practice was different, his first three words after initial introductions eliminated all doubt. "Shall we pray?"

Stan and Passion looked at each other briefly, smiled, and joined hands with the doctor. After a brief but heartfelt prayer, the three sat in Dr. Banner's neatly appointed office.

"Thank you for filling out the questionnaires prior to this meeting. I know it is extensive, but I've found it often helps the communication process to write down our thoughts before we voice them and to hear what you believe to be the sticking point in your relationship. I find that while a therapist may assist in bringing certain matters to light, each person is inherently in touch with their own truth. It is up to you two to make the journey of reconciliation." Dr. Banner gave a brief initial assessment based on what he'd read and then turned to Passion. "You wrote about a very acrimonious first marriage and divorce, and then being celibate a large part of your life before meeting Stan. How do you think these experiences have affected the way you approach sex in this marriage?"

"Sex was used as a weapon in my first marriage," Passion began, grateful to unburden thoughts and words that had been lived but not uttered. "By both of us. There was very little intimacy during the last two years we were together, and from the time I became pregnant until we divorced, none at all.

"I recommitted my life to Christ after the divorce, and encouraged by Stan's teachings"—Passion looked briefly at her husband—"vowed to remain celibate until I remarried. I was divorced for six years before Stan and I married. So . . . I would say that the effect celibacy had on me was that I very much wanted an active sex life when I got married."

Doctor Banner made notes while Passion spoke. When she finished, he simply nodded and turned his head to Stan.

"Stan, you write that you were molested as a child. How do you feel this violation impacted your sex life?"

Stan looked at Passion and then back at the doctor. "In every way. Being molested from the age of eight until I turned twelve impacted not only my sex life, but also my whole life."

"I know this is difficult, Stan. But we're going to keep talking, day after day, week after week, month after month if we have to—until we get a breakthrough. Tell me about this aunt who molested you."

Stan stared hard at the doctor, but when he answered, he looked at Passion. "I can tell you about my aunt, but in truth, the person who molested me was my uncle."

In the forty years since the abuse began, Stan had never been totally honest about what had happened all those years ago. Whenever he'd recounted his abuse story, he'd said it was a

woman who'd molested him. He'd repeated the lie so many
time until sometimes he'd convinced himself that it was true.
But seeing Bryce after all these years forced him to revisit the
painful memories he'd buried.

"It was a man, not a woman, who abused you?" Doctor
Banner asked.

"He would make me take off my clothes—" Stan paused
and looked at Passion before looking away, out the window
and into a distant past—"and then make me put on women's
underwear. Then he would . . . make me do things."

Passion swallowed a gasp as realization dawned. The panties
that she'd so smugly thrown in his face at the restaurant were
part of the residue that remained from his childhood trauma.
Instinctively, she reached out a hand and placed it on Stan's
arm. He flinched but didn't pull away.

Doctor Banner's voice lowered to almost a whisper. "Why
did you tell your last therapist it was your aunt who abused
you?"

"You know why."

"There could be many reasons, Stan."

"I'm a Christian, Doctor, a pastor. To be molested by a
woman is bad enough, but to be assaulted by a man, well, it
would change how my members view me, how the world
views me. That's why no one will ever know."

Stan took Passion's hand. "Thank God I've been delivered,
Doctor, and have a supportive wife in my life. So that those
things from the past can stay in the past."

"But are they in the past?" Doctor Banner probed. "Or are
they in the present, interfering with you and your wife's intimacy and driving a wedge into your marriage?"

When the Lees returned home, there was a FedEx package
waiting just inside the storm door. It was addressed to Stan,
sent from an LA address. He went into his study to check

phone messages and e-mails. Once he'd finished that, he opened the package. He recognized the writing at once.

Stan:

I knew you wouldn't open a package from Detroit, so I asked Ryan to mail this while he handles some business in LA. I'm sorry if our last meeting was difficult for you, but I'm fighting for true love . . . what I know exists between the two of us.

I hope that you enjoy the enclosed, and know that I'm thinking of you every moment, of every day.

Bryce

PS. I've waited twenty-five years, but I won't wait forever . . . all my love.

49

Don't Let Me Down

"Don't be nervous." Carla reached over and gave Princess a re-assuring squeeze.

"I'm not," Princess replied.

Carla looked pointedly at Princess's rapidly shaking leg.

"It's just a habit," Princess said, laughing.

"Uh-huh."

In actuality, Princess was more excited than nervous. The last two months had gone by in a whirlwind: finals, graduation, and now this—the debut of her first book. She'd been too busy to think about all that was going on and what could potentially happen once the book released. But she was getting ready to find out.

Lavon spoke into Carla's earpiece. "You look beautiful, baby. I'm gonna tear you up tonight."

Carla smiled and discreetly gave him a sign to cut it out. He knew she couldn't respond, because even though they weren't yet rolling, the audience members were all staring at her, and her mike could go live anytime. The spontaneity experienced in the studio was one of the treats that awaited the lucky guests who obtained tickets to her always-in-demand tapings. That this show would air live was an even more spec-tacular event.

Princess looked out into the audience and smiled at her mother. Tai smiled back, as did the twins, Tee and Timothy, and her aunt Vivian. Several friends from college, including Princess's roommate Sarah, sat nearby, as did Joni and Brandon. A few rows behind them, editor Serena and publicist Adele from the publishing company sat beaming like proud parents. Princess's newly hired agent, Natalie, typed rapidly into her BlackBerry.

The assistant director quieted the studio audience. The director counted down and pointed to Carla.

"Good morning, afternoon, evening, whenever you're tuning in. Baby, we have a fantabulous show for you today, introducing an exciting new author and her debut novel. I'm excited about this book for several reasons. But most of all, I'm excited because in reading this memoir, I believe spirits will be lifted and lives will be changed.

"In an age when so many young people are trying to live the thug life, or get sexed up, or go after the bling, there are a group of young people out there who are holding it down for their generation and trying to make a difference. Please help me welcome one of them—Princess Brook."

The general audience applauded politely. Princess's friends and family showed their enthusiasm. Once the applause died down, Carla continued. "Let's get right into it, Princess, starting with the title of your book, *Jesus Is My Boo.*" Carla turned toward the audience. "Everybody in here knows what a 'boo' is, right? Your sweetheart, your main squeeze, your number-one man?" Some audience members laughed, others nodded. "How did that title come about?"

Princess looked out at the audience. "I guess it happened after I dumped my cheating boyfriend and fell back in love with Christ."

Those forty-four television minutes went by faster than Princess could have imagined. The interview was easy. Talking to Carla was like talking to one's best friend. She made it easy for Princess to share the painful details of that first year on campus, and she celebrated with her as she provided sketches of her comeback. As her agent, publicist, and Carla had suggested, she gave out just enough information to lure those watching into buying her book. Viewers knew she'd been cheated on but would have to read the book to learn that the other woman got pregnant around the same time Princess had an abortion. Tears on the faces of audience members let Princess know she was not alone in the pain of betrayal, with teenagers, twentysomethings, and older women as well. Midway through the show, she knew that whatever challenges she faced as a result of telling her story would be worth it. If one woman made different choices because of what she'd written, she'd deem her book a success.

"You were fabulous!" Tai said once they were back in the greenroom. "I'm so proud of you, Princess."

"Thank you, Mama."

"Aw, she was aw-ight," her younger brother, Timothy, interjected.

"I told you the blue would look better on television than that sicko green you were going to wear," Tee added in her usual, know-it-all tone.

"And you were right, little sister," Princess said.

For the next thirty minutes, she was swamped with well-wishers. Her agent's BlackBerry and iPhone were blowing up. Other television and radio stations were calling, as were newspapers, including *LA Gospel*. She didn't know it, but Princess's phone was blowing up too. By the time she'd check it an hour later, both her cell phone and her dorm phone mailboxes would be full.

"You've got a bestseller on your hands," Lavon whispered to Princess when he briefly stepped into the greenroom. "Hope you're ready for the ride."

Kelvin sat staring at the now-muted television. He couldn't believe the poised, confident woman he'd just watched on television was the same girl he'd turned out when she was eighteen. And was she that beautiful when they dated? He'd always thought Princess was hot, but her hair had grown longer, past her shoulders, and the loose, big curls accented her heart-shaped face. But it was her eyes that had him mesmerized from the beginning: large, brown, almond-shaped, and sparkled when she talked about her "boo."

His ringing cell phone brought him out of his reverie. "Speak."

"Did you see her?"

"No."

"You're lying." Brandon laughed. "I bet you even TiVo'd it."

"Who?"

Brandon couldn't answer for laughing.

"Forget you, dog," Kelvin said, smiling. "Damn, she looks good."

"Even better in person. And you should have seen her after the show. Everybody in the audience got a copy of her book, and she stayed out front to sign some of them. They were clamoring for her autograph like she was already a celebrity!"

"Who is she seeing now?"

"Jesus is her boo. Did you listen to the show or just watch the images?"

"Yeah, I heard all that. But who's she with?"

"You want to find out any of Princess's business, buddy, you're gonna have to wobble your crippled behind up here and ask her yourself!" Kelvin's casts had been removed, and the doctors said his leg and arm had healed perfectly. But he was still on a crutch for the next three weeks. "Look, Joni just pulled up. I'll hit you back later."

Kelvin tossed his phone on the couch and reached for his TiVo remote. He went back to the segment where Princess was talking about leaving the man who'd broken her heart—talking about him. His heart clutched as he watched the tears fill her eyes and knew he'd stop at nothing until he could wipe them away.

In that moment, it all became clear. Every girl since Princess had simply been a distraction, something to make him forget that his heart already belonged to somebody else. Kelvin picked up his phone and dialed his agent.

"Look, man, get me in touch with Princess Brook. Yeah, the girl who was just on Carla's show. I don't care how you do it, dog—that's why you get paid the big bucks. But don't call me back until you either have her on the line or you have her personal phone number. I'm counting on you, bro. Don't let me down."

You're my boo, Princess, nobody else's. And I'm getting ready to make sure you realize.

Kelvin frowned as his phone beeped again. "Fawn, Little Kelvin all right?"

"Kelvin, we're at the hospital."

Kelvin sat up straight. "Why, what's going on?"

"He got sick again, even sicker than last time."

Kelvin jumped to his feet and began to pace the room. "I thought you said it was just an infection!"

"That's what those other doctors told me. But now they've referred him to some specialists." The confident arrogance Fawn usually displayed was replaced by fear.

"Where y'all at, Fawn?"

"St. Joseph's."

"I'm on my way."

Several hours later, a weary-looking doctor approached Kelvin and Fawn, who were waiting in a private lounge.

Fawn rushed up to him. "Is my baby going to be okay?"

"How is he, Doc?" Kelvin asked, coming to stand next to Fawn.

"The little guy's a fighter," the doctor said, smiling slightly. "But we need to keep him for a few days, run further tests and try to rush the results on the ones we've taken so far."

Fawn tried not to panic, with little success. "But what is it? Another infection?"

"Maybe. But we want to eliminate all other possibilities. Whatever it is, we've hopefully caught it in its early stages. Technology has advanced to the level where even the most serious diseases can be successfully treated. So take heart, Mom," the doctor finished, placing a comforting hand on Fawn's shoulder and winking at Kelvin. "We're going to do everything possible to help your son."

50

I'll Pray

"I don't want to talk to him." Princess was talking on speaker phone and texting at the same time. She was sitting in her new high-rise condo, just a couple blocks from the ocean in Long Beach. The view from her balcony was stunning. Princess had fallen in love with the place the moment she walked inside, which was shortly after she'd decided to stay in LA instead of moving back home. She was only renting now, but the owner had talked of selling it later. Princess let her know in no uncertain terms that if she could afford it when that time came, she'd be the first in line to buy.

"But his agent has called several times," Natalie responded. "Every day. He says it's very important, Princess, and I believe him. Something to do with his son being ill, very ill. I don't think he'd use his son as a tool like that, just to get to you, do you?"

Princess struggled to go past anger and resentment and find compassion and unconditional love. But it was hard. The boy they were talking about could have been her child. If she'd kept her baby, he would have been just a few months older than Fawn's child.

"Tell the agent I'll pray for Kelvin's son."

Natalie sighed. "Okay, Princess." They talked a bit longer,

about the multibook deal that was on the table at Praise Publishing and the recurring guest appearances Natalie had confirmed with Carla's show. By the time they finished talking, Princess was exhausted. Not so much from their conversation, but from the part of her mind that stayed on Kelvin and his son.

She almost didn't answer the phone when it rang. But after seeing Joni's home number on the caller ID, she quickly picked up the phone.

"Hey, girl."

"Princess, it's me. Don't hang up."

Against her will, Princess's heartbeat quickened, the way it always did when she heard Kelvin's voice.

"And don't be mad at Brandon. He wouldn't give me your number, but he dialed you on three-way. I threatened him to within an inch of his life if he didn't. I need to talk to you, Princess. I need you."

Princess closed her eyes against the rush of emotions that roiled inside her.

"Princess, did you hear me?"

"I'm sorry about your son, Kelvin. My agent told yours that I'd pray for him, and I will."

"What about me, Princess? Will you pray for me?"

"Of course."

"Will you pray *with* me?"

"Sure, we can pray right now."

"That's cool, but I want to see you in person. I want you to pray for my son in person. And for me."

"For you? But Joni said you were doing much better."

"Oh, so you've asked about me, have you?" There was no denying the smile in Kelvin's voice.

Princess had asked about him but felt that he didn't need to know it. "It's not a good idea for me to see you."

"Why not?" Kelvin asked softly. "Isn't it the Christian thing to do, to help out a friend in need?"

"It's not fair to bring up Christianity only when it's convenient for you, Kelvin."

"Does it make what I said any less true?"

"What does Fawn think about me praying for her son?"

"She doesn't have to know. I'm coming to LA in a couple days and bringing Kelvin with me."

"If you can bring him to LA, he must not be too sick."

"I wouldn't lie on my son, baby, not about this. The doctors gave him some medication, so he's okay for right now. That's why I want to come this weekend, before he gets sick again. Can I, Princess? Can I come see you?"

"Call me when you get here," Princess said after a long pause. "I'll pray for your son. And for you."

51

Don't Fall for the Okey-Doke

"Hey, Rafael."

"Hey, superstar!"

"Shut up!"

"You know it's true."

"I'm just God's princess, that's all."

"Don't remind me. I'm trying to get you to be my princess too."

Princess smiled. Even though he'd said it in a joking manner, she knew Rafael was half serious about them getting back together. And lately, she'd actually tossed around the idea. They had practically grown up together, had many of the same interests, and he was her best friend and he loved God. Princess knew that she could do worse in the boyfriend department . . . and had. "Why didn't you call me back last night? I really needed to talk to you."

" 'Cause I was working until almost midnight. There's no rest for the weary, or the brothahs at the low end of the totem pole." Rafael complained with a smile in his voice. After graduating in the top ten percent of his class with a degree in political science, he'd secured a job as special assistant to the mayor of Kansas City. Everyone who knew him said that job would be his one day. Rafael agreed. In fact, mayor was only the first rung on his career ladder. He planned to follow in the footsteps of Barack Obama, go all the way to the top, and bring Princess with him as first lady. "You got me now—state your business."

"I talked to Kelvin."

There was no smile in his voice or on his face when Rafael answered. "How'd that happen?"

Princess told him.

"That fool will try anything to get next to you, Princess. Don't fall for the okey-doke."

"But my agent verified it, Raphael. His son is sick. And Kelvin is still healing too."

"So? Kelvin's father is one of the most prestigious ministers in the country. Let him pray for his grandchild and his son. You stay the hell away."

"He's bringing him here."

"To Los Angeles?"

"Uh-huh."

"This is not good, Princess. I'm telling you. He's just trying to get back in, and the fact that he would use his son's illness? That's messed up right there."

"You're right. I shouldn't meet with him."

"No, you shouldn't."

"Uncle Derrick and Aunt Vivian can supply all the prayer his child needs."

"Exactly. When's he supposed to be there?"

"This weekend, I think."

"I think this weekend is a good time for you to visit the family, come back to Kansas."

"I can't get away right now. My PR schedule is crazy. But I'll be home for the fourth. You're invited over to our house for barbeque. Mama and Daddy's in-ground pool will be finished by then. So throw away those raggedy swim trunks you probably still have from high school, and buy some new ones."

"Don't worry about me. You just make sure your body is tight enough to rock a bikini."

"I'm not the one with the beer gut," Princess teased.

"Beer gut? Girl, you trippin'. You know I don't drink."

Rafael and Princess joked, teased, and talked for a while. When she got off the phone, her side was hurting from laughing so much. She glanced at the clock and was shocked to see it was one a.m. She had three book signings tomorrow, the first one at noon. Princess took a quick shower and went to bed, still smiling about the conversation with her dear, crazy friend.

On the other side of the country, Rafael was not smiling. He was worried about Princess. He'd been there to help pick up the pieces of the heart Kelvin shattered. That's why while Princess felt she could handle an encounter with Kelvin, Rafael wasn't so sure. But he knew one thing—*he* could handle an encounter with him. Rafael wasn't going to sit back and let his friend get hurt again. He logged onto his computer and booked a flight to LA.

52

Count the Cost

Mama Max hummed a gospel tune as she pulled into the grocery store parking lot. Her list was short: mainly ingredients for homemade chicken and dumplings and a peach cobbler. This was one of Obadiah's favorite meals, but that's not why Mama Max was fixing it. The idea of preparing it came after a conversation with Nettie earlier, when she'd talked about missing her mother. No matter that it had been more than a decade since she'd passed, Nettie still felt her loss, keenly at times. And how she missed her mama's chicken and dumplings. That's the comment that sent Mama Max to the store.

Life had been interesting in the Brook household since Mama Max's return and Obadiah's heart attack. For one, their schedule had been busy. Gospel Truth had celebrated the reverend doctor's one-year anniversary the previous week, and at the same time, had announced his retirement effective at the end of the year. While returning to ministry had reinvigorated him, Obadiah realized that he no longer had the stamina to effectively oversee a ministry full-time.

Because of the anniversary, the Brook household had bubbled over with activity. King, Tai, and their children had come down for the occasion, as had Derrick and Vivian Montgomery. While they'd stayed in hotels, most of their free time was spent around Mama Max's dining room table, enjoying great food and good conversation and acting as if everything was all right.

Everything was fine, but not all right. Aside from confirming that the plastic pussy had been removed, along with the rest of his pornographic collection, Mama Max and Obadiah had not discussed their marriage in any depth. The doctors had said not to do anything strenuous, which in Mama Max's opinion included arguing—something that was bound to happen once their marriage became the topic of discussion. For the first three weeks following his heart attack, Obadiah spent much of his time resting or reading the Word. Visitors and preparations for the anniversary had taken up the rest of the time. This was the first week that the agenda was not full and Obadiah was healthy. Mama Max knew it was time for them to clear the air.

She put her oversized purse in the small compartment of the shopping cart and wheeled it inside. She started in the produce aisle, picking up fresh herbs and vegetables. She proceeded to the canned-goods aisle, swept through the baking-goods section, picked up two whole chickens, paid for her purchases, and was out the door.

That didn't take long, she thought, looking at her watch as she rolled her shopping cart to the trunk of her black Thunderbird. *I can get this done in time to invite Nettie over for dinner.* Mama Max placed the items in her car and closed the trunk just in time to see Dorothea Jenkins walking toward her.

Mama Max stood as tall her as her five feet five allowed and glared at the woman approaching. "I don't have a thing to say to you, Dorothea."

Dorothea kept approaching. She stopped a couple feet in front of Mama Max. "I have some things to say to you, Maxine. And since you had your number changed, I guess God has arranged for us to meet right here."

Mama Max had changed the number after hearing the

message Dorothea left for Obadiah, just before seeing him sprawled on his office floor. Mama Max mumbled under her breath, pushed Dorothea out of her way, and reached for her car door handle.

"At least I love him!" Dorothea said.

Mama Max whirled around. "You wouldn't know love if it walked up and slapped you! Lust, maybe. Adultery? For sure. But love don't sleep with another woman's husband."

"Even when she won't?"

"You got a lot of nerve flapping your jaws about what you *think* is going on in my marriage," Mama Max hissed as she stuck her finger in Dorothea's face. "A lowlife tramp with no self-respect at all. And now you've got the nerve to be a preacher's wife. It's a shame before the living God."

"No, I'll tell you what's a shame. It's a shame to have a wonderful man like Obadiah Brook in your house and sleep in another bedroom. It's a shame to think you're too holy to honor your marriage vows."

"Honor? I'm surprised you can say the word. You're just jealous that this nappy-headed Black woman has the man you've always wanted! Well, I told you then and I'll tell you now—Obadiah belongs to me!"

"You think so?" Dorothea responded, her subdued voice in stark contrast to a practically screaming Mama Max. "You may have his body, Maxine Brook. But you will never have his heart. *That* belongs to me!"

"Let me get out of here before I do something ungodly."

Dorothea blocked her. "No, Maxine. This conversation is forty years overdue."

"I'm warning you, Dorothea. Get out of my way."

Dorothea's smile was predatory. "That's exactly what I've wanted to say to you for forty years. Obadiah never wanted to stay married to you. His thoughts were on his kids and the ministry and what a divorce would cost him. You've walked around all these years thinking you did a big thing by threatening us all those years ago. You think it was your ultimatum that kept him with you all these years?"

"Whatever it was, he's still with me and not you. So you might as well give up."

"Oh, believe me, Maxine, I've given up plenty."

"You've given up nothing, except your self-respect."

"You don't know the half of it."

"Oh, I don't? Then why don't you tell me? What have you given up, Dorothea Noble Bates Jenkins, and whatever last names that I don't know about? What do you have to show that you've ever thought of anybody but yourself?"

This time it was Dorothea who turned to walk away, but a fired-up Mama Max fell in step behind her. "Oh, now you're done talking, huh? Because you have nothing to show for all this talk about Obadiah loving you more than me, do you? What do you have to show for it?"

Dorothea finally spun around. "An empty womb!"

This answer stopped Mama Max in her tracks.

"Yes," Dorothea continued. "I was pregnant with Obadiah's child all those years ago, when you came knocking on the door of my hotel room. That's why he'd risked everything to come with me, even with his wife just floors below. I wanted his child more than anything, Maxine, more than my own life. Obadiah wanted it, too, said he'd find a way to take care of two families.

"But then he sought the counsel of an older pastor who told him that an illegitimate child at that time would effectively ruin his ministry. Obadiah was distraught, torn between his love for God and his love for me. *Me,* Maxine," Dorothea said, pointing to herself. "When he got back to Kansas, he called to let me know that he'd made his choice. He was going to leave you and the ministry, to be with me and our child."

Mama Max was unconvinced. "If this story is true—and I don't believe it for a minute—then where is this child, this baby that Obadiah loved so much?"

"I killed it." Dorothea's haughty attitude faltered, and tears filled her eyes. "I thought I was doing what was best for Obadiah. I didn't want to be the cause of his leaving what he loved so much, and he loved the ministry. I justified it by saying he and I could have another child, the right way, after he divorced you. I went to a woman known for herbal potions that helped . . . release the fetus from the womb. I drank her poison, and two days later, our son came out. Obadiah was devastated when I told him. That's when I realized what a mistake I'd made, in not leaving Obadiah a choice in the matter. And even though I tried to get pregnant again, *we* tried to get pregnant again, it was the first and only time I conceived. So whatever you think you've given up, Maxine Brook? I've given up more.

"I'm not asking for your pity. I just want to give you something to think about, tell you something you didn't know about the man you take for granted: sleeping in another bed, forcing him to seek inanimate objects to satisfy a need you should be fulfilling. Yes, you may love him, you may have him, but you will never love him more than me. You count that cost, and then you judge me. Because no matter what, as long as there's breath in my body, I will be a part of Obadiah's life."

53

Come Monday

Reverend Doctor O maneuvered his car into the garage and turned off the engine. He extracted his keys from the ignition, reached over for his briefcase, and sat still. He didn't relish going into the house where a stalemate had existed for the past month. For most of the years of his marriage, home had always been his sanctuary. Maxine was good at keeping the house clean and food on the stove. Unfortunately, the kitchen and the fireplace in the living room was the only place a fire burned. The one in their bedroom had died out decades ago.

Obadiah unbuckled his seat belt but still did not move. Instead, he passed a strong, rough hand over weary eyes and tried to rein in his temper. Anger had been the fire Obadiah had felt since having his heart attack. All that time flat on his back had given him time to think and realize that while he certainly was guilty of many sins regarding his marriage, he wasn't the only one. Maxine carried her fair share, too, but she'd walked around these past few weeks like she walked on water. *And I'm sick of it. I'm sick of being made out to be a pervert when all I want is what the good Lord made.* "I never thought it would turn out this way, Max," Obadiah whispered. "Never."

★　★　★

"There go that girl," Obadiah's seventeen-year-old neighbor whispered.

"Ain't nobody stuttin' her," a sixteen-year-old Obadiah replied, his eyes glued to fourteen-year-old Maxine Brook's swaying backside.

"Hey, Maxine!" the neighbor cried out. "Obadiah says he wants to take you out, girl!"

Maxine kept walking, head high, back straight. She acted as if she didn't hear them when in truth, she'd been all too aware of Obadiah watching her and discreetly slowed her pace. Obadiah had to be one of the finest boys in the state of Texas, but she'd never let him know she thought so. He already thought he was God's gift to women, with his praying and preaching skills and all. Plus, she knew at least five other women who liked Obadiah, and more than one he'd slept with. Maxine Brook was going to finish school and save herself for marriage.

"Guess she ain't taken a shine to you, partner," the neighbor teased. "That's one piece of poon you ain't gonna get to sample."

Obadiah slid his lithe frame off the fence, grabbed his jacket off the post, and without a good-bye to his neighbor, began walking down the dusty road in the opposite direction from where Maxine walked. But that was only until he came to the fork in the road around the bend. Then he quickly cut through the tall weeds, darted around the tall black walnut trees, and rounded Old Man Jenkins's catfish pond (Reverend Reginald Jenkins's grandfather). After wiping the dust from his trousers, he casually threw his jacket over his shoulder, put a hand in his pocket, and began whistling a tune as he sauntered down the road. His timing was perfect. He reached the crossroads just as Maxine was turning down the lane to her family's farm.

"Miss Maxine," Obadiah drawled in as manly a voice a sixteen-year-old could muster at the time. "You sho looking good today, girl."

"Well, you ain't," Maxine quickly replied, quickening her pace at the same time.

"Is that so? Then why you trying to run away before you kiss me?"

"Ain't nothing wrong with running away from trouble. And you're trouble with a capital *T*."

"Ain't nothing about me for you to be scared of, Maxine. You not like those other girls."

"That's right, I'm not."

"I know you're not. You're special. That's why I'm gonna marry you."

Maxine's heart skipped a beat, but she acted nonchalant. "How many girls have you told that lie?"

"Aw, girl, why you got to act like that? I'm serious. I'm gonna be a big-time preacher, and you'll make a good preacher's wife."

"What makes you think I'll marry you?" Maxine asked, even as she worked hard to keep the smile off her face and out of her voice.

"Maxine, get on up to this house!" Maxine's mother's yell cut through the flirty atmosphere surrounding her and Obadiah.

"Yes, ma'am."

Maxine gave Obadiah a slight smile before turning to walk toward her mother's hard stare.

"I'ma marry you," Obadiah whispered confidently before walking in the opposite direction.

A little more than two years later, that's exactly what happened. A barely seventeen-year-old Maxine had stood before their Cherry Hill Baptist Church preacher and exchanged vows with almost twenty-year-old Stanley Obadiah Meshach Brook. He had already gained a reputation as "that boy preacher." Maxine's staunchly religious parents approved of the union.

Maxine approved of the union, too, but not of how one's marriage was consummated. Her mother's lesson regarding marital relations had been brief: "He's gonna want to put a baby in ya. It's your Christian duty to oblige." That was it. No further explanation of how this act was going to happen, no instruction for how to make it pleasurable or even that it should be. Maxine had grown up on a farm, so she'd seen animals mating. Still, even as she lay under Obadiah that first night, she could hardly fathom what Obadiah had done to her. Now she understood the late-night arguments she'd heard between her parents, and her mother's hissed whispers to "leave me alone."

No matter how hard Obadiah tried, Maxine never warmed to the act of making love. They never talked about it, such an act being something respectable people didn't mention. He tried romance, flowers, and candy, but that was about as far as he got. Obadiah wasn't an overly sensitive or romantic man himself. But knowing Maxine had been a virgin when they married, and therefore untrained in the art of love, he tried to be patient. After the birth of Esther, the Brooks' fourth child born a year after King, that's what Maxine started telling Obadiah to do—leave her alone.

Obadiah's patience grew thin. He had meaningless affairs following the births of each of his children. Maxine would use the child's birth as an excuse to beg off sex for months at a time, leaving a frustrated Obadiah no choice in his mind but to seek pleasure elsewhere. It was during one of these sexless stretches in his marriage that he'd met Dorothea, a hot, sexy woman whom he'd bedded the first night they met. He fell in love instantly and had loved her ever since.

For years, Obadiah bore the brunt of guilt for the actions he took to assuage his sexual appetite. But no more. The phone call he'd taken just before leaving the church office continued to weigh on him. Dorothea was right. It was as much Maxine's fault as his for the state of their marriage. And if she refused to do anything to change what was happening, then he was out the door.

Mama Max stopped knitting and looked toward the kitchen. *I thought I heard Obadiah pull in a long time ago.* She continued for another minute and then heard the door slam. "I thought I heard that garage door," she said aloud. She continued knitting, although in happier times, she would have risen from the couch and began heating the food. She'd been a dutiful wife while he recovered from his heart attack, but since he seemed no worse for the wear from the weeks she'd spent in Kansas, Mama Max figured he must have been able to turn on a burner himself just fine. So she stayed put.

As Mama Max listened to Obadiah bumping around in the kitchen, without coming to greet her, words from her earlier run-in with Dorothea flitted in and out of her mind. *At least I love him! No, I'll tell you what's a shame. It's a shame to have a wonderful man life Obadiah Brook in your house and sleep in another bedroom. . . .* Mama Max had prayed earlier in the day, after returning from the grocery store. She'd asked God what to do about the situation, and hadn't felt she'd heard an answer. But she didn't feel right just sitting here while Obadiah ate in the kitchen. So she lay down the sweater she was making and rose from the couch.

"You ain't one for greeting no more when you come home?" she said as she entered the kitchen and walked toward the stove. She immediately turned down the too-high fire from under the chicken and dumplings and stirred the pot's contents.

"I'm not the only one ain't greeting," Obadiah replied, reaching into a cupboard for a plate. "Didn't hear you say hello."

"Did you see Nettie at church?"

Obadiah sighed but did not answer. He walked to another cupboard, pulled out a glass, and filled it with sweet tea from a pitcher in the refrigerator.

"Look, if you are going to come in here eating my food, the least you can do is speak and thank me for dinner!"

Obadiah filled his glass, drank half, filled it again. He walked over to the pot under which Maxine had turned down the heat, determined the food was warm, turned off the burner, and fixed his plate. He then took his plate and glass to the table where Maxine now sat and joined her. He said a quick prayer, blew on his forkful of chicken and dumplings, and took a bite.

Maxine looked on in amazement. *Is this man really trying to ignore me? Is he actually going to sit at this table and not speak to me?* After the confrontation with Dorothea, Mama Max had thought to act civil to Obadiah. Not that she took seriously one word of what the tramp had said, but because it was the Christian thing to do. After all, walking around and barely speaking or just talking on the surface wasn't cute after forty-nine years together. That's why instead of taking the entire pot of chicken and dumplings over to Nettie's, she'd placed half in a container and took that, along with a dozen homemade rolls and one of the cobblers. Nettie had mentioned going by the church later, which is why she'd asked Obadiah if he'd seen her. Subconsciously, Mama Max had also been trying to confirm Obadiah's whereabouts. She had no reason to believe he was stepping out on her with Jenkins's wife, but Mama Max put nothing past Dorothea. Yes, she'd totally planned to be civil to Obadiah this evening, but now it was him showing his ass. "Why are you acting like you've got a hair up your butt?" she said with attitude.

"Because I'm tired of feeling like a step-somebody in my own home!" Obadiah said. "Tired of you acting all high and mighty, like you've never sinned, never come short of the glory. I've apologized for the stuff that was in this house, Max-ine. But there's more than one 'I'm sorry' that you could say too."

"Is this about Dorothea? Because I ran into *Miss Adulteress* today!"

"This is about you, Maxine, and about a conversation we need to have that is long overdue. And if we don't have it right here, right now, then come Monday, it'll be me filing a petition in family court."

54

Can We All Get Along

Princess stood in front of her closet trying to decide what to wear. She was also second-guessing her decision to let Kelvin bring his son over to her condo. He'd always had the ability to talk her into anything. But how much trouble could they get into with a three-year-old in the room? She'd figured not much, which is why she'd finally agreed to "lay your hands on him like those TV preachers do," as Kelvin had asked.

Twenty minutes later, she was dressed and waiting, in a pair of acid-wash jeans and a light yellow, oversized T-shirt that read JESUS on the front and IS MY BOO on the back. Her hair was in a simple ponytail, and she wore no makeup. She'd purposely underdressed to underscore the fact that this visit wasn't special. *I'm just ministering, that's all,* Princess reminded herself as she did a final check in the mirror. By the time the doorbell rang, she almost believed it.

Princess tried to still her racing heart as she walked to the front door. It had been almost three years since she'd seen Kelvin face-to-face. It didn't matter that she was no longer in love with him; he'd been her first love. She hummed a Tonex tune as she tried to bring on a casual mood. Looking in the peephole didn't help. She opened the door more befuddled than ever.

"Rafael!"

"Hey, baby girl!" Rafael grabbed a stunned Princess around the waist and twirled her in his arms. "I know, I make you speechless. I've been told I have that trait."

It took Princess a couple seconds to find her voice. "What are you doing here?"

"What does it look like? Moving in." Rafael kissed a still-stunned Princess on the cheek, then reached for his carry-on and moved past her into her living room. "I thought I was due for a weekend getaway. This is nice, girl. Look at you, coming up and thangs . . ." Rafael walked to the window and looked with appreciation at the ocean view.

"Boy, what are you doing here? You didn't mention anything about coming here when we talked last night. And no wonder I couldn't reach you this morning!"

"Well, I'm here now, and I'm hungry. You know they barely feed a brothah on a plane these days. So hook me up with something to eat and then tell me why you've been blowing up my phone."

Princess went into her kitchen and returned to the living room shortly afterward with a half dozen menus. "I have a private chef," she teased, knowing that Rafael was well aware of her lack of cooking skills. "What do you feel like—Mexican, Thai, Chinese, American . . ."

Rafael decided on the Mexican restaurant that Princess said was right down the street, and after placing the orders, Princess took Rafael on a brief tour of her one-bedroom apartment. During this time, they chatted about their families and Rafael's work at the mayor's office. They ended up in the living room, sitting on the couch.

"Watch your back, Rafael. Women don't like to take no for an answer," Princess said after Rafael had finished his latest insider tale of political hanky-panky. And then, "I still can't believe you're here!"

"But you are happy to see me, right?"

"I guess so . . ."

"You guess so? What do you mean *you guess so?*"

Princess sighed. "That's why I was calling you, to get your advice about something."

"About what?"

A knock on the door interrupted Princess's answer. "Hold that thought. That's our food."

Princess picked up the twenty-dollar bill Rafael had given her to cover the order, walked to the door, and opened it. The sight she saw immediately stole her appetite. Kelvin stood before her, six feet five inches of chocolate perfection, even with the crutch that was under his arm. He was finer than she remembered, decked out in a Sean John, smelling of Hugo Boss, the large diamond stud flashing from his left earlobe matching the sparkle emanating from his pearly whites. Princess's eyes traveled down to the child standing next to Kelvin. His son had the same coloring and lanky build as his father, but his facial features resembled Fawn. Princess felt an unexpected twinge of pain, and another one of guilt, as she silently eyed the boy who looked at Princess, then up at his father. When she continued to stare at him, Little Kelvin buried his head in his father's jeans.

"Hey, baby," Kelvin said softly. "You look good."

"You're early," was all Princess could say. Considering the myriad of thoughts that were vying for attention in her mind right now, it's a wonder any words came out at all.

"I couldn't wait another minute, baby. I had to see you. Actually," Kelvin continued with a sheepish, innocent grin that was incredibly sexy, "I've been down in the parking lot for twenty minutes. So now, at least, I'm just an hour early."

"Hurry up with my food, woman!" Rafael yelled from behind the door.

The smile on Kelvin's face scampered away, quickly replaced by a scowl and narrowed eyes. "Who's here?" he asked, taking a step forward.

"No, wait." Princess stayed Kelvin with a hand on his chest. She glanced back toward the living room and prayed that there would be no confrontation.

"Girl, what's the . . ." Rafael's words trailed off as he came up behind Princess and looked out the door. Instinctively, he placed a protective hand on her shoulder and pulled her back against him.

The air fairly crackled in that moment: Rafael and Kelvin glaring at each other, Princess looking from one to the other, Little Kelvin staring up at Princess. A mere second later, the energy shifted in an unlikely manner by an unlikely source— Little Kelvin. "Daddy, I gotta pee."

But the shift didn't last long. Kelvin's eyes kept boring into Rafael as he addressed Princess. "Baby, can you take him to the bathroom?"

"She's not your baby," Rafael responded, taking a step toward Kelvin.

"Oh, and she's yours?" Kelvin queried, taking a step forward as well. And then to Princess, "Baby, I need you to help me."

Princess eyed Kelvin and the crutch. "Come on, let me show you where the bathroom is."

Rafael was just getting ready to block Kelvin's entrance when the elevator dinged and the smell of Mexican food preceded the delivery boy down the hallway.

"Here, El," Princess said, shoving the twenty in Rafael's hand while retaining her position between him and Kelvin. "Can you pay him while I handle this?" Her eyes begged Rafael to chill out. He looked at her a long moment, cut his eyes at Kelvin again, and turned to pay for the food.

"He needs to bounce," Kelvin said as soon as he, Princess, and Little Kelvin had turned the corner. "What's happening here today is between us. We don't need an audience."

"Rafael is my friend and is welcome here." They reached

the bathroom. After turning on the light, Princess left the two Kelvins to handle their business.

"I knew I needed to get out here and save you from yourself," Rafael said under his breath, as soon as Princess entered the living room. "Thought you told me homeboy was going to get prayer over the phone. I thought that's what we decided was best."

"That's what I was getting ready to tell you," Princess responded, keeping her voice low as well. "Kelvin wants me to lay hands on his son, and I agreed."

Rafael snorted. "Please don't tell me you fell for that bullshit. Where Kelvin wants you to put your hands has nothing to do with his son."

"Please don't start nothing, Rafael," Princess pleaded. "I'm going to tell Kelvin the same thing. This is my house and I'm not having it. So if y'all can't act civilized, y'all can get to steppin'."

Princess heard the toilet flush, and soon afterward, Kelvin and Little Kelvin walked back into the combined living/dining room. The little boy immediately eyed the unopened food bags on the dining room table. "I'm hungry, Daddy."

"We'll get you something in a minute, Little Man."

"He can have some of this food," Princess said. "But that's only if you two think you can chill out the madness and act like men with sense. I'm not having any drama in my house, all right? Now, Kelvin, this is Rafael. Rafael, Kelvin. Do you think we can all get along here, or will I be throwing both you nuckas out?"

55

My Boo

Princess looked from Kelvin to Rafael. "Well?"

Rafael spoke first. "I'm cool," he said, walking over and pointedly taking a seat on the couch, where he assumed Princess would sit. The only other seating in the living room was an oversized stuffed chair.

Kelvin turned to Princess. "I didn't come here to have it out with anyone. I came here for my son. *And for you.* No offense to your boy here, but, Princess, can I speak with you privately for a minute?"

"Daddy, can I have some food?" Little Kelvin piped up again.

Princess had forgotten about the Mexican food quickly growing cold on the dining room table. "Let me fix him something to eat. Rafael, you want me to fix your plate?"

"No, I've lost my appetite," Rafael said pointedly, but without looking at Kelvin.

Princess fixed Rafael with a stare before kneeling in front of Little Kelvin. "Do you like tacos?"

Little Kelvin nodded.

Instead of responding to Rafael's taunt, Kelvin followed Princess into the kitchen, where she placed a taco and some rice onto a plate before putting it in the microwave. When she turned, Kelvin was right behind her. Her breasts brushed his chest, and her body immediately reacted. She backed up against the counter and refused to meet his heated gaze.

"Princess, I don't want any trouble," Kelvin said, his voice low. "But I want this moment to be between you, me, and Little Kelvin. Maybe I shouldn't have asked you. My dad has prayed for him, and my grandmother has him on her church's prayer list. I just know how special you are, and I felt your personal vibe would be good for him. I can understand it if dude comes first, but I didn't bum-rush you, Princess. You invited me over. This is a private matter, and your boy's a stranger to my son. I don't want him here."

"But this is my house," Princess replied as she removed the food from the microwave. She reached for a soda in the refrigerator and poured half of it into a plastic cup.

"Maybe you'd better make that to go," Kelvin said finally. "I thought ministry came first with you, but I guess I got that twisted. On second thought . . . c'mon, Little Man. I'll get you something at McDonald's. You want a Happy Meal?"

"I want taco!"

"I'll get us some tacos, then." Kelvin picked up Little Kelvin and started for the door.

"Kelvin, wait."

Kelvin stopped and turned around.

"I'll pray for him, just wait a minute." Princess took a deep breath and walked over to Rafael, who'd turned on the television and was watching ESPN. "Rafael, I want to pray for Kelvin's son, and Kelvin would be more comfortable if you weren't here for that."

"Of course he would."

"Please." Princess placed a hand on Rafael's arm. "Just for twenty, thirty minutes. There's a crosswalk to the beach just a half a block down. I'll call you as soon as he leaves. I'll be okay," she whispered. "Please, do this for me."

Without another word Rafael rose from the couch, crossed the room, opened the door, and left. The ensuing silence was deafening. Princess stared at the closed door for a moment before walking back into the kitchen, retrieving the plate and cup of soda, and setting the items on the dining room table. "Here, Kelvin," she said softly to the child.

Kelvin remained quiet as he picked up his son and placed him in the dining room chair. He saw a spool of paper towels on the counter, reached for one, and tucked it into his son's shirt. He watched Little Kelvin pick up the taco and take a large bite. "Good?" he asked. His son nodded.

Finally, Kelvin looked at Princess. His eyes drank her in, from the perfection of her makeup-free face to the newly done manicure on the toes he used to love to suck. He only had to imagine how those jeans were fitting her nicely rounded bottom underneath the big T-shirt—a shirt Kelvin was sure she'd worn to hide herself. *But you can't hide that body from my memory, baby. And you can't hide your desire either.*

"Do you want something to eat?" Princess asked, walking over to the sack on the table still filled with guacamole, refried beans, and meat-filled quesadillas.

"Yes."

Kelvin's soft answer whipped around Princess's body like a gentle breeze. It heated her as much as his hands on her body ever could. *Help me, Jesus.* She stiffened her back and turned around. "You know what I meant, Kelvin."

A hint of a smile played across Kelvin's face. "Did you ever love me at all, Princess Brook?"

"What kind of question is that?"

"It's the kind of question that's asked when a man who hasn't seen a friend for three years comes over and doesn't even get a hug."

"Let's not play games, Kelvin. You didn't come over here for a hug. You came over here for prayer. Let's stay on course with the reason for this visit, and I think everything will be okay."

"Just one?" Kelvin pressed. Instead of advancing toward her, he leaned against the refrigerator.

"That might be one too many," Princess honestly replied. She walked over to the table and noted that Little Kelvin was almost done with his taco. "You're almost finished, Little Kelvin. Good job! You want some more soda?" She hoped to divert the dangerous direction in which the conversation was headed.

Kelvin's heart clinched as he watched Princess interact with his son. He imagined what it would have been like if they'd had a child together, instead of him and Fawn. Chances are, he thought, he and Princess would be married by now. He'd been so quick to suggest Princess have an abortion when he found out she was pregnant. He'd never imagined himself with a child, especially at such a young age. But Little Kelvin was his heart and had added immensely to his life. If he'd known then what he knew now, he never would have put Princess through the pain he now knew his impulsive suggestion cost her. The reality of Princess's pain became real to Kelvin in that moment. *I hurt her badly.* Now all he wanted to do was make everything better, to make her better. That became his singular goal.

Kelvin moved toward her without thought, reached for her waist, and enveloped her in his arms. Princess did not fight him. Instead, she welcomed what until this moment she'd refused to acknowledge she'd missed. He hugged her tightly, and then, walking them to the portion of counter space that was not visible from the dining room and Little Kelvin's prying eyes, he kissed her.

Princess's body reacted before her mind could form an appropriate defense. Her arms reached around and rubbed Kelvin's strong, lean back. Kelvin's hard tongue pressed against her closed lips, demanding more. She opened her mouth, and he quickly plunged inside, lapping her essence like nectar, their tongues dueling, engaging, remembering.

Leaning his weight on his right leg to protect the one that had been broken, Kelvin lifted Princess onto the kitchen counter and continued his assault. He placed himself between her legs, pulled her forward, allowing her to feel his rapidly hardening heat. He reached for the band that held her ponytail, pulled it out, and buried his hand in her hair. He pressed them closer together and reveled in the feel of her hardened nipples against his chest. This was his Princess, hot and hungry, just as he remembered.

"Baby, I've missed this. I've missed you," he whispered into her mouth.

He felt so good; this felt so good. Princess's body was on fire, her private paradise begging for a visitor, the one it so intimately remembered. Princess deepened the kiss, totally caught up in the moment. Somewhere in the far reaches of her mind, she heard a warning, felt that something was wrong, out of order. A part of her could only focus on what felt right—this, being in Kelvin's arms. But the other part persisted, even as Kelvin reached beneath her long T-shirt and fumbled with the snap at the top of her jeans.

Her top. *My top.* Her JESUS IS MY BOO T-shirt. That was the reminder that Princess needed. Jesus, not Kelvin, was her boo, her man. Princess broke the kiss and fought against every ounce of flesh that was screaming to let Kelvin unzip her pants, begging to be touched, fondled, stroked, licked.

"No!" Princess hissed between clenched teeth. At the same time, she pushed Kelvin away and jumped off the counter.

"Daddy, can I have some more?" Little Kelvin asked, totally oblivious to the tsunami of passion swirling around him.

"Yes!" Princess answered, glad for the diversion. She swept a shaking hand through her disheveled hair and walked on equally shaky legs over to the table. "Do you want some beans? Or another taco?"

"Taco!"

Without daring to look at Kelvin, Princess scraped the uneaten rice off the plate, placed another taco on it, and put it into the microwave. Kelvin brushed past her and walked to the bathroom to handle what was now a very inconvenient hard-on.

When Kelvin came back into the dining room, he saw that Princess had found her hair band, swept her unruly locks back into a ponytail, and was sitting at the table watching Little Kelvin eat. "I'm sorry," he said as soon as he sat down.

"As soon as he's finished, we'll pray," Princess responded. "I'll be right back."

"Princess!" Kelvin grabbed his crutch and rose to follow her.

"No, Kelvin, stay in here. I've got to . . . I'm going to fix my hair and get myself ready to pray." Princess rushed into her bedroom, closed her door, and leaned back against it. "Forgive me, Jesus," she whispered, even as tears threatened. Just as she was about to give in to a full-fledged boohoo, her cell phone rang.

"It's been fifteen minutes. He still there?"

"Yes, Rafael."

"Why's he still there? How long does it take to pray?"

"Little Kelvin was hungry and—"

"How long does it take for a child to eat? What's really going on, Princess?"

"Nothing."

"I'm coming back."

"No!"

"Why not? What are you hiding?"

"Nothing, Rafael, and stop acting like you're my daddy or my older brother. I already got both of those, and their names are King and Michael!"

"All right, calm down. See, that fool's got you trippin', Princess."

"You're the one trippin' right now!"

"Don't do nothing crazy, girl. I'm going to give y'all ten

more minutes and then I'm coming back. And I'll beat the door down if I have to. So you better pray quick."

Rafael had no sooner hung up in her face than Princess heard a knock at the door. "Baby, you all right?"

These men are 'bout to drive me crazy! What was I thinking to have Kelvin over? And what the hell was Rafael thinking to fly out here unannounced? "I'll be out in a minute," Princess managed. Without further ado, Princess kneeled by her bed.

"Father God, I need You. I thought I was doing the right thing, but I'm in trouble. I'm not over Kelvin, and I'm feeling really weak right now. I need You to help me, Jesus, because I want to do the right thing and pray for his son. So please help me."

56

Almost as Beautiful

Princess finished praying, walked into the bathroom, and washed her face with cold water. She ran a brush through her hair and tidied up her ponytail. Then she took a deep breath and rejoined Kelvin and his son in the dining room.

"Rafael will be back shortly," she said as she walked into the room. "So let's pray."

"Is that your boy now?" Kelvin inquired. "Because, baby, I'm telling you, we've got some unfinished business right here."

"That shouldn't have happened, Kelvin," Princess replied. "Please forgive me for the weakness of my flesh. Are you done, Little Kelvin?" she continued, her voice softer as she walked over to the child. "Do you mind if I pray for you? Kelvin, why don't you go clean his hands?" Without waiting for an answer, Princess, back in relative control, walked into her living room and over to the stereo. Soon, the sounds of Yadah, a Stellar Award–winning, Destiny's Child–sounding gospel group, filled the air. It was a worship song, a remake of an old classic. Princess walked over to the window and looked out at the ocean before closing her eyes and getting lost in the words:

I surrender all, I surrender all. All to thee my Blessed Savior, I surrender all.

Kelvin walked back into the room and watched as Princess

swayed back and forth, her arms uplifted. The way she held her arms caused the T-shirt to caress her butt, the one he remembered palming with both his hands. She turned slightly, and he noted the single tear running down her cheek. He started toward her, but something stopped him. Even Little Kelvin was silent, as father and son watched Princess and listened to the melodious voices in perfect harmony. As the music died, Princess turned around. Kelvin detected a change; her whole demeanor was different and her face glowed. "Why don't you sit in that chair, Kelvin, with Little Kelvin on your lap?"

Kelvin did as she'd instructed. Once they were seated, Princess walked over, knelt in front of them, and lightly placed her hand on Little Kelvin's leg. For a moment, all was silent, and then Princess began praying for Little Kelvin's healing, for Jehovah Rapha, the God who heals, to wrap His arms of mercy and arms of love around this child.

Kelvin watched, spellbound, as Princess implored the God of heaven and earth to guide and protect his son. He had no doubt that Fawn loved Little Kelvin, but he'd never seen such passion, such fervor, shown for his seed. Kelvin raised up a hand to stroke Princess's hair, but again, something stayed him. He was afraid to touch her, afraid that he would shatter the spell of the moment and lose this closeness, this rightness, he felt right now.

"In Jesus's holy name we pray. Amen." Princess opened her eyes to see Little Kelvin's eyes closed in sleep and his father's eyes boring into her. They eyed each other for a long moment, before Princess rose from her kneeling position. "That's it," she said, a bit of discomfort returning. She'd prayed for God to help her not give in to Kelvin, and she believed God answered her prayer. But now, more than ever, she hoped for Rafael to knock on the door.

"That was beautiful, babe," Kelvin said softly, earnestly.

"It's the least I can do," Princess said with a laugh, trying to break the intimacy of the moment. "Ooh, I'm hungry," she continued, simply for something to say, something to do. "I'm going to warm up the rest of this food. You want some?" Remembering where that question had led the last time it was asked, Princess reframed it. "I mean, there's enough in here for two," she finished from the kitchen, where she was placing the quesadilla, rice, and refried beans into the microwave.

Kelvin lay his son down on the couch and then joined Princess in the kitchen. "Thanks again for praying for Little Man."

"You're welcome." Princess reached into the refrigerator. "Want some soda? I've got a grape and an orange left."

Can't you feel me, baby? All I want is you, is what Kelvin thought. "No, thank you," is what he said.

Despite the silence, Princess could feel Kelvin reaching for her, wanting her. Theirs had been a powerful connection from the beginning. That Princess still felt this connection keenly was more than a little disconcerting.

"I want to spend time with you, Princess."

"Look, Kelvin, I don't think—"

"I wish he was yours."

Princess stopped, set the soda can down on the counter.

"Little Kelvin, he was supposed to be our child, yours and mine. I'm sorry I asked you to get rid of our baby, Princess. We should be doing the family thing right about now. Can you forgive me, baby? I know I hurt you, caused you a lot of pain, but can we get past that? I need somebody real in my life, somebody who's around me for me, not for the status or my paycheck. I need you, Princess."

Princess tried not to be moved, but Kelvin's words touched her deeply. They'd never talked about what happened, about the abortion. They'd both come back from Germany—where the procedure had been performed after spending the Christmas holiday with Kelvin's family—and acted as if it never happened. Now, Princess realized she wanted to talk to him about it, needed to discuss it. "Kelvin, I—"

The sound of heavy knocking on the front door interrupted her. "That's Rafael," Princess said, her nervousness causing her to state the obvious. "I need to let him in." But she didn't move. She and Kelvin stared at each other, unsaid words creating a barrier between them and weaving a web that ensnared them at the same time. Rafael knocked again, even harder. "I'm coming!" Princess yelled, and hurried to the door.

"Shh! You're going to wake up the baby," she hissed as she opened the door.

Rafael looked over at the sleeping toddler. "My bad," he said, taking in the worried expression that Princess was trying so desperately to hide. But it didn't work on Rafael. He'd known Princess since they both were seven years old. "You okay?"

Princess nodded.

Kelvin came around the corner. He and Rafael eyed each other, but the earlier tension was not there. "So . . . I guess I'll be leaving, then." When Princess didn't answer, Kelvin walked over to the couch, picked up his still-sleeping son, and proceeded to the door.

"You need me to help you to the car?"

"No, I'll be fine." Kelvin leaned against the wall to reposition the crutch and adjust Little Kelvin in his arms.

"I'll keep praying for both of you," Princess said, helping him place Little Kelvin's head on his shoulder.

"I appreciate that," Kelvin said.

"You've got a beautiful child, Kelvin," Princess whispered as Kelvin passed her.

Kelvin leaned down and whispered something into Princess's ear. *I love you,* he mouthed. And was gone.

Princess watched Kelvin's long strides eat up the space between her door and the elevator. She breathed deeply once, and again, trying to get herself together before walking back into the room. She knew Rafael would have a thousand questions for her to answer, but right now she simply wanted to be alone.

"What happened?" Rafael asked as soon as she turned around.

Princess leaned against the door. "I prayed for Little Kelvin. And now I'm really tired. We'll catch up, I promise, but right now, I'm going to take a nap. Make yourself at home."

Princess didn't wait for an answer but instead walked into the bathroom, took off her clothes, and stepped into the shower. There, under the steady spray of water, she let the tears fall—tears of longing, regret, sadness, joy, confusion. She reached for her sponge and thought about Kelvin's answer when she'd said he had a beautiful child.

He's almost as beautiful as the one I'm gonna have with you. . . .

57

Raw and Nasty

Things were better than before. Change hadn't occurred by leaps and bounds, but improvement was visible. It had been a little more than two months since Passion and Stan began visiting Doctor Banner, and in that time, she and Stan had grown closer. He still didn't talk much about the molestation by his uncle, but he'd opened up more about his strict, conservative upbringing. Passion still had her suspicions about Bryce Covington, but because she and Stan were making love almost once a week, she'd decided to leave well enough alone.

Passion's mind whirled with thoughts as she stepped out of the master suite shower and toweled herself dry. Today was a first: The Lees and the Chapmans were going to celebrate the Fourth of July as one big happy family. If someone had told Passion a year ago, even six months ago, that she'd be breaking barbeque with Carla Chapman, Passion would have asked what they were smoking.

But time, and Stan's challenges, had indeed brought about a change. Carla and Passion had talked more since their heartfelt conversation regarding Stan back in April. They hadn't discussed him anymore, at least not directly. Passion had told Carla that they were back in therapy and that Stan was determined to make his marriage work. And where once a hasty greeting was all that was exchanged before Passion passed the phone on to Stan, now the two women discussed topics held in common: kids, church, the latest diet. Even more surprising than Carla and Passion becoming friendlier was the fact that this Lee/Chapman gathering had been Stan's idea, prompted by a casual comment his son Winston made one evening after fighting with his brother, Shay.

"You two are family, and you're going to get along!" Stan had said after his ten-year-old son, Shay, announced he no longer wanted to let seven-year-old Winston play with his Wii game.

"I don't care that he's family. I still don't like him!"

"You heard what I said," Stan continued. "You will let your brother play with that game, and you will stay in there and play together!"

"Why? You and Mama don't! Y'all barely talk to each other and y'all are family too!"

Stan had made the boys put the game up and sent them to their rooms, but what Shay said lingered in his mind. Later he'd talked about it with Passion. "I'm not setting a very good example," he'd concluded. "I need to do better." A week later, while coordinating calendars, Stan had broached the subject with Carla, who readily agreed.

"Mama! Mama! Grandma and Grandpa are here!" Passion's daughter, Onyx, ran up the steps and pounded on the bathroom door in the master suite. "Mama!"

"Onyx, I hear you! And so do half the neighbors. Now, go back down there and see if they want something to drink. Can you be a big girl and do that?"

Armed with a challenge, Onyx didn't even answer her mother before storming back down the stairs. Several minutes later, Passion followed. She was dressed for the eighty-degree weather in a loose, mint-green sundress with a flowered bodice and dark green piping around the neck and arms. Knowing any intricate style would be sweated out by noon, Passion had curled her hair and secured it with bobby pins on the top of her head. A few loose tendrils had escaped and even now stuck to the light layer of moisture on her neck and forehead. If anyone had asked her, she would have lied, but she'd taken special pains with her appearance. She no longer had the hots for Lavon Chapman . . . well, not much anyway. But she still wanted to remind him of what he'd passed up. Passion walked into the living room, greeted her parents, and then whisked her mother into the kitchen to help with the fruit salad while Stan and her father took their places at the patio grill.

A half hour later, happy chaos at the Lee home was in full effect. Carla and Lavon had arrived, along with Carla and Stan's three children, Brianna, Shay, and Winston; Lavon's eighteen-year-old daughter, Felicia; and Felicia's best friend from Minneapolis, where Felicia and her mother lived. Several neighborhood children joined the kids in the pool, supervised by Felicia and Carla's mom, who was also in town visiting. A few church members rounded out the party. There was enough food to feed half of LA.

"Where do you want me to put this food?" Carla asked as she and Lavon walked into the kitchen with a large pan of baked beans, homemade coleslaw, and one of Carla's famous berry cobblers.

"Just set it anywhere," Passion replied. She quickly noted Carla's playful, sexy outfit—bright red capris with a multicolored halter top. The bottom of the top flared out, hiding bulges and rolls, while the slim-legged pants emphasized Carla's wide hips and shapely calves. Her hair was straight, with newly created bangs adding a devil-may-care look to her face. *I almost look matronly next to her,* Passion mused. But Passion knew Stan would have been uncomfortable if the "woman of God" he married ever dared to bare her back.

"Hey, Lavon," she added after greeting Carla with a light hug.

"Hey, yourself," Lavon replied. After helping Carla carry in the dishes, Lavon joined the men outside. The afternoon was filled with great food, good conversation, and games of miniature golf on the Lees' massive back lawn. No matter how they tried otherwise, the ladies inevitably ended up in the kitchen, chatting around the island about kids, church, and the day's headlines.

"But did the mother really sleep with her daughter's boyfriend after they got caught smoking crack?"

"That's what I read in the *National Enquirer*!"

"I see it's time for my baby to come out from among all this gossiping," Lavon said playfully, coming up and hugging Carla from behind. "Come on, baby," he said, nudging her ear. "I've got something to show you."

Carla swatted Lavon's hand away from her backside. "Stop acting out in front of these mothers," she scolded. "We were just in here talking about folks fooling around."

"But that's what married people are supposed to do." Lavon winked at the two older women while placing a firm hand around Carla's waist and leading her out of the kitchen.

As the couple turned the corner, Passion saw Lavon's hand slide down to Carla's backside before she let out a squeal. Passion couldn't help it. A few seconds later, she excused herself from the kitchen with the pretense of checking on the children. She walked outside to the backyard and looked around. The men had stopped playing golf and were now gathered under a shade tree, talking and laughing. Stan was a few feet away from them, on the phone. *Probably a church member sick from too much greasy barbeque.* Some of the kids had abandoned the pool for video games while Lavon's daughter and her friend conversed as they floated on pool chairs. There was no Lavon or Carla in sight.

Passion stepped back into the house just in time to see the guest bathroom door open. Out walked Carla with a wide grin on her face. Directly behind her was Lavon, his arms still around Carla while nuzzling her neck.

He's an animal, probably never gets enough, Passion thought. A surge of jealousy went through her, even as she pasted a smile on her face that she hoped didn't look as fake as it felt. "Hey, you lovebirds," she called out, and kept walking down the hall and up the stairs. Once in her master suite, she closed the door and walked slowly to the full-length mirror in the corner of the room. She turned this way and that, noting how the folds on her back were evident in the cut of her sundress and how her butt didn't look as big and juicy as Carla's. Still, she had a voluptuous pair of "sistahs," a nice head of hair, and a pretty face, just like Carla did. They were both pretty in their own way, Passion decided. *So what was it about Carla that made Lavon choose her over me?*

Passion walked over to the sitting area, sat down, and gazed out the window. Onyx and Winston were riding bikes now, while Shay and one of his friends bobbed their heads to some beat on their headsets. Passion knew she had a lot to be thankful for. Stan was a good man and was trying to be an even better one. Their lovemaking was steady, yet uneventful, and Stan was not yet ready to try some of the things that Passion had suggested. When she'd mentioned a tutorial lovemaking video for adults, Stan acted as if she'd asked him to star in a porn movie. She tried to tell him what felt good and how to please her, but Stan was still too hesitant and closed to sex being pleasurable to listen. Still, he was trying. She had to give him that. But would she ever have with Stan what she knew Carla had with Lavon? Would there ever be passion, raw and nasty, sweaty and breathtaking, in the Lee bedroom?

58

And Then It Happened

Stan sat in his car and looked at the lobby, wondering for the umpteenth time if he could handle this meeting. The call from Bryce's friend Ryan had been a surprise. He'd answered it because it came through on a 310 number, a common Los Angeles area code. The conversation was brief, succinct, and when it was over, Stan knew there was no choice but to see his old lover at least one more time.

Stan and Bryce hadn't talked or seen each other for almost three months, since Stan had resigned from the Cathedral's executive board. And while Stan had refused to take Bryce's calls, he'd thought about him every single day. Every day was a struggle, to stay on the side of right and deny his flesh. Every day was a new, inner war waged with himself, to not go after what his very soul seemed to cry out for—Bryce Covington.

Stan's cell phone rang. He checked the ID even though he knew who it was. "I'm here."

A sigh on the other end of the line. "I'm glad."

Silence. "I shouldn't have come."

"I never would have called you. I promised I wouldn't."

"If it weren't for the news about your mother . . ."

Frances Covington had been Stan's stand-in mother during his years at Howard. He'd spent endless nights at her dining room table, eating food that reminded him of his own home. Even after ending communication with Bryce in the eighties, Stan had maintained contact with Frances for years. She was one of the kindest, gentlest, most compassionate people he'd ever known. Her death had shocked friends and family alike. It was only afterward that they'd learned she'd been silently suffering from heart failure for six months. She'd kept the news from everyone, even her husband.

"Ryan knew I needed you," Bryce whispered, his voice breaking. "He's tried, but he didn't know her. You knew Mama, loved her and . . ."

Hearing Bryce choke up yet again, Stan ended the call and reached for the car handle at the same time. Within minutes, he was outside the door to Bryce's suite. The door was ajar. Stan pushed it open and stepped inside.

Bryce was just on the other side. As soon as the door closed, Bryce stepped into Stan's arms. He cried silently, while Stan held him in a firm grip. "It's all right, man," Stan whispered, his own voice choking up. "She was a one-of-a-kind mother. It's all right to cry."

After several moments, Bryce stepped away from Stan. "It's good to see you," he said, the merest of smiles crossing his face.

Stan nodded. He saw a Kleenex holder on the other side of the room and went to retrieve one for Bryce. Bryce took it, wiped his eyes, and blew his nose as he walked over to the bar. "The usual?" Bryce asked.

"Club soda."

Bryce fixed the drinks and joined Stan on the couch.

"To Frances Covington," Stan said as he held up his glass. "One of the best mamas on the planet."

They clinked glasses. Bryce drained his brandy and immediately rose to fix another.

Stan followed him. "I know you're hurting, my brother, but do you think alcohol is the way to handle your grief?"

"I'm cool," Bryce said, dropping a large helping of ice into the tumbler before filling it with dark brown liquid. "This is only my second drink of the night. I knew you'd scold me, so I held off until you came."

"How long have you been in LA?"

"Just a couple days."

And you didn't call. Stan knew that that was a good thing, even though it didn't feel like it.

"Ryan and I spent the holiday here, on a friend's yacht. We were supposed to have left this morning for London. But then I got the call. My plane leaves in a couple hours. But . . . I'm glad I could see you first."

The two men returned to the couch and spent the next thirty minutes talking about Frances Covington. They laughed and cried over shared memories, especially those that involved diverting Bryce's mother's well-placed suspicions that he and Stan were "too close as friends."

"Remember that time she came downstairs and we were dancing to—"

" 'Time Will Reveal!' " they both said together. Bryce sang the lyrics to the timeless DeBarge classic as he stood and reached for Stan. "C'mon, man," he said softly. Sing it with me. 'More precious than silver . . .' "

"Naw, man," Stan said, smiling. "That's not me anymore."

"Wait a minute, check this out." Bryce walked over to an iPod set in its stereo base. He punched a few buttons. Suddenly the sounds of the '80s R&B group DeBarge wafted into the room. "C'mon, man, one time. For my moms."

Against his better judgment, Stan rose from the couch and stood awkwardly as Bryce danced over to him. Bryce immediately wrapped his arms around Stan's waist, while Stan's hand instinctively went around Bryce's shoulders. For a moment, they just stood there—Stan, unbelieving that an embrace could feel so good, and Bryce, reveling in a moment he thought would never come again. They both began moving, at the same time, as El DeBarge sang their story, talked about special love, and how in time all would be revealed. For the first time in twenty-five years, Stan let down his guard and allowed himself to simply feel. Emotions that had been buried, crushed beneath Scriptures and societal pressure, taboo and guilt, came seeping through his pores and into the moment. He and Bryce remained quiet, listening to the music, soaking up the words of the entire song. Bryce must have known what impact it would have, because he'd put the song on repeat. They continued dancing while it played again.

"You never opened it, did you?" Bryce finally whispered.

"What?" Stan was so full of emotion he could barely talk.

"The package I sent."

"I read the letter but didn't look at the contents inside."

"This song was in there," Bryce said. "I'd made a CD of all our favorite songs from back in the day, remember? 'Let It Whip,' 'Sexual Healing,' 'Love Come Down,' anything by the Gap Band?"

"I haven't heard those songs in years," Stan admitted. Since the time he was twenty-three, he'd listened mostly to gospel music, with an occasional classical or jazz piece thrown in. Gospel music kept him on course, kept his mind stayed on Jesus. Stan was already feeling what could happen when one listened to "memory lane" music.

Bryce broke their embrace once more and walked over to the iPod. He turned off the repeat feature, and soon, Smokey Robinson was talking about being with you. While songs from the eighties provided the backdrop, Stan and Bryce continued to talk, and dance, and talk some more. By the time Diana and Lionel started singing about an endless love, Stan was enjoying himself more than he had in years. And when Bryce reached over and kissed him on the cheek, and then on the lips, he didn't stop him.

Buoyed by not being rejected, Bryce moved over and deepened the kiss. He rubbed Stan's smooth, bald head, the head he'd longed to touch in just this way since laying his eyes upon it in a Detroit boardroom. He reached for Stan's belt buckle, hurriedly undid it, and then placed his hand on the long, thick tool that he remembered. He moaned into Stan's mouth and deepened the kiss even more.

While Mtume talked about "Juicy Fruit," Bryce pushed Stan back on the couch and pulled Stan's penis out of his pants. Stan knew he should stop him, knew he couldn't do this, but he felt totally incapable of stopping what was going on. Instead he lay passive, his eyes tightly closed, his breath coming in short, uneven gasps as he anticipated what was to come.

And then it happened—Bryce's mouth on Stan's manhood—the first time such an act had occurred with Stanley Morris Lee in a quarter of a century. He'd refused to let his wives go down on him, convinced it would unleash what defrocked minister Ted Haggard referred to as "homosexual tendencies." He'd denied himself oral sex, yet here he was, being pleasured by a man. And not just any man, but the only person he'd ever loved so deeply. Bryce took his time, lavishing decades of love upon his one and only. Bryce remembered certain things that Stan liked and did them all. When Stan climaxed, it was intense. A loud hiss escaped from his mouth, even as he reached for Bryce and grabbed him in a bear hug, almost crushing him in its force. Little spasms of aftershocks continued to shake him. He struggled to regain his breath.

When he did, Stan said only one thing: "I have to go."

59

A Heartfelt Request

Passion pounced as soon as the bedroom door opened. "Where have you been?"

Stan walked over to Passion and hugged her tighter than he'd ever hugged her before. "I've been with Bryce. We need to talk."

Later, Passion would swear that her world stopped spinning in that moment. *Bryce? You said you were going to pick up something at the church. And that was three hours ago!* "I called you," she said simply.

"I turned off my phone," was Stan's honest reply.

"Why?"

"Passion, we need to talk."

And that's what they did, for the next two hours. Stan told Passion everything: details about the repeated rape by his uncle, about being with Bryce from the time he was nineteen until just before his twenty-fourth birthday, his secret homosexual longings, and, most importantly, what had happened just hours before. When he finished, he was cried out, drained, yet strangely relieved. He never could have done it without the conversation with God he'd had on the way home.

★ ★ ★

"Father!" Stan uttered passionately as soon as he got into his car. "Forgive me! I'm so sorry. I was so wrong!"

You were forgiven before the earth was made. . . .

"I've sinned again!" Stan continued, crying openly now. "But I tried so hard, God! So hard to obey your word and do Your will. It's been twenty-five years, Lord! Please don't hold this night, this moment of weakness, against the work that I've done!" Stan beat his hands against the steering wheel, his cries turning into heaving sobs. For the first time, he cried for the loss of his childhood, for the uncle turned monster whom he once loved, for the fact that he loved men more than women, and for the decades he'd remained sexless to deny his true longings. "Forgive me!"

All is forgiven, said a voice filled with love.

"I am a sinner, a wretch undone!"

You are my beloved son, in whom I'm well pleased.

"I can't undo what I've just done. There's no way I can pay the cost for these transgressions!" Stan, in a very uncharacteristic way, was hollering almost at the top of his lungs.

My son, the cost was paid by Christ at Calvary. You are mine.

"I am an abomination to the throne of Grace."

You are my child, made in my image, and after my likeness. And no man can pluck you out of my hand.

Stan's tears had dried shortly after hearing this, enough for him to put the car in gear and drive home. Once he arrived there, it was clear what he had to do. He had to get real with himself and stop hiding from the truth of who he was. Until he did that, he couldn't take control of who he chose to be. To do that, he'd have to come clean with Passion, the woman whom God had sent as his helpmate. That's why, after walking through the door, he hadn't been able to talk fast enough.

"Can I hug you?" Passion asked tentatively after Stan had drained his soul. He nodded, and Passion enveloped him in her arms. "I love you, Stanley Morris Lee. And I will be here for you until death do we part. Believe that."

Stan basked in the love of his wife, his partner. Yes, it felt different than Bryce's embrace, but it also felt like the embrace he desired, the life he wanted to lead. He wrapped his arms around her and pulled her tighter, finding her mouth and plundering it with his tongue. He showed more ardor in the next few moments than he'd shown in the past three years. Passion's desire flared like the firecrackers they'd heard earlier as she returned her husband's kiss, their tongues dueling, their hands searching.

"I want to please you," Stan breathed, surprised that after climaxing with Bryce that he was ready to love again.

"And I want to please you," Passion replied.

Stan stopped suddenly, so quickly that Passion had to catch her breath. *Oh, no, is he having second thoughts? Is he thinking this is wrong? Please, God, he's never acted like this before. Please don't let it end this way!* "What's wrong, Stan?" Passion asked. "Is it something I did, a way that I touched you?"

"No, nothing like that," Stan replied, staring into her eyes. He was silent, and stared at her for so long that Passion began to worry if he'd lost a part of his sanity. When he spoke again, she wondered if she'd lost a part of hers. Because he said words she never thought she'd hear in this marriage.

"Passion, I want you to go down on me."

Passion was taken aback. "Youwantmeto what?" The sentence came out sounding like two words instead of five.

"Never mind, you're a godly woman and—"

"No, Stanley! I mean, yes, I am godly but I like, I mean, I don't think that . . . Well, what I'm trying to say is, I would be glad to help you out with . . . whatever you need."

Stanley took a breath and began again. "I want to have oral sex. Can you do that?"

Could she do that? If it wasn't for the fact that it would

ruin the moment, Passion would have broken into a rendition of Handel's "Hallelujah" in the key of G! Instead, her response was quiet, almost demure. "I can do that for you, Stanley," she replied honestly. They undressed, and Passion proceeded to show him just how well she could handle his heartfelt request.

60

Something Else

Princess lay in her old bed, still reeling from the events of the past twenty-four hours. To say what had happened surprised her would be an understatement. Princess turned on her back, stared at the ceiling, and tried to figure out how a casual trip home for the Fourth of July had turned into . . . something else.

The beginning was normal enough. Little sis, Tee, showed off her driving skills by picking Princess up at the airport. They'd made a side trip into Kansas City for a slab of Gates Barbecue before continuing on to Overland Park. When Princess arrived home, Michael, Timothy, and her parents were all there to greet her. "It's going to be a small gathering this year," Tai had told her as they sat in the dining room sharing the slab of spicy ribs. "Mama Max and Daddy O decided to stay in Texas, and your other grandparents are spending the holiday in Ohio with your aunt Rita." Rita was Tai's sister. "So it's just going to be our family, Rafael's parents, and a few others from the church. Oh, and I invited Sandy. Remember her?" Princess shook her head. "She and I used to work together, years ago."

"Oh, the White woman with the red hair."

"Yep, that's her. She just got remarried and wants me to meet the new mister. Oh, and Jan's coming over."

"How's our neighbor doing?" Princess asked as she licked sauce off her finger and polished off a whole fry.

"Busy as ever. I keep telling her to slow down before she has a heart attack."

The next day, company had begun arriving around noon, and by two o'clock, the Fourth of July celebration was in full swing. Folks swam, ate, played spades, and conversed until into the evening. That's when Princess showered and dressed for a night out with her best friend, Rafael. And that's when the surprises started.

"Where are we going?" Princess asked after getting into Rafael's Pontiac Solstice and fastening her seat belt.

"I thought we'd go have a drink on the Plaza, watch the fireworks, and then maybe go to the boat."

"The boat?"

"Yeah, the ca-si-no."

"What? I didn't know you gambled."

"Just a little blackjack when I'm feeling lucky."

"Oh, and you're feeling lucky tonight, huh?"

"Why not? I've got my good luck charm here with me." He took Princess's hand in his, brought it up to his lips, and kissed it.

"Boy, stop!" Princess said playfully, disengaging her hand from his.

"What do you mean, stop?" Rafael asked seductively, reaching for Princess's hand once again. "I'm not ever gonna stop loving you, Princess. I mean that."

Princess didn't know quite what to think about this new Rafael, this flirty, suave, confident version. The evening after Kelvin left her apartment in Long Beach, Rafael had expressed his true feelings for her, how he wanted them to see if they could have something deeper than friendship between them. Princess had suggested to just let things flow, take matters one step at a time. She couldn't give him the firm commitment he wanted, but there was no logical reason Princess could think of for not at least trying things out with Rafael. Not only was he handsome, smart, and spiritual, but he was also her best friend. They'd talked far into the night that evening and cuddled—nothing more. And they had talked on the phone almost every day since then.

Because they had only a couple hours before the fireworks started, they decided to skip the Plaza and head straight to the boat. Once there, Rafael sat down at a blackjack table. He ordered a Sprite, and Princess ordered an orange juice. Within minutes, Rafael won a hundred dollars.

"Wow! It's that easy?" Princess asked.

"That's what they want you to believe." Rafael gathered his chips and rose from the table. "C'mon, baby girl. I'm gonna cash this in, and we can get out of here. That's how you keep your money—win and walk."

"Ooh, I want to try something!" Princess had never been to a casino, and all the flashing lights, bells, and whistles fascinated her. Rafael walked to a cashier, cashed in his chips, then reached for Princess's hand as they walked around the casino floor. That it was a holiday was evident in the large crowd. Most of the machines were taken, and the tables were full. Princess stopped at a nickel machine that bore her name. "What about this one?"

After asking the woman next to Princess how the game worked, Rafael gave Princess a twenty-dollar bill to slide into the money slot.

"You wanna play max bet," their gray-haired, cigarette-smoking friend informed them. "That's how you win the big bucks."

"More like how you lose them," Rafael whispered in Princess's other ear.

"I'm going to play the big money!" Princess said, agreeing with the "expert" sitting beside her. At $1.25 a pull, the twenty-dollar bill got eaten up quickly. She'd win a little, lose a little, and was down to her last $2.50 when the video game seemed to lock up. "What happened?"

"You've got a bonus!" the woman playing next to them replied. "Just listen, and do what it tells you."

Princess squealed with delight as the game gave her a choice of treasures to open, each leading to another level. When the bonus was over, Princess had won almost two hundred dollars. "I won! I won! Look, El, I won more than you!"

"Beginner's luck," he teased. "Okay, cash out and let's go."

"No, I want to keep playing!"

"Oh, boy. See, I told you. That's how they get you—let you win the first time so that you can keep playing and give them back all your money. C'mon, you little gambler. Let's get out of here."

Rafael left the casino, which was located by the airport, and headed to Kansas City, Missouri.

"Where are we watching the fireworks?"

"Just hang with your boy. I've got a prime spot."

The two continued chatting until they came to Union Station. Rafael parked the car. He went to the trunk and pulled out a blanket and a small tote.

"What's that?"

"You know you stay hungry. I packed us a little sumpin', sumpin'. . ."

"Awww, you're so sweet!"

They walked up a large hill. Rafael found a spot near the top, away from the rest of the crowd. He spread the blanket and held Princess in his arms as they watched the fireworks. As they watched the last one, a kaleidoscope of colors timed to exhilarating music, Rafael casually reached for Princess's hand yet again. But this time, he put something on it, or more specifically, on the third finger of her left hand.

"What are you . . ." Princess began, and then looked down at her finger. She gasped. "Rafael! What is this?"

"Girl, that orange juice got you buzzin' or somethin'? What does it look like?"

"It looks like an engagement ring, but . . . but . . ."

"But nothing. You my girl, and I'm marrying you. End of story."

"Uh, excuse me?"

"Don't even think I'm doing that traditional down-on-one-knee, ring-in-the-champagne blah, blah, blah. That stuff is for sissies, and half the time, those marriages don't last six months. I love you, you love me, and when I get through with you, you'll be *in* love with me as well. Now, do you like the ring, 'cause I'm not buying another one. I'll be paying for that one the next five years as it is. Brothah ain't got it like that yet." Rafael changed his joking manner and became serious. "But I will. I'm going places, Princess, and I want you with me. I'll give you everything. Everything you've ever wanted." He stopped and looked over at the cluster of buildings nearby. "What is that fool doing?"

Princess turned to look and gasped again. There, spelled out in lights across the top of the Crown Center Shopping Center, was a question: PRINCESS, WILL YOU MARRY ME?

Princess was speechless. "Rafael, I don't know what to say!"

"It's not a hard question, baby," Rafael responded, again hiding his nervousness behind a smile. "There are only two answers. And unless what you're getting ready to say is yes, don't even say it. Because yes is the only answer I'm going to accept, and I'm willing to wait until that's the answer you've got for me."

That's how it had happened. That's how Princess's world had gotten turned upside down in one day. And now her mind was in turmoil. She loved Rafael and would never want to hurt him. But his proposal had forced her to acknowledge something she'd tried to ignore—she was still in love with Kelvin Petersen.

61

A Testament

Carla embraced Lavon's face and kissed him tenderly. "What did I do to deserve you?" she asked while planting kisses across his face.

"Be born," Lavon responded simply. He pushed himself up against the backboard of the king-sized bed, and brought Carla up with him. After three years, their lovemaking was still intense and constant. They were intimate almost every night—it was a favorite aspect of their relationship. That they could work together, play together, pray together, and love together was a blessing that neither took for granted.

"This turned out to be a great weekend," Lavon said after a pause. "Except I know one thing: I need to have a talk with Felicia's mama. That girl is trying to move too fast."

"That girl is grown," Carla gently reminded him. "Eighteen with a bullet, as they say."

"Yeah, well, that girl is still my daughter." Lavon had observed his daughter while picking her and her friend up from the mall. There were four hardheads gathered around them, as if they were holding court. And Lavon hadn't missed how Felicia swung her behind for the boys to check out as she walked away from them. She would be entering Ohio State University at the end of the summer. Lavon knew from personal experience what the college life could be like. He didn't want his only child "wilding out."

"Baby, I hate to be the one to tell you this, but if she takes after her daddy, she will definitely be getting her groove on, if she hasn't already." Carla remembered their recent conversation regarding Brianna and didn't miss the irony that she was basically telling Lavon the same things he'd said to her. "I feel for you, though, trust. I'm always having to cool Brianna's fast butt down. I even heard Shay talking about 'his girl.' I'm just praying that nobody makes me a grandmother before I'm ready."

"Naw, you don't look like anybody's grandmother," Lavon said, tweaking Carla's nipple with his fingers. "But what about mother? Are you ready to do that again?"

Carla sat straight up. "Where did that come from?" When Lavon remained silent, she continued. "Surely you jest."

"Think about it, baby. We're still young, both under forty. Don't you think it would be nice to have a little Lavon/Carla creation walking around? I mean, I love Shay and Winston, but I'd be lying if I didn't admit that I want a son of my own. But even more, that I want a child with you."

Carla turned fully to look at Lavon. She studied his face and noted the sincerity there. "You're really serious, aren't you?"

"I know, it's probably crazy. What with your career and all, and the fact that your youngest is seven right now. You're probably counting down the years until he graduates high school. The last thing you need is a newborn."

"It's just that I've never thought about it. You've never mentioned us having a child before."

Lavon shrugged. "Never thought that much about it either. But this weekend, hanging out with the family and all . . . just got me to thinking about us leaving our own little legacy, a testament to our love."

Carla rested back against Lavon. "You'd want a son, huh? What if I have another daughter?"

"I'd love her almost as much as I love her mother."

Carla turned her body toward Lavon and kissed him lightly. "And what if I have twins?"

"Then we'd need to get a bigger house."

Carla reached down and squeezed Lavon's manhood. She massaged it gently, reveling in how it hardened beneath her expert ministrations, even though they'd just made love. "And what if I said I didn't want to have any more babies?"

Lavon scooted down, until he and Carla were once again in a horizontal position. "Then I'd have to let you be all the baby I need." He dipped his head and grasped first one and then the other of Carla's nipples in his mouth, even as he gently opened her thighs with his hand. He found the paradise he'd only recently vacated, parted her folds. and slid a finger inside.

"Awwww." Carla widened her legs and deepened their kiss. She reached for his backside, kneading it firmly, just the way Lavon liked it. "Lavon?" she whispered hoarsely as her husband found one of her sensitive spots.

"Yes, Carla," Lavon breathed as he rubbed her pudgy stomach before rolling on top of her. He teased her with his manhood, rubbing it between her legs.

"Lavon?" she breathed again, squirming with the anticipation of feeling him inside her.

"Yes, my love?"

"Let's make a baby."

62

Not a Game

Kelvin wasn't used to not getting what he wanted, especially when it came to females. Which was why not being able to reach Princess was so frustrating. Since praying for Little Kelvin, they'd talked on a fairly regular basis. He'd even invited her to Arizona for the Fourth of July. But she'd already had plans to visit her parents. Kelvin had been cool with that, even knowing that Rafael would be sniffing around her during the entire visit. Kelvin wasn't worried. She tried to hide it, but Kelvin knew Princess was still in love with him. Just like he knew that they were going to get back together. It was only a matter of time.

And in the meantime, another of his girls was back. Stephanie and her family had handled the island controversy and, according to her, they could take up exactly where they left off. Until Kelvin got Princess back in his bed, that is exactly what he planned to do. He reached for his iPhone and began to dial Stephanie's new number. *I need to program this shit in.* Just as he got to the next to last number, Fawn's number showed up on his screen. He thought about not answering it but was always concerned it could be about his son.

"What up?"

"Kelvin, I'm at the hospital."

Kelvin sat up. "Again? What's wrong with him this time?"

"I couldn't wake him up this morning and drove over to emergency."

"And you're just now calling me?" Kelvin jumped up and walked toward his room. He just needed to put his shoes on, and he'd race to the hospital.

"Can you come down here?" Fawn didn't want to tell Kelvin why she hadn't called immediately, that Guy had been by her side until now. The only reason he'd left is because his wife had called, gone ballistic as usual, and threatened to drag his name through the tabloid mud if he didn't come home right then.

"I'm on my way."

It was two hours before the doctor emerged from working on Little Kelvin. Both Fawn and Kelvin jumped up at once.

"How is he?" Kelvin asked.

"Is my boy all right? Is he going to live?" Fawn had been on edge since arriving at the hospital, and after no food and little sleep, she was near hysteria.

The doctor placed a reassuring hand on her arm. "Your son is stable," he said gently but firmly. "Take a few deep breaths, Ms. Carter. There's something I need to discuss with the two of you."

Fawn took deep breaths and tried to slow her rapid-beating heart. The doctor directed them down a hall and into his office. Once they were seated, he got right to the point.

"Kelvin has hemolytic anemia, a condition where red blood cells are destroyed and removed from the bloodstream prematurely."

"What's that mean?" Fawn frantically asked.

"Let him explain!" Kelvin said.

"The red blood cells carry oxygen and remove carbon dioxide," the doctor calmly continued. "In a normally functioning body, these cells are replaced every three months or so by new cells created in our bone marrow. However, when one has severe anemia, like your son, then the bone marrow fails to create new blood cells to replace the old ones. That's why your son has experienced chronic fatigue, dizziness, and other symptoms.

"The good news is that while your son's case is severe, it is treatable. But we have to act immediately."

Fawn sat on the edge of her chair. "What do we need to do?"

"Kelvin needs a blood transfusion."

"What?" Fawn jumped up, her heart racing once again.

"Fawn, stop trippin'!" Kelvin yelled. "We don't need this hysterical bullshit. Now calm the fuck down!"

"I think you both need to calm down," the doctor said slowly and clearly. "Your son is young and otherwise healthy. We're confident that with the transfusion, he'll make a full recovery."

"So what do we do, Doc?" Kelvin asked.

The doctor explained. "I'll have my nurse draw blood from both of you and see which one is the best match for your son. We'll have your blood tested and do this procedure immediately. It's relatively painless and shouldn't take more than a few hours. Afterward, you'll feel groggy and lethargic for a couple days. Other than that, you won't even know that blood has been taken. Now, who wants to go first?"

It was early evening when the doctor asked Kelvin to join him in his office. He'd already consulted with Fawn, who believed the doctor had decided on Kelvin as the best donor match to give blood. Kelvin was more than ready to do whatever it took to make his son better. His back was straight, his stride purposeful, as he walked into the office.

"Sit down," the doctor said, motioning to the chair that Kelvin had occupied earlier.

Kelvin sat. "You don't even have to ask, Doc. I'm ready to give blood, do whatever to help my son. Just tell me where I need to sign and then where I need to go."

The doctor sat down behind his desk and looked at Kelvin intently. "This is a rather delicate matter," he said.

Kelvin didn't doubt that. He'd spent more time in hospitals this past year than he had in his whole life. When it came to saving lives, it was not a game.

After another moment, the doctor leaned forward. "I guess there's no easy way to ask this. But . . . is Kelvin your biological son?"

Kelvin sat back as if the wind had been knocked out of him. Surely he hadn't heard what he thought he'd just heard. "Of course he's my child! What kind of bullshit is this?"

"Kelvin Junior has a rare blood type, one that neither you nor Ms. Carter possess. It's not uncommon for a child to have a different blood type than either parent, but . . . well, the fact is, the best donors normally come from within the biological family."

"Look, Doc, I'm sure you know your job and all, but I've already taken a DNA test. Kelvin is my son."

The doctor studied Kelvin a long time. "In order for us to be absolutely sure, do you mind taking another one?"

It was after midnight when Kelvin returned home. He was exhausted but tried yet again to reach Princess. He'd tried to reach her on the way home but had been unsuccessful. After taking a quick shower, he tried her again and was surprised when she answered.

"Hello?" Princess said in a groggy voice.

"I'm sorry, baby. I didn't mean to wake you up."

"Kelvin?"

"Uh-huh."

"It's late. Is something wrong with your son?"

"I just came from the hospital, but he's going to be okay."

"Oh, praise God. I've been praying."

"That's why I called you."

Princess smiled. "To tell me my prayers are working?"

"No," Kelvin said, his voice somber. "To tell you that Fawn lied to me. Kelvin is not my child."

63

Stay Faithful

Mama Max sat in her living room, watching a rerun of *Murder She Wrote*. Her stomach was bothering her, much as it had for the past two weeks. Ever since Obadiah's ultimatum for her to come back into his bedroom and, even more, into his bed. "The only reason I had all that other stuff is because I was trying to stay faithful to you," he'd admitted during one of the most personal conversations they'd had in years.

"I ain't never liked it," Mama Max had responded.

"Never?" Obadiah had asked, wriggling his eyebrows.

"Well, not much anyway," Mama Max replied. She would have blushed if she could.

Truth was, there were times in those early years when she wasn't so opposed to Obadiah "doing his business." But it seemed that once the babies started coming, part of Maxine—the sensual, passionate, womanly part—just went away. She'd always despised Dorothea, and that was partly due to how effortlessly that aspect of her nemesis's personality came to her. It took her a while to admit it, but some of what Dorothea said in the parking lot had gotten to Mama Max. Obadiah had been a patient man when it came to . . . that. And even now, when she'd asked for a couple weeks to think about what he said and get used to the idea, he'd said okay.

"You want some ice cream, Maxine?" Obadiah asked from the doorway.

Maxine jumped. "Reverend, walking up on me like that. 'Bout to scare me to death!"

"Didn't mean to."

"Yes, I'll take some ice cream. You want me to heat up some of that pecan pie to go with it?"

"That sounds nice."

After warming up the pie, Mama Max and Obadiah settled at the kitchen table to eat.

"It's been two weeks," Obadiah said.

"I told you I needed time."

You've had about fifty years. I think that's time enough. "I told you I wasn't going to go on this way, Maxine."

"And I told you that you didn't have to!" Mama Max huffed, and her lips thinned before she forced herself to calm down. "I'm sorry, but this situation has gotten me all flummoxed."

"How do you think I feel? Having to beg my wife to give me some lovin'."

"Now, don't you go off spouting nonsense, Stanley Obadiah. You know good and well I love you."

"Well, prove it!"

"Remember when King and Queen were little?" Mama Max said, abruptly changing the subject. "And how we used to go pick pecans? You'd climb up in the tree and give it a good shake. The kids thought it was Christmas. They'd pick pecans awhile."

Obadiah chuckled. "Then we'd find a big tree with lots of shade and pull out those cheese and bologna sandwiches the kids loved so much."

"Not just the kids. You'd put back three or four yourself."

"Wasn't that how King broke his arm that time?"

"Unh-huh. Climbing trees and shaking them, trying to act like you."

Obadiah reached over and put a hand on top of Maxine's. "We've had some good times, Maxine. I'll grant you that."

Maxine looked at the man she'd loved for two-quarters of her life. How could she continue to deny this man the one thing that would keep their marriage going strong?

"Reverend, I—" Mama Max was interrupted by the phone ringing. She reached for it and frowned when she saw the caller ID. *This woman has some kind of nerve.* "Yes?" she asked when she answered the phone. "What in God's name gives you the right to be calling my house? And how'd you get the number?"

"Uh, excuse me, Sistah Maxine. This here's Deacon from over at First Baptist. Sorry to bother you, but Sistah Jenkins asked me to get a hold of Reverend Doctor. It's an emergency. They just rushed Reverend Jenkins to the hospital. She asked if he could come right away."

Five minutes later, Obadiah was reaching for his car keys on the table by the garage.

"I'm going with you," Mama Max said, reaching for her purse, which was sitting next to the keys.

"No, now, this is preacher business. I'm going alone."

"Not when it comes to Dorothea. I'm going with you."

It took them less than ten minutes to reach the hospital. They walked straight to the desk, where Obadiah introduced himself as clergy and asked for Reginald Jenkins's room.

"Sorry, ma'am, but you'll have to wait here," the nurse told Maxine when she prepared to follow Obadiah. "Right this way, sir."

Obadiah knew it was serious as soon as he walked into the room. When Dorothea saw him, she rushed into his arms. Obadiah didn't think twice about embracing her, even though a couple other of Jenkins's church members were in the room.

"How is he?" Obadiah whispered, even as he relished how good Dorothea felt, as if she belonged there.

Dorothea looked up at Obadiah, her eyes shining with tears . . . and something else. "He's dead."

64

I Am Not the One

"No, don't leave me," Dorothea whispered as Obadiah shifted his position on her couch.

"I wasn't going anywhere," he said. "But my arm is going to sleep."

It was nearly one in the morning, and Dorothea had barely left Obadiah's side since he arrived at the hospital. As soon as he heard that Jenkins was dead, he'd sent one of the deacons out to tell Maxine and to tell her to go home without him. She'd protested, told the deacon she would wait, but when Obadiah and Dorothea walked into the waiting room almost two hours later, Maxine was gone.

Now, it was Obadiah who seemed unable to leave. Even as he sat in Reginald Jenkins's living room, the man's body not yet cold, his thoughts were untoward, on the warm, willing flesh cuddled up next to him.

"It was horrible, Obadiah, just awful!"

"Now, Dorothea, don't get yourself riled up again."

"I can't help it. I keep reliving it over and over. How he begged me to . . . you know, have sex. We'd only done it once before because the man couldn't get it up! But he kept asking, had been asking for almost a month. So I bought him some Viagra, and he could finally hold an erection. He got on top of me and started pumping, and the next thing I knew, he was slouched down and . . . and I could barely push him off me!"

Dorothea turned and buried her head in Obadiah's shoulder, sobbing quietly. Obadiah reached up and patted Dorothea's hair. *God forgive me.* Because for the life of him, Obadiah could not conjure up a sad feeling about Jenkins's demise. Instead, all he could think about was how good Dorothea felt.

Dorothea turned herself more fully into Obadiah and began kissing his neck. "I need you, Obadiah," she moaned. "I need you to help me make a new memory, to get that memory of Jenkins's dead body out my head."

"Now, Dorothea . . ."

"I need you, man! Please, don't turn me down tonight."

"I'm not gonna turn you down, Dorothea. I'm going to take care of you, girl."

It was six o'clock in the morning when Obadiah pulled his car into the Brook garage. No sooner had he opened his car door than the kitchen door opened and Maxine lit into him.

"You done gone and done it now, mister! Shaming me to my face, knowing everybody saw you at the hospital with her, and some probably know'd that you spent the night. And don't lie. Don't even think about coming up in here trying to lie to me! 'Cause I know where you been, you filthy rascal. Whoremonger!" Maxine spat as Obadiah brushed past her.

"I am *not* the one! You not gonna treat me any kind of way and think I'm gonna just roll over and play dead. Aw, hell to the n-o, no! I'm getting ready to file those papers right back at the courthouse. I mean it, Obadiah, and I don't care who knows it. You've been with that skank heifah bitch for the last time!"

At these words, Obadiah stopped and turned around. "No, Maxine. I've been with you for the last time. Don't worry about filing the papers, 'cause tomorrow, I'm gonna file some of my own. And then I'm gonna spend the rest of my life with Dorothea."

65

That's What's Up

Kelvin's eyes anxiously scanned the passengers coming from the Jetway. Because airport security knew him, they'd given him a special pass that allowed him to go to the gate and wait for his passenger. As people began filing out, Kelvin grew worried. Where was she? Had she changed her mind? He'd booked her a first-class ticket; she should have been one of the first ones out!

Just as he reached for his iPhone, he saw her, walking next to a stooped-over old lady. The two were in deep conversation, as if they were old friends. When they stepped through the Jetway, Kelvin waved. "Princess!"

Princess smiled and put up a finger that said she'd be right there. Then she walked with the old lady over to the counter and spoke to the airline personnel standing behind it. She hugged the old lady, reached into her purse, and gave her something. Finally, she walked toward Kelvin.

"Baby girl!" Kelvin said, picking her up and twirling her around.

"Kelvin, put me down!"

He did, sliding her purposely along his firm, lean body in the process. Princess felt her cheeks grow hot, and as soon as her feet touched the floor, she pushed away from him. "Don't do that!"

"What, I can't hug my girl, who I haven't seen in a month?"

"It hasn't been a month since you've seen me and . . . I'm not your girl."

Kelvin reached over and hugged her to him. "You'll always be my girl, Princess. You know that's what's up."

"How's your leg?" Princess asked, changing the subject.

"It's all right. Doctor wants me to continue therapy, though, so I can be ready when the season starts."

"You're blessed to even be walking, Kelvin. I especially believe that after you showed me pictures of your wrecked car."

"I think it was your prayers that healed me and little Kelvin." Both Kelvin and Princess were quiet a moment, thinking about Fawn and the paternity lie that led to their breakup. Her child's father had attended UCLA but hadn't graduated. Ironically, he'd been at the same party where Princess had caught Kelvin and Fawn screwing. The situation was complicated. Kelvin loved the child, so while little Kelvin bonded with his biological father, Kelvin continued to support Fawn and the child until the courts could sort everything out.

"God is the healer," Princess corrected. "I'm simply the messenger giving life to His words."

They continued small talk as they walked to Kelvin's car. Princess could not believe how incredibly hot it was.

"Why you trippin'?" Kelvin asked her. "It's only a hundred and ten today."

"Dang, Kelvin," Princess exclaimed when they reached Kelvin's car. "Is this big enough for you?"

"It's insurance that my ass don't get banged up again," he said, tapping the lock-release button on the customized Hummer. "I call it the monster."

"Well, it's that all right."

Inside, the car was outfitted with everything a person

could dream of: televisions, a computer, a game console, and a top-of-the-line stereo system that Princess imagined she could hear in California if Kelvin turned the up the volume.

"You like?"

"Yeah, it's tight, no doubt about that. A little too big for me, though."

"That's cool. I've got something else for you."

Princess gave him a sideways look and rolled her eyes. "Still the cocky KP," she said.

"Just stating facts, baby girl."

It was Princess's first time in Arizona, and she marveled at the beauty of the desert. "I didn't think it would be so pretty," she admitted. "For some reason, I was thinking flat and barren, everything a drab tan color. But these mountains are beautiful."

After a twenty-minute drive, Kelvin entered an obviously exclusive area and pulled up to the gate. He waved at security, punched in his code, and drove inside the subdivision, then punched in another set of codes to the gate that surrounded his house. Princess couldn't help but be impressed. Kelvin had come a long way from the condo near UCLA.

At the top of the drive was a sporty Mercedes, powder blue, with white interior. "Now, that's more like me," Princess said as Kelvin pulled the Hummer up next to it. There was also a Porsche, a Jeep, and an Infiniti in the driveway. "You got company?"

"No, these are all my cars. Except that one." Kelvin pointed to the Mercedes.

"Who's that belong to?"

Kelvin's cocky smile returned. "You."

"Quit playing. Whose car is it?"

"I told you!" Kelvin reached into his pocket and then tossed a set of keys to Princess. "Get in, see how you like it."

Princess loved the car. It was perfect. Kelvin got in and they drove around the neighborhood. "This car is the stuff!"

Princess said as she searched different stations on the satellite radio. While not as extravagant as the Hummer, the Mercedes was equipped with TV monitors, a computer, and a satellite phone.

Fifteen minutes later, Princess pulled back into Kelvin's driveway. "You like it?" he asked.

"What's not to like? It's amazing."

Kelvin leaned over and kissed her on the cheek. "You're welcome."

"Kelvin, stop it. You know this isn't my car."

"Yes, it is, girl," he said, laughing. "I bought it for you. You're going to need something a little sportier than what you're driving in Cali. I can't have my girl rolling up to the games in a Honda."

"Look, Kelvin, I am not your girl."

"Aw-ight, whatever. Let me show you around."

"I have to get my bags."

"Housekeeper took care of that. C'mon."

The next two days passed by in a whirlwind and was one of the best times Kelvin and Princess had ever spent together. They'd both grown up, and for the first time talked in depth about their past relationship. Kelvin again apologized about the abortion, along with the constant infidelities Princess had endured during their time together. Princess admitted that she had missed him. She refused to go to Myst or any other club, but they dined at some of the finest restaurants. After turning down his offers to buy up what seemed like half of each boutique they entered, she allowed Kelvin to buy her a dress, a beautiful pantsuit, and a pair of Gucci shoes.

"So you gonna stay in my room tonight?" Kelvin asked. They'd just finished watching a movie and were chilling out on the couch.

"Uh, that would be a no," Princess playfully yet honestly replied.

"C'mon, girl. You don't have nothing I ain't seen already."

"You just don't get it, do you? I am abstaining from sex until I get married."

"Well, hell, that can be arranged. Let's go to Vegas, do the shit, and then *do* the shit."

Kelvin made a face and Princess laughed. "You're so goofy, still acting a fool, I see. So you're serious, Kelvin?" Princess asked after a moment. "You'd fly us to Vegas and get married, just like that?"

Kelvin shrugged. "I don't see why we have to be married to do what we've already done hundreds of times."

"It don't matter anyway. The man I marry will be saved and living for God."

Kelvin turned and lay down, placing his head in Princess's lap. "Then save me, baby. But give me a kiss first."

"Kelvin, stop."

"Just one, baby. Can I just have one?" He reached up and tenderly caressed Princess's cheek. "You know I love you, baby. I want to give you the world. And I meant what I said back in California. I want you to have my baby. So, will you give me a kiss?"

Princess sighed. "Just one."

Kelvin smiled. "And will you have my baby?"

"After you get saved and if we get married, then I *might* think about it."

As soon as the plane touched down in Los Angeles, Princess turned on her cell phone. She checked her messages and had several new voice mails, including one from Adele saying that Princess's book was an *Essence* bestseller. After deciding to wait until she reached her car to return the calls, she couldn't help but smile as she walked up to her trusty Honda. *Kelvin dogged my car, man!* Her smile faded, however, as she placed her luggage in the trunk and thought about what else had happened, just this morning. Princess had gone into the situation with her eyes wide open and had no regrets. Because she knew that life as she knew it was getting ready to change.

After calling her publicist, her agent, her mother, and Jodi, Princess hit one more speed dial. Her smile returned as she waited for the phone to be answered.

"Hello?"

"Yes."

"Hello?"

"Yes," Princess said, laughing this time. "My answer is yes."

Rafael started laughing too. "Girl, are you serious? You're going to marry me?"

Princess continued smiling, through the tears of joy now streaming down her face. She'd gotten a glimpse of the glamorous life and all that it entailed. Kelvin could give her everything she wanted, but Rafael would give her everything she needed. The three late-night phone calls, obviously from females, that had come back-to-back-to-back in the middle of Kelvin's seduction, and the subsequent calls from Fawn the following morning, was what Princess would later call a godly interruption. Princess didn't know if Kelvin would ever be faithful to one woman, but she believed with all her heart that when Rafael said "I do," it would only be the two of them in their marriage bed.

66

Time Will Reveal

Passion stood and paced the length of her master suite. Had it not been for the fact that she was hearing it with her own ears, she never would have believed it. "I'm so sorry, Mama Max. I never would have dreamed that you and Reverend Doctor O were having problems in your marriage."

"Yes, I worked hard to keep up that front, child. But Mama Max could tell you a story or two 'bout marriage, sure could. And now I've got a chapter called divorce I'm getting ready to add to the end of it."

Mama Max tried to sound cheerful, but Passion heard the sadness in her voice. "I'm worried about you, Mama Max," she said softly. Passion didn't know Maxine Brook well—they'd talked only a few times since meeting in Texas—but what she did know, she liked. "I can't imagine what happened, but whatever it was, I'm sure you didn't deserve to have the reverend file for divorce."

"Well, child, it is what it is. I just wanted to call and tell you myself, before the news makes its way through the church grapevine. What about you? You and Stan doing all right?"

"Much better, thank you," Passion said. "We're in counseling, and it's helping."

"Well, I'll pray your strength in the Lord. Staying together ain't easy. But I'll be praying for you. In fact, let's pray now."

While Passion was upstairs, receiving prayer from Mama Max, Stan was downstairs, in his office, needing prayer himself. He stared at the piece of paper he held in his hands, a copy of a letter written a long time ago. It had come from Bryce, in another package with an LA address. *He didn't believe me when I told him it's over, for good this time.* No, Bryce hadn't believed him and had made another package to replace the one that Stan had thrown away without examining its contents. He wished he hadn't gone through this one.

Hey, Tom, the letter began, referencing the Tom and Jerry nicknames Stan and Bryce had used while dating. Bryce was Jerry; Stan was Tom.

> *I didn't know I could miss someone as much as I miss you. I'm going crazy! What have you done to me? I could hardly get to sleep last night, just had to keep playing our song over and over again, then finally fell off about three this morning. And I had that test in Finley's class too. If I fail, it's your fault! Here's a little something so that you won't forget me. I've got something else waiting for you when you get back. And I know you don't want to forget that! (smile). Me neither, baby. It's so good with you, the best!*
> *Jerry*

Stan sighed as he crumpled the paper. A Butterfinger candy bar, that's what had been included in the package, because when Bryce went down on him all those years ago, he said that's how he tasted. There were other letters in the envelope—turned out Bryce had kept all of Stan's letters to him, still had them twenty-five years later. A tear formed at the corner of Stan's eye and fell. Then another, and another, until his shoulders heaved for the one he had loved and could never love again. Not like that. He'd promised God. He'd spoken vows.

Stan straightened out the crumpled paper, then turned and methodically put it through the paper shredder. He reached for the envelope and shredded the other contents as well. Finally, he picked up the CD that Bryce had included in the package. Stan didn't have to guess what songs were on there or, if there was only one, what song that was.

"It's over," Stan said aloud to the empty room. "God, help me." He wiped his eyes and sat back heavily against the desk. His fingers still twiddled the CD around as he stared blankly at the wall in front of him. Slowly his eyes dropped to his desk, where pictures of Passion, Onyx, and his children sat in multi-sized frames at the corners. Suddenly, a thought came to him. "That's it," he whispered. With a heavy heart but the merest hint of a smile on his face, he left the office and headed for his bedroom.

Passion was just about to step into the shower when she thought she heard the door to the master suite open. It was not unusual for Stan to work late into the night. She glanced at the clock on the vanity. It was just after nine. *Hmm, he finished early.* Passion took a moment and repositioned the shower cap before shedding her robe and stepping into the shower. She turned the water up as hot as she could stand it and turned her back to the showerhead, hoping that the hot water spray would work out some of the kinks she felt in her neck and shoulders. *Boy, I sure could use a massage.*

Minutes later, a hand touched her shoulder. Passion's quick intake of breath was the evidence of her surprise. She turned around to see a naked Stan standing behind her. "Stanley?" she asked incredulously.

"Last time I checked." Stan smiled. "Here, turn around. Let me get your back."

Passion turned around, shocked that Stanley Morris Lee was actually in the shower—with her! He soaped the sponge

and rubbed it across her body (including her butt!), and even
lingered there a moment before soaping her legs. After he'd
finished, he put down the sponge and began to knead Passion's
neck and shoulders. Passion moaned her pleasure and put her
head down to give him better access. The massage felt great,
but what happened next felt even better—Stanley began placing small kisses along her neck, shoulder, and down her arm.
Passion didn't know what had gotten into Stanley; she only
hoped that whatever it was would never come out! Once finished, Stanley began to wash himself under the shower's dual
sprayers.

"Unh-unh," Passion said, taking the sponge away from
him. "May I?" She looked into his eyes, and seeing no message
to the contrary, Passion began soaping Stan's body. She alter-
nately rubbed the sponge and her hands across Stan's strong
arms and broad chest, placing kisses where her hands had
gone. She washed him thoroughly before kneeling face level
with his manhood. "May I?" she asked again. Stan spread his
legs and braced himself against the shower wall. Passion
thought that she'd died and gone to heaven as she took in as
much of her husband as she could. They'd had oral sex only
one other time, on the Fourth of July. This was one of Passion's
favorite ways to make love, and she relished satisfying her husband. She was doing a good job, if Stan's moans and grinding
motion were any indication. But just as suddenly as it began, it
stopped when Stan placed a hand on her head. "Wait, Passion,"
he panted. "Let's get out of the shower."

Passion hid her disappointment behind a big smile. She
knew it would take time for Stan to become totally uninhibited in sexual matters. She was determined to be patient and
not rush him into things before he was ready. "Thanks for
joining me," she said sincerely. "That was fun. You can meet me
in the shower anytime."

Stan dried off and exited the bathroom, but Passion lingered, applying a liberal amount of cocoa butter and aloe lo-

tion on her skin, brushing her hair and teeth, and spritzing herself with her favorite body spray. Then, hoping that she could rekindle what had started in the shower, she tossed aside her cotton gown and slipped into a gold satin negligee, with a lace bodice that did little to hide her breasts, and a flowing gown that felt sexy against her skin.

She turned the corner into the master suite and gasped again. The light was low, and the white candles she'd bought months ago were lit all around the room. Stan was in the sitting area, looking debonair in his black silk pajamas. He stood when he saw her and walked over to the stereo. As the first notes of the music began to play, he walked over to a stunned Passion, who was trying without success to close her mouth.

"May I have this dance?" he asked.

Passion stepped into his embrace, convinced that she was dreaming. What happened to staid Stanley, and who was this sexy creature getting his mack on in front of her? *I can't believe this!* Still, she nuzzled closer, breathing in Stan's fresh scent as they danced around the room. When the short jazz intro ended, another song began.

"Wait." Passion stopped dancing and stared at Stanley. "Who are you, and where is my pastor husband?"

Stan laughed. "It'll all reveal in time."

"Uh, is that the group DeBarge playing on the stereo?"

"Do you like them?"

"I love them! But I've never heard you listen to R & B before!"

Stan pulled Passion back into his arms and began singing the lyrics in her ear. Tears came to Passion's eyes as she and Stan swayed to the beat of the music. "This is all I've ever wanted, and more than I dreamed." She hummed along with the music before turning her face so that she could kiss her man. Stan was a willing participant, opening his mouth to let her tongue in, pressing her close against him.

"I want to make love to you," he said huskily. "I want to make love to you all night long."

Stanley? I still can't believe this is my husband talking this way to me. And the night continued to be incredible as they shed their clothes and moved to the large sleigh bed, where Stan kissed her face and breasts before lying down beside her.

"Now, Passion, I'd like you to finish what you started in the shower. And then I want you to tell me how to love you the right way. I want you to tell me how you like it. I want to please you thoroughly. Can you do that for me?"

Could she do that? *How can I love you? Big Daddy, let me count the ways!* "Of course, Stan. I'll be more than happy to love you and to tell you what pleases me." This is all that Passion whispered before kissing her way down Stan's chest, lingering briefly on his thighs before running her tongue up and down the length of his shaft. Her husband had asked her to finish what she'd started. She would do that and then some. After all these years, would she dare not honor her husband's request? Hadn't her marriage vows bade her to honor and obey? And hadn't God's Word said to do the same? Would she not lavish love on her husband's shaft and then whisper succinct instructions on how to have her singing in the key of C by playing her G-spot like it was an instrument? Would she dare deny her husband when what she'd always wanted was now what *he* wanted? Heaven forbid!

HEAVEN FORBID

LUTISHIA LOVELY

ABOUT THIS GUIDE

The following questions
are intended to enhance
your group's reading
of this book.

DISCUSSION QUESTIONS

1. What were your first thoughts when Passion pulled ladies' underwear out of Stanley's luggage?

2. Why do you think Stanley acted so strongly to Passion's demand for sex, to the point that their argument became physical?

3. Happily married couple Lavon and Carla Chapman met and began their relationship while Carla was still married to Stan Lee, yet they both feel the relationship is a spiritual one that God has blessed. What are your thoughts about their soul-mate relationship?

4. When Dorothea Noble Bates Jenkins first came to Palestine, Reverend Doctor O assured Maxine that their affair was long over. Of course, we found out it wasn't. Do you think it's ever possible, or okay, for two people who've been involved in an affair to remain "just friends"?

5. When Mama Max found the sex doll in Obadiah's den, she was very upset. What is your view on various sex toys used within the confines of marriage?

6. Bryce told Stan that King James, the royal subject who commissioned the world's most popular Bible, was gay. It is a possibility that has been debated for decades. If this is true, what are your thoughts on it? Would King James being gay change your view of these holy scriptures?

7. Once Mama Max discovered the sex toys, she left the reverend and returned to Kansas. Do you think she had a right to leave him, or do you think she should have stayed?

8. During a time when Stan opened up to Passion, he admitted that his conservative upbringing prevented him from enjoying himself sexually. Has there been anything in your life—or the life of someone you know—that impacted your sexuality or matters of intimacy? If so, what and how?

9. Stan Lee accepted the position on the Cathedral's board knowing that Bryce Covington was a participant. Do you think he had ulterior motives for doing this? Or do you believe he felt strong enough to work alongside him, given his feelings?

10. Passion knows that her past actions played a significant part in Stan and Carla getting divorced. After three years of marriage, she feels a camaraderie with Carla Lee. What do you think about this "what goes around comes around" realization?

11. African American women make up the greatest number of new HIV cases in our country. Many of these cases are from men on the "down low," and many of these DL men are God-fearing, churchgoing Christians. What part do you think the strong antihomosexual stance within the church has in this growing statistic?

12. Part of the reason why it was hard for Passion to get a handle on her problems with Stan is that she'd lost herself in the marriage and—in her own words—had become a shadow of the woman who'd attracted Stan in

the first place. Has this ever happened to you? In the effort to find someone, have you ever lost yourself?

13. Molestation, especially when it involves family members, is often hidden and not talked about. Have you, or someone you know, been sexually molested? Now is the time to claim your strength by releasing the secret!

14. What are your thoughts regarding Dorothea's revelation about aborting her and Obadiah's love child forty years ago? Does this event somehow validate her love for this married man? Why or why not?

15. Lavon and Carla Chapman have a satisfying, uninhibited sex life. How is yours? Has your religious upbringing caused you to be conservative when it comes to sex? Why or why not?

16. Carla saw sexually suggestive pictures on her daughter's screen saver, and then checked out her MySpace and other social networking sites. Would you view your child's site without their knowledge? Do you feel this is an invasion of privacy or the right of a parent?

17. What are your thoughts about Kelvin Petersen? Do you think he really loves Princess, or did the competitor in him rise up when he saw her with Rafael?

18. Princess chose Rafael. Do you think he is her true love? Do you think their relationship will last? Would you rather have seen her with Kelvin?

19. Kelvin Jr. is not Kelvin's biological child, but he is the only father the child has known for three years. What role, if any, do you feel Kelvin should play in this child's

future? Should he be obligated to continue paying child support? Why or why not?

20. Stan chose Passion instead of Bryce. Do you think his love for God is enough to calm his homosexual desires? Do you think their marriage will last? Why or why not?

Lutishia Lovely dishes up a sexy new series
following the hot tempers and tantalizing temptations
of a family whose restaurant is *the* place for a tasty meal. . . .

All Up in My Business

Coming in March 2011 from Dafina Books

Here's an excerpt from *All Up in My Business*. . . .

1

"The way to a man's heart is through his stomach."
—Amanda Long, grandmother of Taste of Soul
restaurant board member Candace Livingston

Adam Livingston loved the taste of her thighs. Tender on the inside and crispy on the outside, nobody could fry chicken better than Candace, his wife. Even now—after living and working together for more than three decades—his mouth still watered at the thought of this juicy dark meat. Whether the succulent morsels on his dinner plate or those he hovered over when between the sheets, Candace knew how to please him. Unfortunately, the way she sexed him and handled a bird aside, Adam knew that Candace in the kitchen wasn't necessarily a good thing. His wife rarely cooked these days, preferring to either eat at one of their restaurants or have their on-call personal chef whip up an intimate lunch or dinner with guests. Now, when Candace graced the kitchen with her presence, it usually meant a conversation was coming regarding something he'd rather not discuss with her—namely her extravagant spending sprees, plastic surgery, or the ongoing competition between their sons.

Technically, money wasn't a problem. The restaurant his parents had opened in Atlanta fifty years ago had grown into a soul food empire—with ten highly successful restaurants in seven Southern states. The barbeque sauce his grandfather had created, which was used to slather on their most popular menu

item, baby back ribs, had been sold in grocery stores nation-
wide for the past five years, and the Livingston empire now included upscale liquor stores and high-end real estate. Still,
Candace could spend money faster than Usain Bolt ran the
hundred-yard dash. Just last year she'd renovated their kitchen
to the tune of fifty thousand dollars, had their backyard reland-
scaped to resemble the scenic islands they'd visited on their
thirtieth wedding anniversary, and had one of the guest bedrooms converted to a closet to handle her almost daily jaunts
to Nordstrom, Bloomingdale's and Saks. These renovations had
increased the value of their mansion and had made Candace
happy. So Adam hadn't complained . . . too much.

When it came to plastic surgery, Adam thought his wife
had had enough. She'd always been beautiful in his eyes, ever
since he saw her walking across the Clark Atlanta campus back
in the seventies. She'd looked like a Fashion Fair model to him
that day, her dark caramel skin enhanced by the beige mini she
wore along with similarly colored thigh-high boots. Her long,
thick hair had moved with the sway of her hips as she'd casually chatted with a friend. A couple days later, when he saw her
in the cafeteria, he'd immediately gone over and introduced
himself. She was even finer up close than she'd been from a
distance, and after taking one look into the almond-shaped
brown eyes that sat above a wide yet nicely shaped nose and
luscious lips, Adam had gotten the distinct impression that he
was looking at the mother of his children. This feeling proved
prophetic—Candace became pregnant during her junior year,
when Adam was a senior. They'd married that summer and
welcomed their first, Malcolm LeMarcus, the following De-
cember.

Even after having their second son, Toussaint LeVon, Candace stayed slim. Into her forties, when she finally gained thirty
pounds that didn't shed easily, Adam still thought she was fine.
She was five foot seven, and to him the extra weight hardly
showed. Candace hadn't seemed that bothered by it, either,

until her sister-in-law, his twin brother's wife, Dianne, had commented on Candace being "fat" during a family get-together and had suggested liposuction as a quick way to take the weight off in time for their cruise to the Fiji Islands. Candace had been so pleased with the results that a tummy tuck soon followed, and breast implants followed that. Any brothah would be pleased to squeeze a set of firm titties, even if he'd had to pay for them, and Adam was no exception. But a couple weeks ago, when Candace started complaining about her wide nose, Adam had shut her down immediately. "You're becoming addicted to this shit," he'd warned. "If you don't stop cutting on the body God gave you, you're going to become as obsessed as Michael Jackson was, may he rest in peace. You look fine, Can. Give it a rest." So he hoped she'd gotten the message, because he didn't intend to pay the highly skilled and equally expensive cut-and-paste doctor another dime.

That left the topic of his and Candace's sons. The midyear company meeting was in two weeks, right after Juneteenth, so most likely, Candace would want to butter him up regarding some plan in the works—probably another of Toussaint's outlandish ideas. Adam loved his youngest son, but he swore that boy didn't have a fear bone in his body. Where Malcolm was more like Adam, in looks and demeanor, Toussaint was definitely his mother's child. Like her, he was brilliant, but he'd also inherited her traits of impulsiveness and flamboyance. Toussaint had run an idea by him some months ago, an idea that Adam had nipped in the bud as quickly as he had Candace's nose-job suggestion. The economy was too unstable to do anything new now, he'd explained. Adam wasn't sure how the other players would feel about constructing more Taste of Soul locations across the country, but he hoped that his and Candace's vote would be the same—no f'ing way. The more Adam thought about it, however, the more he thought this might be exactly why he smelled chicken frying. *Damn, I have too much on my mind to argue with Candace about this right now.*

One thing on his mind was the e-mail he'd just received on his smartphone, from the woman who'd been trying to seduce him for the past two years. He'd met Joyce Witherspoon in the clubhouse after a golf outing and had exchanged business cards, because she'd told Adam of her plans to start an event-planning business and her desire to contract with Taste of Soul as one of the catering partners. Her e-mails had slowly gone from strictly business to potential pleasure, even as she launched the successful, high-profile business that kept the Taste of Soul catering arm busy. Adam was flattered, and Joyce was attractive, but he had told the sistah that he was happily married. Joyce's response had been quick and witty. "You're married, but are you flexible?" Even after assuring her there was no room in his bed for a third party, she'd continued her erotic banter in various phone calls and e-mails. Adam reread Joyce's detailed description of what she wanted to do to him with her mouth and then pushed DELETE. He had always been faithful but could no longer ignore the fact that Joyce's constant flirtations and rapt adoration was wearing him down. *I've got to do something about this . . . and soon.* Adam picked up the *Atlanta Journal-Constitution* and pulled out the sports section, determined to swap thoughts of Joyce's mouth with those of his wife's thighs—the ones he'd be eating at the dinner table soon, and in the bedroom later.

Candace Long-Livingston poured melted butter into the baking pan and then sparsely coated each buttermilk biscuit with the warm liquid before spacing the dough out evenly in the bottom of the pan. She loved cooking, especially now that she didn't do it often. It was a love she'd inherited from the grandmother who'd helped support a family of four by cooking for an affluent family in their hometown of Birmingham, Alabama. "The way to a man's heart is through his stomach," Amanda Long would tell Candace as she whipped up a slap-your-mama pound cake or an oh-no-you-didn't peach cobbler. Candace smiled at the memory of those kitchen counseling sessions. Adam may have thought it was her small waist and big booty that had captured his heart, but Candace knew it was those candied yams and collard greens she'd fixed while they were dating. But somewhere between the birth of their first son and the opening of their second restaurant, the thrill had gone. She'd worked long, arduous hours at the Buckhead location, the same tony suburb where they lived, and while it had been a labor of love, her joy for fixing food had been replaced by repulsion. There'd been days when she'd thought that if she fried, smothered, or baked another anything, she'd lose her mind.

Tonight she cooked with love, purpose . . . and guilt. Love because that when it came to cooking, she knew she could "throw down." Adam loved food, and her fried chicken was his favorite. Purpose because she thought Toussaint's latest idea was a stroke of genius, that the timing for said idea was perfect, that Adam would surely be against it, and that if anybody could change his mind, she could by using various types of thighs. And guilt because after months of harmless flirting with Q, the personal trainer she'd hired to help tone the very thighs her husband admired, they'd taken their relationship to another level. During her last two sessions, sit-ups, squats, and running on the treadmill weren't the only reasons she'd sweated. And while Candace knew that she should stop the madness, should never even have started down this road, she honestly didn't know if she could heed the red light and make a U-turn back into monogamy. There was no doubt that Candace loved Adam. But thugalicious cocoa cutie Quintin Bright, who was younger than Toussaint, had turned a sistah out for the second time in as many weeks—with sixty minutes of working out followed by nine inches of love.

GREAT BOOKS, GREAT SAVINGS!

When You Visit Our Website:
www.kensingtonbooks.com

You Can Save Money Off The Retail Price
Of Any Book You Purchase!

- **All Your Favorite Kensington Authors**
- **New Releases & Timeless Classics**
- **Overnight Shipping Available**
- **eBooks Available For Many Titles**
- **All Major Credit Cards Accepted**

Visit Us Today To Start Saving!
www.kensingtonbooks.com

All Orders Are Subject To Availability.
Shipping and Handling Charges Apply.
Offers and Prices Subject To Change Without Notice.

3 1143 00933 2132